CONFESSIONS

CARO LAND

First published in 2020 by Bloodhound Books

www.bloodhoundbooks.com

978-1-913419-58-5

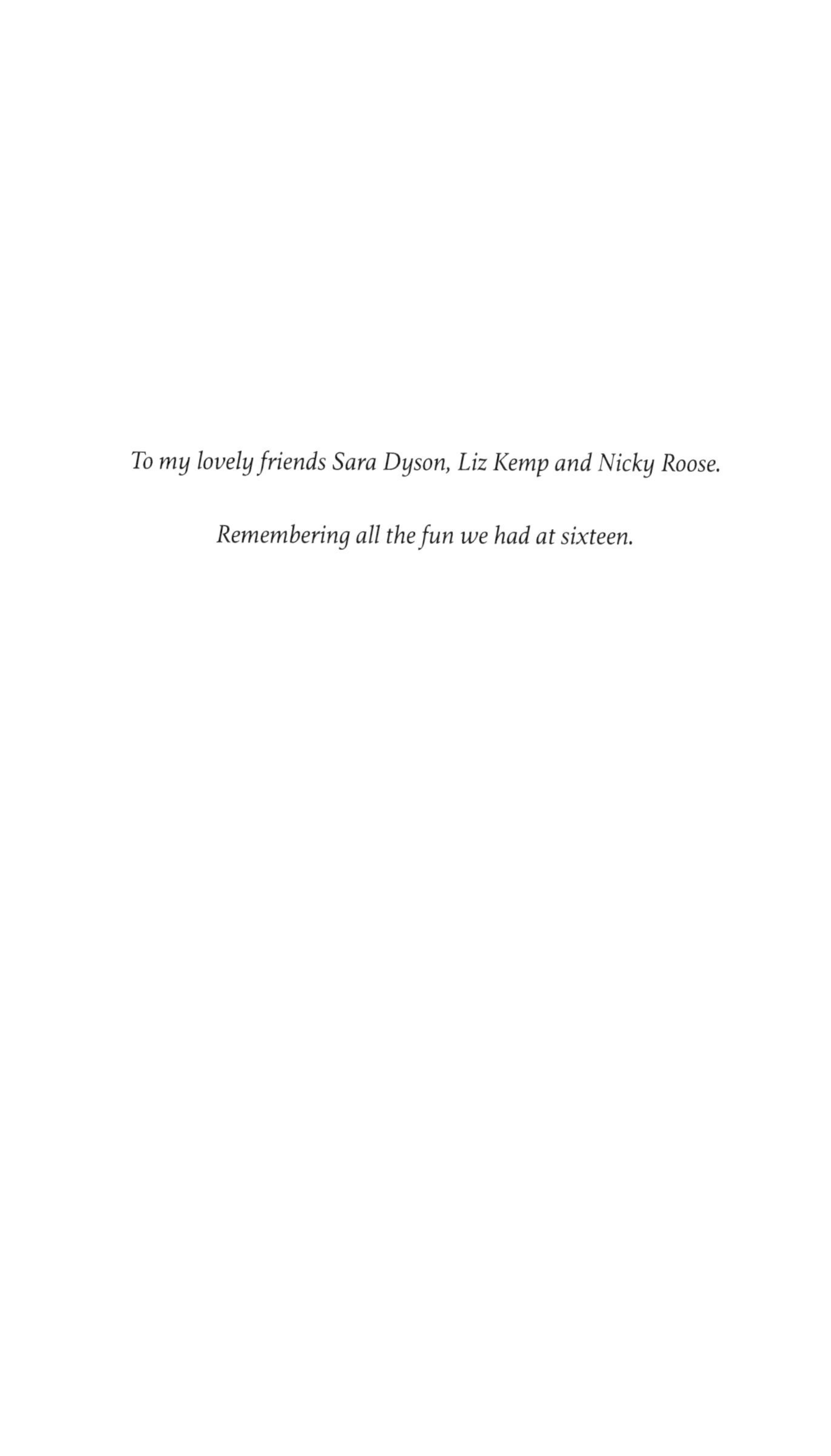

To my lovely friends Sara Dyson, Liz Kemp and Nicky Roose.

Remembering all the fun we had at sixteen.

1

FLUX

Life was in flux, but the nooky was divine. Natalie yawned, stretching her limbs before relaxing again. It was men who were supposed to be unresponsive after sex, wasn't it? Something to do with hormones that made them sleepy? Or perhaps it was just the exertion. Either way, that was the new Natalie Bach, lethargic and dopey like a cat after a night on the tiles, even though it was nearly lunchtime.

Eventually she stirred again, spreading out on her front like a starfish. What was the time? Her lover had left the bedroom some time ago. He'd kissed the back of her neck and said something about her soft skin, a 'quick run' and then food. The grub part was a bonus; her stomach was grumbling, but a man who could sprint ten kilometres after *that* was heroic.

She smiled to herself. Wesley Hughes; beau, boss and married father of two. She had tried to persuade him to stay longer in bed, pinning him with a leg across his warm torso. 'Don't leave me this way,' she'd mumbled, but he had just laughed. 'Don't pretend you won't be asleep in thirty seconds. The crows and the cows are a-calling.'

The Cheshire cows and crows. And sheep, horses, pigs and

goats. She'd accompanied him on his Sunday loop a few weeks ago and had surprised herself by running the whole way without begging for rest. Perhaps those half marathons with Jose in her thirties had put her in good stead. But she was officially in her forties now, so the once was enough. and besides she knew Wes preferred to run alone. He'd been arrested for attempting to murder his wife Andrea last year. The charges had been dropped, but only after the devastating discovery that the woman had deliberately spiked one of their twin son's food to make him ill; she was currently on remand for charges ranging from poisoning to perverting the course of justice.

Wesley Hughes needed the thinking time.

The cottage wasn't overlooked, so she didn't bother with clothes as she padded to the window and yanked open the curtains. The radiator warming her chest, she leaned on the ledge and gazed at the gleaming countryside. Everything was white; white fields, white trees, white bushes and plants. Even the sheep and the goat in the field beyond the manicured garden had a light smattering from the steady snowfall. What a difference a day made.

She took a quick breath. Was Wes okay venturing out in this weather? He'd bought some 'super grip' state-of-the-art trainers, but she hoped he was still taking care. Sure, her life was still in flux, but after six months of hefty buffets and bumps last year, her forty-first had started pretty damn well. She had waved her brother and his family back to Poland after a cramped Christmas in her small terraced house, and Wes had driven his sons over the Snake Pass to Sheffield uni. Nooky was back on the menu; delicious, lazy intimacy with her stunning man.

She looked down at her naked body and blushed; when his brother Sidney was absent from this picture box country home, at least.

The bang of a door reverberated up through the floorboards.

Almost licking her lips like a hungry puppy, she punched the air and hopped back into bed. Beaming broadly, she pulled up the bedding. What would today's delicacy from the Aga be? Yup, things were that good; not only did she fancy the pants off Wes Hughes, it turned out he was a damned good cook.

Inane happiness, she knew. But in fairness the absurd grin wasn't surprising; apart from Wes's crazy wife and her own psychotic ex-boyfriend in Mallorca, life was – astonishingly – hunky-dory. Of course there were the usual complexities of work, not least the decision to keep their relationship a secret from their lawyer colleagues. But the cloak-and-dagger romance had turned out to be fun.

Half closing her eyes, she studied the snow patterns as they stuck to the small panes of the casement. Her mind drifted to Mallorca. What was the weather doing there? At some point last year she had finally stopped loving Jose, thank God, but her home for five years was often in her thoughts. January had been the coldest month in Mallorca, yet sometimes it had been balmy enough to sit outside 'Havana', their beach-fronted café bar.

Willing Wes to appear, she shook her head. Beds and wakefulness were a recipe for morbid thoughts. Yup, anxiety and guilt, still clattering around her skull. She had found out about Jose's admission to a psychiatric hospital last November, but hadn't yet visited him. The self-reproach wasn't so much concerning her ex; it was more with regard to their bar manager, Hugo, who'd admirably picked up the pieces when Jose was sectioned. Over the last few weeks she had been in regular contact with him; he'd advised her to wait because Jose's family, the Harrows, were in Mallorca for the festive season, but Christmas and the New Year had now been and gone.

Nat sighed deeply. There were no more excuses. Yet she was still desperately searching for some.

Loud enough to alert the poor frozen sheep, her belly

thundered again. Then her ears tuned into muffled noises from the lounge below. She stilled and listened to the murmurs. What the...? Bloody Wes had turned on the TV. Football probably; the cheek of the man! Throwing back the duvet, she grabbed his shirt, tiptoed down the stairs, then burst in to surprise him.

'Cheeky sod! You're meant to be–' She clamped her palm to her mouth. 'Oh sorry, I thought...'

His gaze fixed on the television screen and clearly absorbed by the news, the man on the sofa didn't turn. He was broad and black, but unless she'd dozed a hundred years like Sleeping Beauty, he definitely wasn't Wes. Wes's brother was older, but surely not that old? Aware of a slight stab of pique, she felt herself blushing. She hadn't met any of his family. But that was fine, wasn't it? Life was in flux; it hadn't been broached; with the whole Andrea saga, it hadn't been appropriate.

Without looking her way, the man abruptly spoke. 'We'll end up like bloody America if we're not careful.'

Wondering whether to bolt or reply, Nat wrapped her arms around the unbuttoned shirt. Oh shit; its tails were barely covering her modesty. 'Oh?'

'There's been another shooting in Salford.' He shook his head. 'If these delinquents want to kill each other, fine, but this time an innocent young child has been caught up in the crossfire.' Finally turning, he glared. 'Social media, television and particularly American gang culture: that's the cause. Not a brain cell between them. They should lock them up and throw away the key.'

Feeling the usual defensiveness, Nat took a breath. It was on the tip of her tongue to say it was complicated, that society and parenting, schooling and mental health issues, were also to blame, but who was she to make any comment? As a second-generation immigrant, she couldn't help the impulse to stick up for the underdog, but she knew little else about it.

As though finally clocking her presence, the man's eyes focused. 'So who are you?' he asked. 'A friend of Sidney's, I assume?'

Well, that discounted the brother, which meant this was the father. The heat spread from her cheeks to her chest, a mix of embarrassment at the state of her attire and bloody annoyance. She obviously hadn't been mentioned, even in passing, to Wes's mum and dad. On the one hand she understood: he was still married to the 'Cling-on' Andrea; he had eighteen-year-old boys and matters were convoluted by the ongoing criminal proceedings. On the other, he had made some promises on her fortieth birthday – insisted on them, in fact – the sort of undertakings his parents would have to know about eventually.

'No, I'm a friend of Wesley's, actually.' Still gripping her outfit in one hand, she held out the other as though suited and booted. 'Hello. I'm Natalie Bach from Goldman Law.'

Inwardly she snorted. Bloody hell; the lawyerly autopilot must be inbred.

Leaning forward to accept her handshake, Mr Hughes regarded her with a little more interest. 'Ah. So you work for Wesley.'

She held back the loud groan. It was ever thus; people always assumed she worked for a man. She could've been Catherine, managing partner of Goldman Law. But the truth was that she did work for Wes in a way; he was Catherine and Jack Goldman's co-partner, and she was an ad hoc jack-of-all-trades solicitor, recruited by Jack a few months ago. After last year's rollercoaster ride, both personally and professionally, she was still undecided whether to stay with them in their Didsbury high street offices or move on to a city centre law firm.

Another bloody flux in her life.

The lounge door swung open, saving her from a reply. An ample woman sashayed in with a tray, almost spilling its contents as she jerked in surprise. Placing the drinks on a table, she put a hand on her hip and examined Nat with an open, friendly face. There was no doubt she was Wes's mum; although her skin was a touch paler and freckled, they looked strikingly similar.

'What are you like, Joe?' she said to her husband, whose attention was again lost to the headlines. She swept her bright gaze over Nat and smiled. 'I take my eyes off him for a moment and see what happens.' She paused for a beat, lifting her eyebrows. 'Or doesn't,' she said, raising her arms when Joe made no acknowledgement. 'I'm Kathleen, but do call me Kath. Pleased to meet you.' She reached out a plump hand towards Nat's, but instead of shaking it, she pulled her to the door. 'Let's go into the kitchen and leave the old grump to it. Tea or coffee?' She winked. 'Or maybe we could have a cheeky glass of wine.'

Augmenting Nat's sweatiness, the kitchen was warm. Reaching for a high larder shelf, Kath extracted an array of wine goblets and peered into each. She pushed one towards Nat. 'Finally a clean one,' she said amiably, cracking open a Pinot Grigio Nat particularly liked.

After filling both glasses, she pulled out a chair at the small wooden table. 'Do sit, love. You must be Natalie. I would say that Wesley has told me all about you, but you know what boys are like. All the information has to be squeezed out of them.' She smiled, her even white teeth a replica of her son's. 'Like a tube of toothpaste. You know, when the lid hasn't been replaced for a while, which happens every time in my house. You have to press hard to remove the blockage and then it all comes spurting out.' She laughed a deep laugh. 'That's what it's like to have boys.'

Loving the analogy, Nat sat and smiled. Squeezing. Yup, not just boys, but every bloody man in her life.

'He isn't quite there yet,' she continued. 'You know, to squirting it all out.' She put her palm to her mouth and guffawed. 'Oh dear, no innuendo intended,' she started, 'but you know what...' Not able to contain her chortle, she put a hand on her large belly and hooted. Her nerves sliding away, Nat joined in, powerless to stop the hysteria even when a shock of cold air blasted in.

Soaked from head to foot, Wes was standing at the utility room entrance, the Lycra stuck to his body, leaving little to the imagination. Kath took one wide-eyed look, wiped her face with a paper napkin, and set off laughing again. Her ribs aching, Nat watched in wonder, astonished this woman and Andrea had rubbed along as in-laws for so many years. If, indeed, they had been friendly.

Not quite knowing whether his handsome face would show irritation or that enigmatic look she found difficult to interpret, Nat turned back to Wes, but he was grinning and shaking his head.

'I suppose you were just passing, Ma?' he asked, stripping away his wet jacket. 'Only a twenty-mile diversion from Sainsbury's.'

Kath blew her nose loudly. 'Your dad brought some papers for Sidney.'

Wes headed for the stairs. 'I believe you, Ma, thousands–'

The sound of his father's voice interrupted his reply. 'Wesley, come in here. What did I tell you about guns? How you and your fellow lawyers...' Nat heard before the door clicked shut.

Suddenly sobered by the memory of the dreadful headline news, Nat's attention came back to Kath.

'A child,' she said, by way of explanation. 'Shot by another in Salford. Terrible, isn't it?'

2

PRICKLING

Goldman Law's corner offices were quiet on Monday morning. Not that Nat knew for sure; she was still hidden away in the second-floor conference room, a decision made by Jack Goldman because there were more people than space in the suburban village building. Over the last few weeks her caseload had increased to such an extent that she'd been granted a filing cabinet, not the usual bog-standard grey, but a state-of-the-art chrome affair to fit in with the other smart furnishings.

Feeling a strange mix of emotions, she stared at it now. Like her new company car, delivered only last week, it was nice to feel appreciated, but the fetter made her anxious, not so much to the firm, but to Jack Goldman himself. He'd been her mentor and father-figure for over fifteen years, and while she loved him dearly, she doubted he was good for her. Her politically incorrect pal Gavin Savage had his own solicitors' practice in a dank, tatty office a few miles away in Heald Green. He had offered her a job with 'more hours and less pay'. She wasn't entirely sure if his terms were tongue-in-cheek, and she would be acting mainly for his criminal clients, but she increasingly felt that working there would, illogically, make her a better person.

She turned to the sound of laughter beyond the door. She'd taken to propping it open with a legal tome from the small library behind her. Catherine's studious 'commercial' team were in pods on this floor, but the two guys and their typists were considerably quieter than the folk down below. Their open-plan area housed a variety of bodies, ranging from secretary to solicitor and everything in between, so was a hive of gossip and giggles. The same couldn't be said for up here, but the little there was, Nat could now hear, if not see, through the closed blinds. So far she'd discovered that Catherine worked three out of five days most weeks and that she rotated the downstairs 'bench boys' on her cases, but never used the only bench girl. Odd. Perhaps it was because Emilia was Wes's trainee; perhaps she just preferred men. Despite having been married to Jack for the past nine years, Catherine had preferred Wes over everyone not so long ago, but that was something Nat tried not to dwell on.

Her ears pricked to a familiar, eloquent voice saying 'cheers' to someone.

'Max!' she called from her end of the table. 'Come in and say hello before you go.'

Kipper tie loose, he strolled in. 'Hey, Nat. How's tricks?'

'Hunky-dory as it happens, thanks.'

He pulled out a chair and flopped down. In his early thirties and the most senior of the bench boys, Max was undoubtedly attractive in a rugger-bugger type of way. He raked fingers through his thick quiff, but his smile didn't seem to reach his baby blue eyes.

'And you?' she asked, noticing some newly acquired highlights in his already-blond hair.

Sensing girlfriend trouble, she thought back to an office

party last autumn. What might have happened had she not encouraged him to make up with his woman then? Nothing, probably. And just as well. That night had turned out to be magical; she and Wes, getting to 'know' each other again after a nineteen-year gap.

Max took a moment to answer. 'Yeah, good.'

Nat studied his face; his gaze seemed distracted. Definitely something. Family worries? Demands of work? A cock-up on a file? That was something no lawyer was immune to. 'Is Wes keeping you busy?' she asked.

'Yeah, but that's a good thing.' He rubbed the desk and fell silent. Then with a sigh, 'Right, I'd better–'

'Still with...' Nat dug for a name. 'Caz?'

A shadow passed through his features. Ah, correct the first time; girlfriend trouble. 'Yeah.' He lifted a buff folder and gave it a shake. 'Better get on with this.' He looked at her meaningfully. 'It's for Catherine and urgent, so...'

Intending to suggest a drink and chat later, Nat took a breath, but she caught herself just in time. A positive effort not to get involved in other people's lives, remember, Natalie? 'Okey-dokey, enjoy the file,' she said instead.

'Will do,' he replied, leaving the room.

She shook her head. A close call again. Since November, 'butting out' was a daily reminder. She'd got off lightly overall last year, but in truth no good came of interference. Her mum was kind enough to say it was 'helping' and not meddling, but Nat knew from experience that the difference between the two was a very fine line.

Pleased with her miraculous self-control, she went back to the ring binder on the desk. The client was Edward Chaudhury, a fairly recent Goldman Law acquisition. Apparently Jack had first introduced them at Catherine's fiftieth party but, to put it mildly, Nat had been a little worse for wear that evening. In the absence of a face to remember, she had mentally named Edward the 'mill man' and it had somehow morphed into 'Mr DeMille' (without the Cecil B). Though she had met him since, she struggled to call him anything else when she worked on his files.

Passing over both Catherine and Wes, Jack had nominated Nat to deal with Mr DeMille's 'rag trade' needs. The mill in question was located in Stockport, a clothing factory he had acquired not long ago, and he'd instructed Nat to draft employment contracts for the seamstresses. So far so good, but there was something which caused her a 'prickling', as her old mucker Gavin Savage would say. When DeMille gave her a tour of the premises last year, it had felt as though two of the darkly clad workers were deliberately avoiding her. When she'd asked him about the checks required to ensure none of his workers were illegal, he'd stared through his spectacles with magnified eyes for several beats, then asked her to look into it as part of her brief. Whether it was a clever ploy at passing a potential £20,000 civil penalty fine per illegal worker onto Goldman Law, or if it was a genuine delegation, she didn't know, but she had spent the last half hour reading through the relevant UK Border Agency regulations nonetheless, making careful notes of an employer's statutory duties and the documents required.

She sighed. Yes, definitely a prickling. She went back to the ring binder and searched for the company's payroll. Sixteen members of staff. Surely there had been more than sixteen needlewomen when she visited the workshop?

A knock at the door interrupted her scrutiny.

It was Catherine's secretary. 'Hi, Nat. Thought I'd give you the head's up before the boys descend. The sandwich guy has just arrived in reception. Are you hungry?'

3

TASER

Lost in her usual lunchtime game of *Words With Friends* with her mother – who was annoyingly good – the peal of a telephone made Nat jump. She snatched it up.

'Natalie.'

'Your two-thirty appointment is here. Should I send him up?'

Bloody hell; was it that time already? Just goes to show how time flew when trying to create a word with only flipping vowels. 'Cheers, Christine. Don't suppose we could bag a drink? I'm parched.'

'Too much sea salt on the pastrami panini?'

Ah, so that was it. Nat had finally persuaded her mum to stop making her packed lunches fit for an eight-year-old, but the sandwiches brought into the office by the enterprising young caterer were indeed far too seasoned. She inwardly snorted; not sufficient to cause hypernatraemia, she hoped. Shaking her head, she quickly reprimanded herself for the usual black humour impulse. Andrea's intermittent 'use' of salt to keep Wes from leaving her had been far, far from funny.

Pushing those dark memories aside, she stood and brushed the crumbs from her skirt. She had hoped her 'two thirty' wouldn't turn up; she was all for genuine civil claims and grievances, but at times it felt like the 'where there's blame there's a claim' culture had gone too far.

This new case was all Gavin's fault; he'd referred the 'young Ned' to her. 'Bach, glad I've caught you. I need a wee word about a police matter...' he'd said last Saturday when she dropped off his kids.

Gavin Savage, the police and 'wee words' were generally a very bad combination. Nat had felt her buttocks clench, but he had grinned. 'Don't look so worried, I've got a new client for you.'

His boys had darted into his ex-wife's house, but Ruthie had stayed at the porch door, holding Nat's hand, so he had gone on to give them both the lowdown: this particular Ned was the son of one of his criminal clients, and during a pub fracas he'd been tasered by an overeager constable. After an investigation by the Police Complaints Commission, or the PCC, as Gavin had put it, the PC had been charged with assault for using excessive force. The young Ned had been delighted, apparently boasting to his mates on Facebook that he'd be 'going for compo'. Which was where Nat and Goldman Law had come in.

'Just up your street, Bach,' Gavin had said in his gravelly Glaswegian tones. He'd cocked an eyebrow. 'You know; rolling up your sleeves and getting stuck in. Fighting against authority. Looking out for the stooge.'

'I'm not that flipping bad,' she'd replied.

'Says she who defended a sheep killer.'

She'd looked down at little Ruthie. Technically the deceased had been a goat, but she knew better than to say so to her animal-loving seven-year-old friend. 'The client was Catherine's mum, Ruthie, and she hadn't killed a sheep.'

Gavin had stroked his moustache. 'If you say so...'

Looking out for the stooge was usually his area. His phrase

'young Ned', or indeed 'Nedette', wasn't as judgemental as it sounded; that's what he called all his criminal clients, the prefix dependent on variables such as offence, age, size or hair colour. It wasn't unknown for him to employ them too. One who'd tried to burgle his offices was now his sullen receptionist, another mowed the lawn for his wife. Heather Savage was still currently his ex, but both Ruthie and Nat were hopeful that might change fairly soon.

She'd studied her pal's ruddy face and noted the twinkle in his eyes. Still holding his red-haired daughter's hand, she'd given him a hard stare. 'What are you up to, Gav? Why aren't you acting for him? Going for the "compo" yourself?'

Ruthie had peered at him too. She'd shaken her head sagely and breathed her mum's sigh. 'Come on, Daddy, spill the beans.'

'Nothing gets past you girls, does it?' he'd replied. His smile spreading, he'd straightened his six-foot-six frame. 'Guess who's acting for the taser PC Plod? Instructions from the Police Federation, no less. Kosher work, though I say so myself. Possibly the start of much more. Fame at last. Are you impressed, Miss Bach? You'll be begging to work for me now.'

Ruthie had wrinkled her freckled nose. Of course one shouldn't have favourites, but of Gavin's four kids, she was it. 'Begging to work in your office, Daddy?' she said, sounding more seventy than seven. 'I don't think so. Natalie's offices in Didsbury are lovely. Why on earth would she want to?'

As was often the case, the words from Gavin's former wife came straight from her child's mouth. Hurray for Heather, Nat had thought with a smile, but until this moment she hadn't twigged there'd be more Chinese walls, those secrets and conflicts of interest she had determined to avoid this year.

Hearing a knock, she quickly opened her diary. Even Neds had names, as she regularly chided Gavin. Dwayne. The son of Gavin's criminal was called Dwayne.

'Come in,' she called.

A young man's head appeared around the door. 'They said to come up to the... conference room?' he said, stumbling over his words. 'Are you Miss... Miss Hatch?'

Nat had long ago given up pronouncing her surname à la Johann Sebastian. 'It's Bach with a B, Natalie Bach. Come on in.'

Wearing a crumpled suit and looking remarkably like Wes's twin sons, the shy youth shuffled in.

Reminding herself not to make easy assumptions, she held out her hand. 'Hello, Dwayne. Pleased to meet you. Take a seat.' When he'd sat, she dipped her head to meet his eyes. 'How can I help you today?'

Seemingly stuck for words, he slunk lower in his chair.

'I understand you want to make a claim for an assault by the police? An assault by taser gun?' The boy nodded, so she gave him an encouraging smile. 'Great. Start at the beginning and tell me what happened. There's no hurry; take your time. I'll be jotting down notes if that's okay...'

Staring mainly at the table, the young man haltingly described the night of the brawl. Several months ago at closing time, he'd emerged from his local pub with his girlfriend, almost falling into an aggressive stand-off between two groups of men. He and his girlfriend had tried to circumvent the clash, but she'd gone one way and he the other. Concerned for his girl, he'd turned back to find her the same moment as the police arrived. A fight had kicked off big time by then, and the next thing he knew he was falling to the ground in sudden pain, later discovering he'd been tasered on the back by a policeman.

Nat lifted her head from her notepad. 'I have no idea how that must feel, Dwayne. An electrical current through your body must be incredibly painful, I'm sure. Can you describe it?'

Dwayne scrunched his face. 'You know when you get really bad cramp? Playing footie? Like that, but worse. You go stiff and can't move. It came out of nowhere, so the shock made me think I was… I don't know; sounds daft, but I thought I was having a heart attack or something. It hurt really badly, making me fall forwards and hit the ground. There was a bruise for ages–'

'From the impact of the fall?'

He touched his face. 'Oh yeah, that too, but I meant the stun gun.' He appeared bashful again. 'My back was sore where I'd been tasered; the skin had a red scorch in the middle. You know, like a cigarette burn. Kelly – my girlfriend – she took photos of everything. She told her dad what had happened, and he reported it.'

'Bright girl.'

He grinned and finally met Nat's gaze. 'Yeah, she's brilliant.'

'Will she be okay giving me a statement? She can come here, or I'll go to her if it's easier.'

'Yeah, she'd love that. She's a typist at a local builders, so she's pretty hot with that stuff…'

'Excellent.' Nat sat back. The case looked pretty good so far. Liability wouldn't be hard to prove in the light of the findings of the PCC. Damages were the thing. How much would Dwayne be entitled to for the injuries he'd sustained? Not just physical harm but also mental. As well as compensation for any financial loss. 'So let's talk about what happened after the incident,' she said.

Nat continued to ask all the relevant questions. Did Dwayne receive medical help at the time or later? Did he go to A&E or see his GP? Did he miss days at work or suffer salary and any other financial losses? What about the clothes he was wearing or his mobile phone? Did anything get ruined, torn or smashed? How long had it taken his injuries to heal? How did he feel about the attack? Any emotional or psychological issues at the time or still now? Any flashbacks, insecurities, bad dreams?

Once Dwayne had left, she sat tapping her pen for a while.

Of course the assumptions had been hers, Gavin had said very little about him. She had expected a youth with swinging arms, a bad attitude and an arrogant leer. She'd been wrong-footed by the suit and the sweet smile. But neither judgement was right. It didn't matter about the veneer; she'd discovered in the last few months alone that it was often wholly – and sometimes alarmingly – wrong.

Bringing her mind back to Dwayne, she doodled on her pad. His father had had scrapes with the law, that was true, but the boy lived with his mum who worked ridiculous hours in Morrisons to keep a roof over his head. The skirmish had not been of his making. He had simply got in the way of an overzealous PC. She couldn't imagine how painful and shocking it must be to be tasered. Gavin was right; it felt good to be acting for the underdog; she wanted to do her best for him.

'You were the only person to get tasered that night. Why do you think the police officer picked on you?' she'd finally asked, waiting and wondering about his reply.

He hadn't mentioned the colour of his skin. Instead he'd shrugged and smiled, keen to know whether he had a claim, how much he'd get, how soon Nat could start, how long it would take. But her advice was to wait; they had the findings of the PCC, but if the officer was also found guilty of the assault charge, so much the better. And the evidence the PC gave during his trial would give them the heads up for the civil compensation claim.

Dwayne had left with slumped shoulders, but Nat promised to find out more about the criminal proceedings. That was a legitimate request she could ask Gavin about without breaching Chinese walls or client confidentiality, and if he was busy she'd take the short cut by asking his bubbly secretary, Chantelle.

Scooping up her mobile, she tried Gavin first, but it clicked on to voicemail. Then she phoned Chantelle, who answered straight away.

'What's the big man's excuse today?' Nat opened.

'What? Excuse? Sorry?' his secretary replied.

'Gav's excuse for ignoring my call.'

Chantelle didn't reply and it finally struck Nat that her voice had sounded tearful. 'Hey, are you okay, Chantelle? Gav hasn't been winding you up again, has he? Best way is to bat it back fast, so he doesn't know what's hit him.'

'Oh God, Nat.' A pause and a sob. 'Haven't you heard? It's just terrible.'

Goosebumps stabbed Nat's skin. 'Heard what, Chantelle? What's happened?'

When Nat had finished the call, she sat for breathless moments and stared at her hands. They were trembling. Her arms and her legs were shaking uncontrollably. It was too, too dreadful. Focus, she had to focus. Jumping from her chair, she strode to the door, pelted down the stairs, through the first-floor reception, then burst into Wes's glassy office without knocking.

His phone to his ear and his expression grave, he lifted a hand. Clearly listening to the caller, he nodded several times, making notes.

'I'm so sorry again. Thank you for letting me know,' he said finally, turning to Nat.

'You've heard too,' she rushed, her heart hammering her chest. 'What should we do, Wes? Go to the hospital? Or is that too intrusive? We can't just send a text. I don't know what, but we have to do something.'

Wes frowned. He peered at the scrawl he'd just made, as though it would give him an answer. Then he took a deep breath. 'She's dead, Nat. She was dead before the ambulance arrived. There would be no point going to the hospital. I'm not even sure she'll be–'

Nat found herself shouting; yelling and crying and covering her face. 'But Chantelle, Chantelle said she was still in surgery. She said it just now. She can't be dead. That's just too cruel. It's unbearable, Wes.'

He stood, gathering her tightly in his arms. 'It's a shock and terribly tragic…' he started. Then he pulled away and studied her blankly. 'Chantelle?' he asked, clearly perplexed. 'That was… Are we talking about the same thing?'

Wiping her cheeks with shaking fingers, Nat stared, hope upon hope that they weren't. 'Who are you talking about, Wes?'

He stepped back and put a hand on his notes. 'That was Brian Selby's PA. Selby has been arrested.' He rubbed his cropped hair. 'Arrested for the murder of his eldest daughter.' He took a sharp breath. 'And you?'

'Ruthie, Gavin's Ruthie.' The tears were flooding again; it was a struggle to speak. 'Little Ruthie Savage, Wes. She's been shot. The shooting on the news yesterday. It was her.'

4

TRUST

The puzzlement on Wes's face was replaced by disbelief. 'Ruthie? No.' He shook his head and frowned. 'No, there must be a mistake; there has to be.'

'I said the same thing to Chantelle. I wish it were, but it isn't. She's been in surgery on and off since yesterday. I'm so sorry, Wes.'

'No, God, no.' Putting a hand to his mouth he stared with unfocused eyes. 'Heather, Gavin, the boys... How on earth must they...? She's been shot? My God, it's horrendous.'

What could Nat say? She herself was devastated, but Wes had been good friends with Gavin at law school and after; he'd known Ruthie since birth.

He stepped to the window. Gazing out, he was silent for some time. Finally he turned. 'What the fuck, Nat? A petrol station, wasn't it? In Salford? What the hell was Ruthie doing there?'

'I don't know, Wes. Let's see what we can find out online...'

Sharon was perched at her workstation as usual. God knows what she made of the commotion in Wes's office. She'd been Nat's secretary for many years, but for the last five she'd worked for him. Well-meaning and loyal, but hopelessly indiscreet, she made no attempt to close her gaping mouth when Nat finally left with a tear-stained face.

'Tom, Dick and Harry' at the fee-earner's bench made more of an effort to disguise their curiosity, and Emilia wasn't there with her uncanny ability to pick up on gossip, so that was something. Nat wasn't ready to share her sheer shock and dismay. The headline news only yesterday was her gorgeous little companion Ruthie. Unbelievable. Devastating. She felt guilty too. She'd all but forgotten about the shooting; she'd been so wrapped up in the delight of meeting and connecting with Wes's mum that she'd barely stopped to register the enormity of the incident just a few miles away.

She and Wes had read what additional news there was on the internet. A firearms incident at a Salford petrol station, it said. A seven-year-old child had been caught in the crossfire. She'd been hit in the chest and had suffered a heart attack. She was at the Salford Royal Hospital in a critical condition.

Winded, as though someone had repeatedly punched her, Nat trudged back up the stairs. She had never been remotely connected to gun crime before: not a client, a case, or even a friend of a friend. Shoot-outs only happened in television programmes or films in the UK. At least that's how it felt. Injury by shooting didn't feel tangible or real. But a heart attack did. Her father had died from a myocardial infarction when Nat was in her twenties; Jack Goldman had survived one last year. But a seven-year-old, smiley kid? It didn't bear thinking about. Nat had been in the car with Jack when he'd suffered his coronary. For over an hour she'd clutched his trademark retro geek glasses, convinced he was dead. The thought of little Ruthie scared and in pain was intolerable; she wasn't prepared to consider her death.

Feeling disorientated and useless, she tried to focus on her cases, but her mind hopped about repeatedly, her ability to concentrate all gone. She and Wes had agreed to text and leave messages on Gavin's voicemail, offering condolences and assistance in whatever way they could; it didn't seem appropriate to turn up at the hospital. They were friends, not family.

Her impotence frustrating her, Nat stood and paced the room. What else could she do to help? From what Chantelle had said, Gavin and Heather were at the hospital and Ruthie's brothers were with their grandparents. Chantelle was holding the fort at Savage Solicitors until someone told her what to do, but the poor woman was finding it difficult; she couldn't stop crying and the phone had been ringing all day.

Knowing there was no point in staying, Nat collected her handbag and coat, changed her heels for Ugg boots and clomped robotically down the stairs to the slushy pavement outside. Vaguely aware of the sharp wind on her cheeks, she crossed the road and waited for fifteen minutes at the bus stop. It wasn't until she was staring through the grimy window of the 42B that she remembered two things. The first was that her new company car was still parked behind the office. The second was the astonishing news about Brian Selby, the wealthy client she and Emilia had labelled the 'Three Ls'. Lardy, leery and loaded. Not terribly kind, but true.

What the...? Her brain was finally catching up. Had Wes really said he'd been arrested for murder? The murder of his daughter? It was difficult to focus her shattered mind, but what the fuck? The Yorkshireman was a little too tactile and bordered on various *isms* at times; she and Wes had rowed after a sycophantic night out to keep the man sweet; she had been the butt of many jokes about being his 'lucky lady', but overall he'd seemed fairly harmless. A dinosaur, yes, but not a killer, surely? Even worse, a daughter killer. Bizarre, too bizarre. He was married to a woman called Shirley, but Nat'd had no idea he was a father. He just didn't seem the type to have kids.

Flaming assumptions again, she supposed.

Almost missing her stop on Cheadle High Street, Nat hurriedly stood and pressed the bell, then tramped towards home through patches of white that hadn't been walked on all day. As she rounded the corner, she took in her mum's old Ford. Parked in the same spot as the last two weeks, its roof and windscreen were covered in a thick layer of snow. Nat sighed: this was more evidence of her mum's reluctance to venture out of the house. Her friend Barbara had fallen and badly fractured her ankle. Though Barbara was enjoying her hospital sojourn, Anna had become extremely fearful, convinced that a skid, a slide or a tumble was inevitable. Nat was trying her best to be sympathetic, but she was definitely struggling. When Anna had suffered her stroke last summer, being housebound was obligatory, but now she'd recovered so brilliantly, Nat didn't want her to slip back.

'You're being silly about the weather. Don't get old before your time, Mum,' she wanted to snap.

Being tetchy wasn't nice, but at times it was difficult to hold it in. Familiarity, no doubt. She couldn't wish for a better mum, but sharing a small house with one's mother at forty was not how she'd thought her life would be.

Banging the snow off her boots, she stepped into her warm home. The aroma of cooking and Poppy cat greeted her, soon followed by the tom. Holding a tea towel, Anna appeared moments later.

'You're home early. I've just put in...' Then with one anxious glance, 'Skarbie, love, what's wrong?'

It was easy to answer. Plain words. With her mum, that's all it needed. 'You know the shooting on the news yesterday? The child caught in the crossfire in Salford? That was little Ruthie Savage.'

Her mum's face was immediately aghast. 'Ruthie? A shooting? Surely that can't be true.'

'I know. I'm struggling to believe it.'

'Oh, Natalie. It's too dreadful.'

Anna held out her arms. She knew the Savage children well. Every few weeks Nat drove Ruthie and her brothers to a country park. After a couple of hours at the playground, ball games and a paddle in the river, they'd decamp at McDonald's for a Happy Meal, followed by Nat's sofa to munch a few crisps and watch a DVD under Anna's watchful gaze.

The tradition started last year when Gavin had a call-out to a police station. To represent Wes as it happened. Gavin had trusted Nat to take over the play area, races and rapids duties. Keeping two eyes on four children under the age of ten had been heart-in-mouth challenging, but with Ruthie's help, she had turned out to be 'a natural', as he'd put it.

The memory brought fresh tears to her eyes. Little Ruthie. Oh God. It still felt far-fetched, unreal.

Nat told Anna about the little she knew. Their appetite clean gone, they sat in the kitchen and drank strong tea until the silence was punctured by a rap at the door. 'That'll be Wes,' Nat said. 'I'll get it.'

With no plan in mind, the three of them moved to the small console beneath the bay and played rummy. Shaking her head, Nat sighed deeply. Cards and contemplation; another flaming ritual. But this was for when life went awry, crooked or lopsided; like heartbreak or whiplash, misunderstandings or arguments. Nothing remotely like today. Ruthie Savage had been shot; she'd had a heart attack; she was in intensive care. Nat tapped her foot.

God, she wished she could do something to help; perhaps pray for a miracle or invoke divine intervention. In truth spiritual things were more Anna's department than hers, but she longed to do something practical: organise, provide, drive or shop, even answer the phone or reply to a message.

Dropping her cards on the tabletop, she gave up her hand and shifted her thoughts. 'What did Brian Selby's PA want you to do, Wes?'

'I don't think she knew, really. She was shocked; she'd only just heard herself.' He rubbed his face. 'Bloody hell, Brian arrested for murder? Seems crazy, but the police must have grounds. It's not every day you get a call like that.' He smiled wryly. 'Present company excepted...'

Nat nodded. Gavin Savage was the master of dark humour. Taught by him, grim comedy had been their way of coping after Wes's brush with the law. Then there'd been the discovery of what Andrea had done to Matty. Dry drollness enabled them to talk about the traumatic repercussions. Mostly, anyway.

'So what did you advise her to do?' she asked, noting how tired he looked.

'I said that Goldman Law would help in any way we could, but that we're not criminal specialists.' He grimaced. 'Shit; I've just realised; I recommended Savage Solicitors...'

They fell quiet again, Anna quietly collecting their cups and leaving the table. Knowing she'd be thinking about food and what vegetables to prepare, Nat watched her pad to the kitchen. She was actually glad; her treacherous stomach was rumbling. Bad though it was, she was ravenous.

She came back to Wes's dark gaze and smiled thinly. 'There'll be no one quite as unique or tenacious as Gav, but I'm sure Brian will find someone else to represent him. I'll ask around for a recommendation and phone Chantelle later.' She paused, a sardonic quip surfacing, as it always did. 'Though Gav will be really pissed off missing a "juicy murder case" as he'd put it. A wealthy Ned too.' She caught Wes's wince. 'Inappropriate, I know. Sorry. It just doesn't feel real, does it?'

Returning the smile, Wes reached for her hand. 'You're itching to do something, aren't you? To help Gavin and Ruthie. You're no good waiting around, doing nothing.'

She threaded her fingers through his. 'Except when I'm with you...'

The smile spread. 'Yeah. Don't I know it. I'm turning into a domestic goddess, pandering to your every need.' He laughed. 'Feeding you too.'

Feeling a surge of desire, she looked down to hide her embarrassment. What was it about this man? Was it love or just lust? Perhaps she'd been blessed with a perfect combination of the two. Could Natalie Bach really be so lucky?

'Your dad didn't seem fazed by a virtually naked woman appearing in your brother's lounge.' She took a breath, a little stab of disappointment still there. 'He thought I was Sidney's girlfriend.'

Wes lifted an eyebrow. 'Clearly Sidney has good taste.' Then, studying her face, 'We both let Mum filter what she thinks Dad needs to know.'

'Why?'

He shrugged. 'Mum's the boss. It's the way it's always been. Don't all mothers do that?'

Nat thought of her own mother and the 'filtering' about her father. She knew little of his history. He was some years older than Anna and he'd been in a Polish camp sometime in his youth, but that's all she'd been told. On the rare occasions she'd asked about him, her mum had been evasive. But then again, had she tried very hard with her questions? Probably not. She hadn't had an easy relationship with her dad. He'd been angry and distant, and she hadn't felt very loved. When he died, she'd felt more anger than grief.

Bloody hell; what a rotten daughter.

She shook those thoughts away and focused on one more positive. 'Your mum knew my name…' she said, aware of colour flooding her cheeks.

And there it was, Wesley Hughes's inscrutable look: a combination of a frown and backlit eyes. 'Of course she did,' he replied.

Her stomach clenching with apprehension, she waited, wanting more, needing to know what the future held for them; if he'd really meant the promises he'd made on her birthday. She saw him draw breath, but the loud peal of her mobile interrupted the moment. She scooped it up with trembling fingers: the caller was Gavin.

'Nat.'

'Oh, Gav, how are you?' Then, her utterance croaky with nerves. 'How's Ruthie?'

'Still unresponsive.'

'I'm so, so sorry…'

She paused for him to speak further, but he was silent, which said more than words.

Tears were at the surface, but she inhaled deeply to stop them. 'What can I do, Gav? Wes is here too. Tell us what we can do to help. Anything at all. Anything we can do for you, Ruthie, Heather, the boys. Just say the word.'

For a moment he didn't speak, then finally he sighed. 'She had a heart attack, Nat. My little girl. Right next to me on the petrol forecourt.' His voice was hoarse. 'And it was entirely my fault. I got a call-out to collect some paperwork from a client and I took her with me for the ride. Salford, Nat. Bloody Salford. Why the hell didn't I think?'

Fighting her own wobbling emotions, Nat swallowed. She

wanted to say that no one could have possibly predicted what had happened in a million years, to soothe words of comfort and make him feel better, but she sensed that wasn't what was required right now.

He cleared his throat and continued to speak. 'I went to pay for the petrol and left her in the car. How bloody, bloody stupid was that? I even saw the lads on their bikes and still didn't think. Nothing until the sound of fireworks when I paid. I turned to look, just a curious glance, wondering what was going on. Then I noticed the car window. It was smashed and I just knew...'

He stopped speaking again.

'What can I do?' Nat asked. 'How can I help?'

'I can't leave Ruthie. I'm staying here until I know.' His voice dropped to a whisper. 'Until I know either way.' She heard talking in the background. 'The office, Nat,' he said hurriedly. 'That's where I need you right now.'

'Of course, absolutely. So what do you need me to–?'

'Just cover for me. Whatever you think best to keep things ticking over. I have to go. I'll be in touch.'

When she finished the call, she let out the tapped air and met Wes's inquisitive gaze. 'He needs me to help out at Savage Solicitors.'

'Right. Great. So how will that work?'

Nat shrugged. 'I'll be like a locum, I guess.' She stared at her mobile as though it would give her the information Gavin hadn't had time to impart. 'Picking up his caseload and running with it? Or at least sorting out anything urgent and doing the necessary, I suppose.'

He nodded slowly. 'Good; that's good. And I'll do the same for you.'

She put her hand on his. 'You can't take on more work, Wes. You're mega busy as it is, still catching up from...' Anxiety rising, she studied his drawn face. She had done her best with his files during his time away from the office, but he was still working late every night, struggling to keep on top of a heavy caseload, even with the help of Max, Emilia and the bench boys.

Deep in thought, she rapped her fingers, an idea slotting into place. The answer was obvious. She looked at Wes and nodded. 'But I know someone who can.' She lifted her eyebrows. 'Someone who has too much time on his hands and needs a mission.' She smiled. 'And he is the real boss, after all.'

Jack Goldman, of course. Catherine had put him under 'garden arrest' since his heart problem and it was driving him nuts. Remembering his words when he'd saved her from a similar fate last September, she scooped up her mobile.

'Goldman Law, first thing tomorrow morning,' she said when he answered. 'I need someone I can trust.'

5

JUICY MURDER

After a night of surprisingly solid sleep, Nat was up early, determined and ready for the day ahead. She chipped the icy snow from her mum's car windscreen and almost climbed in, only remembering at the last moment that she had her own transport, still parked at the back of Goldman Law's offices.

Of course, Jack had been behind the new company vehicle. He'd phoned her late at home, the Friday before last. 'Expect a delivery tomorrow,' he'd said, as cryptic as ever.

'Are you going to give me a clue?' she'd asked, knowing a 'delivery' from Jack could mean anything. The last dispatch to her house had been Jack himself on the way to his heart attack.

'An A-Class,' he'd replied. 'I thought the Jupiter Red would suit you.'

Which was great, it really was... It just felt a little too permanent, that's all. Still, Jack had risen to the challenge yesterday.

'I would be delighted,' he'd said in reply to her request to look after her files for a few days. 'How come I have the honour?'

'I need to do a spot of locum work for a solicitor friend in Heald Green.' She hadn't really wanted to go into Ruthie and the shooting in detail on the phone. 'His daughter is seriously ill in intensive care.'

'Ah,' he'd replied without inquiring further.

But she'd given him enough information to understand. After his hospital admission, Jack had surprised himself by going through the emotional trauma other mere mortals suffered after illness: sadness, anxiety, guilt, loneliness and regret, but most of all he'd been frightened, 'crippling fear' as he'd described it.

She now stared absently at her mum's car keys. To use it or schlep into Didsbury to get her own? But thoughts of Jack were still prodding. Yes, he had taken up the gauntlet of her cases, but was that an entirely good thing?

She sighed. Indulgent and coaxing, punctilious and strict, he'd brought her up in many ways, shaping the adult, as well as the solicitor, she'd become. Nat had found herself bending the rules or turning a blind eye far more often than she should. Interfering too? Yup, that was something else she could lay at his door. Jack had always meddled, a finger in every pie, and now she'd *invited* him to poke around in her files. God, was she insane?

Decision made, she returned to the house and posted Anna's keys back through the letterbox. Then she gingerly trod in the slush towards the shops, slipping more than once and wryly acknowledging her mum's refusal to step out. Rubbing her hands against the cold, she watched the bus take its time up the high street. Dismayed to see Clipper Man through the murky window, she finally climbed on. For God's sake; the bloody man was cutting his nails again. She gave him what she hoped was an extremely disapproving frown and brushed past. Lucky for him she had more urgent matters pressing this morning, but one day she'd do flaming something, even if it was sweeping up his DNA and sending it to the transport police.

The ten-minute journey was held up by road works on the Mersey bridge, yet again. Conscious of the ticking time and the imperative to start her assignment for Gavin, she'd planned to walk straight to her Mercedes, but when she arrived at the corner building, she decided a few scribbled instructions to Jack would be sensible. Naturally he would ignore any suggestions and do exactly as he wished, but the thought of at least trying made her feel marginally protected from a Jack Goldman tampering overhaul. Removing her heels, she jogged up the stairs and swiped into the second-floor offices, but her diversion was too late; the man himself was already at the conference table, clearly comfortable in her seat.

She glanced at her watch. Bloody hell; only eight forty-five and he was already in full throttle on the telephone. She leaned against the door frame and watched him in action. Hmm... was he doing her a favour or the other way around? His bright eyes suggested the latter. Despite his recent setback, he looked good for his sixty-one years. His thick black hair was peppered with grey, but it added that 'silver fox' appeal many women found attractive. Not that she'd ever seen him in that light. His current wife had, of course. The discovery that Catherine was his secret mistress had been a shock and their friendship never the same; each time they had tried to rekindle it, the flame had flickered but ultimately died. Then there was her old friend's 'mutual need' with Wes, but Nat wasn't thinking about that.

Nat nodded at the filing cabinet when Jack finally put down the phone. 'Is there any point?' she asked with a wry smile.

'Nope,' he replied, leaning back in the chair. 'I think you'll find–'

'That you have taught me everything I know.' She snorted and turned away. 'Have fun,' she called before the door closed. 'And call me.'

The Mercedes was probably the newest car on Finney Lane; if not, it was certainly the most expensive. Indicating right, Nat peered up at the Savage Solicitors sign. Over the Christmas period, one of Gavin's Neds had risked life and limb by hanging out of the window above to decorate it, and the second S was still entwined with tinsel. The green chlorosis hue looked like she'd felt after boozy nights out with its owner.

Parking outside the bookies, she hoped for the best. She didn't want her new car to get stolen or scratched just yet. Last year Gavin had left his recently bought mountain bike in reception and the client he'd just interviewed stole it.

'Not a very subtle career criminal,' he had commented with a grin, but at least he'd known the identity of the thief and had demanded the cycle back with 'interest'. The punishment in that instance had been cleaning; the Ned had been required to scrub and polish the Cannondale after Gav's cross-country jaunts for the following six weeks.

'I see. Prosecution, judge and jury,' Nat had laughed at the time, but as she greeted his floppy-haired ex-offender receptionist, she thought there was something in Gavin's own brand of justice. With the one eye she could see beneath his fringe, the boy was making contact; there was almost a smile, albeit of relief.

'How's the boss?' he asked immediately, following her in to Gavin's office. He looked at his feet. 'And his little girl? Is she going to be okay?'

It brought Nat back to reality with a thump, to the reason she was here. After their conversation yesterday, she had received a single message from Gavin: *I won't be texting much, so don't expect to hear from me. But no news is good news, okay?*

Every time a text had come through last night, her heart had raced with alarm. Ironically it was the opposite of six months ago when she'd stared at her mobile for hours, willing it to beep, buzz or ring. She had thought Jose's ditching her, and then his silence, were the worst things in the world, but of course she was wrong. The possibility of losing a child was.

Breathing in the usual mushroomy smell, she went back to the youth, whose anxious face was now mottled with red patches. 'I really hope so,' she replied. 'Ruthie is very poorly, but they're taking it a day at a time. I think that's the best way to put it...' She couldn't remember his name. It seemed rude to enquire when she'd met him several times. 'Where's Chantelle?' she asked.

The boy opened his mouth, but a loud gurgle of flushing and vibrating pipes answered for him, then the lady in question appeared, adjusting the hem of a shiny black dress more suited to a nightclub. She was still as rotund as the last time Nat saw her, her face a replica of the young Elizabeth Taylor's.

'Natalie!' Holding out her arms, she tottered towards Nat as fast as the Lycra would allow. 'Thank goodness you're here. Robbie's been brilliant, but there are only so many Neds he can advise in a day–'

Nat cringed. 'Maybe call them "clients", Chantelle, just for this week? And who's Robbie?'

The burglar-cum-receptionist held up his hand, testing Nat's assumptions big time. She stared. 'You're Robbie and you've been seeing the clients?'

Chantelle smacked his head playfully. 'He is a paralegal,' she answered for him. From Robbie's expression, Nat suspected the slap was harder than his workmate had intended. 'A *certified* paralegal, just passed his diploma or whatever,' Chantelle continued obliviously. 'Turns out he's a smart bloody Alec.'

'Oh fab. Congrats,' Nat replied. Taking in his flicker of pride, she made a silent promise not to let anything in this office astonish her again. She flopped down into Gavin's leather chair. 'Okay, let's get started. Who's going to bring me up to speed? Where should I begin?' Staring at the messy desk, she thought for a moment. 'Well, let's put it this way, what definitely can't wait?'

Gavin's two employees looked at each other with saucer eyes. 'Robbie instructed Larry to cover this morning's mags, and I've put off this week's old dears...' Chantelle said eventually.

Knowing she'd have to get used to this surreal, goose-bumpy feeling pretty damn soon, Nat took a deep breath. She gathered the 'mags' was a magistrates court somewhere, but 'Larry' and 'old dears' were a mystery.

She put a pencil behind her ear, Savage-like. 'So who is Larry?'

'Larry Lamb.'

The pinpricks increased. There were only three Larry Lambs she knew of. Her childhood knitted sheep, an actor and– 'Not Lawrence Lamb QC?'

Chantelle and Robbie nodded.

Trying to quell the surprise, Nat swallowed. Lawrence Lamb had been the doddery head of a barrister's chambers when she'd first qualified. He had to be a hundred and three; he'd retired years ago, surely? Maybe this Larry was number four. 'No, it can't be the same one. Not the Queen's Counsel Larry. He must be–'

'He only works part-time,' Chantelle said reasonably, as though reduced hours for a centenarian made it perfectly normal. 'Gavin can't always be in two places at once and it gets Larry out and about.'

'Well that's all right then. Does he get paid?' she asked. 'No, don't tell me. What about the "old dears"?'

'Gavin's OAP session every Wednesday morning. Robbie does silver surfer sessions on the laptop while they're waiting to see Gavin.' Playing with one of her hoop earrings, Chantelle glanced at Robbie, who was shuffling his feet.

'And?' Nat asked, the prickling turning to perspiration. 'Come on, guys, spit it out.'

Chantelle's cheeks pinked. 'Well, you asked what couldn't wait. We have a new, er... a new "client" you need to see PDQ...'

An actual client, alleluia! Glad to have something solid to deal with, Nat looked at her watch. 'Okay, great.' She rubbed her hands. 'What time will he or she be here?'

Sounding distinctly Mancunian, Robbie finally piped up. 'He isn't here. He's in custody at Salford West. He was arrested yesterday morning for murder. His name is–'

Wanting to smack her own head Chantelle-like, Nat winced. Oh hell, she knew what was coming and it was her own stupid fault.

'Brian Selby,' Robbie continued. 'I've no idea who referred him to us, but his PA was really upset, so we said yes...'

Oh God, Brian Selby, the 'Three Ls' from Doncaster. They hadn't turned him away. Nat had forgotten to speak to Chantelle about it. And the poor man had been arrested yesterday. More to the point, one of Goldman Law's most wealthy clients had been in a bloody police cell for God knows how many hours.

Though Robbie's sore blotches had resurfaced, he was peering at her carefully. 'Thing is, Mrs Bach... it was a personal recommendation.' His eyes flickered to Chantelle. 'And we thought, me and Chantelle thought the boss wouldn't want to miss out on a–'

Nat nodded. 'On a juicy murder.' Feeling a surge of near hysteria, she smiled stiffly. Part of her wanted to shout at this pair, but the other wanted to kiss them both for their loyalty to Gavin.

She took a deep, calming breath. 'Okay. Okay...' Talk about starting at the drowning end; it was only a murder; what could possibly go wrong? She eyeballed Robbie. 'The first thing: Mrs Bach is my mum, and I'm Natalie or Nat. The second: tell me absolutely everything, whether or not you think it's important. What do we know so far?'

Chantelle was now filing letters in the dented grey cabinets, but she spoke over her shoulder. 'Joshim said he'd call back if he finds out anything more.'

Nat spun around. 'Joshim? What? *My* Joshim?'

She stared at Chantelle's placid profile, and her heart fell to the floor. Oh God, it had to be him. A couple of months ago, she and Gavin had met up with their old law school mate, Joshim, for a few pints and a curry. Immediately smitten with his 'boy band' good looks, Chantelle had invited herself along and had spent most of the night smashed and squashed on his knee, determined to 'make him straight'. She hadn't, but they'd clearly remained friends.

'Please say it's not Joshim Khan. He's a CPS solicitor, Chantelle. A prosecutor! That means he's the enemy, poised to lock Brian up for as long as humanly possible. What did you say to him?'

Chantelle put her hand on what should've been a hip and looked at Robbie with raised eyebrows. 'We're not stupid, Natalie. Besides, we don't know anything.'

'Except this.' Robbie turned the laptop towards Nat.

'Facebook? Not now, Robbie.'

'It's the Greater Manchester Police Facebook page,' he replied patiently. He read it aloud. '*A fifty-four-year-old man has been arrested for the murder of his twenty-nine-year-old daughter.*' He looked at the time on his mobile. 'That was posted yesterday. He asked for legal advice, so the police can't question him until he's seen you, and before that they have to give you disclosure of all the allegations. Mr Selby knows to say nothing until then. Because it's murder, they can hold him for thirty-six hours before charging him.' He clicked another tab. 'Route planner to Salford West. The motorway's the best way, it's actually in Swinton.'

Nat stared. True, she hadn't brushed shoulders with 'crime' since her mid-twenties, but a flaming police Facebook page. Too loved-up and busy, she hadn't bothered much with social media in Mallorca, but clearly she had to up her game. Big bloody time. She turned to Chantelle, now humming a tune as she sashayed about her chores. 'Right. Are you okay to hold the fort? I'm off to Swinton, apparently. Smart Alec is coming with me.'

6

MORPHINE

Where was Gavin Savage when you needed him? Nat thought during the half-hour journey to the police station. Her criminal law expertise was pretty much zilch. Though she'd never fist-fought with the long arm of the law, she had been on the periphery once or twice, mainly defending Jack Goldman's obdurate son – a charge of criminal damage for smashing a shop window, and his refusal to take a breathalyser only a day or two after passing his driving test. Those had only involved a plea of mitigation, trying to persuade the stony-faced magistrates, with a suitably simpering smile, to be lenient: Julian had been young and foolish; his parents had recently split; he'd been too easily influenced by peer pressure; he had asthma. The usual baloney.

Of course there had been last year's shocking wallop with proper crime: a charge of assault against Julian, upgraded to attempted murder, and Wes's arrest, but they had been passed on to Gavin, as it was his speciality. He'd played a blinder with both, using the old 'Savage charm' to get them bail, and eventually persuading the police to drop the charges.

God, Gavin, poor Gavin. Of course the resolution of both cases had been more than just his tongue-in-cheek personality.

It had involved long hours, hard work, determination and sharp intelligence. She took a deep breath; she'd do everything in her power to do the same.

The beep of her mobile interrupted her thoughts. She glanced at her companion. Pale and clutching his seat belt, Robbie was staring fixedly through the windscreen. He had been so quiet she'd almost forgotten he was there.

'Grab my phone and see who that's from, would you, Robbie? It's in my handbag.'

His Adam's apple bobbed, but he duly complied, holding it up with trembling fingers. 'It's a message from Mr Khan.'

Nat's heart sank. 'Okay, read it out.'

Robbie cleared his throat. 'On the QT. Thought it might help to know that Brian Selby has already confessed. Call if you need me.'

Her ticker fell even lower. 'No, Joshim, it doesn't damned well help!' she wanted to shout, but from Robbie's tight expression, she sensed he was already terrified. She was pretty damned anxious herself, but a brave face was the thing.

'Okey-dokey. No worries.'

She smiled and dug for something hearty that Gavin might say. Nah; she couldn't find anything that wasn't an 'ist' or an 'ism', so she settled on the old Scots proverb hung up in Gavin's office loo: 'If ye like the nut, crack it.'

The traffic was heavy, every light predictably on red, but Nat finally managed to drive into the police station car park and pulled up next to a police van.

Her nerves tingled. 'A "Big Black Mariah",' she quipped to her companion. Not surprisingly his pale face was blank. In fairness she was an infant when the song came out, so he wouldn't have even been a twinkle in his dad's eye, if indeed his dad had been born.

Oh God, she was internally blathering. Thoughts of Ruthie had been prodding in between her general panic, but she also had to block out the constant worry of how she was progressing. Focus, Natalie, and get a grip. She took a huge gulp of air; she was *not* going to cock this up for Gavin. Or for Brian Selby; whatever had happened, he was now her client and it was her legal duty to represent him to the best of her ability.

She nodded briskly to Robbie. 'Come on, then. Let's do this.'

Standing as tall as her five-foot-five would allow, Nat announced herself to the sergeant at the counter. Her eyes swept the room as she waited, coming to rest on the far wall. Her stomach lurched as she stared. Bloody hell; a firearms surrender poster. She prayed Gavin and Heather would never see it; the irony of their child's shooting during an amnesty period would surely heap on the agony.

Pursing her lips, she tried to blow out her anger. Over the last twenty-four hours she'd found herself having murderous thoughts of her own. Jack had often said she found 'excuses where there aren't any' when it came to bad or criminal behaviour. Nat disagreed; considering the bigger picture was important to her; not excusing the offence or offender, but searching for reasons: poor parenting, poor education, poverty, peer pressure and, of course, mental illness. But she had discovered that her reactions were very different when the crime was close to home. She'd had no forgiveness for what Andrea had done to Wes and their sons, and if someone gave her a pistol now, she'd happily mete out an eye-for-an-eye punishment to whoever had shot Ruthie.

Tapping their feet in unison, she and Robbie sat side by side. A weary-looking female detective eventually appeared and showed them through to an office. She didn't ask them to sit down.

'So disclosure,' she said, shuffling her papers. 'Your client smothered his adult daughter to death at 2200 hours on Sunday night. He admitted it to his local GP who duly informed the police.'

'And...?' Nat asked.

She shrugged. 'As mentioned, he told his doctor. He'll be charged with murder.'

'That's your "disclosure"?'

The woman had the good grace to look sheepish. 'Pretty much.' She again lifted her shoulders. 'Your client has confessed, Ms Bach. I'll ask someone to take you through.'

Nat frowned. Wasn't the law meant to be equitable these days? Weren't the other party to any case, either civil or criminal, supposed to show their hand at the outset in the interests of fair play? But the word 'smothered' was interesting.

Following an officer who wasn't old enough to shave, they were shown into an echoey interview room. Brian Selby was sitting at a table attached to the wall. If he was surprised to see Nat, he didn't show it. Indeed; he didn't show any recognition at all. He appeared deflated; still a large man but sagging within, completely diminished from the braggart she'd spent a boozy dinner with only a few weeks ago.

Breathing in the stench of body odour mixed with pine disinfectant, Nat held out her hand. 'Hello, Brian. It's Natalie, if you remember? Natalie Bach.' She resisted describing herself as his 'lucky lady'. His luck was clearly all out. 'I'm on a secondment with Savage Solicitors. Gavin Savage is currently indisposed, but I'm here to help.'

She looked at his pasty face and felt a surge of emotion. His eyes were empty. It was as though he was insubstantial, just the plump body shell with nothing inside. She inhaled sharply. It was hardly surprising: whatever had occurred at the weekend, his daughter was dead. Until that moment, the dreadful reality hadn't sunk in. This man had lost his child: she wasn't just gone forever, but had also died by his own hand.

She waited for some acknowledgement, but none came. 'Did you hear what I said, Brian? This is Robbie...' She didn't know the boy's surname. 'Robbie Smart,' she said, improvising. 'We're here to represent you. Because a period has passed on account of Mr Savage's unexpected absence, we don't have much time before the police...' She cleared her throat. 'They intend to charge you with murder, Brian. It's important that you focus and tell us exactly what happened. Do you understand?'

He nodded, his eyes momentarily focusing. 'It was me. I...' He stretched out his large hands and pressed them on the table. 'I suffocated her.'

Nat waited for him to elaborate, but he'd drifted again.

'Why, Brian? Why did you do that?' she asked, the same time as her mobile beeped.

The text was from Joshim Khan. *Ask for disclosure of the GP's statement*, it said.

She passed her phone to Robbie and nodded. 'Why did you call your doctor, Brian? Why did you tell him about what you'd done?'

Brian's sudden sob made her start. He covered his face with shaking fingers, his grief so intense that Nat had to quickly swallow to hold back her own tears.

'She wanted to die. My Melanie. She'd asked him, our doctor, but his hands were tied. He could only prescribe pain relief. She, she...' He made motions with his hands on his forearms, but Nat didn't understand.

'What did she do?'

'Morphine, she collected the morphine. Went without for

days. Used it that night to end the suffering. But she was still alive, still breathing, so I...'

Robbie pushed a note along the table towards Nat. 'Mercy killing? Assisted suicide?' it said, an echo of her own thoughts since she'd heard the word 'smother'.

She put her hand on Brian's arm. 'Listen carefully, Brian. The police say you admitted to it. But "it" wasn't murder, was it? If I understand what you're trying to say, it was an assisted suicide. Am I right? You aided and abetted your daughter to kill herself. But that isn't murder, is it?'

7

EVERYDAY LIVES

Nat sped along the motorway, spouting off about the police and justice and mercy for a good ten minutes before realising that Robbie hadn't said a word.

'Are you okay, Robbie?' she asked, suddenly twigging he hadn't volunteered a word on the way to the police station either.

His tight, pallid face didn't match the nod of his head, but Nat couldn't focus on him right now. After finishing with Brian, she had spoken to the detective in charge again. She'd refused to disclose the doctor's witness statement 'at this stage', but conceded that Melanie had been seriously ill, bedridden for years with an extreme case of ME.

'Irrespective of that,' she'd said, stifling a yawn, 'your client, Mr Selby, has admitted to killing her. In the absence of evidence to the contrary and considering the time limits, I have no alternative but to charge him with murder. In view of the seriousness of the offence, police bail is refused and any future application for bail will have to go before the magistrates.'

Nat's temperature had dropped by the time they reached Heald Green. The rant had been more about the police keeping information up the long sleeve of the law rather than the outcome. Even if the charge was reduced to assisted suicide, it was still a severe offence which attracted a long prison sentence; she hadn't for a moment supposed they would let Brian walk free. But there were feelings of shame too; she'd made blithe assumptions about Brian Selby in the past, the 'Three Ls' in particular. She hadn't even known he had children, let alone a family tragedy; she couldn't imagine how crippling it must be to have a perfectly healthy daughter who'd lived life to the full until a routine immunisation at thirteen had changed her life.

Watched by two long-faced men smoking outside the bookies, it took Nat several attempts to reverse into her previous slot. At the first opportunity, Robbie bolted from the car, but she stayed for a few moments, picking up her mobile to call Wes. But before she'd had a chance to do so, a message appeared on the screen. Shit; the text was from Gavin. Feeling breathless and sick, she closed her eyes. However much her heart had hurt over Jose, it was a drop in the ocean compared with this. She peered at his name again. Oh God, Gavin had texted when he said that he wouldn't.

Inhaling sharply, she opened the message quickly, as though speed would make a difference.

Police have made an arrest, it said.

Her heart thumped and her hand trembled as she typed a reply. Not bad news, thank God. But nothing she composed sounded quite right. Her relief was immense and the murderous thoughts were still there, but it didn't seem appropriate to text them. She wanted to ask after Ruthie too, but was fearful of a negative reply. So she just kept it simple: *Good. Thinking of you all. Here if you need me.*

Gazing at people going about their everyday lives, she remained in the Merc. A woman in a woollen bobble hat was examining a tray of apples outside the fruit shop, a small child in red wellies was tugging his mother's hand towards the newsagents, an elderly man was emerging from the charity shop, holding a book about crochet. Then there were all the passing cars, people listening to music or the radio, perhaps thinking about dinner and developments in *Coronation Street*.

She shook herself back. The mobile was still clutched in her hand, her knuckles white. There were a million questions she had wanted to ask Gavin: about Heather, about his other kids, and particularly about Ruthie's prognosis. Would his little girl live? But even if it had been appropriate, she'd been too frightened to ask. She still felt winded; just opening one text had knocked her so badly. Suppose it *had* been bad news?

She sighed deeply. Approaching her fortieth had been hard. It had felt as though everyone but her had a family, children. She had wasted five years with Jose and she'd missed the baby boat. At Christmas Wes had touched on them trying for one, but nothing more had been said. Perhaps it was just as well; maybe she was better suited being the indulgent spinster aunt, loving her nephew and nieces and Gavin's kids dearly, but not having the terrifying responsibility of that umbilical attachment.

Still needing to talk, she called Wes, chatting to him for several minutes about Brian and Gavin. Eventually realising he had said very little, she paused and looked at the clock. It was nearly teatime, and yes, her stomach was rumbling. 'Sorry, Wes. Is this a bad time?'

'Of course not. Just listening. You've had quite a day.'

'How about you? How's yours been?' she asked. 'Are you doing anything tonight?'

She flinched the moment the words were out. It sounded like a hint, but it wasn't. She wanted to go home and be fed by her mum, then lie quietly on her sofa until bedtime.

Wes's silence went on for too long for comfort. She found

herself filling it. 'Sorry, I know you're madly busy. You'll be signing your post. And the rest. It was a stupid time to call.'

'No, not at all. It's just that...'

The sense of dread spread, heavy in her limbs. Certain something unpalatable was coming, she rested her head on the steering wheel and waited.

'Andrea has been in touch. She wants to see me, to talk.'

So there it was. The ghost of the Cling-on, alive and kicking.

No. Whatever she wants, say fucking no! her head screamed inside. 'Right. And what did you say?' she asked instead.

A pause, then a sigh. 'I'm thinking about it.'

'What's to think about, Wes?' The surge of anger was sudden. She couldn't have stopped the words even if she'd tried. 'I know it's none of my business, but that woman has tried to ruin your life, not to mention what she did to her own flesh and blood–'

'It's complicated, Nat.'

'No it isn't. It isn't *complicated* at all. She poisoned Matty last year. In all likelihood she'd done it when he was just a little boy. She made your son ill, Wes. That isn't normal. That isn't forgivable. That isn't something you can cure by talking–'

'Well, as you say, Natalie, it's none of your business.'

The call abruptly ending, Nat stared at the blank screen. What the fuck had just happened? Did Wes really say it was 'none of her business'? The man who'd declared love and a whole lot more? Really?

Trying to shake off the disbelief, she climbed out of the car, stepped over an abandoned brandy bottle and opened the office door. Yes, Wes *did* say that. Quite clearly and crisply.

'Everything okay, Nat?'

She looked up at the voice. Chantelle was buttoning her faux leopard print coat.

'Everything okay?' she asked again, putting a hand on Nat's shoulder.

'Yeah, sure,' Nat replied. Little Ruthie, Brian Selby and fucking, fucking Wes. Life was just fine.

Chantelle cocked her head. 'Everything's tied up here for today, Nat. We could go for a drink if you like.' She grinned. 'I hear Joshim Khan came good.'

Nat nodded, realising for the first time that he had. 'Yeah, he did. Robbie too.' She looked at the reception bench, wondering where he had gone. 'Maybe we could go for a drink tomorrow? It sounds pathetic, but I just need my mum.'

'Aw, mums. That I defo understand.' Chantelle took a breath as though to say more, but clamped her lips when Robbie appeared with a mug. She ruffled his hair playfully. 'You okay to lock up, honey bun?'

'Unless anyone needs a lift home?' Nat asked, jangling her keys.

She clocked Chantelle and Robbie exchanging a glance. Was something going on between them? Unlikely, but nothing was impossible these days.

'Nah, we're good. See you tomorrow, Nat,' Chantelle replied. Then after a moment. 'You do know you're on call tomorrow?'

'As in?'

'The duty solicitor rota.'

Lifting her hand, Nat turned to the door. 'I do now. See you guys tomorrow.'

Feeling unbelievably tired, she headed the car towards home. It was less than a two-mile journey, but the roads were chock-a-block, giving her more time to dwell on bloody Wesley than was good for her. She understood things were tangled in his life. She knew about the flux, but allowing Andrea back, even in the smallest way, was dangerous. The evil woman was on remand for criminal offences, for goodness sake; she was vindictive and manipulative; no good would come of speaking to her, let alone seeing her.

But, as Wes had firmly stated, it was none of her business.

She pulled up the Mercedes behind her mum's Ka. Except for some stubborn icy patches, the slush had gone, leaving the pavement gritty. What a difference a day made, she thought, as she walked into the warmth of her home. She breathed in the aroma, that comforting combination of bacon and cabbage, knowing her favourite dish was in the oven for dinner.

Anna appeared from the kitchen, holding stripy oven gloves. 'Hello, Skarbie,' she said, but her eyes darted anxiously.

Oh God, what now? 'What's happened, Mum?'

'Nothing's happened.' Anna glanced at the telephone. 'I'm sure it's nothing, but you had a call today. I didn't want to trouble you with it. She said it could wait.'

Nat felt an uncomfortable tingling in her toes. A 'she'. Which *she* would perturb her mum so much? 'Okay… Who was it?'

'Isabella.'

Of all the Isabella's in the world, Nat knew only one. Bloody hell, this was nasty icing on the top of a particularly crap day. She dropped into the armchair. 'Not Issa?'

Her mum's face was pale. 'Yes.'

'What did she want?'

She picked up a notepad and handed it to Nat. 'I don't know. She left her number…'

Sighing, Nat closed her eyes. Isabella Harrow, Jose's younger sister. What on earth did she want?

8

A JIFFY

It was drizzling the next morning, the sort of half-hearted rain which didn't appear to merit wipers but actually did. Or so the Mercedes had decided. The auto functions clearly knew better than Nat.

She sighed. Her own auto functions were working too flaming well. Why couldn't she turn them off? She'd relapsed by months: self-recrimination and anxiety, and an unhealthy relationship with her mobile phone. On the one hand she was fearful of a text from Gavin, yet on the other she wanted to hear from Wes. With a bloody apology. Last night she'd tried to think about his clipped words coolly and dispassionately, which of course hadn't happened. She could only feel the hurt. Shock and surprise too, if she was honest. Her last preamble that something about his kids wasn't 'her business' had been met with a swift reassurance that it was; that Wesley Hughes's concerns were absolutely hers too.

Then there was the call from Issa Harrow. She didn't have Nat's mobile number, thank God, but what the hell did she want? Something to do with Jose, for sure, and it was bound to be bad. Nat's omission to visit him in hospital, for starters. A host of other possibilities too; from the reasons for his ill health and why she hadn't noticed it, to her failure to return to Mallorca to deal with the bar. Blame, accusations and finances, no doubt. Though she'd tried to hide it with layers of hustle and bustle, she'd known 'comeback' would happen at some point. Not from Issa, who'd always seemed friendly and chilled, but from her mother, who definitely wasn't.

She glanced at her phone on the passenger seat. None of the Harrow family had her current number because, frustrated and drunk, she'd hurled her old one at a brick wall last year. Wes had later told her that 'everything changed' for him that night. That's what he'd told her, the guy who now said his business was none of hers. She clenched her jaw. He'd known he 'loved' her that night. That's what he'd bloody well said.

Shaking her head, Nat parked up outside Savage Solicitors, or 'SS' as Joshim called it. There was no use dwelling; it was now time for work. She was 'on call' as today's duty solicitor, apparently, whatever that entailed. Pulling back her shoulders, she took a big breath and stepped into the office. Flipping heck, that rotting Penny Bun smell. Surely there was something they could do about it? She had intended to ask her mum if the fungal aroma had travelled with her to Cheadle last night, but other concerns had been more pressing.

Like the message from Issa Harrow. Oh God.

She looked around the chilly reception and rubbed her arms. The plastic seats lined beneath the window and on one side of one wall took her back to her childhood dentist. Feeling that same tummy churning, she turned to the counter. Empty. And no sign of Chantelle behind her partition either. Hmm... a good start. She made her way to Gavin's office and opened the door. A man with more than a passing resemblance to Santa Claus was sitting at the desk.

Immediately regressing fifteen years, the words popped out before she could stop them. 'Oh. Good morning, Your Honour.'

Lawrence Lamb QC had been a county court judge at some point; she'd once appeared before him to apply for a matrimonial ouster injunction against – unusually – an abusive wife. He'd granted it, but the application being *ex parte*, she was the only person there and he had kept her chatting afterwards for a good fifteen minutes. He'd looked benign and twinkly even then.

'A very good morning to you too. Do call me Larry.' He stood and saluted. 'Larry Lamb at your service, Miss Bach.' He motioned for Nat to sit on the chair. 'Don't worry about me, I'm invisible.' He patted his waistcoat pocket. 'If and when the call comes, I will be here in a jiffy.'

Mesmerised, Nat watched him delicately lift a checked tweed jacket from the old hat stand, brush it down and slip it on. Then she rallied. 'The call?' she asked.

'The call for our rota of duty today, dear lady.' He beamed. 'Duty solicitor at our local constabulary, in other words.'

'Ah, of course.' She absently opened the desk diary and peered at today's page. 'Are you coming with me?'

He raised a white eyebrow. 'Yes, but only if you wish.'

'Not Robbie?'

'Young Robert doesn't go in cars. I do go in cars, but I don't drive one.' It was not quite a ho ho ho, but he chuckled. 'Not unless I have to.'

Resisting the urge to ask if he preferred to travel by sleigh, Nat sat in the warmed seat and watched him leave. Then she shook herself back to reality, standing again and giving chase. 'Where are you going now, Your... Larry?'

He turned at the door, gesturing to the selection of newspapers beneath his arm. 'The local public house, dear lady, where else?' He tapped his nose. 'Early doors. The licencee and I are acquainted.'

Shaking her head, Nat retraced her steps to Gavin's office, almost colliding with Robbie who'd appeared from a door opposite.

He flushed and dropped his gaze. 'The boss said it was okay if I kipped here,' he said, shuffling his feet. 'You know, just for now? To keep an eye on the office.'

'Of course; that's fine.' She had forgotten Gavin lived in the flat above. Her stomach clenched; at least he had been until Sunday. Now he slept in a hospital camp bed next to his seriously injured child. The thought reminded her of Brian Selby, his family tragedy and the visit to the police station.

'Thanks for coming with me yesterday, Robbie. You really helped a lot.' She peered at his face, needing to say something. 'Judge Lamb... Larry says you don't go in cars.' Oh God, he was frowning, his blush deepening. 'That was... brave of you and your help was fantastic.' She touched his shoulder lightly and smiled. 'Hope my crazy driving didn't freak you out even more...' Bloody hell, she was talking too much; there were times she should just keep flaming shtum.

Robbie messed with his long fringe, pulling it over one eye. 'It was okay, actually.' He nodded towards reception. 'The phone's ringing. I'd better answer it.'

'Okay. I have a question...' Grabbing Gavin's diary, she followed him in. 'There's an appointment for a Mr Lee. What's that all about?'

'A mental health tribunal hearing next week. He's the dad.'

She read further down the page. 'And Marcella Bates?'

'Went to the pub for a day, leaving her kids home alone.'

'And Chantelle?'

He looked perplexed for a moment before smiling. 'Photo shoot today. She does some work for an online magazine.'

Nat nodded. She now remembered. Chantelle modelled clothes for 'the larger lady' to supplement her 'bloody minimum wages'.

'So if I need any typing?' she asked Robbie.

He shrugged. 'DIY?'

Nat was reeling from sheer concentration by noon, but she was wiser too. First up had been Mr Lee and his wife. She had taken them through the psychiatric reports with a fine-tooth comb and discussed their application to the mental health tribunal for the discharge of their son. Four years previously he'd lost his rag in their restaurant and had stabbed an abusive customer in the chest. The psychiatrist they'd instructed was firmly of the view it was an isolated psychotic episode and that he was stable now. Second up was Marcella. The petite, softly-spoken woman had overcome her alcohol addiction for the best part of a year, but her recent relapse and arrest for soliciting had resulted in her infant children being taken into care.

Nat sipped her tea and sighed. Neither 'criminals' were bad people, but both cases were difficult. The Lees loved their boy and wanted him home, but the tribunal had a duty to safeguard the general public from harm; Marcella was mortified to lose her kids, but social services had a duty to protect them. More than ever she understood Gavin's politically incorrect humour was his way of coping. She could picture him grin and say, 'I like the Lees, but I won't be going to their restaurant for a takeout,' or 'Marcella's a good kid, but I doubt I'll ask her to babysit this week.'

The air outside was fresh and crisp at lunchtime. She strolled along Finney Lane, bobbing in and out of the local shops. She was really after a (non-salty) healthy sandwich, but found herself waylaid by a craft store selling hand-knitted teddies and baby clothes. Trying to bat away thoughts of Wesley and all 'that', she spent several minutes looking at the tiny jumpers and cardigans, brushing a soft finger across the cute farm animals embroidered onto the soft fabric. Forcing herself away from the alluring socks and booties, she picked up a knitted toy dressed in colourful layers of clothing. A version of a Russian doll, she bought it on impulse; a little person she knew would love it. If she regained consciousness; if she got well.

Arriving at the office with the gift, and something resembling a pork pie which had caught her eye in the butcher's window, two things struck Nat, both of which were worrying. First, she seemed to have become immune to the champignon smell already and, secondly, why did Larry's nose now resemble a strawberry?

'Perfect timing, dear lady,' he said graciously from his seat. 'The call has come! We are Wythenshawe bound. Are you ready, my dear?'

Oh God, Wythenshawe police station. She had never been there, but Wes had. Bloody Wesley Hughes who thought his arrest and overnight stay in a police cell, never mind the subsequent charge of attempted murder, was none of her business.

She batted that thought away. 'I am, Larry, absolutely.'

Ready for another foray into the criminal world, she inhaled deeply and shook her limbs. 'So, do we know anything about the client or the arrest?'

'I didn't ask. Similar to book blurbs; I don't like spoilers,' he replied with a glint. 'I prefer the unknown. It's part of the fun.'

Like wrapped Christmas gifts, Nat supposed, but she was with him on that score. She watched him stiffly rise and sway to the door. His voice sounded steady and as eloquent as earlier, but he was undoubtedly pissed. Catching Robbie's eye, she found herself stating the obvious.

'Larry, you're drunk.'

'Good point!' He wobbled back to Robbie's bench and accepted the proffered Styrofoam cup. 'Nothing this won't cure.' He took a swig of what Nat hoped was exceedingly strong coffee and walked on. 'I believe I'm what people call a "functioning alcoholic". Rest assured, I function well.' He saluted Robbie at the door. 'Hold the reins, young man. We'll be back in a jiffy.'

The 'jiffy' turned into four hours at the nick. First up was a woman charged with criminal damage to her (now ex) boyfriend's beloved and expensive camera.

'It was an accident. One minute I was holding it, the next I dropped it. It just slipped through my fingers. Honestly.'

'And this happened where?' Larry asked.

'In our flat. In the bedroom.'

'And on what floor do you and the complainant live?'

'The fifth...'

Larry lifted a white eyebrow. 'Might I ask how it ended up, somewhat...' He wafted a small hand. '...irretrievably impaired on the pavement below?'

A little too close to the bone for comfort, Nat found herself glancing at Larry's equanimous expression. Like knowing what kids want for Christmas, could he tell how much she was cringing at the memory of her own 'irretrievably impaired' hissy fit with her phone?

But the second case was somewhat more sobering. The juvenile idly kicking the table leg was called Curtis. He had been arrested, yet again, for shoplifting booze. The boy answered

Larry's questions with an indifferent shrug, but once outside the room, his mum was inconsolable.

'Curtis hasn't been to school for nine months, some nights he doesn't come home. It's drugs, I know it is. I'm at the end of my tether. What have I done wrong?' she wailed.

Delicately stepping to one side, Larry left Nat to deal with this one alone.

'I'm sure you've done nothing–'

'No. Tell me,' the mother repeated. 'Please tell me what I did or didn't do. I've tried everything in my power to get my son back on track, but nothing works. What else can I do to help him?'

A tough one for sure; Curtis had already been on a youth prevention programme but given it up, and he'd refused the Child and Mental Health Services counselling his GP had wangled. Nat's heart went out to the poor mum, but other than assuring her that Curtis was eligible for legal aid as he was under sixteen she had no answers.

She squeezed her hand. 'All you can do is look after yourself; and make sure you're in the best place so you can help him when he's ready,' she replied.

Oh God; did that sound patronising? What the hell did childless Natalie Bach know about these things? But the woman nodded before shuffling away.

Pausing for a quick – and disgusting – cup of coffee at the vending machine, Nat had to give herself a swift reminder that it wasn't her job to solve other people's problems. She was here to offer logical and coherent advice based on the legal position; or at least Larry, the expert, was.

Turning to the man himself, she took a breath to ask if any cases 'got' to him, but he drank his scalding liquid in two noisy slurps and then smiled. 'Ready for customer number three?' he asked with glowing eyes. He rubbed his hands. 'Exciting isn't it?'

Nat blew out long and hard. Exciting it wasn't.

~

'Guess what? We've bagged another murder,' Nat announced to Robbie on her return, not quite believing the words coming out of her own mouth. Since when was a victim's dreadful death a good thing? But she was in Gavin Savage's head these days: a murder case was high profile, a good earner and interesting, this particular one being no exception.

Customer number three, an alleged killer, was called George. He had been positively loquacious in comparison to Brian Selby. A man in his sixties, he'd still lived with his mother. She had waved him off in the car for groceries, but on a whim he'd gone to the pub first. All would've been well had he not jumped a red light with a police vehicle behind him. He'd been arrested for drink driving, spent several hours in a police cell, gone home to face his mother's wrath, and had then strangled her.

From the moment George mentioned his public house diversion, Larry had been all ears, asking incisive questions and making notes which he'd handed to Nat before she dropped him at a gated mansion in Wilmslow. She peered at them now, beautifully written in loopy handwriting. *Manslaughter*? he'd written. *Loss of control? Diminished responsibility. Self defence? Intent? Low IQ. Check causal link.*

Nat took a deep breath which turned into a yawn. Now the exhilaration had waned, she felt both anxious and tired. Trying to tackle an area of law she knew nothing about was, frankly, exhausting. Collecting her bag to go home, she reminded herself she was only overseeing Gavin's files, not trying to effect a miracle cure. And as things had turned out, it was a relief not to be at Goldman Law's offices where she'd bump into Wes. Twenty-four hours had passed and he'd made no attempt to contact her, not even to ask how she was getting on. Clearly the man was a shit.

She said goodnight to Robbie and climbed into her car, the high of bagging a murder left behind in the office. She hoped she'd done some good today, but it was difficult to feel positive. Snoozing in Wes's bed, feeling happy and carefree, now seemed a lifetime ago.

The traffic was looser tonight, a reflection of the later time, she supposed, so she was outside her house in ten minutes. She picked up the pork pie and practised a grin in the mirror. It didn't seem fair to bring her despondency home to her mum. But the smile fell away. Was that a beep? Yes, definitely a beep.

She looked at the passenger seat. Too involved and busy all afternoon, she had forgotten to put her mobile in prime view. She felt her pockets and upturned her handbag. Where the hell was it? There had been a beep, she was sure. The glovebox? Yes the glovebox. With trembling hands, she pulled the phone out and peered at the screen. It wasn't a text from Wes as she'd hoped, but one from Gavin as she'd feared. There was an urgent need to weep, even before she read it.

Ruthie has just opened her eyes, it said.

9

FAIR ENOUGH

Nat found herself doing a 'circular head' and singing with Ed Sheeran in the car. A guy in a van and a red-haired rocker at the crossing gave her a scathing look, but she didn't care. After the brief exchange of texts with Gavin the previous night, she felt bloody happy. So jolly, in fact, that she'd overslept this morning.

The earworm still buzzing, she pranced into SS and smiled at Chantelle. 'Morning!' She was late, but what the hell; she was currently the boss and there were no swipe cards here to keep a check on her timekeeping. 'How was the photo shoot?'

'So so,' Chantelle replied, adjusting her sleek Holly Golightly bun. Then, appearing to think about it more deeply, 'Boring, actually, and I wouldn't wear the frumpy underwear myself in a million years. I'd rather have been here to chat with Larry about Pilates. But hey ho, if I want to do *Vogue* one day, I have to start somewhere.'

'Oust Meghan Markle from the front cover?'

'Absolutely.' Slipping delicately from her stool, she followed Nat into Gavin's office. 'You're...' She squinted at her. '...looking good today.'

Nat snorted inwardly. Flaming millennials! Had she

appeared other than 'good' before? Stress, anxiety, disappointment...? Well, yes, probably. She shrugged the thought away and grinned.

'I'm certainly feeling top of the morning, as they say. Ruthie woke up yesterday evening. After four unresponsive days, Gavin imagined the worst. She's still very poorly, but it's progress.'

Chantelle opened the desk drawer, pulled out Nat's gift bag and shed the pink tissue paper from the woollen doll. 'So cute! I couldn't resist having a peek earlier. She'll love it.'

Slightly stunned, Nat nodded. 'I hope so.'

'Maybe buy something for the other kids too?'

'Oh, right.' Nat hadn't thought about that. 'Yes, excellent idea.' She wasn't very good on the whole children malarkey, but Chantelle was right; the last few days must have been agony for Gavin's boys.

'I'd get something football-related for the older two. And Cameron...' She scrunched her face in thought. 'Yeah, defo a Matchbox car. He collects them. A Tesla Model X. I doubt he'll have it yet.'

'Okay, great. I'll try John Lewis at lunch.' Feeling a jolt of envy that Chantelle knew more about Gavin's kids than she did, Nat opened the desk diary. 'Where's Robbie?'

'College this morning.' Chantelle hovered for a moment before making for the door. 'Jack Goldman's been on,' she said over her shoulder. 'Says can you phone him back on his mobile.'

'Okay, thanks.'

Bloody hell, Jack already? A call from him wasn't generally good news. Best call him back straight away, then the day could only improve.

As though he'd been waiting, he picked up immediately. 'Natalie.'

'Hello, Jack. I got a message to–'

'The police constable with the stun gun.' As usual there was no preamble. 'What do we know about him?'

It took a moment for Nat to orient herself. Right; young Dwayne. Was it really only this last week that she'd seen him? Jack was looking after her files, which meant Dwayne's taser claim was now in his hands...

She glanced at the dented filing cabinets and felt a shiver down her spine. Oh God, the taser PC was Gavin's police federation referral; she'd forgotten about that. It felt horribly incestuous, but Savage Solicitors, and thereby she, owed the PC a duty of client confidentiality – she couldn't say or do anything to breach it, so she had to tread carefully.

'I can't tell you anything other than what you've read for yourself in my file, Jack. You know that.'

'I wouldn't dream of asking. PC Abbot, he's called. Ring any bells?'

'I know and no.' She felt the old prickling. 'Why are you asking, Jack?'

'No reason. I'm just a frail old man wanting a chat with the woman who's deserted him.'

Nat had glimpsed a 'frail old man' a few weeks after his heart attack, but the robust Jack had returned with the birth of his first grandson, thank God. Not that he didn't still drive her nuts at times. 'How's the baby?' she asked. 'How's little Rubin?'

'Fat,' he replied, though Nat could clearly hear the pride in his voice. 'Catherine can't get enough of him. I'm feeling quite... otiose.'

She laughed. That was most definitely a description she did not accept. Jack had never rested on his laurels. Despite Catherine's curfew, Jack would never be fruitless or without a purpose. He'd have been busy with machinations of one sort or another from his frosty rose beds, she was sure.

The word 'fruitless' suddenly hit with a sharp swoop. That's how Catherine had described her life last year. Those low points had resulted in her 'mutual need' with Wes. The fling had started well before Nat's return to Goldman Law, so she'd almost erased the image of them together *in flagrante delicto*, but now it felt fresh in her mind.

'So, other than trying to dig up info about PC Plod, anything else to report?' she asked, trying to shake off the image.

'I'm seeing your seamstresses and their documents this afternoon. I might get measured up myself. Treat myself to a nice dapper suit now I've been let out.'

She paused for a moment. Should she mention her disquiet about Mr DeMille and his workers? Nah. If anyone could sniff out a rat, Jack was the man. Indeed, it would be interesting to see what he'd uncover.

'A nice dapper suit, eh? Superman or Batman?' she asked instead.

'Very droll. Right I'm off. Ciao.'

Feeling a little lost, Nat listened to the dead tone. She had wanted to casually ask about everyone else in the office to see if she could glean anything of Wes. They had kept their romance discreet, but Catherine knew about it. Had she told Jack? Nat had no idea. Despite being man and wife, there was a huge nest of eggshell information she had about each of them, secrets that the other didn't apparently know. It had been hell to juggle them behind last year's Chinese walls.

The high of her and Ed harmonising in the car receded a further notch. She doodled absently on the pad. God, she missed Wes; she wished he would ring. He was right; his life was complicated. And she had to remember the 'squeezing'. He wasn't a person to wear his heart on his sleeve; he was thoughtful and 'deep', as a bench boy had once described him. She sighed. If he'd just call and say sorry, they could talk, get their relationship back on track. Because it was more than just an affair, wasn't it? Much more.

Looking down at her scribble, she sighed. Love hearts. Unconscious love.

Chantelle's presence at the door brought her back from her thoughts. Right; time for work. Nat had already dictated her notes from yesterday's police station sojourn, but the new Neds, ahem clients, would need to go onto the SS system, with files to be opened and retainer letters sent out.

'Would you mind getting these notes typed up…?' she began, rustling in her handbag for the tape. Then she lifted her head. The visitor wasn't her secretary; it was the answer to her wish.

Her elation dissolved as quickly as it had appeared. Wes's expression was grim. Oh God, what the hell? The sound of flushing and Chantelle appeared behind him. She lifted her hands in a 'Sorry' but clearly curious gesture.

Seeming to notice her presence, Wes turned. 'Cheers, Chantelle,' he said, closing her bulging eyes and slack mouth from the room.

He stepped to the desk and put his palms on the top. His dark eyes were intense. 'It *is* your business. I'm sorry.'

Finally breathing, Nat tried to cover the heart mosaic with her hands. She gazed at his tense features, wishing he wasn't so damned attractive when she wanted to milk the apology for all it was worth, rather than go belly-up like a puppy. But he continued to speak before she could do or say anything.

'But you have to understand that it is complicated, Nat. Very. Andrea is the mother of my sons. I can't just pretend she doesn't exist.'

Nat folded her arms, any thought of just letting it go evaporating. 'I know. But there's a difference between that and positively communicating with her, Wes. Even worse, meeting her. You know how manipulative she is–'

'She's still their mother–'

'A mother who poisoned one son and tried to lay the blame at the other's door.' The heat rose to her cheeks. 'I can't believe you're turning a blind eye–'

Wes raised his voice. 'I'm not turning a blind eye, Nat. Don't fucking insult me by saying so. I'm perfectly aware of what she did. I'm just being a realist. She exists, she's their mum. She will always be a part of their lives and therefore a part of mine. It's not how I want it, but there it is.'

Nat tried to keep her voice even. 'She's on remand, Wes. You'll be a witness for the prosecution. I'm sure they won't be happy about you having a tête-à-tête with the woman who set you up for a–'

'*What*? You're my bloody lawyer now?' His jaw set, he moved back and glared. 'It would hardly be a tête-à-tête, Nat.'

'And what do the boys think about this?'

'It's–'

'None of my business. I know. You've already told me. Well, that's fine by me. Perfectly fine.' The sheer anger made her calm. 'Let's leave everything there. No doubt I'll run into you at the office from time to time.' She gestured around the cluttered room. 'As you can see, I'm busy covering for a good friend whose life really is complicated right now.'

Wes stalked to the door, opened it, then closed it again. He turned and sighed. 'I haven't even decided what to do. Don't let her do this.'

'Do what?'

'Split us up.'

'What's to split, Wes? Your sons and your brother don't know about me, neither did your dad. Your mum only knew because she forced it out of you. No one at Goldman Law knows–'

'Your decision too.'

'One you were particularly keen on, as I recall. I guess that's the norm when you work your way around the office, sleeping with the staff.'

'Catherine was–' he started, before dropping his hands to his side.

Nat took a deep breath. She wanted to cry, she wanted to say, 'What about the promises you made on my birthday, the house, the garden, the apple tree. And the baby? You promised me a baby.' But she held back the tears. Instead she looked at him coldly. 'To be honest, I think we've run our course, Wes. The sex was nice, but I'm sure I can find that elsewhere.'

She glanced down at the paperwork on the desk, needing him to stay but wanting him gone.

'Fair enough,' he said eventually, and left.

At home, Anna's eyes were watchful all evening. They ate dinner in silence, then sat together on the sofa to watch an episode of a crime drama, which seemed tame in comparison to life at Savage Solicitors.

'I'll tell you when I'm ready, Mum,' Nat said at the break.

'I know, love,' she replied. Then after a moment. 'Have you phoned Isabella?'

'Not yet, but I suppose I should.'

Knowing the call had to be made at some point, Nat picked up the notepad and stared at her mum's handwriting. Tiny print, as though it would diminish the trauma. She sighed. If it was a demand to fly to Mallorca, so be it; other than covering for Gavin, there was no longer anything holding her here. She scooped up her mobile and punched in the numbers. About to press the green icon, it rang.

Holding her breath, Nat accepted the call. 'Gavin? Everything okay?'

'Heather went home for a few hours today. She had a shower and a kip, saw the boys.'

'So that's good.'

'Yeah.'

Nat tensed. 'And Ruthie? How's she doing?'

'More hours asleep than awake, but that's to be expected, so...'

'Awake some of the time sounds great.' A pulse of time and then, 'What about you, Gav?'

There was no reply, so Nat tried for humour. 'You must be stinking something rotten by now.'

She heard a faint laugh before silence again.

'It wasn't your fault, Gavin. No one could have anticipated–'

'It was, Nat. Heather says the same as you, but it was.'

Understanding he needed to own it, she didn't protest. Instead she changed the subject. 'I bought something for Ruthie and the boys. I thought when they're ready, we could do the park and a cheeky Big Mac.'

'That would be brilliant. I'll ask Heather to text you. Everything ticking over at work?'

'I've bagged you two murders.' The words were out before she could stop them. She paused for a moment, hoping she hadn't been indelicate. 'Though I can't take all the credit. Santa Claus and your Smart Alec paralegal helped.'

'I'd better reclaim my chair before you've changed the nameplate. Good work, Bach. I'll make a criminal solicitor of you yet.'

He was trying for humour, but she could feel his sadness.

'Oh, Gav. I'd like to give you a hug.'

'I'd like that too. Better go. Night, Nat.'

Putting the phone to her chest, Nat inhaled deeply. Tears were stabbing her eyes, brimming at the surface for Ruthie and Heather and Gavin, but also for herself. Something irrevocable had happened with Wes today. She'd forced it, of course, but in truth it had already been there, hadn't it? The End. Though there had never been a beginning, not really. Neither the Cling-on nor her ghost would ever let it happen. That old tenuous triangle of Andrea, Wesley and Natalie would always be there; insidious, destructive, malignant.

Feeling her mum's anxious gaze, she sniffed and lifted her chin. Ruthie was improving inch by inch. Such positive news should be her focus. And in the meantime there was Issa Harrow. There was no point procrastinating.

She rang the number and listened to the flat ringtone for several moments.

'Hello?'

'Hi. Issa? It's Natalie. You left a message with my mum?'

'Yes. I–'

'Sorry for the delay in getting back to you. Long story, but I've had to cover at work for a friend, so... How can I help?'

There was noise in the background, then Issa's lowered voice. 'Now isn't a great time to talk. And to be honest, I think it would be better to speak face to face. I could drive over on Sunday afternoon if that suits you. You live in the same house in Cheadle, I assume? Would that be okay?'

Nat closed her eyes. 'Sure, of course, no problem. I'll see you then.'

10

SCRAPS

Nat had napped at some point during the night; it just didn't feel like it. Her reflection in the bathroom mirror agreed as she yawned repeatedly. There had been so many things to worry about, her mind was spoilt for choice. She'd found herself seeing Brian Selby's empty face; smelling Gavin Savage's funky office; hearing Issa's troubled voice. And touching; touching Wesley Hughes, being touched by him. But that was only when she dreamt.

She shuffled back to her bedroom and threw on her dressing gown. Today it was Saturday, so that was something. A lie-in, crumpets and tea in bed, persuading her mum that it was safe to venture outdoors, then drive Gavin's kids to the playground, followed by McDonald's, had been the plan. Unfortunately, the lie-in hadn't worked; she'd woken at seven and though she'd tried to get back into dream world, her mind had nagged about Issa Harrow. She'd been so busy seeing Gavin's clients back-to-back yesterday, then she'd had a mini reprieve, but the anxiety had now returned big time. What was going on? Nat was very fond of Issa and Jose's genial, larger-than-life father, but their mother had always been cold. She had a horrible feeling Issa was acting at her behest. What did the strange woman want?

Of course Nat had known the Harrow family pretty well over the years, first as Jose's 'friend', though what he'd told them about their on-off relationship she didn't know, then later as his girlfriend. She supposed the description had extended to 'partner' in Mallorca, not only romantically, but in terms of business. Jose had bought 'Havana' with a substantial financial contribution from her. When her mum had the stroke, she'd boarded the first aeroplane to Manchester, expecting him to follow. It was confusing, a surprise, when he didn't, but worse shortly followed. She was to stay in the UK; he didn't want her back. It was a kick in the teeth, a blow to the stomach, a stab in the heart, and every other possible hurt and wounded idiom there was, finally delivered in one single *I don't love you any more* text.

A dreadful, dreadful shock. He'd pursued her since law college; she'd been certain of his adoration. The sudden change from what she absolutely knew and understood had tilted her world; it had made everything move, sliding and uncertain. The muteness made it worse. Jose changed his number and cut her off completely; there was no explanation, no contact, no closure, a limbo which had lasted for months. Even lovely Hugo, their bar manager, was silent.

To find out what had become of Nat's investment, Jack instructed an enquiry agent behind her back. Outrageous interference, of course, but the report had finally given her some answers. Perhaps Jose had stopped loving her, she still didn't know the answer to that, but she discovered he'd been admitted to a psychiatric hospital in Palma after a violent psychotic episode. As far as she knew he was still there.

Trying to shake off the general feeling of gloom, Nat now padded down her narrow staircase. Flipping heck, the house was hot. Her mum had taken to having the central heating on twenty-four-seven, or so it felt, which was all the more reason to get her out of the house. Nat had offered to drive Anna to the hospital to visit her friend Barbara, but she'd firmly declined.

She shook her head. It was definitely odd; the two Polish women were very close. Was it the idea of being in a hospital again? On reflection, that wouldn't be surprising; Anna had been an inpatient for several weeks after her stroke; she'd progressed from near death to an amazing recovery. Flaming Bach willpower, or what? But that was precisely why her mum's current timidity was all the more worrying.

The kitchen door was open, the tea in the pot, the crumpets in the toaster. Anna had beaten her to it.

'Oh, Mum. I thought I'd be first down and bring you breakfast for a change.'

Anna kissed Nat's cheek. 'You're the worker, Skarbie.' She nodded to the table. 'Here or in bed?'

'Here,' Nat replied, not wanting to dwell on lazy, tender meals with Wes in the sack. She pulled out a chair and smeared a lump of butter on her crumpet. Then after a moment, surprising herself, 'Talk to me about Dad.'

Her mum sat opposite and folded her hands. 'What do you want to know?'

Nat took a breath. She didn't fully understand her need for information, but whenever she visited an old probate client in Didsbury village, it occurred to her that she knew more about his eventful life, from birth to old age, than she did her own father.

'Well, the camp in Poland for starters...'

'I don't know that much myself–'

'You must know something, Mum.'

Lifting her shoulders, Anna smiled sadly. 'All I learned came from his brother. Scraps here and there from chatting. Your dad... Well, apparently even as a youth, Tatuś was an idealist and too opinionated...'

'It was a labour camp?'

'Yes, that's right, it was.'

Nat raised her eyebrows. Both her parents had been practising Catholics, but she'd often wondered if her father had Jewish blood like Jack Goldman. This made more sense. She could picture her dad, ranting at the television: the news, *Question Time*, anything political. 'Dad was a dissident? A communist?'

Her mum wiped some crumbs from the table. 'I'm not sure. Socialist, certainly. His brother once mentioned he'd been involved with a trade union.' She looked up at Nat. 'I'm sorry I don't know more, love. I feel that I should, but he never wanted to talk about it, so I respected his wishes and didn't ask.'

Feeling a mix of pride and sadness, she reached for Anna's hand. 'Thanks, Mum. That's really helpful.' She wondered whether to say more, but what would be the point? It was good to hear her dad had firm beliefs and ideals, but it didn't change the fact he'd been a crap father.

'Fancy another crumpet?' she asked instead.

Anna patted her stomach. 'No thank you. Need to keep an eye on my waistline.'

Nat chuckled to herself. Yes, her mum had willpower, most certainly. There was no way on earth she would have respected her dad's wishes if she'd been his wife. She'd have prodded and poked until she had the full, unedited story. Like Wes's mother, Kath? What had she said about her sons? That information had to be squeezed out like a tube of toothpaste.

Suddenly sweaty, she sighed. Oh hell. Squeezing was fairly gentle, wasn't it? Her approach with Wes had been more sledgehammer. Perhaps she shouldn't have demanded answers; maybe she shouldn't have made her opinion so clear. But that was Natalie Bach; he knew that. And wasn't she entitled to know, to be part of his life? That's what hurt: the pushing away, the exclusion.

'Fair enough,' he'd said when he left Gavin's office on Thursday. No argument, no fight, just acceptance. The bastard could fuck off.

She glanced at her mum. She felt guilty about using a profanity, even if it was in her head, but at least it had reminded her to text Joshim Khan. Joshim dealt with any romantic angst in his life, usually flighty men, by using his 'fuck-off' theory. Did it work? She had no idea, but the mental Tourette's was fun.

She pulled out her mobile. *Thanks for being a star*, she typed.

Anything for the big man. How's his kid? he replied.

Nat smiled sadly before composing an answer. Joshim's name for Gavin was usually derogatory, 'Rabid Scot' being one of his kinder versions. And of course Gavin gave what he got. With interest.

Out of danger, I think, she replied. God, she hoped she wasn't tempting fate by mentioning it.

A drink to celebrate tonight? Metropolitan? Nine o'clock?

That sounded a grand idea. She usually got together with Wes on a Saturday. But he could fuck off. Or perhaps he already had.

Anna declined Nat's invitation to stroll into the village to buy a newspaper, but surprised her after lunch by appearing in a bobble hat, anorak and wellies.

'Oh, Mum, look at you. Where are you off to?' she asked.

'I'm coming with you to the park.'

'Great. I'll–'

'Now you have five seat belts.'

'Right.'

As usual her mum had said nothing at the time, but was now making the point that Nat had regularly transported five bodies in a car made for four. She tried to shrug the small irritation away. On the day of Wes's arrest, it had been a question of 'needs must'. And after that, what should she have done? Left one of Gavin's kids at home with a 'Sorry, I can only afford to use my mum's crappy four-person car'? Of course she now had the Mercedes and little Ruthie was missing, so everything was just fine.

By the time they reached Gatley, Nat felt rotten for her tetchiness. Her mum meant well and she had finally left the house of her own volition. She turned to the passenger seat. 'Thanks for coming, Mum. I'll grab the boys and be back in two ticks.'

Anna nodded. 'Take your time, love.'

Catching Cameron's red hair at the window, Nat knocked on the porch door; it was answered by Gavin's ex herself.

'Hi, Natalie. Thanks for coming.'

'A pleasure. Really; your children are brilliant.' She handed over the gift bag. 'A little something for Ruthie, sent with lots of love.'

Heather gazed for a moment. 'Do you want to pop in for a minute?' she asked from the shadows.

'Sure,' Nat replied, glancing over at her mum in the car. She was pleased to be asked, but it felt a little strange. Though they had exchanged texts, she'd never had a face-to-face conversation with her. They had waved at a distance and through Ruthie's grown-up comments and unintentional imitations, she felt she knew her quite well.

Following the woman's slim frame, Nat stepped into the lounge.

'I love the colour of...' she began before clocking the

woman's pallid, drawn features. She pulled her into an impulsive hug. 'Oh, Heather, I'm so sorry about Ruthie. I have no idea how you must be feeling, but if there's anything I can do, please say, any time.'

Heather turned to her sons, lined up on the green velvet sofa. They were already in their coats, the two older boys clutching footballs and little Cameron a rucksack. 'You're doing it right now. Thank you. They've been excited all morning.' She paused for a second, her face thin behind the host of pretty freckles. 'There is something, though.' She turned at an angle and lowered her voice. 'Gavin – he's taken this so hard. I think he needs to talk but...' She spread her hands. 'You know what men are like; whatever's going on, he isn't sharing it with me. But he thinks so highly of you, so if you get a chance to draw him out...'

'Of course I will,' Nat replied, blinking away the sharp burn behind her eyes. She met Heather's desolate gaze. 'And you too, Heather. I'm not an expert at anything, but I can listen. Please do call me. Any time.'

11

AMMO

Nat stepped off the tram and looked down at her stupidly high heels. Why she'd put them on, she had no idea. If she slipped and broke her neck, it would be her own flaming fault and her mum would have the satisfaction of saying, 'I said this weather was dangerous'.

Not that Anna would. Though she'd had a trillion opportunities over the years, she'd never said 'I told you so'. It was one of her mum's many lovely qualities. As well as patience and kindness; compassion, understanding and attentiveness.

Nat flicked open her umbrella. God, she hoped she'd inherited some of her mum's attributes. Attentiveness, surely? She was a good listener, she hoped, which was why her rendezvous for *deux* had turned into *trois*.

Max's surprise text had come through at the park. To ring the changes, Nat had taken Gavin's boys to Etherow Country Park to feed the ducks and have a snack in the café. At that point she'd been carrying little Cameron for over an hour. Though he'd briefly stopped crying when a goose gave chase, he was astonishingly heavy, so it had been a relief to pass him over to her mum for two minutes while she had a look at the message.

Fancy a drink tonight? it had said.

Sounds good. Nine o'clock at the Metropolitan? she had quickly replied.

Now feeling a little hot under the collar, Nat tottered towards the brightly lit corner building. Her response had been sent without too much thought, but once it had whooshed away, she'd had second thoughts. Max still had his girlfriend, right? It wasn't some sort of date, surely? An absurd idea, of course. She was older than him and he didn't seem to be in short supply of admirers. Though there had been that sizzle of attraction last year... If that night had panned out differently, who knows? But right now Nat wasn't on the market, not for him or any other bloody man. And if he harboured ideas in that direction, he'd soon be disabused.

The pub was already hot and heaving, the music just a little too loud. She glanced around to spot her quarries. Both playing with their beer mats, they stood either end of the bar. She looked from Joshim to Max and laughed; a *ménage à trois*, perhaps? They were both attractive men, with quiffed hairstyles as it happened, but the pretty, chiselled slimmer one was gay and the other more chunky, private-school sort wasn't, in truth, her type. She had composed a text telling them both it would be a threesome tonight, but she didn't want it to sound as though she'd invited one as a chaperone because she didn't like the other – or whatever else they might have deduced – so she'd binned it. She now shook her head. Get a grip, Natalie! Stop over-analysing and worrying; chill out and have fun.

She gave Joshim a tight hug, then called over to Max. 'Max, this is Joshim. He's...' She pictured Gavin, but manfully resisted his usual 'the only gay in the CPS' quip in his honour. 'He's a pal from law college. He works for the Crown Prosecution Service, so watch your Ps and Qs. Joshim, this is my colleague–'

'And friend.'

'And my work friend, Max. Well, last week's employment, anyway.' She snorted. 'I feel as though I've been away forever. Right, what are you two drinking?'

The men found a corner table. Though it took longer at the bar than she liked, Nat finally returned with the booze.

'Nearly had a fist fight,' she commented.

Joshim smiled. 'Any particular reason?'

'Men,' she replied.

'God, not those again.'

'Yup. The ones who seem to think it's okay to push in.' It was fine; she'd put the arrogant trio right. 'So what were you talking about?'

'The boss,' Max replied.

Oh hell; he was talking about Wes. Why, oh why did she ask? 'Well, I'm pleased to say I don't have one,' she said, trying to change the subject. 'Cheers!'

'Yeah, Wesley has barely spoken to anyone this week,' Max continued. 'He's had a face like thunder, expecting us to all be telepathic and snapping when we aren't. Of course Emilia thinks it's all to do with her.' He turned to Joshim. 'Why do women do that?' He mimicked Emilia's high southern voice. '"I don't think he likes me, guys. What did I do wrong? Oh golly, is he angry with me?"'

Nat cleared her throat loudly. 'Women? Just this generic clump of–'

'I'm not counting you, Nat.' Max snorted. 'Besides, it's probably your fault.'

'Interesting,' Joshim said, his gossip radar on high alert. 'Because Nat's not in the office the godlike Wes Hughes is Mr Moody.'

Knowing exactly what was coming, Nat tried to intervene quickly, but Joshim had already leaned forward conspiratorially.

'You do know Wes and Nat were an item at law school, don't you, Max?'

'No we weren't, Joshim. He was dating Andrea and then he married her. End of.'

Joshim's almond eyes glowed with mischief. 'The shag hag or the Cling-on as she was known. Little did we know the full extent of her talents...'

Nat wasn't sure how much everyone in the office knew about the whole Andrea saga. She threw back her glass of fizz. 'Your round, I think, Joshim,' she said pointedly, but he didn't move. Instead he lifted his dark eyebrows.

'Just like you weren't...' He made ironic speech marks with his fingers. '"Going out" with Jose, I suppose?'

'I wasn't seeing either of them, Joshim.'

Aware of Max's head snapping from her to Joshim like a Wimbledon spectator, she decided on a diversionary tack. She took Joshim's hand, saying, 'Why would I consider anyone else when I was so in love with you?'

'Good try, Bach,' he said, standing and collecting the glasses. 'As stunning as I was, Max, she never even noticed me. However, when Wes Hughes sauntered into the room...'

Expecting an inquisition, Nat held her breath as she turned to Max, but he was looking vacantly over her shoulder, clearly miles away. Ah, definitely girlfriend trouble. What was she called? That's right, Caz.

'So what's your excuse?' she asked.

He frowned. 'Sorry?'

'How come you're here on a Saturday night and not with Caz?'

He snorted. 'Sadly, I couldn't tonight. I had to meet my boss to discuss urgent developments on a file...'

Nat groaned inwardly. She hated people telling fibs. Well,

lying, in fact. But in truth, everyone did it. She didn't comment but waited for him to elaborate.

He raked a hand through his hair and looked down at the table. 'I should never have moved in with her, Nat,' he blurted, tumbling over his words. 'I can't breathe. She virtually takes notes when I get home: who I've seen, what I've done, what I ate for my bloody lunch. Completely fucking claustrophobic. I'm not sure I can do it a moment longer.' He finally made eye contact. 'What would you do?'

Nat took a breath. Wow. She didn't know they lived together. She'd clearly missed that. And maybe the poor woman was just interested in his life. Still, he did look pretty stressed and unhappy. 'If it's really that bad, I guess you could always tell her it isn't working and move out.'

He glanced at Joshim, approaching with the drinks. 'If only,' he replied hurriedly. 'I can't, she won't let me. Basically blackmail, Nat. And bad bloody timing. Wesley has given me the nod for partnership in April. Brilliant news, yeah? But Caz has ammo that will put it at risk. She's made it quite clear that she's willing to use it...'

12

BAGGAGE

Nat listened to the church bells as she fluffed up the lounge cushions. She'd fallen asleep the moment her head touched the pillow last night and hadn't woken up until eleven. Since then she'd thought of nothing other than Wes, Catherine and bloody Jack Goldman. The treacherous bastards had offered Max a partnership. She had worked extremely hard for ten long years at Goldman Law before she left for Mallorca, and when she came back she'd cleared up everyone's mess, the three of theirs in particular. Yet they hadn't offered one to her; they'd turned to golden-boy Max who was seven years less qualified than her. Even if one took off the five-year hiatus, she still had his better by two.

The patting turned to battering as she focused her anger on Jack. 'Natalie has the sharpest mind I know,' was his opening whenever he introduced her to a new client. And yet she wasn't sharp enough to be offered a bloody promotion.

Observed by the cats, she slumped down on the sofa. The car, of course. The salve of a company vehicle. So that's what the Mercedes had been all about. She wiped away a tear of frustration. But at least that was something, some recognition from Jack. Which left Wesley and Catherine. Cool. Bloody. Catherine. Perhaps they'd rekindled their lonely hearts club in the office flat. Maybe she should mention it to Jack: 'Did you know your perfect wife had a mutual flaming need with Wesley for a year?'

She folded her arms, then thumped them to her chest for good measure. Catching her reflection in the window, she almost laughed. Oh God, she was acting like a sulky child. Of course she wouldn't breach a confidence; she never did. And it wasn't Max's fault. He'd done a fairly long stint at Goldman Law and he deserved the recognition. It was her own shortcoming; almost on a whim she'd jacked in her career to follow her boyfriend. It sounded so pathetic and meek; nothing like her old feminist self. Why the hell did she do it? She still hadn't quite worked it out. Old-fashioned need, probably. She'd grown so used to Jose's obsessive love that its absence left a gaping hole and she'd floundered without it.

Pathetic woman or what? She snorted loudly. Perhaps everything came back to Jose in the end. He'd glued himself to her back at law school and despite her efforts over the years to detach herself from him, he'd never gone away. She hadn't set eyes on the man for well over six months, yet his sister was due, all the way from Liverpool, in an hour and twenty minutes. The reason? A mystery she could do without, especially with a hangover from hell.

She shook her head to test it. She, Max and Joshim had gone dancing in some dodgy basement bar in Withington after the pub last night; they'd moved on to snakebite cocktails which had tasted almost nice after the third. She smiled a little at the memory. How had the two men fared after she left? Despite knowing Max was rugger-bugger straight, Joshim was clearly smitten, and Max was so drunk he'd struggled to cook up a reason why he'd be home so late. She pictured them waking up in the same bed. A possibility? From Max's terror, it might have been easier to fall for Joshim's charms than face his girlfriend's interrogation. Stranger things had happened.

Wondering what had become of her umbrella, Nat swigged back more water. She'd taken two painkillers and the headache seemed to be receding, but the house was too quiet; it would bring on gloomy thoughts if she didn't do something productive. Her mum was out, the slip-free trip yesterday having chivvied her into action. She usually met Barbara every third Sunday to go to their old church in Oldham, but she was visiting her in hospital instead.

Nat squinted through the bay. The pavements were still gritty, but dry. Why the hell not? If the backstabber Wes Hughes managed seven kilometres in fifty minutes each weekend, surely she could manage three?

The jog towards the gardens was slow, but at least Nat didn't collapse before she'd reached the entrance. The wind behind pushed her on, but memories of last Sunday morning wafted back. Lazy, tender lovemaking with Wes; through his lips and his hands, she'd felt sure of his love. How had that evaporated so easily? 'Fair enough,' he'd said the other day. Where was the passion, the fight to keep her? It wasn't there. The same as his promises. Like the snow, they'd disappeared. She just had to move on.

The air was damp, the trees stark, but the grass sparkled as she paced the hard path around the boundaries. The park was surprisingly busy – other runners, lovers hand in hand, dogs taking their owners for a walk. And so many happy families: small children seemed to be everywhere, in papooses, on shoulders, in prams. Zipped up in thick coats, wearing mittens and hats, their noses like cherries.

She pictured Gavin's kids in similar attire yesterday. His two older boys had seemed fine, darting around the perimeter of the lake, then climbing an ancient oak tree, but little Cameron had clutched on to her and cried. 'I want Ruthie, I want Ruthie.' It had brought tears to her eyes, her mum's too.

Nat continued to run steadily, her mind flitting as she grinned at the astonishing variety of canine. A veritable international feast: French bulldog, German shepherd, English springer spaniel. Then there were the mixed breeds: cocks, poos and doodles. Some people stopped to smile at babies, but with her it was dogs, big ones and small, fluffy or smooth, bounding blithely with wet noses and *joie de vivre*.

And the thought spreading through all the others as she strode: Issa Harrow was due soon. What on earth did she want?

The drizzle had started on Nat's last lap of the park, developing into a heavy shower by the time she reached Cheadle High Street. Of course she'd tempted fate: 'The weather is fine, so is life, really. Just one more circuit, you can do it, girl,' she'd said to herself.

So much for positivity. Now she was soaked, knackered and the brain rattle was back. She had no energy left, and though her tracksuit hood was up, she couldn't get any wetter.

Fifty metres from her house, she finally looked up from the soggy, pinpricked pavement. Oh hell. Its driver's door open, a blue car was parked behind hers. An umbrella shot out, followed by Isabella.

Nat found herself trotting through the deluge. 'God, I'm sorry,' she called. 'I lost track of the time.'

Issa turned. 'Don't worry, I'm early.' Clearly taking in Nat's drowned rat appearance, she nodded to the still-open door. 'Should we wait in the car until you've...?'

'Of course not,' Nat replied, searching her pockets.

Oh God, 'we'. She'd supposed her visitor would be Issa, alone. Oh God, what the hell?

Too anxious to look at the passenger, Nat turned to the house. Her hands numb with cold, she fumbled with the key, scrabbling to insert it in the lock. The portal finally opened with a blast of hot air. 'Come on in. Please take a seat.' She made for the stairs. 'I'll be two ticks; I'll just grab a towel.'

Nat perched on her bed. She hadn't expected to feel so heart-pumping nervous, so alarmed. She tried to peel off her wet running kit hurriedly, but it took moments to undo the stuck hoody zip, then struggle to yank the soaking vest off her head. Drying herself quickly, she pulled a brush through her hair, then donned a clean jumper and leggings.

It was time to face the music. Was Mrs Harrow and her sharply set shoulders downstairs? Even worse, was it Jose? Standing tall, she breathed deeply. Come on, Natalie! She could do this and see it through.

Issa Harrow was perched on the armchair. Perhaps a little blonder these days, but with her angular face, chestnut eyes and high cheekbones, she looked remarkably like her brother. Nat cast her eyes to the second seat and the sofa. Poppy cat was curled up on one, her brother, Lewie, stretched out on the other. Her gaze finally rested on the floor. The 'we' was asleep in a car seat: a chubby, fair-haired baby dressed in blue.

'Oh, Issa, I didn't know. Congratulations! A boy?'

She nodded, but didn't smile. Her pale face was tense. 'Yes. He's called Carlos.'

Stuck for words, Nat stared at the tiny tot. Issa had a beautiful child, but didn't appear remotely like the happy parents in the park. 'You kept up the Spanish name tradition,' she commented for something to say.

Issa snorted. 'As though Mum would have allowed anything else.'

She still had a mild Liverpudlian twang, but her bubbly personality appeared to be missing today. Where would this strange reunion go? Nat took a breath. 'I'll make us a drink. Coffee, tea, cocoa, or something cold?'

'A cup of tea would be good, thanks.'

'Me too. Come on through.'

They sat at the kitchen table, both clutching their drinks but saying little. Nat eventually chuckled. 'I think we're as nervous as each other. Whatever you need to say…' She thought of Gavin Savage and smiled. 'Just shoot,' she said.

Issa's lips finally twitched. In all the years Nat had known Jose, he'd had no interest in football, either watching or playing, but Issa was a keen Liverpool FC supporter.

'I always liked you and your easy humour,' she said. 'Which is why I'm here. You're a nice person.' She lifted her chin. 'And a solicitor.'

Nat spread her hands, surprised but mightily relieved. 'That's fine. You can tell me anything. It's all confidential.'

Issa looked at the baby, still asleep in his seat. 'So,' she began, swallowing, 'I met JP at Harrow's retirement party just over a year ago–'

Issa and Jose's father had always been known as 'Harrow', but 'JP' didn't ring any bells.

'JP?' Nat asked.

'Sorry, JP is Carlos's dad, John Paul.' She glanced at Nat briefly. 'Harrow had just stepped down as head teacher after his twenty-five-year stint. They had a big event at the school. So many people came: former pupils, staff, Oxbridge success stories, chief executives, actors, published authors. People stood up and gave speeches about what a difference he'd made to their lives. It was fantastic, heart-warming stuff.'

Nat nodded, thinking back to Mallorca. Yes, she recalled Harrow retiring in his 'silver jubilee' year. Jose had been reluctant to trek all the way to Liverpool, but she'd persuaded him to go home for the celebration. She would have gone too had Hugo been available to cover at 'Havana' that weekend. Indeed, she was disappointed not to go; she'd always liked Harrow. Big-hearted, gregarious and caring, he was exactly the father she would have chosen. Her mental image of him was not unlike Gavin Savage. Tall and solid, a former military man, everyone from the family to his pupils and school staff called him by his surname.

'JP was... is... different...' Issa smiled wryly. 'Not my usual sort. I'm sure you'll remember them. Less louty, more introspective, you might say. Not even a footie fan, let alone a Red. Ironically a bit like Jose.'

Though the mention of her ex's name made her flinch, Nat remembered. Issa had a series of opinionated, die-hard Liverpool-supporting boyfriends her mother couldn't stand. As for Jose, his poetical but uptight sensitivity had driven his sister nuts at times. Nat understood that. Despite his law degree, Jose hadn't held down a job until his late twenties; he was still 'trying to find himself' in his early thirties. He'd seemed to have settled down in Mallorca, though.

Nat pushed that particular rug-pulling realisation away. Yes, the Harrow family had always felt severed between Issa and her personable dad, Jose and their severe Spanish mum.

Issa abruptly covered her face. 'I suppose I should've known.

A handsome and loving forty-six-year-old man without baggage. They don't exist, do they?'

Nat didn't reply. Last year she had joked with Gavin about his 'baggage' of four children, but there was nothing remotely funny about this poor woman's clear devastation.

Issa didn't speak for a time, so Nat waited. Finally, she took a shuddery breath. 'My question is: what if someone says something terrible, something you know without a doubt isn't true?'

Surprised at the change of tack, Nat sat back. 'Do you mean a defamatory statement?'

Issa nodded. 'I suppose so.'

Nat put on her lawyer's hat and gave herself a moment to think. 'Well, it has to be false and made to someone other than that person. If it's published it's libel, if it's spoken, it's slander. If it's so bad that it would make ordinary people think less of them, then the person to whom it's addressed can sue for damages, apply for an injunction and so on.' She searched Issa's pale face. 'Why are you asking, Issa? Has someone said something about JP? You have to know that libel proceedings are only for the super rich; there isn't any legal aid and it's particularly costly litigation.' She paused for a moment, not wanting to suggest anything bad about a man she knew nothing about, but needing to make the legal position clear. 'Truth is a complete defence, Issa, so you'd have to be sure it's absolutely a lie before considering anything legally–'

Issa stood, accidentally knocking the car seat as she stumbled away from the table. 'I am sure,' she said loudly. Woken from his slumber, the baby started flailing and whimpering, but she didn't appear to notice. 'I'm absolutely sure, Natalie; I've known him all my life.'

As though in reply, the baby spluttered, then mewled, so Nat found herself kneeling and scooping the little man from his seat. Rocking him gently, she stared at Issa's wet face.

'Who, do you–' she began.

'JP says Harrow is a paedophile,' Issa blurted. 'He says he was abused by my father when he was just eight.'

13

SCARS

Needing to scrub away the uncomfortable tale Issa had told, Nat spent several minutes in the shower once she'd left.

For moments Issa had stared into space before her baby's cries broke through. If it was possible, her expression had fallen even further. 'Oh, Carlos, I'm so sorry,' she'd said, taking him from Nat's arms and bringing his downy hair to her face.

She'd passed Nat a changing bag. 'There's a box of formula in there. Would you mind decanting it into the bottle, then heating it? I'm all fingers and thumbs today.'

The milk duly warmed and the teat in Carlos's mouth, Issa had finished her story. There wasn't that much more to tell. She had always known something was troubling JP: he was on antidepressants and saw a therapist every month. She'd encouraged him to talk about his issues, persuading him it was far better to get things out in the open. Ironically, she'd argued that he couldn't heal inside until he'd faced his demons, that he owed it to his new baby son to try and beat them. And when he did, it was devastating: he alleged Harrow had sexually assaulted him when he was an infant; he had attended the school retirement party to 'out' his abuser, but had met his daughter and fallen for her instead.

Her mind still whirring, Nat dried herself briskly. What a horrendous situation for Issa; she clearly loved both men and had no idea how to resolve such a tangled set of circumstances. What would Nat do in that position? Lover versus father. What would anyone do?

The sound of the front door opening interrupted her thoughts. Anna was home, her lovely, straightforward mum. She had met Harrow over the years and liked him as much as anyone. Would Nat breathe a word of what she'd just heard to her? Quite apart from breaching client confidentiality, of course she wouldn't. It would devastate Anna, so God knows how Issa was coping.

Slipping on jogging bottoms, a T-shirt and slippers, Nat padded downstairs.

'Hi, Mum. How's Barbara?' she asked.

'Making lots of friends,' Anna replied. 'She's such a character; she knows everything about everyone in that ward, including the nurses. She'll be sad to leave.'

Her mum's expression seemed uncertain. 'But it was fun to catch-up with her?'

'Oh yes, I wheeled her to the café.'

'Sounds nice. Did you buy cake? Don't tell me, lemon drizzle?'

Her mum didn't answer. Instead she frowned. 'And I might be mistaken, but I think I saw Ruthie's dad.'

'Gavin? But...' Ah, of course. Anna had never met him. Though she'd met Wes several times and clearly approved of him; playing cards while Nat slept had been evidence of that.

'Very tall and broad with sandy-coloured hair. Well, I know that could be anyone, but the lovely knitted toy you bought Ruthie – he was holding it, sitting alone in the café, holding that dolly. He looked dreadful, Skarbie. Both Barbara and I... well, our hearts went out to him.'

Gavin, her pal; the one guy who'd seemed oblivious to the usual buffets of life. But Nat knew that wasn't true. He just used dry humour as a shield. Heather had clearly been worried about him too. She peered at her watch. Would it be appropriate just to turn up at the hospital without an invitation? But her mind was already made up. She wouldn't even text; better to give him a fait accompli.

Within ten minutes, she'd changed joggers for jeans, combed her wet hair, dragged on her boots and jumped in the car. The motorway route she had suggested to her mum? No, it was a Sunday; it was just as easy to take the Parkway and the shortcut past the retail parks.

Regent Road was chocka, the traffic crawling past the pub which, she realised with a jolt, was famous for a fatal shooting incident. Hoping she was not tempting fate, Nat tapped her fingers on the steering wheel and tried not to picture Issa's wrecked face.

Her favourite author was right: when *would* there be good news?

The congestion finally clearing, she put down her foot and followed signs to the infirmary. It had been called Hope Hospital back in the day. God, she prayed so.

Similar to the police station she had visited with Robbie, the huge angular building looked fairly new. She took a plastic coin at the barrier, searching for a space in the busy car park. Pulling up next to a walkway, she was on the point of climbing out when a tall figure caught her eye at the pay station: Wesley Hughes. The start of a dark beard had grown since last she saw him. It emphasised his sharp cheekbones, but made him a stranger. Willing him to turn, she watched him walk towards his Mercedes. What was he thinking? What was going on behind his impassive facade? If only she'd been two minutes earlier she might have bumped into him on the ramp. It still wasn't too late if she just... But Wes was lifting his arm to unlock his car; he was climbing in and reversing smoothly away.

Trying to ignore the heavy disappointment in her chest, Nat pulled out her mobile and sent Gavin a text.

I'm here and on my way to the Hope building. See you in the café in ten? Then to lighten it. *I might even dig deep in my pockets and treat you to a slice of Dundee!*

She made her way to the ground floor Café and sat at a table. The ten minutes became twenty-five, but that was fine. The hospital was huge. Who knew where they secreted a very poorly child who'd been shot? Who'd had a heart attack. The shocking words still winded her.

She glanced at her phone again. Gavin hadn't replied. Oh God, had she messed up? Was she interfering again by appearing without being asked?

'Seems I'm popular today.' The Scottish burr made her jump. Gavin. Thank heavens. He pulled out a chair. 'Wes left not long ago.'

She nodded but didn't comment. 'How's Ruthie?' she asked. She had intended to let him talk about her at his own pace, but she suddenly needed to know.

'A fighter,' he replied.

She put her hand on his and grasped it tightly. He'd visibly lost weight. Pale purple grooves beneath his eyes emphasised his tired gaze and his facial hair had spread erratically from his moustache to his chin.

'She's like her dad. I knew she would be,' she said, covering the need to cry with a wobbly smile.

'A fighter who sleeps most of the time.' He rubbed his face. 'Thanks for taking the boys out yesterday.'

'Any time. Really, any time. They're such fun.'

His lips faintly twitched. 'Thought you had a job to go to.'

'Oh, that. Piece of piss.' She took a breath. 'What can I get you? Bun, cake, slice, scone?'

'Just a coffee would be good, thanks.'

'Yes, boss. One of your girly lattes coming up.'

It was a relief to breathe deeply as she stood at the counter. She doubted Gavin had consumed anything but caffeine for the last week.

When she returned with a tray, he cleared his throat. 'Was Cameron upset yesterday?' He peered at her intently before looking away. 'It's fine – I already know. The old man came down from Glasgow yesterday. There's only your dad who'll tell you straight.'

'What did he say?'

'That Cameron cries constantly. That the shooting was my fault. That I shouldn't have taken Ruthie with me to Salford. That I shouldn't have left her alone in the car.'

'And?' Nat asked. Even a dour Scot had something kind to say, surely?

'That it was done now and I should have the courage to move on.'

Nat swallowed back the emotion. 'It sounds like good advice to me. Do you have a mum too?'

'Not since I was eight.'

Bloody hell; the same age as JP when he was allegedly abused. She needed to think about that.

'How awful for you; losing your mum so young. I'm sorry.'

He picked up his mug and took a loud slurp of his drink. 'Don't be. She isn't dead as far as I know.'

Surprised, Nat sat back. So his mum must have left home when he was eight. Good God. Her dad hadn't been the best in the world, but at least he was there. 'I didn't know.'

'Why would you? We only know the best bits about each other.'

She grinned and punched him on the arm. 'Hmm... let's think. Calls his own clients derogatory names, sexist, homophobic, not to mention the loud aftershave. Bloody hell, Gavin, if those are the best bits...'

He snorted. 'See what Heather had to put up with.'

Nat cocked her head. 'Had? Things are good between you two, aren't they? Well, were good before... You know what I mean. Dates out and the like.' She gave him a small kick beneath the table. 'I missed my big chance, of course. A curry and a shag was the undeniably attractive offer, as I recall.'

That was Gavin's proposition when they'd rekindled their law school friendship last year. It brought a small smile to his face and she was glad. She would've danced naked on the café tables if that's what it took to lift the gloom from his whole bearing. But he dropped his head again, picking up a sachet of sugar and pouring it into his empty cup.

She dipped her face to his. 'Just keep talking, okay? To Heather, especially. Communication and all that malarkey. It really does help. And if it's too difficult speak to her, chat to me.' She squeezed his hand again before feigning a yawn. 'You know how I love to be bored to death.'

Folding his arms, he sat back, a hint of mischief in his eyes. 'Communication, eh? Talking of which... What's going on with you and Wes?'

It was Nat's turn to play with the sweetener.

'Nothing. Nothing can come of nothing and all that.'

'Don't think you can quote Shakespeare at me and get away with it, Miss Bach.' He waited for a moment, then tilted his head to the ceiling. 'Guilt is complicated and corrosive, Nat. What happened with Andrea and Matty – the poisoning – happened on Wes's watch.' He puffed air through his nose. 'More than anyone I know how that feels. But mix it with anger, regret, bitterness and God knows what else...' He spread his hands. 'Some baggage there, eh, Nat? But my guess is Wes needs you now as much as ever.'

He stood and pulled her into a bear hug. 'Time's up.' He lingered for a moment, his gaze evasive. 'I would invite you up to see Ruthie, but... Maybe next time.'

She watched him stride away, then remembered a question. 'Why doesn't Robbie like to travel in cars?' she asked, catching him up.

'His mum died in a car crash when he was eleven. He and his father survived.' He lifted his eyebrows. 'The laddie was left with multiple scars, and not just on the outside.'

14

NO SMOKE

Another Monday morning. On her way into the office, Nat made a mental note to arrange a girls' night out with Bo and Fran. She definitely needed some light relief. It turned out that everyone she had come into contact with over the past few weeks was fucked up. Except her mum and her friend Barbara. Since Nat was already at the hospital yesterday, she'd found her ward and popped into say hello.

'Oh, this is my dear friend Anna's lawyer daughter,' Barbara told her bedfellows. 'She's such a clever girl. If anyone needs a little advice while she's here, I'm sure she wouldn't mind...'

Nat had duly chatted about a range of the patients' problems, most of which weren't strictly either theirs or law-related, but they clearly enjoyed the debate. Judith described a personal injury claim she'd read about in the news; the woman, who had claimed to be bedridden after a road traffic accident, was caught out at a Zumba class; was it really true that the insurer's solicitors had filmed her through the window on the quiet? Was that really fair play? Jolivia mentioned her neighbour's lack of contact with her grandkids, and Melinda complained about the shocking cost of the new vet's fees; her

Maisie had placidly gone to the old veterinary year in and year out, but even she was upset. Was there anything Nat could do? It had reminded Nat about the 'old dears' silver surfer sessions. Would she still be at SS for the next one?

Gavin had said nothing about returning to work. It hadn't felt appropriate to ask him, so she intended to carry on driving to Heald Green every day, then sit in his chair until somebody stopped her. She liked Robbie and Chantelle, Larry Lamb too, and although she'd discovered that some of Gavin's Neds weren't misunderstood victims of society, but were actually very bad people, she did like the helping aspect of the work. Being away from Goldman Law also prevented any accidental contact with Wes. She'd mused and mulled on Gavin's words of wisdom last night. While they had prompted her to see matters from Wes's point of view, she'd decided she couldn't 'help' him unless she was asked. There was also the question of Max's offer of partnership. Wes must have known about it for weeks, but he hadn't seen fit to mention it. That was festering.

Still getting used to driving a car which cut out in neutral gear, Nat waited at the temporary traffic lights and tried to fill the silence with a positive thought. She was scraping the barrel, but the fact that Issa hadn't mentioned Mallorca once yesterday was a bonus. On the other hand, the Harrow allegations brought on frequent surges of heat. She hadn't thought it through properly yet, but each time her mind touched on it, she felt a slap of shock that he of all people was accused of child abuse.

She pictured Issa's teary face. She had conceded she was naturally biased as Harrow's daughter, but she'd pointed out her dad had been in education, surrounded by children, parents and staff, his whole adult life. There had never been a whiff of any scandal; he hadn't had one complaint about anything throughout his illustrious career. Even that aside, Harrow had met JP a year ago; there hadn't been a flicker of recognition; he'd been as friendly and fatherly to JP as he was with everyone else.

Before leaving, she'd eyed Nat solidly. 'I know people say there's no smoke without fire and that all these dreadful abusers have been forced out of the woodwork since Jimmy Savile, but you know Harrow, Nat. Hand on heart, can you believe, even for a moment, he would do such a thing?'

Now parked outside the butchers, Nat rested her palm on her chest. Her heart was racing, pumping with anxiety for Issa. It was true; she couldn't believe Harrow was an abuser. The trouble was that JP apparently did and, more to the point, so did his survivor's group pal who just happened to be a journalist for a local newspaper.

Climbing out of the car, Nat headed for SS's grimy windows. She shook her head. What a nightmare for poor Issa. Stuck in the middle, her loyalties were split. At the moment there was stalemate, Issa begging JP to do nothing for the sake of their son; the journalist pal goading him to publish an exposé. Harrow and his wife didn't know anything yet; Issa had held off telling her parents, hoping the whole thing would go away.

'Why do you think JP is making these allegations?' Nat had asked, knowing no other way than just to ask.

Issa's eyes had become glassy. 'JP isn't well. We've never even lived together properly. He's not a bad man, but he's needy and easily pliable. He wasn't even at Harrow's school, Nat. I think there's definitely something troubling from his past, but not this.'

'Good morning, dear lady!'

Still mentally with Issa and on autopilot, Nat jumped at the sound of Larry's eloquent voice. A silver ink pen in his chubby hand, he was perched at Gavin's desk.

She sat in the chair opposite and mirrored his stance. 'What would you do if a small local newspaper had a defamatory exposé rumbling about a client, but hadn't done anything about it yet? A rogue journalist with his own personal agenda?'

Larry took a deep, thoughtful breath. There was definitely a whiff of hops, but no other hint he'd been drinking. 'A swift formal letter to the editor threatening fire and brimstone, with a mention of the journo's personal vendetta not being in the public interest. That'll alert the editor to the 2013 statute.'

'Oh?'

'Has to be in the public interest, balanced, neutral. Facts have to be verified.'

'And true?'

'Of course. Truth is a complete defence, but the onus is on the defendant.' His gaze became beady and sharp. 'Consider these things: Who is the source? What do you know about them? Do they have facts and figures? Same for the journalist. Why is it a personal agenda? What does he have to gain from publication?' His eyes resumed their usual twinkle. 'A bit of digging goes a long way.'

Nat nodded. That's more or less what she'd advised Issa: to write a strongly worded letter, certainly. But Issa wanted to hang fire and think about it; she was clearly hoping for a miracle. Nat hadn't wanted to point out that doctors did them occasionally, but lawyers never. The only thing that could possibly help would be a resolution by conciliation or mediation, but Nat had no idea how that would work without the involvement of Harrow, or even if there was a service which would cover it.

'Now to more parochial matters.' Larry's silver-tongued voice brought her back from her thoughts. 'Pay attention,' he said, as he gave her an update. 'I'm only here for this morning; later I have a tryst with a fine bottle of port.'

Between Nat, Larry and Robbie, they had a productive morning, but Chantelle held back on the usual chatter, frequently looking at Nat with sucked-in cheeks and narrowed eyes.

'Okay. What have I done?' Nat finally asked, watching Larry jaywalk to the pub opposite through the dusty blinds.

Chantelle fired out her vexation: 'You were out on Saturday night with Joshim.'

So that was it. She clearly hadn't given up on her mission to 'turn' him.

'Yes, Joshim and another guy I work with, Chantelle, neither of whom would want a... a "butterhead" to shag.'

God knows what the word meant, but she'd heard Chantelle use it only last week and it brought a momentary smile before the frown returned. 'Joshim said you were in love with him at college. You told him on Saturday.'

'That was a joke and he's just winding you up by repeating it. Surely there's a nice boy out there for you? You know, your own age and straight–'

'Nah, I only want him.' Seeming satisfied with Nat's description of herself, Chantelle flashed a perfect smile. 'Like you and that black guy. What a looker! I take it from the row that he's your fella?'

Nat swallowed. 'You heard the argument?'

'I tried, but not all of it.' She twirled a strand of shiny hair which had escaped from today's elaborate bun. 'He never came here, but I'm guessing he's Wesley Hughes. Poor sod was married to that Andrea looney, wasn't he. I felt so sorry for those boys. How on earth did she get bail?'

Nat hadn't forgotten Gavin represented Wes but, stupid though it was, she hadn't linked it with this office and Chantelle in her mind. No doubt the file and all its nitty gritty was in one of the filing cabinets right next to her. The thought made her uncomfortable.

'I wish I knew how. Or bloody sectioned at the least,' she replied distractedly.

But she did know really. Andrea's case was 'indictable' and so had been passed to the Crown Court for a full trial with a judge and jury, but she had first appeared before the soft touch JPs in the magistrates' court. She was a clever and manipulative operator who'd obviously blinked her baby blues and satisfied them that the charges were all a 'terrible' misunderstanding or a 'dreadful' miscarriage of justice. A next of kin could have asked for a Mental Health Act assessment, but that was for someone who was an immediate risk to themselves or others; while she and Gavin had concluded the Cling-on was as mad as a hatter, she was not, under the law, 'detainable'. Nevertheless, Gavin thought it was a good thing; he wanted the prosecution to prove that her actions were 'capacitous', that she was fully aware of their consequence rather than them being the result of mental health problems. 'Then they can drag her kicking and screaming into a cell,' he'd said with unusual venom after the arrest.

Nat sighed; it was a shame that the woman's husband didn't feel the same.

She came back to Chantelle, still dreamily winding her hair. 'And he's not my fella, Chantelle. Not any more.'

'Who's not your fella any more?'

Nat knew the deep timbre, but swung round to check anyway. What the flip was Jack Goldman doing in her office? Okay, not her office, but Gavin's.

'Sorry to interrupt. There was no one in reception so I followed the sound of chatter,' he said. He offered his hand to Chantelle. 'Hello, I'm Jack Goldman of Goldman Law. How are you?'

'Fine, thank you,' she replied with a bob, almost like a curtsy.

Nat wanted to snigger. This was the effect Jack had on everyone. It was the voice; full-toned, dominant and charming.

'Are we talking about The Spaniard?' he asked.

'Yes we are,' Nat declared, motioning Chantelle to leave. Then, suddenly concerned at his unexpected visit: 'Why are you here, Jack? Is something wrong?'

He sat down on the client chair and placed a folder on the desk. 'A coffee would be nice,' he said, crossing his legs.

Still standing at the window, Nat folded her arms. Her alarm had been replaced by the memory of golden-boy Max and his promotion to partner.

Jack gazed for a moment, then took off his glasses. 'What is it, Natalie?'

'I hear Goldman Law has offered Max partnership. And let's face it, Jack, Goldman Law is you.'

He frowned before replacing his black frames. 'Wesley put his name forward for consideration. He's bright, been with us several years; he's a good, solid and reliable worker…' He smiled wryly. 'However, as is often the case, we were reminded of these things when young Max threatened to leave us.'

'And suppose I did the same? Would I be offered it?' The words came out in a croak. It was ridiculous, but she wanted to cry.

Jack leaned forward, studying her intently. 'If partnership is what you want, it's yours,' he said softly. Then after a few moments: 'What *do* you want, Natalie?'

The tears really prodded then. The baby. The house in the countryside, the apple tree, the things Wes promised me! she wanted to shout. But she was forty, not fourteen. She had to get a grip.

'I don't know,' she said instead, stepping to the desk and blowing her nose. 'Winning the lottery might be a start.'

Jack lifted his hands. 'If you need cash, that isn't a problem, I'm always here. Does the car help?'

She was already feeling foolish; hormonal and girly and very, very stupid. 'It does. Anna is delighted to have her car back at last. Thanks, Jack.'

'And what about The Spaniard and the money he owes you? Have you sorted that yet?'

Nat laughed. 'Don't push it, Jack. I'll get you a coffee. Then you can tell me why you're here.'

In the small kitchen she finally breathed. Wondering if Jack knew what he was in for, she sniffed the 'value' coffee and added two teaspoons to his cup. She splashed cold water on her face, then added another measure of powder to Jack's sherry-coloured drink. By the time she returned, she felt more composed, but had it been wise to leave Jack alone in Gavin's office?

'I had a visitor this morning,' he said once they were settled.

'Oh yeah?'

His face gave nothing away. 'Mrs Brian Selby.'

Nat put down her teacup, all ears. 'Shirley Selby? Really? God, the poor woman. A husband in custody for the murder of their daughter. It can't get much worse. What did she want?'

Jack paused for a moment. He liked dramatic impact, so she knew it was big.

'She says Brian is innocent.'

'As one might expect from a wife–'

'She says he's covering for her. She says that she did it.'

Anna had retired early to read before bed and Nat's cats had formed an uneasy truce, Poppy on her lap, Lewie perched on her shoulder like a parrot, so she wasn't allowed to move from the sofa. She had flicked through pretty much every channel on Freeview, not taking anything in, but enjoying the muted company.

After a bumpy day, she felt remarkably calm, focusing properly on what Gavin had said about Wes. She still wished he had the strength to say no to bloody Andrea, but she recognised that his emotions must be all over the show. And she now knew the full story about Max: he had threatened to leave, so the existing partners' hands had been forced. It wasn't a rebuff as she'd thought; they hadn't chosen him for promotion over her.

She stroked Poppy's soft fur. Partnership. Responsibility. Permanence. If she had been offered it, what would she have said? Even the company car made her feel slightly trapped. And Wes knew she had considered looking for employment elsewhere. She wasn't being fair to him; she was blaming him for what he couldn't give her, both personally and professionally.

She took a breath and punched his number.

'Nat,' he said when he answered. His voice was flat; it betrayed nothing, though certainly not friendliness.

She didn't know what to say. 'How's everything?'

'"Everything" as in what?'

Her stomach clenched; it was hostility after all. 'I just wondered how you were.'

Hearing a sigh, she pictured him rubbing his head. 'What do you want, Natalie?'

The tears were at the surface again. She'd never heard him so disinterested, not since she'd first returned to Goldman Law.

'I just wanted to say sorry.'

'Sorry for what, Nat? For cosying up to Max the moment you'd dumped me?'

'I didn't–'

But he'd already interrupted. 'Because *nice* sex is so easily replaced, isn't it, Natalie? If you don't get what you want the moment you want it, if life doesn't go your way for five minutes, you chuck out the dummy, throw your mobile, have sex with the next man on the agenda.'

Man on the agenda? The phrase was so quaint, it was almost funny, but seconds later his words soaked in. Did he really think she'd sleep with Max? Insulting or what? And what about his comment about the mobile? Yes she'd thrown it just the once when her heart was as shattered as the phone, but Wes had seemed to understand completely that night; he'd picked up the pieces of both.

More hurt than angry, she quickly pressed the red icon to end the call. She had thought he cared, really cared. What a stupid fool; she'd believed it was love.

15

CLOSED DOORS

First downstairs on Wednesday, Nat spent a good ten minutes sweeping up cat litter from the kitchen floor. She glared at Poppy. Yes, she was a princess among moggies, but why she had to kick out the granulated clay so far and wide, she had no idea.

Lost in thought, she reached for the small broom beneath the fridge. How could it be midweek already? Her mind was still buzzing from her meeting with Jack on Monday.

Once she'd got a grip and stopped snivelling, the two of them had discussed the Selby case for half an hour, a 'without prejudice' chat as they'd named it, neither of them knowing what to do about the surprising development of Shirley Selby's confession. They had concluded it would depend on the forensic evidence pointing to either husband or wife. Fortunately for Jack, Mrs Selby had presented him with a fait accompli; she had already asked the GP to inform the police it was her who'd ended Melanie's life, so he didn't have to worry whether her admission to him was a 'sealed lips' communication as per solicitor and client 'legal professional privilege', or if it fell within an exemption. The common law had long recognised that particulars of an 'iniquitous nature' passed between lawyer and client could not be confidential. Indeed, a solicitor had a positive obligation to inform on client criminal behaviour; crime, tax evasion, fraud and money laundering included.

The thought stopped Nat brushing. Had Jack complied with this rule and his duty when acting for some of his less savoury clients such as Danielle and Frank Foster, AKA The Levenshulme Mafia? One thing was for sure, Nat did not want to know.

'Heavens, who'd want the danger of being a GP in Worsley,' Jack had quipped at their meeting. He'd then gone on to say how he'd visited the Selbys' home once, a magnificent modern property on the edge of the local golf course. He'd met a lovely teenager whom he'd assumed was Brian's only daughter, but the poor man obviously had two, one who'd been bedridden and in pain since childhood.

It just went to show that no one really knew what occurred behind closed doors.

Keen to discover more, Nat had telephoned the police station as soon as Jack left, but her request to see Brian had been passed from pillar to post. 'Police wasting police time,' as Gavin often put it. No one had been prepared to give a definitive yes or no to a visit, so Nat had just turned up on Tuesday afternoon with Robbie in tow. They'd both waited with folded arms until the female detective appeared, stony-faced. She clearly wasn't best pleased at the turn of events. A murder-cum-assisted-suicide wasn't the easiest of cases to investigate, but two loving parents claiming it was solely them made it complicated.

'Is it really in the public interest to detain the Selbys?' Nat had asked her. 'Whichever of them did it, it was clearly an act of mercy.'

The officer had looked coldly at Nat. 'People are not entitled to take the life of another person, however sympathetic one might be of the circumstances. That's the law. It's up to parliament to change it.' She'd shrugged her shoulders. 'Two confessions. Someone is playing games. The sooner we find out who, the better. Am I making myself perfectly clear?'

But the visit with Brian was brief. He'd been both taciturn and truculent. 'Shirley is trying to cover for me,' he'd said. 'Tell her to withdraw her statement and go home. That's all there is to it.'

The old dears' session at SS was interesting, not so much from a legal viewpoint, but from a human interest perspective. Nat was now with Marguerite, who preferred to be called Madge. She'd been born at home seventy-five years ago and still lived in the same building. She'd never married, she hadn't had children and she'd lived with her mother until the elder lady popped her clogs.

Nat wanted to stop her there; the back story was a little too close for comfort. Despite the absence of snow, her own mother was refusing to leave the house again, saying she was fine to stay in, that online grocery shopping was just the thing in winter as it saved her from having to face the cold. Madge, however, was glad to be out of hers; after twenty minutes, she was still warming to her tale. Sat with a straight back and wearing a pale blue Crimplene two-piece and pearls, she looked much like the Queen. But unlike Her Majesty, Madge lived in a council house on the huge Wythenshawe estate.

Nat took in the pensioner's papery skin and bright eyes as she spoke. The real help was lending an ear, she knew. So many elderly people had no one to talk to, but there were other clients waiting in reception. She had tried several times to get Madge to the crux, which she assumed was a legal issue, but the conversation had drifted so badly, she gave up trying to steer it and just listened.

Madge had an older brother whom her mother adored; she herself hadn't ever felt loved by her; indeed, the old woman had regularly told Madge she'd been a 'bloody mistake'. Despite that, she'd nursed her father until his death, then cared for her spiteful mum who hung on until she was ninety-six. Madge now had cataracts, and until she was at the top of the list for surgery, she was unable to pursue her true love of sewing and embroidery.

Clearly the old dear had much to feel fed up about, but she told her history with a sunny smile, patting her newly permed hair and diverting to tales of the money her mother had lavished on her brother's kids even though they'd rarely visited. Patting her chest and coughing delicately, she finally turned her thoughts to the reason why she'd come.

'It's so lovely to chat with you, dear, but I'm afraid Alfred will be hungry, so if we could talk about–'

'Alfred?'

'Alfred the Great. He's Persian. Sadly Edward the Elder died last year.'

Madge had cats; of course Madge had cats. All mother-sharing-house-daughters did.

'Lovely. So you have a legal problem you'd like to discuss?'

'Yes, yes. That's why I'm here, dear.'

'Great, so...'

'About six weeks ago, a very pleasant man in a builder's van knocked on my door. He invited me to look at the footpath. It was in a "dangerous state", he said. If the postman tripped, I'd be "in for a claim".' Her curls shook. 'He was right, of course. I could see the chinks for myself. Then he pointed to the roof and the windows and tutted. The house would "fall down" if I wasn't careful, he said, but seeing as I reminded him of his gran, he'd sort them out on the cheap.'

Already knowing the outcome, Nat nodded. Bloody cowboy.

Madge continued her tale: the nice man had filled a few cracks in the paving, then he'd asked for a thousand pounds to buy new UPVC frames and the like. 'Cash would be best', he'd added. She'd dug into her savings to pay him, but he'd never come back. It was two months ago now. She was worried about her missing money; what should she do?

Nat felt the heat rise. For God's sake, the man hadn't just worn a Stetson; he'd carried a swag bag too. Even worse, any vital repairs should have been the council or housing association's responsibility. She inwardly sighed before answering; it wasn't good news for the poor woman. Proceedings in the small claims court would usually be the way forward, but the cowboy-con-man-builder would hardly be listed in the *Yellow Pages*, and if he could be tracked down, cash had been paid, so it was her word against his. Even if Madge did get a judgement against him, enforcing it was a whole other problem. The expression 'blood out of a stone' came to mind, a frustratingly apt one. Madge would have to fund her own legal costs too; the issue fee alone was eighty quid.

Once the disappointed pensioner had left, Nat let out a long breath. It felt as though the process for debt recovery was specifically designed to stymie the likes of poor Madge with her small pond of lifetime savings. Good old Gavin had a collection box on reception to cover the cost of court fees, so at least it gave the oldies a start. Occasionally the tin got stolen, but it was surprising how quickly it filled with coins. Nat had found herself sliding in a fiver each time she called in a new silver surfer. The other day she'd seen Jack slip in a couple of twenties.

She shook herself back to the sweet aroma of cocoa.

Chantelle was holding out a mug of hot chocolate topped with a mountain of whipped cream and marshmallows.

'Midweek treat,' she said, licking a long talon which had changed shade since this morning.

'Wow, thanks. It looks delicious.'

It clearly contained three weeks' worth of calories, but Nat took it and shrugged; with her sudden taste for the local butcher's pork pies, she was going to be enormous by the end of this secondment, but who bloody cared.

Chantelle watched her negotiate the fluffy candy and fail. Then she laughed and held out a teaspoon. 'This might help.'

A sudden burst of sound from reception made her turn. 'The old guys are having fun with Robbie,' she explained. 'They've worked out how to Google images of those busty film stars from the fifties. Ready for the next customer?'

'Yes please.'

Wondering what the 'old guys' made of Savage Solicitors' own busty film star, Nat watched her sashay to the door. A swell of laughter filtered through, then the words, 'Rosalind Russell, now she was a stunner!'

The hum of conversation reminded her of the old days at Goldman Law. The fee earners had box rooms back then, but they'd gather for frequent chats between clients and cases. The current open-plan area seemed to have the opposite effect; other than whispering at the fee-earners' bench, Nat had found an absence of laughter.

She snorted. It was probably why Goldman Law made reams of money and Savage Solicitors didn't.

Nat stood at the sound of a rat-a-tat tap. The OAP was a man this time, looking dapper in a flat cap and cravat. He held out his hand. 'Borys Gorski at your service.'

'Hello. Please sit. Is it okay to call you Borys?'

Recognising his accent as Polish, she fleetingly wondered

about her mum. What on earth did she do cooped up in the house all day?

Borys nodded and sat. 'My son is a waster.' That got her attention. 'But I love him.'

'Okay. How can Savage Solicitors help?'

'Not a lot about his...' He looked to the ceiling, apparently searching for the right word. 'Idleness.' He laughed easily. 'I discover there is no cure for that.' He took off his cap and flattened his thin white hair with an age-spotted hand. 'But tell me, how can he owe double this week what he owed last week, and next week it will be double again, in three months he'll be in debtor's court? You get my drift.'

Nat didn't really. 'So, your son has money problems?'

'He takes one loan and swaps. They are both still there. He's a bloody fool.' He spread his arms. 'But I love him.'

'Okay, let's start at the beginning.' Nat grabbed a biro. 'Try to explain it one step at a time. So, what's your son's name?'

'The waster is Michal,' he started, then he launched into his animated story in Polish. Nat had dutifully learned the basics of the language as a child, but she was lost almost immediately.

She chewed the end of the pen, thought of her mum's pale face, her refusal to leave the house, her loss of appetite... 'Have you got twenty minutes to spare?' she asked when Borys paused to take breath.

He stroked his neat moustache. 'For you I have all the time. What do you wish?'

'I have a translator who might be able to help with the lingo. She can be here in twenty minutes.'

He grinned. 'Lingo, I understand. I will wait.' He stood from the chair and made for the door. 'I expect as pretty as you, though.'

Nat called Anna, but her excuses were immediate and inevitable: it was very kind of Nat to invite her, but she was in the middle of sorting whites for the washing machine; the cats needed feeding; the postman might call; she had a cold coming on.

'This is business, Mum, not pleasure,' Nat said steadily, trying to keep the exasperation from her voice. 'I have to go now, but I'll see you in twenty minutes. Thank you, Mum.'

Nat finished the call, sat back and thrummed her fingers on the desktop. Then a sharp stab of guilt hit her. So busy with the highs and lows of her own life, she'd forgotten to keep an eye on her mum, hadn't she? The medics had warned them both about emotional changes and depression after a stroke, and not necessarily immediately. Oh God, she'd been a bad daughter; it was time to pay more attention.

Unable to settle, she stood at the window with mentally crossed fingers, hoping for a sighting of turquoise. But she needn't have worried; her mum's old Ford appeared in fifteen minutes; Anna Bach hated to be late for anything.

Nat rushed outside to greet her. 'Thank you so much for coming, Mum.' She kissed her cheek and stood back. Anna's face was tense; it had been quite cruel dragging her from her comfort zone, but it was done now. 'Come in and meet Borys; he seems a lovely man.'

The two Poles sat together in Gavin's office and Nat watched, interested to see the interaction between her mother and a man. Anna had been a widow for fifteen years, and though she was now seventy-three, she didn't look it; smaller than Nat, she was slim and neat, and her elfin-style haircut suited her petite face.

As she waited, Nat doodled: love hearts again. What was happening in Wes's life? Had the boys been home? Did he still live with Sidney?

Had he seen the bloody Cling-on?

Didn't he miss her at all?

Coming back to the Polish chatter, she smiled. The

conversation didn't appear to be strictly about business. Borys was stroking his moustache and her mum's cheeks were pink. She didn't want to spoil the fun, but time was ticking.

'So?' she asked, glancing from one to the other.

Borys held out a hand, inviting Anna to speak.

'He says his son is a waster–'

'Yup, got that.'

'The son, he's called Michal, got himself into financial trouble.' Anna turned to Borys for confirmation. 'He had several credit cards and a car loan. He lost his job and couldn't afford to pay the monthly payments. Demand letters kept coming, and though he got different employment eventually, the debt got out of hand. Then he saw an advert about a debt management company.'

Aware of a tingling sensation at the back of her neck, Nat nodded. 'Go on.'

'They told Michal they would take on his loans and pay them off, then he would pay them at a much lower rate, one that was manageable.' She looked at Nat and lifted her eyebrows. 'But presumably for a much longer time. No one can make debts go away.'

'That's true. So...'

'So Michal signed up for this "debt management plan". For the last year he has been paying the agreed payments to the company, but somehow Borys has discovered that the car loan and the credit card debts are still current and earning interest, so instead of going down they've increased massively. It appears that he now has more arrears to pay off than when he started.'

Borys bowed and clapped. 'Perfectly put as I wish. My son Michal doesn't like opening letters. I go to fix his boiler and find a pile of post this big. His head is in the sand.'

Nat picked up her pen again. 'And the name of this debt management company?'

Opening his smart jacket, Borys plucked out a stuffed wallet. He scattered scraps of paper, business cards, photographs and two fivers out on the desk.

'Ha!' he said eventually, finding the item he was looking for. He slipped the folded note towards Nat and she opened it. It was an advert from the free local newspaper.

She read it aloud: '*Write off your debt! Complete protection from creditors! Low monthly payments! Stop interest and charges! Honest and free friendly advice.*'

The familiar prickling was now stabbing her skin. 'And all the other exclamation mark miracles, no doubt,' she said dryly, reading on further. 'Let's see who the veritable saints are. Ah, here we go. DFL Debt Advisers.' She nodded, unsurprised. Surely not a coincidence? DFL: those damned initials she'd seen before.

16

FAVOURS

Nat sped along the M62. The car guy had told her there was a way to operate the radio from the steering wheel, just by telepathy probably, but it was easier to do it the old-fashioned way. Searching for some lyrics she could belt out to ease her nerves, she flicked through the stations. Where was Mr Sheeran when you needed him? In sheer desperation, she settled on Smooth Radio, singing along with 'I Just Died in Your Arms' for a few moments. But thoughts of Brian Selby and his dead daughter soon prodded, so she surrendered to her agitation about Borys's son and DFL Debt Advisers.

Perhaps she was barking up the wrong tree completely. She doubted it, though. The combination of the initials 'DFL' and 'money' could not be a coincidence. She groaned at the memory of last year's Chinese walls. She didn't want to dwell on the favours she'd done to keep the Goldman clan happy. The stack of secrets each of them had, which only she knew about, would come crashing down one day. She didn't want to be around when it did, which was why she declined Jack's frequent invitations to join the happy family for lunch or brunch or 'supper'.

Nat snorted to herself. Suppose she had a psychotic moment and let out all the secrets over smoked trout and quail's eggs? 'Jack, you paid out a huge sum of money to protect Julian from a conviction of attempted murder, but he didn't do it. Aisha did the dirty deed; it was she who ran over the debt "enforcer". Catherine gave Aisha a false alibi because she felt guilty about lying; she'd told Julian you'd refused to help him out of his financial mess when you hadn't. Which is why Julian had gone to a loan shark in the first place.'

She'd prefer to consign the whole episode to history, but unfortunately she couldn't. Not the loan shark part at least; her mum's new number one fan Borys Gorski had made it topical.

Anger rose from her toes to her cheeks. The bloody Levenshulme Mafia; she'd only been thinking about them yesterday when sweeping up cat litter. Pretty apt, really. Frank Foster and his sister Danielle were indeed shits. Nat had acted for their estate agency's 'needs' over time. She'd done her best, of course, but had always felt grubby. Then last year she'd discovered Julian's 'problematic' loan was made by DFL Financial Services Ltd, a company owned by Frank, Danielle and her son Lewis Foster. An old school pal of Julian's, Lewis appeared to be a reputable, upmarket financial adviser with glossy offices in Wilmslow, but underneath he was a loan shark. Like his mum and uncle, he was a money-grabbing, heartless crook.

Going back to Smooth Radio, Nat sang 'Freedom' along with George Michael as she neared her destination. How satisfying would it feel to play even the smallest part in the Foster family's downfall? It would never happen, though. Apart from Danielle's amazing ability to manipulate and charm the pants off the hardest candidate, Goldman Law had been her solicitors for years. She was protected by that old chestnut of legal professional privilege. While Nat suspected there were plenty of communications between Danielle and Jack which were of an 'iniquitous nature', and thereby grounds to waive the confidentiality, they would be pretty damn hard to prove.

The main obstacle to any justice was flaming Jack Goldman himself. He, Danielle and Frank Foster had agreed the financial deal to keep Julian out of prison. Nat didn't want to contemplate what legal and ethical crimes her old boss had committed. If everything went pear-shaped, he would be behind bars himself.

So, all in all, Nat had to stay shtum about anything remotely related to the Levenshulme Mafia. Gavin Savage of Savage Solicitors, though... Well, that was a whole new ball game. Trouble was that Gavin had much more important things on his mind.

Indicating left, Nat took the slip road for the motorway services. What the hell was she doing? The last time she'd tried a mini-mediation, it had most definitely gone pear-shaped. But then again, she'd been dealing with Jack and his son, two of the most stubborn and proud people she'd come across since... well, since her dad. It had all come good in the end, however, albeit with a whole street of Chinese walls.

She parked up the car and looked at her watch. Too early, so what now? To say she was nervous was an understatement. A flaming mediation. Not one between JP and Harrow, which might have done some good, but between JP and Issa. When Nat had suggested it as a possible way of resolution last Sunday, she hadn't for a moment expected a call from Issa asking her to be the piggy in the middle.

'I've had a long think, Nat,' she'd said last night. 'I think the mediation idea is a good one.'

'So you're going to tell your parents about the allegations?'

'God no. Just one between me and JP. And I'd like you to be… well, the mediator, I suppose.'

Nat had been temporarily stuck for words. When she found them, she tried to explain that she was no expert, and as a friend of the family she was far from independent. Besides, she wasn't sure what either of them hoped to gain from a mediation without Harrow's participation.

But Issa had begged. 'Please, Nat. JP needs to talk and I haven't been able to listen. I could do it if you were there. Please, it's worth a try, surely? If JP can let it all out, we might nip it in the bud before Harrow has to know.'

Now tapping the steering wheel, Nat sighed. 'Nipping in the bud' was, she suspected, a tad optimistic. And her stomach was churning with both hunger and nerves. She glanced at the M&S Local. Her mum had become super-efficient with online grocery shopping, reordering her 'favourites' without having a quick scoot for goodies or bargains. No wonder Nat had taken to Chantelle's treats with such relish.

Should she be tempted? Even when they'd done the supermarket shop in a store, Anna put just one BOGOF item in the trolley on the basis of 'need'. So Nat had to discreetly slip in the second, along with something sweet. Sure, her mum baked various Polish delicacies, but there was nothing like mass-made saturated fat products. She missed a sneaky Battenberg behind her mum's back! There was also the pork pie phase; she was over it now; she needed a change.

Having overspent on Percy Pigs, teacakes, Kettle crisps and two-for-a-fiver tubs of Rocky Road (yup, marshmallow again), Nat slung the carrier in the boot and sighed. No more procrastinating; it was time to face the music. She understood why Issa had covered her ears and refused to 'listen' so far; she thought her confession touchingly honest and her willingness to do something about it brave. But she wasn't at all sure about the meeting today; she was all for communication, but she had a horrible feeling it might do more harm than good.

She made her way to the café area, sat at a corner table and pulled out her mobile. Though the habit of holding her breath whenever she checked for messages was now ingrained, the anxiety had lessened. Another week had passed and Ruthie was steadily improving, thank God. As for Wes, she didn't expect to hear from him any more. Polar opposite to her need to pelt her angst and anger out, he was from the 'least said, soonest mended' style of intercourse, and she had gone too far. But then so had he. They'd both breached the Queensberry Rules; she couldn't see a way back.

Tapping her nails on the Formica, she glanced around. Issa had suggested here because it was generally empty midweek and she was right. Only one other couple were there, huddled over a plate of spicy wedges. Were they lovers? She and Wes had intended to share chips the night their affair began, but she'd chosen gravy and he curry sauce. Potato and potato. Perhaps their relationship had floundered even then.

At the sound of voices, she turned her head. A man resembling a middle-aged rocker appeared, holding Issa's hand. Sporting long hair and wire-framed tinted glasses, he wasn't what she had expected. Not a Jose clone after all. Externally, at least.

Trying to look confident, she stood on jelly legs and thrust out her hand. 'Hello. I'm Natalie Bach. John Paul, I assume?' After a pulse the man accepted it, but didn't quite meet her eyes. 'Drinks before we begin anyone?' she asked, suddenly realising her throat was sawdust-dry.

'No thanks, we're fine,' Issa replied.

'Right-oh.' Bloody hell, there was no option but to start. 'Thank you both for coming. If you'd like to take a seat either side, and I'll sit at this end...'

She took a deep breath when they'd settled. 'You've both come here voluntarily, so that's great. Maybe some ground rules?' There were no directives for this situation; she'd have to make them up as she went. 'Everything you say will be kept confidential, both by me and each other. This is an opportunity to say what has happened in the past, where you are now, and how you'd like things to be in the future. While my role here today is independent and I won't be partial or take sides, strictly speaking I'm–'

'I know. You were Jose's partner. That's fine.'

Nat paused for a moment. *Interesting; not 'girlfriend', but Jose's partner*. She shook herself back to JP's intent gaze.

'Great, thanks, JP. There's a possibility that either or both of you will get upset and that's fine. If you need a break or time out, just say so. But no shouting or swearing, please. Try to stay calm. Okay? Now each of you has five minutes uninterrupted time...'

She continued through the spiel. Would she be more successful than the last time? Julian had taken seven long minutes to say his piece, and in fairness Jack hadn't cut in, but when it was his turn to speak, Jack had immediately stood, pointing and aggressive. It hadn't ended well.

'So who would like to speak first?' she now finished.

'Issa, you go first,' JP said. He had a rich Welsh voice, but the tremor was clear.

Issa looked down at her knees. 'There isn't a lot to say, JP. I want us to be happy with Carlos. I want this dreadful trauma to go away. I love you; I love Harrow.'

Nat nodded and waited for more, but there it was in a nutshell; Issa wanted the pain to disappear. 'Your turn, JP.'

He reached an arm across the table. 'I know it's hard for you, Issa, but I need to be heard.'

'I know, that's why I'm here.'

'I need to be heard by him, by Harrow.'

Issa lifted her head. 'Harrow didn't do anything, JP. I think deep down you know that.'

This wasn't going to plan, but Nat let it run.

JP withdrew his hand. 'See, Issa? You're not listening.'

'How can I listen when I know it's a lie?'

'Then why are we here?'

They both turned away at an angle and were silent for some time.

Nat inwardly sighed. Communication was the key to so much in life, but it could be bloody, bloody difficult. 'Do you understand JP's need to be heard?' she eventually asked Issa.

She nodded.

'And do you understand how painful it is for Issa to listen?'

JP nodded.

'Taking that into account, do you both want to try again?'

Her features pallid and tight, Issa lifted her chin. 'Say what you need to, JP. I'm listening.'

He inhaled deeply through his nose. 'When I was eight, I started piano lessons with your father.' The words rushed from his mouth. 'In the house your parents have now. The same piano, same room. He was kind, just like he's kind now. I trusted and liked him. He was far nicer than my own father, who was unloving and cold.' He took a shuddery breath, then carried on doggedly. 'Your father was my saviour. He gave me treats to encourage my progress. Told me I was special and talented. Then the rewards turned to something else, something intimate. He called them "favours".' His voice broke. 'My saviour became my abuser…'

Nat turned to Issa. Her head was bowed. 'Are you okay?' she asked.

She nodded. 'How long did this go on for, JP?' she asked quietly.

'I don't know exactly. Six months? No more than a year.'

'Why did it stop?'

JP didn't reply for several beats. His knuckles bone-white, he put them to his temples and tapped. 'We were caught,' he said eventually. 'He was caught.'

'Who by?' Issa asked.

His hair fell around his face. 'By... by your mother,' he replied.

17

HAPPY MOMENT

Nat stretched and yawned. Thank goodness it was Saturday, a whole day of not having to juggle cases and problems and people and... She stopped herself there. Well, almost. She was spending this morning with Robbie, of course. She had offered to collect him from his father's house – wherever that was – but he'd declined, saying that he'd walk to hers. Was it because he was camping in Gavin's place full time? She had no idea, but she'd decided it was better not knowing too much about his background and fear of cars. Gavin had given her the heads up about his mum's death and that was enough.

Robbie was in her kitchen, devouring a teacake when she finally came down. He wiped the butter from his lips with the back of his hand and nodded a greeting.

'Morning,' she mumbled. Was she crazy? Had she really offered to give him driving lessons? No, not lessons, more a foundation course of where the pedals and handbrake were located in her mum's Ka.

She glanced at Anna's passive face. Surprisingly, she was all for it, and what was the worst that could happen in her tiny car? Well, a collision, a crash, the death of them both, a pedestrian or another driver was the flaming worst that could happen. Or maybe a bump and having to pay the huge excess over and above the extortionate cost of the insurance she'd paid yesterday.

She sat down and inwardly sighed. But if she didn't do it, who else would? This was a boy who preferred kipping in Gavin's mangy flat rather than going home to his dad, a young man with reams of potential. The job ladder was difficult enough without being held back by an inability to drive.

Robbie gulped back the last of his drink. 'I brought my provisional licence like you said. So what happens now?' he asked.

'Well…' His knee was jerking, his face ashen. 'There's no hurry about any of this. Let's just sit in the car today, get used to the gears and stuff. Does that sound okay?'

'Or drive up and down our road. Maybe have a go around the pay-and-display car park? If I can do it, so can you,' Anna added.

The car park that was always chock-a-block? Nat stared meaningfully at her mum, but she'd already turned away, tossing a tea towel over her shoulder and humming a tune. Invited by Borys, she'd joined an OAP dancing group at a church hall in Bramhall. Last night had been their first outing and had clearly gone well. What Borys had lacked in talent, he'd 'made up in enthusiasm', she'd told Nat with a sunny smile last night. From her glowing reticence, she suspected her mum had been a dancing star. It made Nat's heart swell. Go Mum!

Finally sat in Anna's car, Nat introduced her student to the ropes in the same order as a sweaty and smutty driving instructor had a million years ago to her. Robbie tucked his long fringe behind an ear, and for the first time she noticed a puckered scar on his temple. His expression was tense and he didn't say much, but he practised turning the engine on and off, then putting the car into gear.

'Practise for as long as you like,' she said several times, but boredom soon set in. What was that old Scottish proverb? *If ye like the nut, crack it.* Well, she and Robbie were going to crack this particular nut. She glanced to the pay-and-display across the road. Yup, this one was heaving; the cheeky buggers had even parked on yellow lines to pop into Sainsbury's for a loaf, or a Quality Save bargain.

'Are you up for actually moving?' she asked Robbie, and when he nodded she said, 'Okay, let's swap seats.'

Nat drove to the only local business park she could think of. Ignoring the gym kit bunnies keenly hopping towards the David Lloyd, she drove to the empty far end and parked up. 'Right, let's change places again...'

Hoping Robbie couldn't tell just how clenched her buttocks were, she gave a mental salute to the patience of (even sweaty and smutty) driving instructors, and encouraged him to inch forwards and back. Once he seemed to get the hang, Nat found her mind drifting.

From their hand-holding yesterday, she'd supposed Issa and JP had travelled to the motorway services together, but it turned out they'd come in separate cars. Sensible really, when there was a high probability they wouldn't be leaving as friends. After JP's shocking revelations, Nat had stayed in the café for a while, buying herself a fizzy drink to quench her thirst and her agitation. What the hell would Issa do about the horrendous situation now it included her mother? But when she'd returned to the car park, Issa was waiting in her own car.

Nat had hurried over and climbed into her passenger seat. 'Oh my God, I'm so sorry. I thought you'd gone home with JP.

Are you okay?' she'd asked, taking in Issa's tight face and hair, newly scraped into a ponytail.

'Not really. What do I do now?' she had replied, staring through the windscreen.

Nat had been stuck for an answer; she'd still been spinning from the blow herself, but Issa had continued to speak.

'What did I tell you? It's all up here.' Tapping her temple, she'd focused on Nat. 'JP is forty-six. He's talking about something that happened thirty-eight years ago. I wasn't even born then. We didn't buy our house until I was five. I can remember moving in because of my new swing. Dad didn't give piano lessons; the Steinway was bought for Jose when he started playing.'

It had taken Nat a moment to add everything up. 'So that means...'

'It means it didn't happen, Nat. It can't have. When JP was eight, we didn't live in Lower Heswall, so he can't have been in our house. Jose was two, so there was no piano back then.' Her eyes had glazed for a few seconds, then she'd nodded. 'JP asked me to listen and I did. I hope that's enough.' She turned to Nat again and blew out her release. 'Thank God I did. I knew it wasn't Harrow, Nat, and now I know for sure. Not that for a moment... but it's a relief, a huge relief.'

Nat had wanted to punch the air. She was so pleased for her, glad that Harrow wouldn't have to be dragged into the horrible mess. Issa had been right after all; the less her parents knew, the better. Like her with Robbie and his fear of cars, which he'd temporarily put behind him.

She came back to her pupil and glanced through the wing mirror. 'Whoa, Robbie!' she declared, pressing an invisible brake in the passenger footwell. She stared at the wall he'd almost mowed down, took a deep breath and tried for the patient voice of an instructor, rather than the harridan inside who was itching to shout.

'Remember to look in your mirrors, Robbie. One more go, then let's call it a day.'

A panini was waiting on the table for lunch. *Szynka* and gherkin on seeded bread; it looked and smelled delicious but she'd be eating again soon at McDonald's. Truth be told, she was getting pretty sick of cheeseburgers and fries, but Gavin's kids objected if she didn't join in.

Taking a break from her tune, Anna turned from the sink. 'You could wrap it in foil and take it with you,' she said, as ever reading Nat's mind. 'Then you could blame your mama for making you eat proper food.'

Nat smiled; it was lovely to see her mum rosy-cheeked and happy. Borys was clearly a charmer, not unlike Hugo in Mallorca. Lovely old Hugo used to guide the ladies around 'Havana's' small dance floor with a firm hand; he'd even managed to make Nat feel like a natural. It was a happy memory, but reminded her of Issa's parting shot the other day. Did Nat know that Jose's condition was so improved he'd been discharged from the clinic in Palma? He was deciding his future, but in all likelihood he'd be coming home at some point.

Liverpool was thirty miles away, but the thought still made her feel queasy.

The sandwich duly wrapped, Nat drove the short journey to Heather's house. She parked outside the frosted glass porch. Would she be invited in again? There was always that instinctive desire to help. Or was it to interfere? She wanted to say, 'I talked to Gavin. I said that I'm here if he needs me. Don't forget it's the same for you too.' But her father would've said she was 'blowing her own trumpet' and 'seeking approval', and that real charity was when other people didn't know about it. He was probably right, but who didn't enjoy appreciation and applause?

Gavin answered the door, his head almost hitting the frame.

'Gav, it's you! Don't tell me you've gone and had a shower, you old devil.' Surprised and pleased to see him, she laughed. Newly shaved and with a pink shiny chin, he looked about fifteen.

'Watch it, Bach,' he replied. 'Though I think the nursing staff were on similar lines. They pretty much kicked me out.'

'Good for them.' She put her head in the lounge and waved at the boys duly lined up on the sofa. Stepping back, she lowered her voice. 'Seeing as you're home, shall I postpone the park for another day?'

'God, no. They'd never forgive me.'

Picking up a rounder's bat from the corner, she lightly prodded him. 'Come on then, big man. There's room in my charabanc for five.'

Over the past few outings Nat had tried different parks, but today she drove to Wilmslow, where the tradition had first started. She'd been touched by Gavin's trust that day, alarmed too; he'd abandoned her with four young children and without any instructions. But little Ruthie had been there to show her the ropes. The thought made her sniff. Sure Gavin felt the loss too, they watched his three sons tumble from the car and charge towards the tall climbing frame. The two older boys shimmied up, halfway in seconds, leaving Cameron behind. She glanced towards their dad, wondering what he would do; the metal structure was too advanced for the three-year-old, his legs not long enough to manage the first rung.

'He'll learn,' Gavin commented, not moving.

Her heart in her mouth, Nat watched. The bigger boys were hanging from the top and shouting down to their little brother. Was this the way Gavin's dad had taught him? Her father had been strict too, but she'd had the softness of a mother.

She itched to help. Poor little Cameron was now on his knees; she couldn't see his face but could tell by his slumped and heaving torso that he was sobbing. Thank God she didn't have kids; it was all too emotional, there was too much to lose. Turning away, she searched out the ice-cream van, a constant presence, whatever the weather.

'Here we go.'

She spun back at the sound of Gavin's voice. Cameron had picked himself off the ground and was swinging on the bottom tier, lifting his legs high and catching another. The little tyke was on the damned frame! His red, blotchy face was a picture of delight, and his brothers were cheering.

Nat had to blow her nose this time. Gavin put an arm around her shoulder. 'What are you like?' he said with an amused chuckle. 'This is a happy moment.'

The grass was boggy and wet, but that didn't stop a muddy game of rounders; Gavin and Cameron against Nat and the older boys. Perhaps it shouldn't have been a surprise, but all the Savage's were competitive, even little Cameron, who pelted around the make-shift bases like a spinning top.

Having declared it a draw, they headed for the River Bollin. Already in wellies, the boys hurtled down the bank and splashed into the shallows. Though the sun had cracked a smile, Nat lifted her collar as she sat on the bench.

'Are you cold?' Gavin asked when he joined her.

She eyed him. 'You're going to say something about me being a soft... female? Southerner?'

'Nah, not me.'

She tried for a Scottish accent. 'We're not all made of *girders*, you know!'

'Not bad for a southerner.'

Keeping an eye on the boys, they fell silent.

'How's Ruthie?' she asked eventually.

'Not Ruthie yet.' He turned and smiled a small smile. 'But glimpses.'

'Oh, brilliant. I'm so pleased. And Heather?'

He gazed ahead, watching his sons skimming stones along the water's surface, but after a few moments he spoke.

'They've arrested the shooter. He's fifteen.'

Nat nodded; she'd heard this already. On the news, or maybe from him.

'I've had the heads up he'll be pleading guilty. The police picked him up that same evening. Gun residue on his hands and clothes. He couldn't not admit to it.' He sighed heavily. 'So, there's this gun amnesty going on, and in the same spirit the police are encouraging restorative conferencing...'

She nodded again; it seemed to be the latest thing; bringing offenders and victims together in a safe environment to 'repair harm and promote healing'. All great in theory.

Gavin abruptly covered his face with his hands. 'Heather wants to do it; she's prepared to forgive, but I can't.' After a moment he took a breath and looked at Nat with burning eyes. 'I've sent my children to a catholic school, I've attended church with her and the kids, but if I'm honest...' He thumped his fist on his chest. 'It isn't there. I want to believe, but I don't. So all this claptrap about forgiveness and healing.' He shook his head. 'Fifteen or not, he shot my girl. She nearly died. I can't... I won't do it.'

18

ABRUPTLY SOBER

The Saturday night threesome had turned into five. Chantelle had got wind of the gathering and it felt unfair not to invite Robbie. Nat had assumed he was in the region of thirteen, but having asked for his date of birth for the car insurance, she'd discovered he was twenty-one. Still young enough to be her son, she supposed. Her flipping son! That had been Gavin's interpretation earlier at the park. She had entertained him with the whole driving malarkey and he'd deduced it was all to do with her need for kids. Her motherhood hormones were crying out for action before it was too late, apparently.

Only Savage could say something so outrageous and get away with it. She'd decided not to rise to the bait. 'Think I'll just stick with my surrogates, if you don't mind,' she'd replied, nodding towards Cameron who'd just fallen flat on his face in the freezing murky water.

It had been comical watching Gavin pluck him out at arm's length as he tried not to get saturated himself. Her laughter had faded when she remembered they would be in her brand-new car, so she'd suggested races, hoping the wind would blow away some of the damp. She'd impressed everyone with her speed.

Smiling at the memory, Nat now looked around the bar. Misty, grimy and damp. She sniffed. Yes, and even more pungent than Gavin's office. God knows why after last time's deadly hangover, but Joshim and Max had decided on the Withington dungeon again, so she was on the snakebites. She lifted her glass and squinted at the contents. It was half lager, half cider with a blackcurrant top, apparently, though in this light, she could be drinking pretty much anything from treacle to tar. She'd left her mum at home with Borys, ostensibly playing cards, but who knew what those OAPs got up to? Her lips twitched wryly. It seemed the motherhood worry hormones extended to the older generation as well.

'So what are you smiling about?' Joshim asked over the loud music. He was drunk, but then again, so was she. Chantelle had gone to the ladies, so he was allowed a two-minute break from the dance floor.

'My mum, actually. Seems she's got herself a boyfriend.'

He nudged Nat's arm clumsily, causing some venom to spill out. 'So there's hope for you yet.'

They both stared at the sizzling bubbles.

'What the fuck do they put in that drink?' he asked, the same time as Nat spoke.

'You sound like Gavin.'

'How is the Rabid Scot?'

Joshim's use of Gavin's nickname was a sure sign that Ruthie was getting better, a joyous thought which prevailed over the other doom and gloom consciousness sloshing around in her head. Along with the hiss of snakebite, of course.

Joshim was still speaking. 'Talking of which, causation.'

Nat tried to drag her stunned mind to the legal term. 'Causation?'

'Not *who* done it, but *what* done it,' he managed, before being plucked off his chair by the indefatigable Chantelle.

Nat turned to Robbie, her surrogate child. He was talking to Max, his stutter noticeably pronounced, but Max's quiff had fallen forward and his eyes were rabbit-pink, so she doubted he'd notice. She'd told Robbie that Max was someone to keep in with, a man of the legal future, the next generation Jack Goldman. Not that Wes wasn't. He was as clever and as forward-thinking as anyone; it was just that Wesley Hughes was scrupulously fair, he did everything by the book, whereas she sensed that Max would cut corners or bend the truth if he had to.

'Max the man,' she said, leaning over. 'I've got a bone to pick with you.'

He swigged his beer and wiped his damp mouth. 'Oh yeah?'

With a look of relief, Robbie stood. 'I'll just...' he said, swaying towards the dancers.

'What did you say to Wes?' Nat asked Max. 'He thinks, you and me...' She circled her fist and poked it with her other forefinger. Putting a hand on her belly, she cackled. She hadn't done that since she was twelve.

'What, me?' he replied once she'd finally stopped hooting. He lifted his eyebrows, all innocent. 'I didn't say anything, Your Honour. A little jealousy doesn't hurt, though.' He looked at Nat meaningfully. 'Unless you're in a relationship already, in which case sleeping around with someone as handsome as me isn't so good.' He gazed for a moment then rolled his eyes. 'I might have said something to wind up Emilia.'

Nat snorted. 'And whatever you tell her goes straight to Sharon–'

'Who can't help but mention it to Wesley. Sorry. Do you want me to put him straight?'

'Absolutely not.' She lifted her glass in a salute. 'He can fuck off!'

He groaned loudly. 'God, I wish it was that easy.'

Some erratic movement caught Nat's eye. What the...? Dancing pogo-style, Robbie and Joshim were clearing the dance floor. She brought her attention back to Max. 'Talking of which, how come you've been allowed out again?'

'She's at some posh medical event.'

'She's a doctor?'

'Oh yes. Super clever, attractive, plenty of dosh. I should be counting my–'

'Fingers? Bunnies? Testicles?'

He pulled out his mobile and showed Nat the screen. 'There you go. Six missed calls during the last two hours.' He burped. 'I won't bore you with the texts–'

Nat leaned forward and crooked her little finger. Yup, she was really, really pissed; the last time she'd done that, she was older than twelve but under twenty. 'Come on, spill the beans. What's the ammo, Max? You've got a small dick?'

Sniggering, he spurted out a mouthful of ale. 'You're closer than you think.'

'You snore and dribble when you sleep? Nah, that's all boys. Cheesy willy? Spotty bum? Porno?'

'Very warm.' He banged the table, still shaking. 'I don't know why the fuck I'm laughing about this. Like I said. Blackmail. Basically blackmail to stop me from leaving.' He lifted his phone and waved it in the air. 'A moment of madness.'

'Not a sex tape?'

He nodded.

'With her? Your girl? If so, surely she wouldn't want–'

He winced. 'No, just me.'

'Oh, right.' Nat laughed. 'Beating the old bishop, eh?'

When he didn't reply, she thought for a moment. Posh private-school guy who played rugby... 'Oh God, don't tell me it was a 'Piggate' moment?'

Putting his head in his arms, he groaned. 'No, but along those lines...'

Smirking, she ruffled his hair. 'Fifteen minutes of fame on your way. Couldn't happen to a prettier boy.'

Max lifted his head. 'It's not funny though, is it?' he said, his face abruptly sober. 'It isn't "conduct becoming a solicitor". This partnership offer is my big chance, Nat. Put that on social media and it would fuck everything up. And she knows it.'

19

SILVER SPOON

A brand-new week at Savage Solicitors. Nat had bunged Chantelle a tenner for air fresheners on Friday, so the smell of mould was now mixed with sweet, cloying scent. She sniffed. Better or worse? She couldn't decide.

His head down at the laptop, Robbie was already on reception. He greeted her with a grunt. He was suffering from the excesses of Saturday night, no doubt. Nat herself felt fine; indeed, she was full of energy and an idea. The others had continued to drink steadily at the bar, but she had decided to match them glass for glass with tap water. It was impressive stuff; peeing several times in the night was a nuisance, but she'd awoken on Sunday looking half human and without even the hint of a headache.

It had been nice to have a work-and-stress-free day at home on the Sabbath. She, Bo and Fran, had a 'Jacob's Table' every few weeks, and it had been her turn to host it. As usual they'd each contributed a few surprise food items with a flourish, hoping no one else had the same idea. It wouldn't have mattered if they had: bread and jam would have done. The joy was catching up, exchanging funny stories, news and irritations, and more often than not, telling each other tales they'd heard many times before.

Her mum usually flittered in and out of the conversation and kitchen, but yesterday she'd driven Borys to a garden centre for a 'coffee and a browse'. Nat had raised her mild concerns with Fran and Bo.

'Should I drop a few hints that neither Anna nor I have any money?'

'And you need to do that because...?' Fran asked.

'Long story, but Lover Boy has a son who, by his own admission, is a waster.'

'And...?'

Nat laughed. 'Well, I don't know; it might be a hereditary condition!'

The waster, and particularly the villains who'd conned him, had been in her sofa-thoughts yesterday evening and they were here again today as she studied Gavin's stationery-cum-storage room. His ground floor premises comprised the reception area with a partition for Chantelle and her word processor, his office, two smaller rooms and a loo. There wasn't a lot one could do about the tiny kitchen, but in here, albeit deeply hidden, she found just what she was looking for: a desk.

She nudged Robbie from his elbow malaise. 'Come on, Smart Alec, it's time for action.'

He followed Nat to the stationery room and loitered at the door, watching her lift a crate with a puzzled expression. His shoulders hunched even further when she passed it to him.

'Chop, chop, Robbie. You'll be pleased, just you see. You might even crack a smile,' she cajoled, the words intriguing Chantelle sufficiently to honour them with her presence.

'So what's going on?' she asked.

'We're making space for a beauty salon,' Nat replied.

'Very funny. Though...' Chantelle held up her sparkly aqua

nails. '"Self-made mermaid" today. What do you think? Could make us some money…'

'Tempting, but some wild instinct tells me manicures aren't Gavin's thing…'

They spent most of the morning moving boxes, Chantelle simply watching on the grounds of said nails and the need for someone to man the phone and reception.

'Are you still here?' Nat asked from time to time, but she didn't blame Chantelle for her lack of manual labour. She was wearing a figure-hugging shimmery blue dress with eye shadow to match, and in fairness she regularly brewed up, imperative for de-clogging the dust from their throats.

Feeling a tad naughty, Nat couldn't resist lifting lids and peeking in. Some of the contents were old client files which Gavin was obliged to hang on to for six years, but others contained miscellaneous items, from Christmas decorations, which she could see the merit in keeping, to a dead Bonsai tree, which she couldn't.

She sent the tatty suitcases with Robbie to the upstairs flat. Suspecting they contained Gavin's life before he moved out of the matrimonial home, she had no desire to open them. It gave her pause for thought as they stopped for another tea break. How hard must it have been to pack his bags and leave the children behind? Gavin did fathering in his own feral way, but the love and affection between him and his kids was plain to see. She didn't know the ins and outs of why he and Heather had split, but he had once mentioned Andrea's influence. She and Heather had been close friends at one time. No wonder he'd celebrated her final downfall with gusto. She sighed. If that's what it would eventually be; who knew with the Cling-on?

The room finally rearranged to her satisfaction, Nat sprayed the desk with another 'value' product from the kitchen and rubbed hard with a cloth. 'Ta da!' she said to Robbie when she'd finished. 'What do you think? You now officially have your own office.'

From what she could see behind his fringe, he appeared relatively pleased, but Chantelle's orange lips were turned down. 'A pile of boxes along one wall. Pretty damned dark. No window, no telephone, no computer...'

'A desk, two chairs, pen and paper.' Nat glared at her meaningfully. 'And a brilliant paralegal to go in it.' She handed a fiver to Robbie. 'There's a spare lamp in Gavin's office. Nip to the pound shop and buy some light bulbs. The highest wattage you're allowed these days. You've got a mobile and you can bring in the laptop. All sorted.' She glanced at her watch; bloody hell, her nosiness had added an hour or so to her mission. 'Heck, look at the time. You'd better be quick, Robbie, your first client arrives in twenty minutes.'

Hopping from foot to foot, Nat hid in Gavin's office and peered through the blinds. Trying to clean them had been a mistake; it turned out that the dust was glued to the slats and they were now covered in fluff.

Michal Gorski was fifteen minutes late for his appointment. Had she not heard him introduce himself to Chantelle through Gavin's open door, she wouldn't have known the scowling guy walking past was the son of charming Borys. She felt ridiculously nervous. She'd prepped Robbie and he was bright; he understood what he needed to find out from Michal, the instructions he should take and the terms of his retainer, and he especially knew the importance of keeping Nat's name well out of it. Of course she wanted to do the best for Michal and help him out of his financial pickle (even if he was a waster whose father was after her mum), but if she could get some ammo, as Max had put it, on the Levenshulme Mafia, so much the better.

What she would actually do with the information was a whole other thing.

Holding her breath, she listened to Robbie greet him. 'My office is this way,' she heard him say without the hint of a stutter. Fantastic. Go Robbie!

Intending to work on the Lee's file for next week's tribunal hearing, she returned to Gavin's desk and picked up the latest medical report, but the word 'ammo' took her on another tack. Saturday night's drunken conversations: she'd knotted two things of significance in her mental handkerchief. What were they?

Yup, that was the first: Joshim and Brian Selby. But she'd made an appointment to take a witness statement from Brian's GP tomorrow, so she could shelve that for now. The second was Max, his girlfriend and 'conduct befitting a solicitor'. She'd mused on that for some time when she awoke on Sunday. It was a tricky one, for sure. Historically, she'd always stuck up for her own sex. Women hadn't had the same political, economic, personal and social equality as men for too many aeons, so she'd had a default button in that regard. These days she might, if pressed, admit that she *might* have been a tad blinkered at times. However, with age had come reality: some females were plain bad – Danielle Foster, for example. Others downright evil: Andrea was evidence of that. As for Max's Caz, she had felt a little sorry for her at first; the poor woman was clearly insecure; maybe Max gave her good grounds to be. But stealing a private video from your boyfriend's phone, then threatening to expose it? Nah, Nat didn't like that one bit.

She searched for his number. He'd know the law as much as she, but would it have occurred to him? She'd speak to him now while the thought was fresh. She stared at the screen. Hmm...

probably not a good idea to call his mobile after what he'd said about his girlfriend's monitoring. Best try him at work.

She put a call through to Goldman Law.

'Nat! Hi. How's it going?' Christine asked. 'We're missing you. It feels like ages. When are you coming back?'

It did feel like forever, and for a moment Nat felt quite sentimental. Silly though it was, Goldman Law was like a first love; it would always be there in her heart; she'd move on at some point, but never really get over it.

'I know, it feels like months. How's my conference room?' she asked.

'Max is in there now. I took him a pizza and drink earlier, and he's not half as tidy as you are. You know what boys are like, files all over the floor, screwed up paper that doesn't quite reach the bin, feet on the table...'

'Definite breach of the office manual. Good job for him that Wendy's still on maternity leave,' Nat replied to cover the jolt of pique.

Of course Golden Boy would be in *her* room, waited on hand and foot. He was a partner-to-be, important now. They were hardly going to leave him on the fee-earners' bench downstairs with young Tom, Dick and Harry. And here she was trying to help him. She took a sharp breath of self-reproof. He was her mate; that's what mates did. 'Is Max there now, Christine? I just need two minutes of his time.'

He came on the line straight away. 'Nat. Can I call you back later? I'm just tied up with Catherine right now.'

'Sure,' Nat said, putting down the receiver. Max was 'tied up' with Catherine. Of course he was.

Larry was in her chair when Nat returned from her usual lunch walk. She had discovered that John Lewis was closer than she'd thought. If she walked briskly, she could make it there in fifteen minutes, spend thirty just touching mugs and throws and cushions and vases in the Homeware department, then be back at the office within the hour. Not that the sixty minutes was mandatory; she was at SS after all. There were no swipe cards, time-recording or hundred-page office manuals. No salary either, as far as she was aware. She hoped she'd be paid by someone at the end of the month; she and Wes hadn't worked that one out when they'd hatched the secondment – when they'd still been friends.

Of course she was happy doing Gavin the favour for as long as it took, but she needed an income to pay the bills; her mum only had her small pension and Nat had given her ill-gotten gains to Jose to buy 'Havana'. Having spare cash to buy delicious colour-coordinated bedding and curtains, Le Creuset Cookware, a lover's armchair and matching pouffe and a new flat screen TV would be great, but in truth she didn't need any of those things; her small terraced house was packed to the rafters as it was, a rattle bag combination of her possessions and her mum's. These days it felt more like Anna's home than hers, but in fairness her mum had lived there for five years on her own. Neither she nor Nat had expected her permanent return.

Nat inhaled the mouth-watering smell of her bacon barm 'with a twist' from the sandwich shop. She had been hoping to discover the twist while it was still warm, but Larry was clearly impatient to fill her in with his morning's endeavours at the magistrates' court. After all, at two o'clock, it was way past his usual pub date time. The poor man's glint had been replaced by trembling hands; she could feel his need for ethanol-related sustenance before he expired.

'George, the mother murderer?' he started. 'Remember the one?'

It wasn't as though Savage Solicitors had so many homicides she wouldn't remember them all, but she let it pass by nodding.

'An indictable offence, so the case was sent to the Crown Court for a plea and case management.'

'Okay...' Nat watched the movement of his white whiskers, glad that Larry had everything in hand, but distracted by her rumbling stomach. Cranberry sauce was her guess; yup, the twist was definitely cranberries.

'Had a little chat with George while I was there. A veritable witch, the mother. Wouldn't let him have a life, dictated his every move, demanded complete loyalty and attention. My interpretation, mind you, not his words.'

Nat grabbed a notepad and pen. It sounded similar to Madge and her mother. But of course the difference was that she hadn't resorted to strangulation.

Larry was still speaking, his tremor receding as he warmed to his subject. 'Mother love. So *intensioris* and *complicatas*, especially between mothers and sons...'

Nat duly scribbled. Was he really speaking in Latin (or perhaps Greenlandic)? She tried her best with the spelling; she'd look it up later.

'Yes, young lady, I've seen it before, that unconditional and suffocating love *matres* have for their *filiorum*; that inbred willingness to go to the ends of the earth. That's what brings the men to the final ghastly deed. The need to escape.'

'Not yet a legal defence to murder,' Nat replied dryly, though she was thinking about Gavin's mum. What type of mother left an eight-year-old boy with his puritan dad?

'Very true,' Larry replied, the twinkle surfacing. 'But I think we have an excellent argument for manslaughter. We'll have to see what our expert psychiatrist will say, and it will be for us to prove it, but my money is on diminished responsibility, abnormality of mental functioning.' He stood and paced, his fingers in the lapels of his checked jacket as though it was a court gown. 'Did he understand the nature of his actions? Was he able to form a rational judgement? Could he exercise self-control? No, we will say, he did not!'

He looked to Nat as though he expected applause, but she was too busy making notes to oblige. 'Very good,' she said instead. 'Please go on.'

'Then we have loss of control, the old provocation defence. He had bruising on his face and his body that he's currently unable or unwilling to explain. Was there a qualifying trigger? Was he in fear of serious attack? Were things said or done to cause him that loss of control? I realise *Matre* was elderly, but that is certainly no bar.'

Wondering about Larry's relationship with his own mother, Nat eyed him; this case had certainly hit a chord, but he was still in mid-speech.

'But for now dear George is not saying much. Even in the four walls of his cell, the poor man doesn't want to be disloyal. It will take careful handling to bring out the full story. Which brings me to my third point.' He started pacing again. 'How did she die? Strangulation, you may say, but we don't know that yet. George said that she "fell to the floor". Was this before or after he had his hands around her throat? Causation, young lady. Did those hands *cause* her death?'

Causation. So, that's what Joshim had been mumbling about on Saturday night.

'So, you're saying–'

'I'm not saying anything, dear girl. But it's something we must investigate. What exactly did she die of?'

'Asphyxiation?' she tried, unsure if it was a rhetorical question.

'It may well be,' Larry said, patting her shoulder. 'But one must keep everything sharp. I think a nice forty-year-old tawny is calling.'

Nat sat at the desk when he'd gone. There was a sour aroma of alcohol in the air. Perhaps the smell was imbedded in Larry's clothes, but if that was how sharp his mind was by the afternoon, God only knew how whetted it was when he woke every morning.

She took a bite of her cold butty. She had been fooled by the colour. The bacon was accompanied by sweet onion relish mixed with beetroot, delicious all the same. Putting her feet on the table, she ruminated on the information Larry had given, but she was interrupted mid-flow by her mobile. It was Max. She was tempted to ignore it, but he'd become a good friend. Wes had left a large hole in her life; she didn't want another.

'Yup,' she said.

'You called me.' Then after a moment. 'What are you eating?'

'Bacon and beetroot.' She sighed. It had to be humour; it was the only way to cope. 'I had to brave the cold to buy it, whereas I hear a handmaiden brings in your lunch and feeds you from a silver spoon.'

He laughed. 'Well, who'd turn it down?'

It was true, very true. Nat put down the floury bread. 'So, I was thinking about you and your girlfriend's... well, manipulation.' She nodded to herself. Yes, the woman sounded far too much like the Cling-on.

'God, don't,' Max replied. 'I'm trying not to think about her. I'll have to delete my call history before I go home.' He paused. 'Not all of it, but some. All of it would look dodgy, wouldn't it? That would look suspicious and she'd harangue me for hours.'

'Just leave her.'

'She'll use her ammo.'

'Bluff it out.'

'I can't take the risk.'

'Then there's only one option. From what you've said, she's threatening revenge porn. I don't want to teach my grandmother to suck eggs, whatever the hell that actually means, but it's illegal to share sexually explicit images without the owner's consent.' Squinting, she tried to remember the wording of the statute. 'It's something like, "Non-consensual sharing of any explicit film depicted in a sexual way..." or, and I imagine this is the crux, "with their private parts exposed..." It's a potential two-year prison sentence, Max. Put that in her pipe and invite her to smoke it.'

20

MONEY TALKS

Although Nat had already done her research, the posed portrait on the waiting room wall named Doctor Peter Woodcock as the senior partner of the modern Worsley practice. It also stated he was a Justice of the Peace.

The receptionist took her through to his surgery. Smart and regular-featured with neat grey hair, he stood when she entered and held out his hand. From his patterned Pringle jumper, the golfing celebrity photographs adorning one wall and the selection of putting irons lined up against the other, Nat guessed he mainly dealt with the upper echelons of Worsley society. Not that she judged him too much; he seemed a very thoughtful, if guarded, man.

After inviting her to sit, he tapped his lips with steepled hands. 'I have agreed to speak to you because I've been asked to by...' He cleared his throat. 'Brian and Shirley aren't just patients, they are friends and have been for many years.' He paused for several moments. 'However, I have to be circumspect. How do they put it in American legal dramas? I wouldn't want to incriminate myself.' He flushed slightly. 'Not that I have anything to hide, but...'

Nat sensed he wanted to help, but was struggling. Perhaps he'd seen a solicitor who'd told him to keep quiet. Or maybe he'd learned caution from his voluntary work as a magistrate.

'I don't know how the police operate,' she replied. 'But I'm talking to you on behalf of my client, Brian Selby. Anything to help me understand his daughter's condition can only help him.'

He nodded and leaned forward. 'Then I'll be frank. I was and I still am the whole family's general practitioner. As I say, we are friends too. But I have a responsibility to this practice, my patients and my partners. If there was any suggestion that I knew about what Brian, or indeed Shirley, had in mind, that I conspired or colluded in any way...'

Nat met his gaze. 'I understand. And of course it was you who quite properly reported it to the police.'

He looked at her steadily with intelligent, clear eyes. 'Indeed.' He took a breath. 'I was asked by Melanie herself many times if there was anything I could do to relieve her suffering. I did all that I could, which was to prescribe levels of morphine in accordance with guidelines. I carefully documented everything in the medical records together with the clinical reasons for it.'

Nat nodded. Yes, morphine; that's what Melanie's dad had told her and Robbie at the police station. Still on remand, Brian had been transferred to HMP Risley in Warrington, so Nat had visited him this morning en route. If it were at all possible, he'd been even more reticent than the last time. Though Nat had emphasised she was on his side and that everything he said was protected by solicitor–client confidentiality, all he'd been prepared to say was: 'My girl was suffering. She wanted to die; she asked me to help her and I did. If that's a crime, so be it. Shirley should go home; Lucy needs her. That's all there is to it.'

'Lucy is Melanie's younger sister?' she'd asked him.

He'd nodded briskly. 'A daughter needs her mother at a time like this.'

Nat came back to the GP's face. He wasn't telling it, but the tension in his jaw told a tale. He was worried; more than just worried. What had Brian said? That Melanie had stockpiled the morphine? This upstanding member of the community would have to appear in the coroner's court; his name might be mentioned in the tabloid press; even worse he could get into trouble with the police and his own profession by allowing an overdose to happen. How did the prescribing and management of drugs work? Was the pain relief left at the house for the patient to use when needed, or did the rules require administration by a medic? The latter, surely? But even then, Harold Shipman had demonstrated *that* was no bar to prevent abuse. She considered asking the good doctor, but didn't want him to clamp up. Today's visit was to extract as much information as she could about Melanie's illness. To fill in the gaps Brian wasn't supplying.

She took a breath. 'What did Melanie mean by "relieve her suffering"? Are you saying that as a euphemism? And if you are, what did she say exactly?'

'Melanie told me many times that she wanted to die. This was also made clear to her family and friends.'

'Do her medical records reflect this?'

'Of course. There's a "do not resuscitate" notice clearly stated at the front of her notes. But at no time did she express the desire to shorten or take her own life. If this had been the case I would have swiftly switched morphine capsules to patches or even a syringe driver. I had no concerns; indeed Melanie and I had a good rapport. At times she told me she had less pain, so the dosage was reduced–'

'And at others?'

'If it became worse, she told me that too.'

'And you would up the dosage?'

'Yes.' He cleared his throat. 'It isn't uncommon for prescribing to go up and down. It's part and parcel of pain management.'

Nat nodded. So, Melanie had been on oral medication; not injections as she'd supposed. 'The friends you mention. Can you name any of them?'

He looked at his surgery door as though it might give him an answer. 'No, I'm afraid not. Of course Lucy would know but the poor...'

His voice trailed off, so Nat waited. Lucy was Brian's younger daughter, the 'lovely teenager' Jack had mentioned meeting a while back. Nat didn't know a great deal about her yet, but her heart certainly went out to her. 'Would you be happy giving me her mobile number? Her address?'

Doctor Woodcock brought his focus back to Nat. 'She's staying with us, actually. But I would want to ask her first. She might want me there...'

'Of course,' Nat replied. Would a young woman actually want her older doctor there? A boyfriend, a husband, a friend, perhaps?

'She's just turned seventeen, technically a minor,' he commented, as though reading her thoughts. 'A late blessing for Brian and Shirley.' He pinched the top of his nose and was silent. 'What else would you like to know?' he asked eventually, reaching for a tissue.

Bloody hell. Only seventeen. No wonder Brian wanted Shirley to go back home. 'Melanie's illness. Can you tell me more about it?'

'It was diagnosed as chronic fatigue syndrome by the specialist many years ago. You might be aware it's also known as myalgic encephalomyelitis or ME. The family believe it began when Melanie was given a routine BCG vaccination at school.'

He frowned thoughtfully. 'I'm very much a proponent of immunisation, and in my view that was purely coincidental, but one can forgive her family for suspecting otherwise. The causes of CFS/ME are varied – from viral infections, such as glandular fever to bacterial infections, such as pneumonia; then there are problems with the immune system and hormone imbalances. Sadly we'll never know, but over the years Melanie declined to such an extent that she became bedridden, then eventually lost her voice, the power to speak. For her that was the final straw. It was horrendously tragic to witness it.'

'How did she communicate?' Nat asked, aware of a huge lump in her own throat.

'Written notes, her iPad, her laptop – when she could summon the energy.' He looked at his watch. 'I'm sorry but I'm due a patient now. Is there anything else I can help you with?'

Nat took a breath. Was it appropriate to ask? She had her own view of the matter, but it would be interesting to hear his. 'You spoke to them both, Brian and Shirley. They came to you to confess. Who do you think did it?'

His expression stony, he stood and guided Nat to the door. 'That is something I would prefer not to comment on.'

Finally back in Heald Green, Nat strode to the office, stepped over the threshold, then stopped in her tracks to fully absorb the comical scene. Would she get away with taking a photograph? Just for a reality check, if not to post on Instagram? She snorted. Yup, this could only happen at Savage Solicitors. Sitting cross-legged and revealing red knickers through her tights, Chantelle was atop the reception counter.

'So...?' Nat began.

'A mouse,' Robbie explained with a shrug. 'So she says.'

'There was a mouse, if not a rat, in his...' Chantelle motioned quotation marks with her fingers. '...office.' It caused a worrying wobble. 'I am not coming down until someone catches it.'

'Don't go in there, then,' Robbie replied reasonably. 'And if you insist on using my desk for your break, don't eat cake like you did this morning.'

Nat thought about Goldman Law's office manual with a smile. There would surely be an answer within that tome to deal with this unexpected situation, not to mention the fifty-eight clauses which dealt with health and safety.

'Look I'm sure the mouse is more scared of you than you are of it...' she began. 'If it was an actual live and kicking one. Robbie and I found a whole load of stuff in there.' She laughed at the memory. 'Seems the boss used to do magic tricks. It wouldn't be at all surprising if a pretend rodent was part of the act.'

She was ad-libbing, but it was true, there had been a box stuffed with magician's paraphernalia, adult-sized. She made a mental note to rib Gavin about it big time. Robbie had stashed it upstairs with his other personal effects. It had felt too invasive to go up there herself, but she did wonder what his living quarters were like. Was his flat as threadbare as the office or had he made it homely with soft furnishings, nice curtains and cushions à la John Lewis Homeware floor? Somehow she doubted it.

She reached out to Chantelle. 'Come on, girl, there's work to be done. I was stuck in blasted traffic, so here's the tape from today's meeting with Melanie Selby's doctor. You won't believe what the poor woman had to go through before she died. It's unbelievably tragic.'

That seemed to do the trick. Taking both her and Robbie's hands, Chantelle uncrossed her legs and dropped delicately to the floor.

Robbie followed Nat to her office. 'What do you think about restorative justice?' he asked, his stutter making a comeback.

Surprised, she turned. Had Gavin mentioned it to Robbie? After their park conversation, she'd tried to put herself in her pal's shoes, but really couldn't. She had wanted an eye for an eye, the shooter shot, if not hung, drawn and quartered, not so long ago, but now she knew Ruthie would make a full recovery, albeit a slow one, the idea of forgiveness felt different.

She studied the paralegal's flushed face. 'Restorative justice? I don't know much about it,' she replied. 'But I understand that if both parties want to do it, it can be very rewarding. I've read that it can help victims feel empowered and give them a sense of recovering what they've lost, but it's not for everyone; sometimes the anger is too much, I suppose...'

He looked at the floor and shuffled his feet. 'Lecture this morning.'

'Of course, I keep forgetting you're a college boy.'

It hadn't been part of Nat's learning at uni or law school, but conciliation, mediation, restoration and the like were very much part of the legal process these days. She liked them, but knew that other lawyers didn't. Some older diehards viewed them like their medical counterparts viewed alternative medicine. There were also the legal fee implications. Alternative dispute resolution, if successful, was a very effective cost-saving measure. Not every barrister or solicitor wanted that. What was that joke? Ah yes. Question: What's the difference between a good lawyer and a bad lawyer? Answer: A bad lawyer can let a case drag out for several years. A good lawyer can make it last even longer.

'What about you?' she asked Robbie. 'What do you think from what you learned today?'

He played with his fringe. 'Sounds good,' he said, quickly

changing the subject. 'You wanted to have a chat about Michal Gorski today–?'

'God, yes. How did it go? Tell me everything,' Nat replied, sitting down.

What with all the other things rattling around in her head, she'd temporarily forgotten about Borys's son and the Levenshulme Mafia. If, of course, they and DFL Debt Advisers were one and the same... Though deep in her bones, she was certain.

Perching opposite, Robbie took a big breath. 'He brought what documents he could find, basically the warning letters from the car loan and credit card companies–'

'The ones his dad finally opened?'

'Yeah. But he'd downloaded all the debt management documents from the internet, signed them and sent them to a PO box address without keeping a copy. The DFL crooks arranged the direct debit payments which have gone out ever since.'

'What did the credit card people say?'

'That they don't know anything about any...' He crinkled his nose, clearly searching for a word. 'Any... *assignment* of the debts, or debt management plan. They say Michal still owes them in full for the loan, penalties, interest and recovery costs. They were just about to go for a judgement, but I explained everything and they said they'd hold off for now.'

'Good work, Robbie. So at the moment we've got no documents; we can't actually prove the name of the debt management company?' He nodded. 'Right; you need to do some digging on the internet and Michal needs to find out what he can from his bank.' She thought for a moment. 'Though it might be much quicker – and effective – for Michal to just cancel the direct debit. Money talks. I'm sure that will get the bloody worms out of the woodwork.'

Robbie flushed. 'I've already suggested that to him.'

Nat grinned. 'Great minds. No flies on you are there, Robbie.'

He made for the door, then turned. 'Say no if you want to...'

Replaced by a frown, his happy smile from seconds earlier had vanished.

'Okay, go on.'

He tried to meet her gaze. 'This restorative conferencing thing. When my mum died...' He swallowed. 'The man who crashed into us. Well, back then, he wanted to do something like that. He asked to meet my dad. To say sorry, I suppose, but Dad refused.' He took a breath. 'If he still wanted to do it, would you come with me?'

21

HERE AND THERE

Until the sudden influx of chatter at eleven, Nat had forgotten it was silver surfer morning. Looking at the huge 'to read' pile of letters, she sighed. At least forty envelopes had been fired through the office letterbox this morning. Not just correspondence, but medical reports, CPS disclosure, utility bills, pleadings and court orders. The *Magic Circular* magazine too. Had Postman Pat been hoarding them? And that was on top of the million emails which were waiting in the firm's inbox. But at least she'd had a couple of hours reading through files, making calls and staring at Gavin's diary. Lists being the answer to every admin trauma, she'd compiled another one, prioritising his cases in order of urgent, urgenter and urgentest. God knows how he managed to spin all the plates full time. The help of Larry and Robbie was invaluable, but she still hadn't got a handle on when they worked and when they didn't.

'Gav has a brain the size of his penis,' Joshim Khan once quipped.

Gavin and Joshim's humorous fencing was usually derogatory, so she'd assumed he had meant both were small, but now she wondered. She hadn't known the Rabid Scot that well at law college. He'd shared a house with Wes and some other lads on the same Chester street as her and her friends. Thinking back, there was some mention of Cambridge, but she'd thought the others were taking the piss; a burly, beer-guzzling, non-PC Glaswegian didn't seem the usual recipe for Oxbridge.

The thought of asking Wes popped in her head. Her stupid mind still did this from time to time; that split second of thinking everything was fine until she registered it wasn't. She pushed the discomfort away; Wes had made his position quite clear, and far more pressing things than an aching heart were going on in the folders on her desk, let alone beyond the office.

She peered at her tally of 'calls to return'. Jack's name was included. Should she begin with him or keep that conversation for the end? There were pros and cons to each, but in truth Jack Goldman was always number one. She couldn't say whether it was affection and loyalty or irritation and annoyance, but she called him first anyway.

'Seventh hole,' he said. 'I birdied the third and fourth. Got an eagle on the fifth.'

'What is this? The Master's latest leaderboard hotline?'

'No, it means I'm busy and we should have a drink later to celebrate my hole-in-one.'

'Wow, a hole-in-one too?'

'Not yet, but I will. I'll text.'

Smiling, she swung on the seat. Sod it, it was affection and loyalty every time. A dose of annoyance and irritation, certainly, but at the end of the day, love. Her dad had died the same month she'd joined Goldman Law; she'd swapped an angry old father who'd never appeared to give a damn, for a younger, charismatic and encouraging one. The thought reminded her of the Harrow saga. She tapped her nails on the desk. She and Issa hadn't spoken since the car park conversation. Her name wasn't on the list, but all the same, Issa had to be the next call.

'How's it going?' Nat asked when she answered. 'Is little Carlos growing bigger and even more beautiful every day?'

'He is; thanks Nat, you're sweet.'

'And everything else?'

Issa sighed. 'I don't know. I thought it had settled down. You know, now I've listened to what JP needed to say. But he was out last night at his survivors' group. I haven't seen him yet, but whenever Chen turns up, he's always unsettled afterwards.'

'Who is Chen?'

'The whole bloody problem. He's the journalist.'

'Oh right. Funny name, Chen...'

'It might be a nickname or his surname. He's part Chinese, I think. I've only met him a couple of times.'

'What's he like?'

As though thinking, Issa paused. 'If I'm being honest, I thought he was nice, friendly, interested. But I could tell he was ambitious. We met in a big group and he seemed to go from person to person, asking questions. Really intense with everyone, wanting to know about their lives. Digging tenaciously, when I look back. I now reckon he was looking for a headline.' She sighed. 'But at the time I felt a bit sorry for him, thought how hard it must be to get on in journalism. I almost wanted to make up a story for him. God, Nat, how little I knew.'

'You can smile and smile and still be a villain.'

'Precisely.'

'Well, fingers crossed for JP and last night. Keep me posted. And give Carlos a little kiss from me.'

Hearing a surge of noise from reception, Nat stifled another yawn and walked through to investigate. She chuckled with pleasure. The scene was akin to ants swarming around something sweet. OAPs and flipping Gavin Savage! Opening his long arms, he scooped up three purple-permed ladies into a group hug. Once he'd released them, he moved on to two elderly men.

Quickly returning to the office, she glanced around. Oh God, was everything in order? All the trinkets and toys made by his kids were still in situ on the desktop, but whether she'd done the correct thing procedurally, or made the best decisions on his cases, was a whole other thing.

'Do I get one?' she asked when he eventually appeared.

'Still gagging for it?' he asked as he complied, hugging her tightly for several moments.

It was lovely to hear his old quip and have him back, but tears were near the surface as she took him in; his cheeks still looked sunken, his clothes far too big and there wasn't even a hint of his bracing cologne.

He sat down opposite her. 'I tried to resist between the ages of nine and nineteen, but my grandma made me cuddle her every time we met. She said that no one wants to touch you, let alone hold you, when you're old. I'll never forget that.'

Swallowing, Nat nodded. Gavin was wearing a jumper, not a suit. 'Are you back?' she asked, not sure how else to put it.

He shrugged. 'Here and there, I guess. See how it goes.' He smiled a thin smile. 'The staff at the hospital seem to think I should visit less often.'

'What does Heather say?'

He picked a hair off his sleeve. 'Not a lot. We're not often in the same place at the same time.'

Nat nodded. It wasn't a surprise. When she'd chatted with Cameron at McDonald's on Saturday, he said that his mummy was sleeping in Ruthie's bed to keep it warm until she came home. The relationship was clearly under strain. Whose wouldn't be under the circumstances? But at least Gavin was there with his boys rather than in the flat upstairs.

'So, what's this?' he asked, pulling one of Nat's lists towards him.

Feeling like a schoolgirl, she tensed. The head teacher was marking her work; God, she hoped for an A star and some praise. But Gavin read the sheet without making any comment.

Her heart raced. 'Obviously crime's not my area of the law, but I hope I haven't made any irretrievable cock-ups. Larry and Robbie have been great–'

'Who the hell is Larry?' he asked, looking up from her next inventory with a frown.

The alarm spread. 'Larry who does the court work...'

Gavin's face was blank.

'Lawrence Lamb QC. He was a...'

But by then Gavin was laughing. She aimed a kick which he deftly avoided. 'Bloody hell, Savage. You got me really worried.'

'Father Christmas, eh?'

'I know. Absolutely!'

He smiled a moment longer, then went back to her scrawl and made notes with a pencil. He slotted it behind his ear. 'Right, need to look sharp, there's work to be done.'

Supposing that was a dismissal, Nat made to stand, but Gavin lifted a hand.

'Nah, stay there, you're not going anywhere.' He continued his jottings, then lifted his head. 'And I've a wee bone to pick with you.'

Tensing, Nat waited. He pointed his pencil. 'What the hell have you done to my storage room?'

Feeling carefree and light-headed, Nat drove straight from Heald Green to Mobberly. Alleluia, she was no longer in charge! Though her relief was immense, she was incredibly tired and her pasty face in the mirror agreed. What Gavin's 'here and there' meant, she wasn't sure, but that was nothing new at Savage Solicitors. For the present she'd just continue to turn up every morning and see what happened. Right now there was no alternative; she didn't want to bump into Wes; Jack had her files; and Max had her office.

Turning into the golf club car park, she pulled up and watched two ladies tee off the first hole. She had played herself a few times in years gone by, mostly at Goldman Law 'client entertainment' outings. Fortunately a poor performance on her part hadn't been the 'entertainment' – she'd had a damned good swing and had whacked the ball steadily up the fairways. Finishing the game had been her weakness. 'More practise on the putting green, Natalie,' Jack always said. 'As you sow, so shall you reap.'

The memory reminded her of Doctor Woodcock's surgery. Did he perfect his putting between appointments? Because despite so many tragedies, life did go on. It was a sobering thought, but people had to live and be happy, despite the grim reaper doing his worst all around them.

She pinched her cheeks for some colour and climbed from the Merc. The men's changing rooms appeared to be on this side of the building, so she walked towards the manicured greens, looking for the entrance.

'Natalie.' It was the usual bass tone. 'Up here.'

A glass in his hand, Jack was standing on the veranda above her. Was the drink alcoholic at this time of day? It was one of the things he'd been advised to cut back after his heart attack, or his 'rogue artery', as he preferred to call it. Should she ask and reprimand him if it was? No. Though it felt like it at times, she wasn't his daughter.

She joined him on the balcony, but even with the warmth

from the outdoor heaters, it was still bitingly cold. 'What can I get you?' he asked.

'Do they do hot chocolate?'

He smiled. 'They will if I ask them. Nothing stronger?'

Jack nodded to her cocoa once it arrived. 'This isn't the Natalie I know and love,' he commented.

'But it's warming and I'm driving. I have a nice company car someone arranged and for which I'm very grateful.'

'Must be quite a boss.'

'He is. So, what did this boss want?' she asked. Alcoholic snifter or not, Jack was looking good; bright eyes, glowing skin and trim.

'A drink and a catch-up, of course. How's Anna?'

'She's great, actually.' Nat laughed. 'Stepping out with a dashing Pole, would you believe.' A quip about the waster son almost leaked out, but she muffled it with a cough. God, that was close. Michal and the possible DFL connection was a definite Chinese wall alert. It was a good job she wasn't drinking alcohol. As the Yanks put it, 'loose lips sink ships'.

'Good for Anna.' Jack studied her for a moment. 'And how are you, Natalie? How's life treating you? How's work?'

She snorted. 'Come on, Jack. You want me to tell you something that I shouldn't. Pass on confidential information. Fact is, I know nothing about anything which might be useful to you. I haven't seen hide nor hair of the taser PC's file and Brian Selby isn't talking. How's Shirley doing?'

'See how smoothly you did that,' he replied, deftly avoiding the question himself.

'I must have learned from the expert.'

'So, just a drink and a chat, then?'

She clinked his glass with her mug. 'Certainly looks like it.'

22

AN ASS

Wondering whether Gavin would be in the office and where she should sit if he was, Nat headed straight to Worsley in the morning. She had mentioned the Lucy Selby interview to him yesterday and asked if he still wanted her to go.

'Business as usual, Miss Bach,' he'd replied, which she'd taken to mean a yes.

'By the way, your suitcases are now upstairs,' she'd mentioned before leaving to meet Jack. Then, worried he might think she'd been snooping. 'Robbie took them up.' Itching to mention her magic kit discovery, she'd studied his profile for a few seconds, but the pencil was back behind his ear, his head down towards a file.

'They contain my best bib and tucker for when I need to leave the country,' he'd said without looking up. 'Need to launder the money first. If you have any bright ideas, let me know.'

'You could try opening a dodgy solicitors' office in Heald Green,' she'd replied.

He'd turned and cocked an eyebrow. 'Not bad, Natalie. You know, for a girl.'

She now smiled as she manoeuvred the Merc from lane to lane. If Gavin was hoarding ill-gotten gains, he was making a good show of it. Still, she had heard of villains living like paupers for many years to avoid alerting the police. If she came into a shed load of dosh, she'd want to enjoy it. Though could anyone really 'enjoy' money they'd stolen, or received through menaces, extortion and blackmail, selling drugs or other illegal acts? Well, yes; Danielle Foster, if her several-million-pound (and annoyingly tasteful) home in Prestbury was anything to go by.

There had been several expats in Mallorca she'd wondered about. Fat-bellied Londoners splashing the cash with the mandatory boob-op-blondes on their arms. She and Jose had been pretty scathing: 'I expect she adores him for his love of ornithology,' he'd say.

But Nat knew there was no accounting for love. Who would have thought down-to-earth bubbly Issa would be attracted to an ageing sensitive rock star type? But then again, Harrow and his wife were a similar mix of extrovert and introvert. Could the same be said about her? Had she been like Issa and Jose like JP? Maybe. But as the years went by she'd contained her friendliness whenever Jose was watching. He hadn't approved of it; without her even noticing, he'd become the dominant one in their partnership. His need for submission and control had filtered through to their sex life. Funny how one only saw these things in retrospect.

The surgery car park was full, so she parked along a grass verge, tucking the Mercedes in as closely as she could without denting the manicured lawn. She took in the variety of high spec vehicles. Was Thursday a popular day for appointments? Or were the residents of this upmarket area particularly prone to illness? Not that Nat knew much about doctors and their patients. It was eight months on and she still hadn't re-registered at hers. It had been hope upon hope that Jose would have her back for the first four, lucky good health for the second.

Lucky good health. She sighed at the thought. It was so incredibly arbitrary. Some people lived to be a hundred and three, whereas others suffered a short, painful existence. What if the stroke had left her mum in constant agony and without a life worth living? What would she have done if Anna had begged to die? Such a dreadful decision. Lose the relative you deeply love, forever and ever? Or grant them their desperate wish and allow them peaceful, painless final moments? And what about potential medical cures just around the corner? Oh God, it didn't bear thinking about.

She brought her attention back to the modern building. Dr Woodcock had suggested meeting Lucy Selby here and that was fine. At only seventeen, she would be entitled to have a parent or a guardian with her in any interview, and perhaps the formality would be easier than at her home. The poor, poor girl; how would anyone cope when they had effectively lost their whole family? Even worse, at such a tender age? Nat had been twenty-five when her father died, and though she'd left home on bad terms before then, it had upset that delicate balance of duty and love, resentment, expectation, disappointment, loyalty. And a whole host of other emotions she still felt guilty about.

Focusing on today's mission, she strode up the path and waited for the glass door to swish open. 'Hi, I'm here to see Lucy Selby. I'm Natalie Bach,' she said in a low voice to the receptionist.

'Of course,' the woman replied. 'Doctor Woodcock is waiting. Give me a minute and I'll take you down.'

Hearing the usual coughing and spluttering, Nat glanced over her shoulder. A memory bounced back. Her dad again, watching *Casualty*, *ER* or any medical drama. 'Bloody hospital and doctors' waiting rooms,' he'd say. 'Germs, illness, death. If you're not ill when you go in, you will be when you come out.'

The smile fell away. She and her brother used to laugh at his ridiculous grumbling, but who knew what his past had held? Almost combusting with anger, she'd shouted at him on the day he died like never before, berating him for his refusal to go to hospital, for what he was doing to Anna.

She quickly snapped back to the counter. She hated thinking about that day, but inevitably did whenever heated words were near the surface with her mum. Suppose this was the last day? Suppose those were her very last words?

The receptionist led Nat to a door at the end of a corridor. She opened it before turning back. 'The staffroom,' she said over her shoulder, 'so help yourself to drinks.'

'Thanks.'

Taking in the aroma of fresh coffee, Nat looked around. Easy chairs and magazines; sink, microwave, fridge, kettle. And, to her surprise, two girls on a sofa. They both turned their heads.

'Oh, hi.'

Nat stepped towards them, then stopped, unsure which was Lucy. They were both fair-haired and pale, but on second glance one was older, her foundation not quite concealing a bruise beneath her eye. The woman stood and held out her hand. 'Hello.' She gestured to the other. 'This is Lucy. She's asked me to sit in, if that's all right.'

'Of course. And you are?'

She smiled pleasantly. 'Sorry, I assumed my father had explained. Typical Dad. We thought Lucy might be more comfortable with someone her own age.' She gave her companion a friendly nudge. 'Well, sort of. I won't tell if you don't.'

'You're Dr Woodcock's daughter?'

'Yes, Cassandra. And you must be Miss Bach.'

Nat handed over Gavin's business card. She'd added her name and mobile number in biro, which looked pretty naff. 'Please call me Natalie.' She sat down in the armchair nearest to Lucy. Close up, she appeared even younger. 'Hi, Lucy. Thanks for seeing me. I understand this must be incredibly hard for you. I'm the solicitor who represents your dad. Someone else represents your mum.'

'I know.' The girl stared at her hands. 'Peter – Doctor Woodcock – said you had some stuff you wanted to ask.'

Nat took a breath; should she ask the vital question at the outset? She felt bad, but she needed to know. 'Your mum and dad both say they helped Melanie to die. Can you shed any light on what happened that could–'

Cassandra leaned forward. 'Sorry, Natalie. Lucy wasn't there, so there's no point asking.' She looked at Nat meaningfully. 'With both her parents currently... away, it's too upsetting to think about it, let alone speculate. Dad said you wanted to ask about Mel's friends and what she told them about her condition and her wishes. You're okay with that, aren't you, Lucy?'

Lucy's shoulders flinched but she nodded.

Feeling shamefaced for asking her opening question, Nat moved towards the girl and briefly touched her knee. 'Thanks, Lucy. In your own time, can you tell me what she said to you and her friends about her ill health. Did she mention ending her life? If so, when did she say it, how and to whom did she say it? I'm sure you understand we need as much evidence as possible to show her intentions.'

Nat pulled up in her usual spot outside Savage Solicitors. Her heart was still thrashing. She'd hoped it would calm down, but she'd felt hopelessly out of her depth talking to Lucy Selby. She now had a list of Melanie's friends, her social media information and passwords, details of a living will and online forums she'd used. It was a useful trip in that regard, but she'd felt ill-equipped, both as a human being and as a lawyer; she had never experienced such personal tragedy.

She groaned wearily. From her research, the law was uncertain too. It seemed that juries were loath to convict genuine assisted suicides or mercy killings, yet a recent attempt to make it legal had been rejected by parliament, so the police were duty bound to pursue every reported case. Then there were two potential defendants; would the CPS prosecute both or neither? She supposed it would come down to the evidence the police were obliged to reveal, the 'golden rule' of disclosure. Whether good or bad, they were required to hand over their witness statements, reports and documents. From what she had researched each evening at home, those statutory duties hadn't yet kicked in, but the common law duty to be open in the interest of justice and fairness was already there. She most certainly hadn't seen any 'fair play' to date. But what did she know? Thank God Gavin was back, at least to oversee the case, if not to take command.

She rested her head on the steering wheel. She felt inadequate, an imposter; she should have done better. But at least she'd been cheered by Cassandra Woodcock. Catching Nat up by the car, she'd taken her hand.

'Thanks for being kind and... accessible,' she'd said. 'Lucy was really scared about talking to a lawyer. Of course you guys are just humans like the rest of us, but you showed her that. Well done, and thank you.'

Nat had wanted to keep hold of her fingers and ask: 'How did you get that black eye? And that small cut on your lip?' But of course, like many other things, it was none of her business.

She opened the car door and stepped out. After a positive

start to the week, she felt drained, tired and lethargic. Rather like the bloody law, in fact. It wasn't only the Selby case. As far as she was aware, there still wasn't a date for Andrea's trial. She'd been arrested and charged last November, but after being granted bail, she'd gone back to her life in Cheadle Hulme, not two miles away from where she was standing now. Whether that still involved coffee mornings and cake with her local 'Jam and Jerusalem' chums, she had no idea, but when she thought of the Selby family's plight, Andrea's flaming liberty didn't seem fair.

As Mr Bumble had said, the law was an ass.

'Hello, Natalie, I was just about to give up.'

Nat turned to the voice. A large lady was walking from the office towards her. Chantelle? No, of course not. More than twice Chantelle's age, this woman had darker, freckled skin and that warm grin Nat remembered from aeons ago. But not really that long. Just a month, probably, when life had shifted in so many ways.

Like an idiot she stared. What was Wesley's mum doing here? After a beat of gaping, the surprise turned into alarm. Oh God, had something happened? To Wes or the boys?

Finally bursting from the trance, she found her voice. 'Hello, Kath. Lovely to see you. How are you?'

But she needn't have worried. Kath Hughes was smiling and holding out her arms.

'I'm good,' she said after a warm and firm hug. 'I've been waiting for you in Gavin's reception, chatting to the paralegal.' She lifted her eyebrows. 'Bit pongy, in there though, eh? Shall we find a café? I'm sure the boss won't mind.'

Feeling the sharp irony, Nat drove the short distance to the Roasted Coffee Lounge and climbed out. She peered through the glass windows and pictured her and Wes at a table for two. Yup, she'd met him here to 'talk'. About Andrea, of course. Lies, manipulation, attempted murder, no less. But this time it was his mum who clearly had something on her mind.

They sat on opposite leather sofas and ordered a cloudy apple juice and barbecued pork paninis. They sounded delicious, but Nat's appetite had been replaced by a swarm of butterflies.

'Gavin seemed a bit wobbly,' Kath said conversationally. 'But it's hardly surprising after what he and Heather have gone through these past weeks. Wesley has been so worried for them. It's such a relief to hear Ruthie's on the mend.' She shook her head. 'And who'd have thought a small child would get shot in this country? If you wrote it as fiction, no one would believe it.'

Nat inwardly sighed. Similar to an apparently nice middle-class mum poisoning her son with salt. 'True,' she replied.

Kath's sunny disposition clouded with a frown. Had she had the same thought?

'So Gavin's in the office today, then?' Nat said to fill the silence. 'I haven't been in yet.'

'He left an hour or so ago. Off to the hospital, he said,' she replied.

The belly insects fluttered big time. Oh God, Kath had been waiting for that long. It was nice to hear Robbie had introduced himself as a paralegal, and that he'd been 'chatting', but what the hell did she want?

Kath seemed to shake herself back to the redolent café. She turned to the book-lined wall and pulled out a Second World War hardback. 'Nice touch, isn't it? With all these tomes, I could tempt Joe in here. There wouldn't be a lot of conversation, but he'd be a happy bunny. Bloody men, eh? They're not good at talking, are they?'

Nat wondered about the generalisation. There was poor JP

who was desperate to tell his story, but it was probably true; the men in her life did struggle to 'share': her dad and his history, Jack Goldman with his expertise at changing the subject, Gavin and his politically incorrect deflections, not to mention laconic Brian Selby. But of course Kath was talking about Wes, the son she'd had to 'squeeze'. That's why they were here.

They waited quietly as the drinks and sandwiches were served. Kath picked up hers and took a bite. 'Ooh, nice,' she said. Then she continued to chat as she chewed. 'I've been pressing the best I can, but I'm not getting much out of Wesley. He's told me about Andrea's ever-changing stories about what happened with poor Matty, but not much else.' She cocked her head. 'Mainly by telepathy, guesswork and his miserable mug, I've worked out you and him aren't currently friends.'

Leaning forward abruptly, she grabbed Nat's hand. 'Which shows what a bloody idiot my son is.' She released it and fell back with a sigh. 'Not just Andrea but Sidney's ex too – two daughters-in-law I didn't warm to, but I liked you even before I met you. I could see from his face and his whole being that you were good for him. You made him happy and carefree. Just like he was before that bloody life sentence.'

After the criminal charges against Wes, her choice of words weren't the most tactful, perhaps, but Nat knew what she meant. She too, had seen the difference in him. She'd known and fancied the pants off the snake-hipped and light-hearted Wes Hughes at law college. He and the moody man she had met eighteen years later at Goldman Law were like two different people.

Wiping her mouth with a napkin, Kath chuckled. 'Who would have thought I'd end up with two bachelor sons living together like *The Odd Couple*? I love that old film; you should watch it if you haven't and you'll know what I mean. I don't suppose Sidney wants his little brother cramping his style, but until Wesley's house is sold, they're stuck.' She scooped up her juice and threw it back. 'Now, you can tell me if it's none of my beeswax,' she continued, 'but you and Wesley... I'm guessing it's to do with her, Andrea?'

Nat couldn't help snorting at the similar phrase, but she replied sincerely: 'Of course it's your... business. You're his mum.'

Kath's face abruptly darkened, her eyes shiny with anger. 'God, that bloody woman. I could kill her for what she's done to his family; I would if it didn't make things worse. I hope you find out for yourself one day, but that intense love you have for each baby never goes away. You want to do whatever you can to make your child happy; constancy, care, sacrifice; you fight their corner with all your strength...' Her voice broke, so she stopped, patted her cheeks with a tissue, then took a deep breath. 'As well as making an idiot of yourself over a pulled pork panini.'

Nat squeezed her arm. It resonated with what Larry had said about mother love. Strong, reliable and pure, and yet for some it was hollow or corrosive. Then there was Andrea. She had put her obsession and desire to keep Wes above her sons. The notion was still incredible.

Kath lifted her eyebrows. 'My guess is that you said something similar to me. That Andrea is an evil and manipulative bitch who deserves to be locked up. That he should stay well away from her...'

Smiling thinly, Nat nodded. Though a little shocked at Kath's aggressive tone, she couldn't have put it better herself.

'...and I'm sure he's given you the same reply, that it isn't simple, that she's the mother of his sons and so on. It's undeniably true, but...' She looked at Nat steadily, her face remarkably smooth and unlined for a lady well into her sixties. 'I think there's something else, something Wesley isn't saying. Of course we have the benefit of hindsight now, but Joe and I should've seen it. Andrea set him up from the moment she met him. She got her claws in and was not going to ever let go. Nothing has changed, Natalie. By hook or by crook that woman wants to control my son. Manipulation, lies, blackmail. That's her game and we need to stop her.'

23

AN EXPLANATION

Friday felt like a Goldman Law desk share. Gavin was already in his office with the door closed when she arrived, but Robbie's room was empty, so Nat grabbed the laptop and sat at his desk, wondering what she should do to justify her salary, if indeed she was getting one.

Since yesterday, she'd been mulling about Wes. Why had Kath travelled all the way from Congleton and waited for an hour to speak to her? Nat certainly liked her for it, but what could she do? She and Wes were no longer friends, let alone romantically involved. She could hardly pick up the phone and say, 'Your mum thinks your wife has something she's using to keep you dangling. What is it?' That would surely justify a 'none of your business' retort, and quite frankly she could do without the rejection.

The tables had veritably somersaulted at home. Anna was dusting, vacuuming and cleaning the house with a cheery smile, delving into her cookery books to hunt for new Polish recipes, fluffing her hair and applying a nude lipstick, whereas Nat felt weary and despondent. Even worse, she looked it; her face was waxy and wan, and she couldn't be bothered to do much about it. It was the lack of sunshine, probably. Bloody miserable British February weather; no doubt her whole body was protesting the lack of vitamin D. Apparently Borys's son had seen her in the office at some point and had commented on what a 'fine-looking woman' she was. That didn't help her general malaise; if the best she could do was a waster with debts of twenty grand, then she preferred to stay single.

Half listening to the regular peal of the reception telephone breezing in, she watched a grey mouse go about its business between the boxes along the wall. Cute, but not terribly hygienic. Perhaps she should bring in Lewie cat for a spot of consultancy work like she did with her mum. No, Poppy would be better; though she had the sweetest possible face, the old girl was definitely the best mouser.

Doodling on her pad, Nat smiled at the mental image of Chantelle and her precarious perch the other day. Yup, she should have taken a pic to show Gavin. Talking of which, where was the fashion queen? She listened again. Oh hell, the calls were diverting to the answerphone.

Pleased to have a mission, she left the miserable Natalie in Robbie's office, settled behind the counter, and amused herself by trying different ways to greet the Ned clients: 'Savage Solicitors, good morning'; 'Savvy Savage Solicitors. How can I help you?'; 'Top of the morning to you', rather than the 'What?' Robbie had employed before he was upgraded to paralegal.

Most of the callers responded in kind, buoyed up by that #FridayFeeling, she supposed. No one asked for her, which was pretty impressive of Gavin when he'd only been back in for three minutes.

'Good morning, Savage Solicitors. How can we be of assistance this fine Friday?'

'Why aren't you answering your mobile?'

'Because I'm answering this phone. Why are you calling it?'

She was being dry with Jack Goldman as usual, but it was nice to hear his voice.

'To invite you for brunch on Sunday. You still haven't met my grandson. I won't accept a "No" this time.'

Flaming heck; this was the trouble with landlines and missing staff; one couldn't filter the calls, or at least prepare a wild excuse before answering.

'I'll have to look at my diary...' Nat started, but she was saved by a knock and the outline of a figure through the frosted glass. 'I'm the only human here and someone's at the door. I'll call you back.'

With a smile of relief, Nat clicked up the latch and greeted a middle-aged man.

'Sorry, it's usually open at this time.' The bloke was scowling, so she tried for a jolly tone. 'Lovely morning. Can I help you?'

Wearing a donkey jacket, his hands were stuffed in its pockets. 'You can. Is Natalie Bach here?' he asked.

Alleluia! She was needed at last. 'Hello, I'm Natalie. How can I help?'

Closing the space between them, he bared his teeth and pointed a finger. 'Yeah, you can. You can help by keeping out of things that have nothing to do with you.'

Immediately alarmed, she stepped away. 'I'm sorry. I have no idea what you're–'

'Just fucking back off, right? Everything was settled. We'd put it behind us. Then you put in your oar, causing trouble. One minute driving lessons, the next minute...' The man's palm had clenched into a fist. 'Fucking keep out. Have you got that loud and clear?'

He marched to the door, then spun round and glared. 'Who do you think you are, anyway?' he hollered, striding back towards her. 'Fucking Mother Teresa? Or maybe you're just a sad old spinster paedo who gets off on being a busybody.'

Her heart clattered with fear. She'd moved as far from him as she could, but she was trapped against the bench; he was so close to her face, she could smell his stale breath.

His skin was puce, the veins bulged in his neck. 'Do-gooders like you make me sick.' He lifted his arm.

Oh God, oh God. This aggressor was going to strike her and there was nothing she could do except cover her head to protect it. Cowering, she scrunched her eyes...

'That's enough, Jed.'

Letting out the trapped air, she finally breathed. Oh God, thank the Lord. Gavin had appeared. His hands on the man's shoulders, he was pushing him back.

'That's enough, Jed,' he said again.

Though considerably shorter than Gavin, the man held his ground, his chest puffed out and anger distorting his features. 'I want to hear it from her. That bitch has been–'

'Helping your son. Being kind; charitable; altruistic. Go and look them up, Jed. Don't come back to this office until you've got a hold of yourself and have apologised.'

Following him to the door, Gavin opened it to let him out as Chantelle sauntered in. She was holding a white box.

'Thank God it's Friday. Cake day!' she said, bustling to the counter and opening the lid. 'Chocolate eclairs for Gavin and Robbie because they're boring boys who're happy to have the same old, same old. But for us girls...' She stopped and glanced from Nat to Gavin. 'What's going on? What's happened?'

Gavin nodded to the window. 'Jed just had a go at Nat.'

Chantelle made a whistling noise. 'Oh God, poor you, Nat.' She picked up the carton. 'I'll put these on plates and brew up. Tea with sugar is what you need.'

Trying to hide the tears and badly trembling, Nat turned away and made for Robbie's office. 'A *go*'? Is that how Gavin saw it? She was absolutely in no doubt that Jed would have hit her if

Gavin hadn't intervened. And from his aggressive bearing and sheer rage, it wouldn't have been just the once.

'Hey.' Gavin was pulling her around and into a tight hug. 'I know that was frightening. Come into my room and let me explain.'

Her limbs like jelly, she followed him in. He dug into his pocket, passed her a handkerchief, then sat at the desk. The thought that Gavin Savage was probably the only forty-year-old guy in the world to carry a hanky these days flashed through her mind, but she was still too winded for humour.

He tapped his pad with a pencil. 'The crash that killed Robbie's mum. Both he and Jed suffered head injuries from the impact. The other driver was completely liable – he'd been drinking and was well over the limit – so there was a civil claim for damages. I didn't act, so I don't know much about the ins and outs, but what I do know is that part of Jed's personal injuries claim related to the impairment of his cognitive and executive functioning, his emotional responses and impulses that he now has difficulty controlling.' He spread his hands. 'I've seen the medical reports because I've had to refer them to the magistrates once or twice in mitigation. To date there hasn't been any actual violence, but he's pleaded guilty to verbal assaults, threatening behaviour and breach of the peace. It doesn't make it right, Nat, but it's an explanation. Yeah?'

She blew her nose. Bloody Savage was ridiculously like her. What did Jack always say? That she found too many excuses for people who behaved badly. And her reply? They weren't excuses but reasons. But right now she didn't care about either. She still felt afraid and vulnerable and wanted to hide. Nodding to the phone, she stood on shaky legs. 'I think you have a call waiting.'

Still clutching Gavin's hanky, she returned to Robbie's office and picked up her handbag. Needing to hear Wes's voice, she searched for her mobile. No bloody luck. Today of all days she'd forgotten it. Narrowing her eyes, she thought back. Yup; she could picture it by her bed, untouched and unloved. She rested her head in her arms. How had things come to this? Her phone had been a lifeline between her and Wes, yet the rupture was so final she no longer bothered to even look at it, never mind realise it was missing.

The mouse appeared again, close to her feet, a harmless little creature in far more danger than her. Trying to get a grip, she took several deep breaths. Everything was fine; she could have been hurt, but she wasn't. Sure, she'd been frightened and alarmed, but it had come to nothing. Not like whatever had happened to Dr Woodcock's daughter.

An image of Aisha's bruised face popped up in her mind. Despite being pregnant, Julian's girlfriend had been belted hard by the debt collector last year. Until this moment, Nat hadn't realised just how mentally strong and brave the young woman had been: not only facing up to such an aggressive bully, but doing something about it. It made her feel quite ashamed; Nat had listened many times to victims of violence and domestic abuse; she'd been horrified, appalled, sympathetic, but until now she hadn't really understood; until now, she hadn't felt it.

Chantelle's voice at the door broke her thoughts. 'Are you okay, Nat? You seem miles away.' She handed over a mug. 'The cure to every ailment, as my nana always says.'

'Thanks; you're a star.'

'No probs.' She rolled her pretty eyes. 'Better get back to the usual grind.'

Remembering her promise to call Jack, Nat slurped her tea. Flipping heck, how many spoonfuls of sugar was in there? Not wanting to offend its maker, she glanced left and right, then slunk to the kitchen to make a replacement. Ambling back, she glanced at the bench. Still no sign of Robbie. College? Holiday? Or prevented by that angry brute of a father?

Digging for positives, she took a shuddery breath. At least she knew what the man looked like now. She was forewarned and forearmed, and all that malarkey. If she sat here in reception, she could clock who was at the door before letting them in. And besides, she didn't have her mobile; if she wanted to make a call, this telephone was the only way.

Feeling a little naughty, she called Goldman Law.

'Hi, Christine.'

'Nat!'

'Can't talk; I'm blocking calls. Is Jack in?'

'I think so...' Then after a moment. 'Line engaged.'

'How about Wesley? Is he around?' Oh God, the words were out. What the hell was she doing?

'I'll put you through.'

'Nat, hiya!' It was Sharon.

Feeling a sharp mix of relief and disappointment, Nat briefly closed her eyes.

'Hi, Sharon. How's things?'

She heard her take the usual huge breath. 'Well... Emilia and me were only saying this morning how much we're missing you. There's loads of gossip. Did you hear about...'

Nat breathed, the tremulousness ebbing away as she listened to her old secretary's Mancunian tones. She smiled wryly. It seemed Sharon and Emilia were currently bosom pals, so that was one good thing. And Wes was clearly engaged or out; she'd been reprieved from her error of judgement, so that was another.

Talking nineteen to the dozen, Sharon filled her in about the surprising colour of Wendy's baby, Jack's temporary new glasses, the alleged snog between the ginger bench boy and Catherine's (recently married) secretary, finally moving on to Wesley and his rotten mood. '...he's working at home today, which is a relief if

I'm honest. He's been so grumpy. Course Emilia thinks it's all to do with her...'

Aware she was still preventing incoming calls, Nat tried to interrupt, but only half-heartedly. Good old Sharon. Indiscreet as ever, but nice, safe, dependable.

Gavin's spicy presence hastened the end of her call. 'Sorry,' she said, the heat rising to her cheeks. 'I had to make a call and I've forgotten my mobile.'

He nodded. 'Fair dos,' he said. 'Let's have an hour or so brainstorming with cake, then you can go home, recover your mobile, go shopping at John Lewis, whatever.'

Chantelle popped her head around the partition. 'That isn't fair; it's favouritism.'

'So it is. Don't think I don't know what time you arrived this morning. Get on with your work.'

Surprised at his tone, Nat followed her boss to his office again. She sniffed. Yes, she hadn't noticed earlier, but the heady smell of his aftershave was almost masking the fustiness. A pre-Ruthie aroma. It made her both happy and sad; she was glad of his hanky.

Thumping down in his chair, Gavin scooped up his plate and ate his eclair in two bites. He licked the chocolate from his fingers and nodded to the door. 'Half a day for everyone,' he said with a grin. 'Bit of fun winding her up first.'

24

SUDDEN DIVERSION

Pleased to find a bottle of water in the passenger footwell of her car, Nat slugged it down. In one morning she'd imbibed more sugar than a person needed in a lifetime. A cream horn to start, followed by another mug of excessively sweet tea (which Chantelle had watched her drink like a bloody nurse). Then there was the box of chocolates one of the old dears had left as a thank you. She'd felt obliged to take one or two; Gavin had helped himself to a handful from the top, but by the time she left, Chantelle had demolished the whole second layer.

Should Nat say something to her? Everyone knew that sugar was the new devil, worse than salt, butter, even lard. Diabetes was a very real problem these days. But it wasn't her place to comment. Chantelle was a fully grown adult. And Nat had to butt out. Jed had gone the wrong way about it, but he was probably right about her being a 'busybody' or a 'do-gooder'. The latter sounded infinitely better.

Feeling the start of an uncomfortable heart flutter again, she peered through the windscreen and scanned the pavement. What would she do if Jed appeared right now? He'd clearly been furious about Robbie's suggestion of restorative justice. It hadn't been her idea as it happened, but she could see why that would unsettle him, bringing the tragic accident back in Technicolor-like PTSD. And not just the crash, but his feelings of anger, rage and revenge.

Oh God, like Gavin's.

The thought smacked her like a slap. If it came out, would Gavin know she hadn't actually put in her oar this time? Of all people, she didn't want to upset him by insinuating he was wrong to refuse Heather's request, or let him believe she'd been indiscreet by telling Robbie about it, when she hadn't.

Trying to ignore her trembling fingers, she lifted her chin. Get a grip, Natalie; everything was fine; they'd had a fruitful session just now. She'd brought Gavin up to speed about his files, especially the two fatal cases she'd bagged. The 'mother murderer' action wasn't as troubling as the other. As she'd explained to him, Larry seemed have everything in hand, identifying with George in more ways than one. The assisted suicide was another matter. Apart from its obvious entanglements, she already knew Brian, so she felt a personal responsibility. She shook her head. To think she was once his 'lucky lady'. Poor sod; she wasn't giving him much luck right now.

'Every case is only as good as the client,' Gavin said reasonably. 'You can't change the facts; you can't influence what they say or do, even though you'd like to.' He'd raised his sandy eyebrows. 'Getting too involved or emotional is not good either for you or for them. That's why we're called professional.'

Another headmaster's reprimand. Though she'd tried not to show it, she had felt quite offended.

'Who do you think did it? Brian or Shirley?' he'd asked.

She had wanted to say something prickly in reply like, 'Oh, my opinion *is* worth something, is it?' or perhaps, 'Shouldn't we just look at the facts?' But in truth she was still overwrought from earlier, and further ripples wouldn't be good for her still-jangling nerves. 'I don't think for a minute that Brian did it, he's covering for her, but he's bloody stubborn,' she said. 'He wants to do the old-fashioned gentlemanly thing. Touching, but stupid. You'll have your work cut out there.'

Gavin had picked up the phone then, mouthing that it was fine for her to go, to have a good weekend. And now she was here, sugared-out and feeling lost. What to do? Where to go? Home for a snuggle with Anna and Borys? No thanks. Perhaps Gavin's suggestion of John Lewis was a good one. Not the café, definitely not the café and a cake, but she could browse, even buy a lipstick or a frivolous pair of knickers, neither of which would break the bank.

Trying not to catch her dejected face in the mirror, she put the car into gear and finally found a gap in the lunchtime traffic. At the end of Finney Lane she intended to turn left, but she didn't. Instead she made a right, flicking on the radio and driving steadily past Lakeland and the garden centre, over the Majestic Wine traffic lights and down the tree-lined hill to the Wilmslow roundabout.

She couldn't explain the sudden diversion, so she didn't try. Instead she kept her thoughts shallow, listening to today's tittle-tattle in Ambridge and searching for signs of spring as the countryside trundled by. As ever, she wasn't sure when to take the sharp turn, but eventually a few familiar landmarks from her single 10k run told her she was near, and suddenly she was at the entrance to her picture-postcard dream home.

She stared at the 'kissing gate'. It felt too intrusive to open it and drive in, so instead she found a dent in the bushes further along the scenic lane, parked up, inhaled quickly and climbed out.

Her heels were inappropriate for the squelchy ground, her blouse too thin to keep out the chilly breeze and three eager chicks almost escaped from the yard. But despite nearly breaking her neck on a claw of hidden knotweed, she resolutely headed towards the patchwork path and down to the stable front door.

Holding her breath, she lifted the knocker and rapped. No reply for several seconds. She looked over her shoulder. Like the characters from *Chicken Run*, the hens were eyeing her expectantly. Female solidarity or clucks of disapproval? Oh God, what to do. Turn tail or try again? She came back to the door, but the choice had been made for her. A handsome black guy had answered. He peered at her enquiringly, then lifted his arms to gather a young boy and girl who'd appeared either side.

Oh fuck; it wasn't Wes.

She blew out the air snared in her lungs. This was clearly the brother Sidney and his kids, the guy who owned the house. What the hell had she been thinking? Just turning up had been crazy. She stared at her muddy shoes. Shit. And no doubt her blouse was now stuck to her chest from perspiration. Blame the sugar, excessive glucose and insanity? Instead she smiled politely as though her unexpected presence was perfectly normal.

'Hi, is Wesley in?' she asked.

Lifting his eyebrows in a knowing way, Sidney grinned. 'He is.' He stepped back and hollered, 'Wes, there's a visitor for you.' Then, apparently not receiving a reply, he pointed upwards. 'I'll go and get him.'

Studying her with obvious interest, the children didn't move, so Nat waited on the doorstep with a fixed polite smile. Was it really too late to bolt? Tell the kids she was really a Jehovah's Witness? But Wes had appeared from the stairs, a puzzled frown on his face before recognition set in.

'Nat?' Then after a moment, striding forward. 'Has something happened?'

'No!' The word came out ridiculously loud. She tried again. 'No, not at all. I just...'

She actually wanted to say, 'Yes, someone nearly attacked me today and I really, really needed you to hold me'. But she could see how it looked. Why would anyone appear at your front door, unannounced, unless someone had died. Struggling to hold back the tears, she nodded towards Sidney, shuffling away the gawping kids. 'I'm so sorry to turn up like this, I didn't know that Sidney would be here; I didn't think. It was a half day at work so I... came.'

His expression betraying nothing, Wes nodded. He reached out his hand, led her down the hallway and into the kitchen. He glanced at her shoes, then disappeared into the utility room, returning with two pairs of trainers which he placed at her feet.

'It's all we've got.'

Unable to cope with the silence, Nat found the power of speech. 'The girl whose foot this Nike fits...'

Wes didn't smile. 'Something like that.' He seemed distracted. 'Try them on. I'll find a coat and...'

She heard him bound up the stairs as she tried on the sneakers. Neither fitted, but she figured slipping out of the larger pair was preferable to bunions. Too agitated to sit, she glanced around the tidy kitchen and inhaled the sweet aroma of baking. *The Odd Couple*, Kath had said. She'd already guessed which one was fussy Felix.

Eventually returning with an armful of clothes, Wes sorted them out on the table, passing her a jumper and socks. 'They should do.'

Nat nodded to the Aga. 'Is something due to come out?'

'Shit.' Wes grabbed an oven glove and pulled out a tray of slightly over-baked cookies which he eased off the parchment and onto a Sheriff Woody platter.

His attention on the task, Nat finally looked at him properly.

Her tummy flipped. He had a proper beard. Did she like it? She wasn't sure. He was attractive as ever and it emphasised his sharp cheekbones, but made him that stranger she'd spotted at the hospital. She inwardly sighed. And his expression was definitely tense; it seemed she'd be blamed for burning the biscuits as well as interrupting his work.

Wes disappeared with the plate. By the time he returned she was dutifully attired: chunky socks, huge jumper and an oversized coat. Along with her best work skirt, they looked super stylish. She would have said so with a huge dose of sarcasm had Wesley not appeared so stern.

Her emotions dipping yet again, she followed him through the utility room and out of a side door. The icy wind whipped her cheeks. Why didn't he just ask her to leave, make up some excuse or tell her to fuck off? He clearly wanted to bundle her out of the house. Was her presence so embarrassing?

After taking a few steps, she glanced up. Wes had already stalked ahead. Bloody rude, actually. She clenched her teeth. Should she leave? To hell with her shoes. Just tromp to the car and drive back the way she'd come? But at the side of the garage, Wes turned and folded his arms. He looked so heartrendingly handsome, she couldn't have resisted the pull if she'd tried.

'What took you so long?' he asked when she reached him.

She gesticulated to the trainers. 'You try walking in these.'

He pulled her into his arms and held her tightly. 'What took you so long?' he said again. He peered at her intently. 'You have no idea; you have no bloody idea how much I've missed you.'

Needing to sob with relief, Nat buried her face in his jacket. 'You've dressed me up like a bag lady just to say that?' she managed to croak.

'Pretty much,' he said into her hair. But then he fell silent, so she pulled away to study his expression.

'And?'

He didn't quite meet her eyes. 'Nothing.'

Feeling nauseous, she swallowed. 'Wes? What is it?'

He rubbed his head and sighed. 'You and Max.'

'There is *no* me and Max, Wes.' She took a step back. 'In fact, the suggestion is bloody insulting. As though I'd do that.'

He lifted his hands. 'According to Sharon, you've had a few dates–'

'With Joshim Khan and others. Or am I sleeping with them too?' Laughter bubbled up. 'Since when did you take any notice of Sharon, let alone her gossip?'

His jaw tight, he didn't answer for several beats. 'Since my girlfriend said she'd find *nice* sex elsewhere.'

Her smile fell. He was right; it had been a low blow. 'I didn't mean it; I was upset and I lashed out.'

'I thought...' He looked at his feet. 'I *had* thought you and I–'

'Liked each other?' It was the euphemism they'd used last year. And eighteen years ago.

He snorted lightly. 'Yes.' Then after a moment. 'It hurt, Nat. Really hurt.'

Remembering their brief, hostile call, Nat closed her eyes. He was right; she hadn't got what she had wanted; she had thrown out the dummy. And if he'd said the same to her? She'd have been devastated, for sure. But... But... It was her turn to examine the soft ground. 'I was hurt too, Wes. You pushed me away, made me feel excluded. And when I thought it through, I realised you'd hidden me away; I hadn't met your parents, your brother, your kids...'

He massaged his forehead. 'You didn't say anything about wanting to, so I didn't push it. I didn't want to freak you out. With everything else going on, you were my lifeline, my ray of hope. The last thing I wanted was to lose you.'

'You said it was none of my business, Wes.' Her voice

sounded choked and small; she didn't want to mention *her* name.

'I know and I'm sorry.' Circling her waist, he pulled her in. 'Why am I talking when I want to do this?' Putting his lips to hers, he softly kissed her.

Relenting, she reached up her arms around his neck. 'I'm sorry too.' She nuzzled his face. 'Not sure about this beard though...'

He grinned. Finally, that stunning Wesley Hughes smile. 'Give it time; you'll grow to love it.' He held out his palm. 'Let's walk before we freeze.'

Absently traversing the thistly fields and soggy paths, they strolled hand in hand, chatting intermittently about Gavin and Ruthie and work, about Wes's cases, the bench boys and Jack. Everything but Andrea.

When the cottage came in sight, Nat stopped and took a breath. She didn't want to spoil the moment, yet it had to be said. 'You know we have to talk about...' But Wes placed his fingers against her mouth.

'I will; I promise, but not now. Come and say hello to Sidney and the kids. They've had a teacher training day, but he'll be taking them back to their mum's soon. I'll cook something nice for dinner. What do you fancy? A risotto or pasta? I have steak and salad; I could rustle up a stir-fry.' He kissed her forehead. 'Or we could go out if you'd rather. A meal or the pub. What's your heart's desire?'

Nat smiled at his sweetness, but he was talking too much. Kath was right; he was hiding something. Oh God, what was it?

25

THE GHOST

Nat's sleep had been so deep that it took several moments to remember where she was. She was naked, toasty hot and Wes Hughes was watching her from the pillow opposite.

'You're meant to fall asleep after sex, not before,' he said with a smile.

She turned onto her stomach and thought about last night. She and Wes had had an enjoyable dinner with Sidney. Before that, Wes had gone to do his thing with the Aga, abandoning her to his brother's obvious curiosity in the warm lounge.

'As you can tell, Wesley is the wife,' Sidney had quipped, and had then gone on to bombard her with questions. How long had she known Wes? Oh right, Nat was the Chester mystery girl. Didn't they once meet at a party? So why the long hiatus? Ah, it was her job Wes took over at Goldman Law. Where did she go? And why did she come back? Leave the sunshine behind; was she mad?

Nat had tried doing a Jack Goldman by changing the subject, but Sidney was so easy-going, open and guileless like his mum, it had been difficult to take umbrage. She wasn't used to speaking about herself, especially the missing Mallorca years, and she'd found it quite exhausting to filter those bits she was willing to share. Still, like a typical man, he'd abruptly got bored and moved on to talk about himself.

She now laughed at the memory. Surely Kath didn't need to do any squeezing with this son. Within the time it took Wes to produce his beef stir-fry, she'd had a detailed resume of Sidney's career progression, his current job, his kids and why his marriage hadn't worked (too much time away from home on business trips and – allegedly – too messy when he was there). *The Odd Couple* indeed; Nat clearly had the more thoughtful (and tidy) of the two, the one whose dark eyes were so difficult to interpret at times.

Right now wasn't one of them: with those damn clever fingers Wes was stroking her back from shoulder to buttock.

'It was cruelty, actually,' he was saying. 'Having to sleep next to this beautiful body all night and not touch. You are just perfect.'

Nat smiled, her skin tingling with pleasure. 'Fat, you mean. That's life at Savage Solicitors. A diet of pork pies, marshmallows and cream cakes. Not to mention the extra helpings of liquid sugar.'

'Hardly fat. A touch more curvaceous. I like it.'

His hands were replaced by his lips. Sidney had still been holding court at midnight, so she'd given Wes a meaningful glance, then slipped away to the bedroom before him. She'd stripped off her clothes, waiting with an inane grin for him to join her. The last thing she'd remembered before sleep hit was a promise to herself that she'd make him talk first thing this morning, honest pillow talk before anything else. But at this precise moment, talking could wait.

They sat at the small kitchen table, an astonishing selection of cereals – from Cookie Crisp to Crunchy Nut, from Cheerios to Coco Pops – between them like a wall.

'Sidney's kids,' Wes said by way of explanation. 'He spoils them to make up for... well, you can imagine.' He ate a few mouthfuls of muesli, then put down his spoon. 'Talking of which, I had arranged to drive over to Sheffield today.'

Feeling a twinge of the old exclusion sensation, Nat tried for a smile. 'To see Dylan and Matty? That's nice.'

'Yeah. I promised to take them out for some lunch. Why don't you come with me?'

Almost choking on her Weetabix, Nat stared to see if he was being serious.

'Really?'

'Of course. It'll be fun.'

The flare of pleasure was quickly followed by something else she couldn't quite describe. Apprehension? Fear? It was so sweet and unexpected that Wes wanted her to meet the boys, but the thought made her sweaty.

As though reading her mind, he put his hand on hers. 'They'll love you, Nat. And I want to do it properly this time. You've met my mum, you've met Sidney and his kids. Dad too. You should meet my sons. You should've before now.' He frowned. 'I wanted to introduce you last year, but...' He shook his head. 'And after the past few weeks of missing you so badly...' His expression clearing, he leaned forward to kiss her. 'I want them to meet the woman I love.'

The happiness increased, but so did her disquiet. They hadn't spoken yet; it was jumping the gun. The line of breakfast boxes wasn't the barrier; it was Andrea, or as ever, her ghost.

A wave of anxiety sickness hit. Lowering her head, Nat tried to breathe the nausea away.

'Hey, are you okay?' Wes knelt by her chair and peered at her face. 'You're meant to say something along the lines of how much you love me too, not faint.'

The tears prodded then; how she wished she could control them. 'I do very much, Wes, but you're holding back on me. What is it? There's something Andrea is using–'

'Catherine.' Still on his knees, he leaned back and spread his hands. 'Catherine,' he repeated. 'That's what she's got.'

Stuck for words Nat gazed.

Wes rubbed his head and blew out before speaking. 'I haven't seen Andrea in person,' he said eventually. 'But...'

She held her breath.

'Back in January she called, as you know, and after that she continued to phone from time to time. Long winded conversations about the boys, this and that, as though everything's fine.' He snorted. 'Lulling me into a false sense of security...'

Nat bit back the desire to say, 'I told you so.'

'...but she got to the point in the final call.' He sighed. 'She mentioned the office flat in one breath and Catherine in another. She didn't say it outright, of course. We both know that's not her style. But as sweetly as ever, she made it quite clear that if I didn't visit her, Jack Goldman would hear about whatever information she has.'

Wes following in his, Nat drove to Cheadle and parked up the Mercedes behind her mum's Ka.

He had become quite assertive when she equivocated about the trip to Sheffield. She'd found herself sounding worryingly like Anna. Suppose the boys resented her? Or blamed her, even? Wouldn't it be nicer for Wes to see them on his own? Her blouse was sweaty. She had no clean knickers.

Her mobile was at home. Borys might have abducted her mum.

She'd even resorted to the old chestnut of: 'And the cats might need feeding.'

'Dylan and Matty will love you because I love you,' he'd said firmly. 'I'd prefer you not to wear underwear, but if you insist, we'll go via Cheadle to collect some and I'll say hello to your mum. We can drop off your car while we're there.'

As though she'd been watching, Anna flung open the door. Reaching up on tiptoes to kiss Wes's cheek, her delight was plain to see.

'Oh do come in and get warm, Wes. How lovely to see you...'

Nat studied his dark beard while he and Anna chatted. It was full but trimmed short, and added a certain gravitas, but it still made her feel a little unsettled. He'd grown it without her; perhaps that was why.

Rolling her eyes several times, she watched her mum fuss. Her cheeks glowing, she offered drinks and snacks even though they explained they couldn't stay long. Nat admired her restraint. All those weeks ago Nat had promised to spill the beans about her break-up with Wes, but never had. Anna hadn't pried; her pale gaze had been watchful and loaded with concern, but she'd held back. How Nat wished she could do the same, just let things rest, but it wasn't in her nature. She had to examine, to pick and to pull, until she had the right answer.

The latest Andrea problem was examined, picked and pulled during the hour's journey to Sheffield. In Nat's mind, if not verbally. It was a no-win situation: on the business front, Jack, Catherine and Wes were the partners of Goldman Law, but not in equal shares. Jack didn't much care how the other half was apportioned so long as he retained his fifty-one per cent. In short, Jack controlled the firm. If he got wind of the affair, Wes could lose his job, a job he loved, a job he needed. The fall out and gossip would damage his career.

'I want to buy a new house,' he'd explained in the kitchen. 'I'd like to buy us a home, but unless I can remortgage Cheadle Hulme or sell it, financially it's difficult. It's Andrea's house too. She doesn't want to leave. It's Dylan and Matty's home, so that's fair enough, but she won't sign documents to release any equity. I'm saving what I can, but it'll be nothing if Jack finds out and sacks me...'

There was the personal front too. Nat knew without a doubt that Catherine adored Jack, that her fling with Wes was born of a complicated mix of loneliness, childlessness and hitting fifty. But things had now changed; she and Jack had reconciled with wayward Julian; they had little Reuben, a grandson they both doted on.

Then finally there was Nat's own love for Jack. He'd recovered from the coronary and its aftershock; he was in a good place. But it wasn't simply that. Apart from her mum, Jack had been the most constant person in her life for nearly sixteen years. She was his most trusted confidant. If he discovered she'd known about the affair and hadn't told him, where would that leave them?

As the purple moors of the winding Snake Pass hurtled by, Nat asked Wes the obvious questions. Was Andrea just digging around for dirt? Was he sure she really did know about the trysts at the office flat? Did she have proof? Couldn't he call her bluff? Just flatly deny it?

But her queries were ones he'd already asked himself many times. Andrea wanted to see him and until she did, he wouldn't know exactly what evidence she had, but in all likelihood she had something, an exchange of text messages between him and

Catherine, probably. Maybe she had a screenshot of them. But even if she had nothing, she was clever. On the basis of 'no smoke without fire' she could do plenty of damage with the fumes alone.

A weathered road sign welcomed them to Yorkshire. Nat absently noticed it, then did another take. Oh God, they were almost there. Like a radio with only two channels, she tuned her worries from Wes's wife to his sons. The nausea back, her stomach churned. Matty and Dylan. She wanted to meet them; she was intrigued and interested. She *so* wanted them to like her; perhaps even confide and trust her in time. But at the end of the day, they already had a mother they loved. That person just happened to be the bane of her life.

She turned to Wes, needing to ask before they arrived. 'How do the boys feel about their mum now?'

He frowned briefly, but didn't appear to mind the question. 'I'm not entirely sure; I try to ask from time to time, but they barely speak about it at all.'

Hmm... Kath and her squeezing; the sons sounded much like their father.

Wes's expression was thoughtful. 'To be honest, I think they prefer not to dwell on it. Their first year at uni; they want to be carefree, get drunk, have fun.' He caught her hand. 'Discover the delights of pretty girls and sex. God pray they use a condom.'

She nodded, the irony not lost. Wes hadn't intended to procreate with Andrea, let alone settle down at twenty-two. She'd announced the pregnancy when their relationship was on the wane. Yup, the Cling-on had been ahead of the game, even then.

'But I have discovered more info about Andrea from the police,' Wes continued. 'The investigation was handed over to a different detective and she gave me a call to fill me in.' He glanced at Nat. 'Apparently Andrea has changed her story several times. When Matty's poisoning was confirmed by the hospital, she told that officer it was me who'd done it; he pointed out that Matty's illnesses occurred in Sheffield, so she then said it must have been Dylan.'

Shaking his head, he scowled. '"Harmless sibling rivalry," as she put it. Next she asserted Matty's pathology results were wrong, that laboratory errors took place all the time. Then finally, when confronted with the tests on her home-cooked food from the freezer, she said she'd realised what must have happened: it was all a terrible mistake, she liked to decant loose products into containers at home; she must have mixed them up in the cupboard by accident, salt for sugar and the like.' His jaw tight, he smiled thinly. 'And the worrying thing is, she's so bloody convincing.'

Nat felt that familiar prickling on her skin. 'What about throwing herself down the stairs and blaming you? Wasting police time; perverting the course of justice?'

'Ah, that one's easy,' he replied with a bitter snort. 'She smashed her head; she had bleeding and brain damage, so she can't remember what happened on the day of the fall. It's all a fog, evidently. She says that maybe she just tripped, or perhaps she had a dizzy spell, but can't say for sure. As for the allegation against me, she was disorientated, confused when she woke up with a bandaged head in hospital. She pointed out that the last time I was at the house we'd argued, so she genuinely thought I had pushed her; that her statement to the medical staff was the honest truth at the time. Apparently she sent her profound apologies to me through her solicitor.'

Wes's grimace returned. 'God knows what a jury will make of it. In our civil cases we're used to the balance of probabilities test, aren't we. Crime is a whole other thing. I can see some poor sap believing her salt for sugar story. Or at least thinking there's doubt. And people with head injuries do have the sort of problems she claims: forgetfulness, befuddlement, loss of memory and so on. The new detective is determined to bat on, but...'

As he steered the car down one of Sheffield's seven famous hills, Wes's voice trailed off. He didn't need to say what they were both thinking. Nat's tingling sensation had now turned to stabbing and was crawling down her spine. Trying to shake it off, she folded her arms and stared at the sturdy grey stone properties. Why she hadn't thought of it before, she didn't know. The standard of proof required for a criminal conviction was 'beyond reasonable doubt', a pretty tall order for any prosecution, let alone one against someone as cunning and inventive as Andrea. There was room for manoeuvre; space to create dilemmas, uncertainty and conundrums for the jury. The manipulative Cling-on was clearly working on that.

Bloody hell; Bloody hell! Kath's 'evil and manipulative bitch' might well be acquitted.

26

CRUMBS

Nat yawned and reached her arm to the mattress by her side. It was cold and empty. Of course; Wes's Sunday 10k. Remembering the sex before *and* after sleep this time, she curled back into a ball. No, that wasn't quite true. The before had been lovemaking. Sidney hadn't been around last night, so they had 'retired' at eight.

'I'm not risking you falling asleep on me this time,' Wes had said with a grin.

They had chatted and laughed; they'd touched, stroked and kissed. Tender, intimate, glorious. They hadn't drifted off until the early hours.

Catching a glimpse of sunshine through the curtains, Nat smiled. Spring was on its way and life was back on track. And yesterday's trip to Sheffield had been fine after all. Not good, not bad but okay. Dylan and Matty hadn't seemed surprised when she turned up at their flat, but they hadn't been particularly friendly either. Neither were dressed, so she and Wes had sat in the kitchen area, losing count of the scattered shot glasses and bottles. Thrumming her fingers on the table, she'd stared at the dirty pots piled high in both sinks.

Wes had smiled. 'You're itching to do something...' He'd glanced over his shoulder. 'Ah. That's what mine looked like back in the day, believe it or not, but if you wash, I'll dry.'

They'd made a few inroads, Wes replacing the dishes randomly on shelves, with a comment that it would probably 'cause beef, but what the hell'.

Unable to stop herself, Nat had squirted the last of the Fairy Liquid on the fat-and-food-encrusted hotplates, then applied elbow grease with a scrubbing brush.

Still looking sleepy, Dylan had appeared at the door. 'That isn't ours,' he'd stated. 'It's the girls'.' He'd nodded to the other hob, which was pretty damned clean, and shrugged, 'No cooking, no mess.' Then he'd peered in the cupboard Wes had just closed. 'Those plates aren't ours either. That's going to cause beef.'

Wes had caught Nat's eye and half smiled. 'A thank you would be nice,' he'd replied evenly, then, when Matty appeared moments later, 'This is Natalie, by the way.'

Matty had nodded, his expression a touch more friendly than Dylan's. 'Do you have kids?' he'd asked.

'No,' Nat had replied, which appeared to be the correct answer.

Two female faces had bobbed around the kitchen door. 'Do you think the "beef" might be eased by a free lunch?' she'd asked, reaching discreetly for Wes's hand and hoping he didn't mind.

'Sweet,' the boys had replied together.

So the lunch foursome had become nine eventually, Nat trying to work out which of the pretty women didn't belong in the flat of three guys and three girls.

'I hope you didn't mind my... interference,' she'd said in the car on the way back. God, she hated that word; she needed to find one that sounded more heroic.

'Not at all. It was fun.' Wes had cocked a wry eyebrow. 'No problem with you frittering my hard-earned cash.' Then after a minute: 'Actually, I want to spend some on you; I'd like to buy you a ring, a diamond to show everyone you're mine.'

'You can't, you're married,' she'd said, trying to hide the flash of delight.

'I won't be for much longer,' he'd replied.

The moment had felt special, significant. Like an engagement of sorts. Holding on to it tightly, deep pleasure ran through her now. How life could turn on a sixpence. Of course Wes was still a married man and diamonds were expensive, so she'd put a rain check on the ring, but his offer was the thing, and especially the reasons behind it.

She stretched and sighed. There were problems, insurmountable problems with Andrea, that was true, but this moment was good, it was pretty damned 'Gucci', as the boys had put it yesterday.

'Oh shit,' she said, suddenly sitting up.

It was Sunday; Jack had invited her to brunch. She hadn't even phoned him back, let alone thought of a decent excuse. Slipping on Wes's T-shirt, she crept downstairs, her ears tuned for the sound of people, but when she peeped into the lounge, it was chilly, tidy and empty. She thumped down on the sofa, pulled the soft throw around her shoulders and extracted her mobile from her handbag. She smiled as she turned it on. So much for the unhealthy relationship with her phone. It had been switched off since Thursday night and she hadn't missed it a jot.

A series of beeps alerted her to several texts. The first was from Jack: *Did no one teach you that it's rude not to return calls, let alone accept or decline an invitation? Catherine doesn't know how many to cater for. Call me back.*

Then another. *Not impressed, Natalie.*

Then the final one. *No word from you. Are you all right?*

That provoked a whole swathe of emotions as she stared at the decorative hearth. She hated to let Jack down but the last message showed he knew it too. Then there was Catherine; she would be unimpressed as well. Nat shook that particular worry away: Cool Catherine was at the root of Wes's current difficulties with Andrea, and though it wasn't her fault as such, that mix of anxiety, annoyance and, yes, jealousy was buzzing.

Blowing away the bout of dizziness, she lowered her head. In truth, she didn't want to face Catherine right now, let alone the rest of the Goldman clan. How to respond? She didn't know. She'd look at the other messages, then summon the energy to create a viable evasion and apology.

She peered at the screen. Several missed calls, but none from her mum to her surprise. She'd been remiss in not telling Anna where she was on Friday evening. Halfway through the grilling by Sidney, she had suddenly realised, and she'd asked if she could make a call from his landline. Feeling like a guilty schoolkid who'd skipped teatime, she'd apologised to her mum and confessed where she was; Sidney had made no secret of listening, the smiling sod. Good job she liked him.

The two notifications from Jack were expected, but the three from Issa Harrow were not. Oh hell, what had happened now? Could Nat cope with not knowing until tomorrow? Nope. Pulling the throw over her legs, she phoned her back.

'Hey, Issa, I missed your calls. Is everything okay?'

'Nat, hi. Thanks for calling back...'

Issa was almost whispering. Was JP there, or perhaps her mum and dad? Nat still didn't have a handle on the unusual three-way connection. Issa and the baby seemed to be based at her parent's house, but she was still romantically, or at least emotionally, involved with JP. The whole situation seemed pretty odd, even without the astonishing allegations against Harrow.

During her short-lived matrimonial career, Nat had attended a 'family conflict' course and had been taught about triangular relationships; she'd been intrigued to discover that a conflict between A and B was often worsened by the involvement of 'innocent' C. But of course there wasn't yet a triangle in this case; A didn't know about the discord, so all the angst was falling on C, poor Issa, who was still speaking quietly.

'Sorry, I shouldn't have bothered you. Everything is on hold for now, but I really needed to talk and you said to call–'

'Absolutely. Can you speak now? What's happened?'

'Give me a minute.' The line went silent for a time, then Issa returned. Her deep sigh was audible. 'Yesterday I had a big fall out with JP. I thought he was in a better place after he'd spoken about... things... at our meeting, and to be honest, I'm sure he was. I had listened and that's what he said he needed. Anyway, everything was fine until he went to his group. Of course he didn't say so, but it's Chen, not him–'

'Hold on, rewind a bit. So the journalist guy was at the meeting? The one threatening an exposé?'

'Yeah. He doesn't always go, but when he does he seems to wind JP up. So, just when I thought everything was settled, JP said that being heard wasn't enough, that he needed to be believed.'

Issa's speech became strangled then. 'Since we saw you, I've tried not to think about it. I've just buried it, I suppose, hoping that somehow it would go away. You know, listening but forgetting, moving on. But actually being asked to *believe* it? How can I even pretend? I know my parents; I knew it was a fantasy, even before I heard the when and the where. But the facts make it irrefutable; whatever JP has imagined simply couldn't have happened, Nat.'

'I know. It sounds a nightmare.'

'So we had a big fall out, going round and round. His feelings, my feelings, hurt, anger, the lot. I cried, he cried, he apologised. He said he understood why I couldn't believe it, that he was hurting me, that he should never have asked me to try.' Her voice cracked again. 'I thought I'd finally got through to him, but he said the answer was for me not to be involved any more. It would be between him and Harrow from now on.'

'Oh no,' Nat replied.

Yup, the triangle theory. It was hard for poor Issa, but JP was right. The way forward was for him to challenge Harrow and get it out there; Issa's involvement had probably clouded everything and made the situation worse. But it wasn't Nat's place to say that. She was just listening as a friend, and she understood Issa's desire to protect her parents from the grim allegations.

Issa spoke again. 'But for now it's fine. Mum and Dad are off on holiday today. It's their belated ruby wedding anniversary cruise. I begged JP to wait until they come back in three weeks and he's agreed. So there it is; stalemate for a little while longer.' She was now clearly crying. 'This isn't the way I expected to spend my maternity leave. It's meant to be a happy time, isn't it? My breast milk has completely dried up and I can't tell anyone why. I feel so isolated and–'

'Oh, Issa, at least you have me. Listen, I'll drive over to you one day or evening; let's have a few drinks, or a meal out. Text me some dates, and in the meantime, call me any time...'

Relieved she'd managed to hold back her own tears, Nat ended the call, then searched in her handbag. No damned tissues, but at least she found Gavin's hanky. When she looked up, Wes was at the lounge door, holding a brown paper bag and watching her silently. He sat down and pulled her close. 'You're a good person, you know that, don't you? Trying to fix everyone.'

'You've put that very nicely,' she replied, sniffing. 'Some things can't be fixed though, can they.'

She stared at Gavin's handkerchief. The last two days had been so perfect, she'd forgotten about the confrontation by Jed and her fear. It felt too self-indulgent to mention it now.

They sat silently for a few moments before Wes roused himself. He kissed her hair. 'At least I can fix breakfast. Full English or continental? I've bought croissants, but there's bacon in the fridge.' He gazed, then grinned. 'In the kitchen or would m'lady like hers on a silver platter upstairs?'

'If you don't mind crumbs, continental in bed please.'

'Happens I love crumbs. A quick shower and I'll be with you.'

Propped up against the pillows, Nat waited. It was lovely to be spoilt with delicious food, and whatever was coming with it, but she was distracted by a dull tummy ache. It felt as though her anxiety and tension about all the things she couldn't 'fix' were appearing as cramp.

Like Jack and his heart attack. Although he described it as a 'dodgy artery', she was sure the stress and anxiety about his son had brought it on. Oh hell, she hadn't called or texted him yet. What should she say? Hoping for inspiration, she fingered her mobile. A bad stomach? Food poisoning? It wouldn't be far off. She sniffed the air. She could think about it later; her breakfast was on its way.

The acrid smell of bacon appeared before Wes. 'Best of both worlds. Continental with a twist,' he announced, presenting her with a tray.

'That looks delicious,' she said. He'd wrapped the meat around the croissant. It was very pretty, but how would she manage to eat it? The cramps were getting worse; she didn't feel hungry at all.

The sudden peal of her phone made her jump. She peered at it, still in her hand. Oh shit; the caller was Max. Not wanting to cause 'beef' when things with Wes were so perfect, she turned it to show him.

'It's fine; take it,' he said, putting the food on the chest of drawers.

'Max, hi, I'm just busy right now, so–' she began.

His voice clipped, Max interrupted. 'Do you know what you've done?' He mimicked Nat's voice. '"Just leave her, Max." Oh, and then threaten her with legal action for revenge porn. Fucking great idea, Natalie! Thanks a million.'

The ache was getting worse. 'Hold on. Why? What's happened?'

'I did what you told me to do. I threatened to report her to the police if she did anything with the... private stuff. Then I packed my suitcase and I left.' He was shouting now. 'And guess what? I get a knock at the door. Only the fucking cops at my parent's house. She got in there first, didn't she, accusing me of some made up crap. Why the fuck didn't you keep your nose out?'

Nat's heart raced. 'God, I'm so sorry, Max. It was only a thought. You seemed so unhappy; I was trying to help–'

'Call this fucking help? What if they charge me with some trumped-up offence? I have the partnership coming up. My parents have completely freaked out.'

'I'm so sorry.'

The line fell silent, only the sound of his breathing still there. 'Right,' he said eventually, his tone a little calmer. 'I have an appointment at the police station to give a statement next week. You're coming with me. You need to tell them what happened. That it was me who should've been reporting her to them. That she's just fucking lying.'

'Yes, of course I will. I'm sorry, really sorry.'

The call finally ending, she glanced towards Wes. His face stony, he turned from the window and folded his arms.

'Max,' he said in a flat voice. 'What was that all about?'

She inhaled deeply. Oh God, what to say? She had meddled again; Max was her friend; he was up for promotion; Wes was a partner; she could damage Max's prospects if she said anything. The stitch was bloody hurting; she wanted to puke.

Stepping to the bed, Wes gently lifted her chin. His expression had softened.

'He's upset you, Nat. If you're upset, I'm upset.' He rubbed his head and sighed. 'I was stupid when I thought those things about you and him. You were completely right; what I said was insulting. But do you see how important it is for us to talk? To be open and honest? I don't find it easy with the whole Andrea shit, but I'm trying.' He reached for her hand. 'We're a proper couple now. What hurts you hurts me.'

Nat took a breath to explain, but the mix of stomach pain and nausea had become intolerable. Darting to the bathroom, she reached the toilet just in time to feel yesterday's dinner slide from her body. As the spasm slowly eased, she staggered to the sink, battling the urgent need to vomit.

Wes was behind her. 'Are you okay? What can I do?'

Breathing deeply, she lifted her head. 'It's fine. I'm fine. It's under control. I just need some tissue.' Shuffling back to the holder, she unravelled the last sheets of toilet roll. 'If you could just find me a new one, please?'

When he'd gone, she automatically wiped. Something felt wrong. The tissue was red, her fingers bloody. What the hell? Freaked out by the severity of the tummy pain, her mind madly jumped. Rectal bleeding; what did it mean? Bowel cancer?

Colitis? Crohn's disease? Then she laughed at her ridiculousness. Bloody bad timing, but it was just a heavy period.

She flushed the loo and looked at the shower. Was she strong enough to stand for several minutes? Not really; both her and her legs were feeble, insubstantial. She'd have a thorough wash, and maybe a bath later.

Feeling foolish and embarrassed, she perched on the wicker chair and waited for Wes. Only she could turn a romantic morning upside down within minutes. And the T-shirt she was wearing – his T-shirt – was soiled with blood. 'Sorry,' she said, when he appeared with a packet. 'I'm not a pretty picture.'

He was gazing, his eyes glassy. 'I think we should go to A&E,' he said.

'No, I'm fine. I had bad stomach ache, but it's gone. I just feel a bit weak and stupid...'

He took a deep breath, like a shudder. 'When did you last have a period?'

She thought back. Why was he asking? Nope; life had been so intense and busy since Ruthie's shooting, she couldn't pinpoint a date. Perhaps that was his point; miss the curse and get two for the price of one at an inconvenient time.

He was still looking at her steadily. 'Come on, let's get you dressed. Better safe than sorry. It won't take long to drive to Macc.'

'Macclesfield hospital? That's silly. It's just a heavy period–'

He glanced at the toilet, then he put his hands either side of her shoulders. 'I'm so sorry, Nat, I think it was more than just that.'

27

FORGIVENESS

Her eyes sore and swollen, Nat ignored the alarm on Monday morning. It was the shock, that was all. She hadn't known she was pregnant, but looking back, things added up: she and Wes had often met at the cottage last minute, or had been longer there than they'd anticipated, so she might have taken the pill late or not at all. And when she gave it some thought, she hadn't had the curse for at least two months; her breasts had been fuller and tender; she'd felt nauseous from time to time; she'd been overly sensitive to certain smells. All a natural consequence of working at Savage Solicitors, she'd thought.

It shouldn't matter, she'd said to herself repeatedly through the tortuous night hours. She hadn't actually lost anything; you couldn't miss something you didn't know you had. And yet she'd cried and cried and couldn't stop.

She pictured Wes's anguished face yet again. So worried for her, he'd begged her to go to A&E, but she'd just wanted to come home for a long bath and, though she couldn't say why at the time, a good old sob. In the end they had compromised; she'd call 111 to find out what one did in the circumstances, then have her soak at the cottage.

The conversation with the NHS adviser had been surreal, as though she was talking about a friend or a client. But she'd been fine, remarkably so, as she listened to the bloke hurriedly read from his miscarriage script. Perhaps he had a Sunday lunch date, she'd randomly thought. Like the one she'd missed at Jack's. She'd had to make herself tune into the man's speech.

'You're right, Accident and Emergency isn't appropriate,' he'd said, 'especially for pregnancies in the early stages. It sounds like a complete miscarriage, but if not, in the majority of cases, the remaining tissue passes out naturally in a week or two. It's probably best to consult with your GP next week.'

'Why?'

'Your doctor might recommend medication to assist the passage of the tissue, or you could choose to have minor surgery to remove it if you don't want to wait.'

The idea of 'surgery' had felt alarming and Nat particularly didn't like the sound of the word 'tissue'. Until then it'd had a nice floaty feel, something that was helpful in times of crisis, not the cause of it. She hadn't liked to ask Wes what the 'tissue' looked like, and he wasn't happy about the adviser's dismissive advice.

'Let's call your GP now. There must be an out-of-hours number,' he'd said, pacing.

Of course, she didn't have a flaming GP. She had 'lucky good health'. But she'd promised she'd re-register at her old surgery today. That had appeared to appease Wes who'd been far more agitated than her. 'For you,' he kept saying as he held her tightly; 'I'm so sorry for you.'

They had taken the bath together. Just like when they were law students, they had ended up not having sex, but something more intimate. Feeling his erection against her back, she'd leaned on his chest as he tenderly soaped her body. She hadn't understood his sadness then, she hadn't felt the loss or the grief, but Wes had anticipated it for her. He'd known what was coming and it was here now.

She had lost her baby.

She wiped her face yet again. She had forgotten the discomfort, the embarrassment and the blood. All she could think of was what could have been; those most tragic of words 'if only'. Wishing Wes was there to hold her, she pressed her face in the pillow. He'd understood completely; he had seen her intense desire to be a mum, the one she'd almost hidden from herself.

Perhaps knowing the end of the call was nigh, the 111 adviser had eventually been kind. 'Try not to worry, miscarriage is very common. It happens far more than people imagine. You and your partner can try again soon.'

'Partner.' The word brought on a fresh rush of tears. She'd lost her baby but gained a boyfriend over a single weekend. The overwhelming wish was for both. It was greedy, she knew, but she couldn't help it.

She eventually glanced at the bedside clock. It had gone nine o'clock. She'd be no use to anyone at SS today. Flu or a heavy cold was the thing; she'd phone Chantelle and say she was available to take calls, but didn't want to come in and spread her germs.

Chantelle had been easy. 'Poor you,' she'd said. 'I hate having a fever, so yeah, best stay at home.' Then after a noisy yawn, 'My mum always says "feed a cold, starve a fever", so look on the bright side.'

There was no bright side.

Anna was more problematic. She was unusually direct when Nat emerged from her bedroom at eleven. 'Are you going to tell me what's wrong, Skarbie? You go to work on Friday with a long face, come home on Saturday with Wesley and a huge beam. Then you disappear again until Sunday evening. No smiling this time, but Wesley doesn't let go of your hand until I push him out of the door at midnight.'

'Very observant, Mum,' Nat replied, puffing up the sofa cushions and stalling for time. What should she say? The obvious thing was to tell her about the miscarriage, but she knew how much Anna loved being a grandma; she desperately missed the three grandchildren in Poland. Why add to the grief? Like Issa and her parents, there didn't seem to be any point; what she didn't know wouldn't hurt her.

She flopped on the settee. 'I'm just fed up and under the weather,' she replied, realising it was true. 'Though I've loved helping Gavin, it's been... emotionally challenging. I need to have a bit of time out.' She tried to frame how she felt, not about the lost baby, but the verbal assaults by Jed and Max and the unfairness of them both. Like miscarriages too, but of justice.

Though her mum didn't speak, her worried eyes demanded more.

Nat sighed. 'Over the past few of days I've been shouted at by two men. Both about things that aren't my fault.' She thought for a moment. 'Well, not strictly speaking...'

Perching in the armchair, Anna nodded and waited, her gaze steady and compassionate.

'As you know, Robbie lost his mum. A drunk driver crashed into the family car, killed her and injured Robbie and his dad. Anyway, at college Robbie has been learning about something called restorative justice–'

Anna touched the cross around her neck. 'Yes, I know about that. Trying to forgive those who trespass against us. Us Catholics have known it forever, but it seems to be fashionable these days.'

Nat couldn't help but smile at her mum's small show of

conceit. Never for herself, but always for her faith. 'Very true, Mum. So it made Robbie think about it. He asked me if I'd go with him, just for support. Naturally I said yes.' The fear bouncing back, she put her palm on her chest. Her heart was galloping. 'I thought nothing more of it, but on Friday morning, I let a man into the office with no idea who he was and... well, he turned out to be Robbie's father.' The tears prodding, she demonstrated with the flat of her hand. 'He was that close to my face, Mum. I was really scared. He was unbelievably agitated. If Gavin hadn't intervened, I'm sure he would've hit me.'

As though there and ready to defend her child, Anna stood erect. 'That's dreadful, Natalie. Just dreadful. Did Gavin call the police?'

'No, no he didn't. Apparently Jed, Robbie's dad, has a medical condition, a brain injury from the car accident. He has difficulty controlling his emotions, anger included. Gavin told him to go home–'

'I'm sorry, love. Perhaps I don't know a lot about these things, but that can't be right. Not just the way he frightened you, but letting him back on the street to do it to someone else.' Her jaw was tight. 'Why on earth did he think he could treat you like that?'

'He was angry about the suggestion of Robbie meeting the offender, I guess; the man who'd killed his wife. He thought I was...' She cringed; it was that bloody word again. 'He thought I was interfering. He told me to butt out.' She sighed. 'And on this occasion I actually wasn't...' She gave a mental nod to Wes. 'I wasn't trying to fix anything.'

Anna shook her head. 'It seems a...' she struggled with the word '...disproportionate reaction. Perhaps it's something else as well, to make the man so upset.'

Nat thought back. 'You may be right. His manner was so odd. But who knows what goes on in someone's mind.' She thought of Robbie, ensconced in the upstairs flat. 'Or behind closed doors. Jed resented the driving lessons too…' She smacked her forehead. 'Oh no. I missed Robbie's driving lesson, didn't I?'

Anna chuckled. 'I suppose this is what happens when you're so… "loved-up", I think that's the expression.' Her cheeks flushing, she looked pleased. 'It's a good job Borys was here on Saturday. He gave me the confidence and said I could do it. He sat in the back and we took Robbie together to your industrial park–'

'*You* gave Robbie his driving lesson?'

'I did. We spent a good hour at it. Borys thinks he's making very good progress.'

Nat couldn't help smiling again. 'Well you've got the right expression, Mum. "Loved-up", indeed.'

Seeming to understand her grief, the cats didn't fight but stayed on her lap, purring gently and keeping her warm. Anna had wanted to stay in (and hover worriedly, no doubt) but considering her mum's usual telepathy, Nat had got rid of her by a combination of 'cheering up' treat requests and the need for a nap. She didn't actually want to sleep, nor eat; she wanted wishes or magic or prayers to put everything right. Or at least stop the sorrow, the hollowness, the breathtaking feeling of loss.

A red van flashed by the bay window, soon followed by the knocker. An airmail parcel no doubt; her sister-in-law sent regular gifts from the grandkids – clumsy sewing or cross-stitch, a lumpy clay model or smooth stone splattered with colourful paint – very sweet acts of kindness which meant so much to Anna. Nat glanced over her shoulder; it was tempting not to budge, but the cats accepted the inevitable and moved before she did.

She shuffled to answer the door. To her astonishment, Jack Goldman was at the threshold, holding a stunning bouquet of yellow roses.

'For you,' he said, handing her the bunch and stepping in.

Struck dumb, Nat stared at the flowers.

'It seems you've abandoned your mobile, so I called your office. They said you were ill.' He kissed her on the cheek. 'A coffee would be nice.'

Trying to contain the urge to cry, Nat padded to the kitchen. 'I think I might be able to manage that.' Jack followed her in. 'Aldi's best instant or fresh?' she asked him.

'I think you know the answer to that.'

As she struggled with her ancient cafetière, he strolled around the small room, picking up Anna's Polish trinkets and examining them carefully before replacing each one in exactly the same spot. They sat at the table, eventually, and he asked the question she knew was coming.

'What's wrong with you, then?'

'A cold,' she replied, sniffing. 'Maybe flu, so watch out.' She added milk to her tea. 'So, what's happening with Shirley Selby?'

He smiled. 'A very smooth change of subject, Natalie. As it happens I've been talking to your Mr Savage this morning. Very bright, isn't he?'

'The best.'

'It was his child who was shot?'

'Yes.'

'Dreadful, truly dreadful.'

'But she's finally on the mend. I hope so, anyway.'

'That's good.'

Nat inwardly snorted; Jack had deflected her Shirley Selby question beautifully. But he surprised her by coming back to it: 'We've agreed a plan of action; we're both going to make aggressive applications for bail. Put the ball firmly back in the prosecution's court. There's been little or no disclosure so far.'

'Hark at you,' she replied with a grin. 'A criminal specialist at sixty and a bit. Who says you can't teach an old dog new tricks?'

His lips twitched, but he didn't give the expected reply. Instead he removed his glasses and rubbed his eyes. 'What's really wrong, Natalie? You looked dreadful when I saw you last week–'

'Such compliments...' Nat started, trying for a joke and deflection, but the tears had already started, falling from the end of her nose onto her mum's neatly folded pinny.

'You're pregnant,' Jack stated.

She shook her head. 'I was.'

'By Wesley.' He smiled softly. 'I might need these,' he said, replacing his frames. 'But I'm not blind.' He took her hand. 'I'm sorry. How many weeks were you?'

'I've no idea. One minute I was fine, then the next I had severe cramp and... well, blood.' Trying to hold in the self-pity, she took a deep breath. 'I didn't even know. It's stupid to feel so empty about something I never had.' She looked at him and just said it. 'But it was what I wanted, Jack; it's what I've wanted for years.'

He nodded. 'I assumed that's what Mallorca was all about. Catherine always said that you didn't love The Spaniard.'

Glad she'd finally said it, Nat blew her nose. She wanted to be a mum; more than anything, that's what she wanted.

'Liverpudlian, actually. Jose is from Liverpool.' She glanced at him and smiled. 'As if you didn't know that anyway.' Then after a moment, 'I'm sorry about Sunday brunch. You were right; it was rude not to reply. Stuff happened on Friday and I'd left my mobile here, but still, it's no excuse. Please say sorry to Catherine.'

Finishing his coffee, he stood. 'Will do.' He took a few paces before turning back. 'It might help to talk to her, to Catherine.' He glanced up to the ceiling, then spread out his fingers before curling them into a fist and tapping his lips. 'Five,' he said eventually. 'We had five miscarriages. We paid for the best, a lovely consultant called Hirsch, but we never got to the bottom of why. It ripped out Catherine's heart every time.' He cleared his throat and kissed Nat on the head. 'But that was us. We left it too late; we let work get in the way. Look after yourself, Natalie. Learn from us. Don't make the same mistake.'

28

BLACK AND BLUE

Wes had asked Nat to take the rest of the week off work and that was fine. She didn't feel great anyway, and when she looked in the mirror, a pale face and hollow eyes stared back. Even though she frequently reminded herself that many people were far worse off than her, the tears had a will of their own. She kept them to her bedroom, but she knew the snivelling and self-pity would take over completely unless she made a real effort to get out of the sack, get dressed and shake herself down.

Determined to do something useful while Anna was out, she looked in the fridge for dinner inspiration. Over the last few weeks she'd tried to persuade her mum that meat was not a compulsory ingredient for each and every meal (or cabbage, for that matter) but she wasn't making much progress, so she'd make something without either today. Onions, garlic, peppers and tomatoes were a good start; she'd fry them in a splash of flavoured olive oil and see where that took her.

Taking care not to lop off a finger, she finely sliced the veg, but the onion fumes made her eyes water, and by the time she had finished chopping, she didn't know if her wet, snotty face was from desolation or amaryllis-induced. She only understood she was sad, even though there were a number of reasons to be happy. The main one was having Wes Hughes back in her life. He'd driven straight from work to Cheadle the previous night, and the three of them had eaten dinner then played cards as usual. Once Anna was settled in her bedroom, they'd cuddled on the sofa. Inevitably it had brought on the waterworks.

Wes had looked at her intently. 'Everything will turn out right in the end. Honestly, I can feel it in my bones. We *will* have a baby; we'll have lots of fun making it.' He'd grinned. 'And guess what?'

'What?'

'Matty sent me a text saying to pass on his thanks for the meal.'

'Aw, that's nice–'

'And...'

'There's more?'

'There is indeed. He said that Dylan's girlfriend mentioned you were a "complete babe".'

That had brought a smile; she knew from Chantelle that 'babe' was a good thing. 'So one of the girls was Dylan's–'

'Seems so.'

They had speculated on which of the attractive lunch attendees she was. Though they hadn't come to a consensus, it had been lovely to laugh. But later Wes's expression had turned half serious, half wry.

'I'm sorry to bring this up, but we do need to talk about Max.'

'I know. You're completely right, it's just...'

Despite Max's verbal attack, the loyalty – and feelings of culpability – were still there; she didn't want to get him into even more trouble, but she understood Wes's need for her to share. So she'd made him promise to have two hats, one for Wes her boyfriend ('Can it be a Brixton Messer Fedora?' he'd asked) and the other for Wesley the partner at Goldman Law.

'So I'll be telling the story to the former, my "boyfriend". Understand?'

As though he knew how much the BF word pleased her, he'd grinned.

'I do.'

'Good. Then let me begin by saying that you, wearing the fedora, should understand and empathise with him...'

His smile had slipped. 'Go on.'

'You had a mad wife in the attic; Max has the same, except she's his girlfriend.'

Wes had shaken his head. 'Okay, as your boyfriend, I'm listening, but when I met her she seemed very nice.'

Nat had raised her eyebrows. 'So does Andrea.'

'Point taken.'

So she'd told him the whole saga of Max's possessive woman and her sex tape blackmail. The rest of it he'd already gleaned from listening to Nat's side of the Sunday conversation. 'So you have to feign amnesia at work. Okay?' she'd finished.

But Wes was Wes; he played with a straight bat; could he really do otherwise?

'Look, Nat, I won't say anything to him, or to anyone at work, but as someone who loves you, I think he's well out of order blaming you. He's a grown man. Whatever he did or said, both on film and to his girlfriend, it was his decision. I can see why he's stressed, but bawling you out like that just isn't on. I know the two things aren't connected, but...'

She'd nodded. He was right; her miscarriage and Max would always feel linked.

Trying to expunge the smell of onions, Nat washed her hands several times. Dinner preparations were completed, what to do now? It was still only noon. What on earth had her mum done with the yawning hours in her pre-Borys days? She glanced at the blank television screen. Nope, daytime TV was a little too desperate, and anyway there were texts to be sent.

The one to Robbie was tough. She'd had a set-to with his dad; did he know? How did he feel about it and, more to the point, had his dad taken his anger out on him too? She wanted to check he was fine without making a big deal of it. She'd discovered from Chantelle that he'd been at college on Friday, and of course he'd been here, alive and driving on Saturday, but his father had been so irate, he was nevertheless on her mind, the responsibility pecking.

How's life? Hear you'll be driving for Formula 1 soon! she typed.

He immediately replied. *Thx. 1 way 2 get a car.*

It was brief and numerical, but at least he was breathing. Still mulling about his situation, she sighed and sat back – losing a mother so young, keen to stay in Gavin's flat rather than go home to his angry dad. God, she remembered that dread. It was hard being twenty-one, needing your own space, but not having the dosh to move out, let alone buy or rent luxuries like a car.

She thrummed her fingers on the armrest. Money, money, money. The root of all evil. A thought suddenly struck her. Bloody hell; that was a good point. Should she...? No; look how much trouble she'd already landed herself in by poking into other people's lives. And she was no expert. But still, fairness was fairness; wrong wasn't right.

Her finger hovered before pressing the icon. Just do it, Natalie. She wouldn't be interfering this time, more flagging up or passing the buck.

Gavin answered eventually. 'Bach. Are you still skiving?' he asked.

There had been no discussion about whether she remained

seconded to Savage Solicitors. Was she still needed? Did she even have a job at Goldman Law? But she felt uncomfortable addressing it, so she didn't. 'I can come in and sneeze on you if you'd prefer.'

'I'm not in the office at the minute,' he replied.

'God, sorry to bother you.' Ruthie had improved and was now in a Stockport rehabilitation unit. 'Are you with my favourite little girl?'

'No, I'm at court with your boss, Mr G. An application for bail.'

'Ah, Brian Selby.'

'"Lucky lady", eh, lassie?' There was a smile in his voice. 'I know you like to get around, but a man from Yorkshire of all places.' He mimicked the accent. 'Strong in't arm, thick in head.'

'Very droll, Gav. I'd stick to the day job.' She heard a court tannoy. 'Look I'll call you later.'

'It's fine; I've got a few minutes. Shoot.'

'Okay.' She should reconsider?

He must have sensed her hesitation. 'Come on, Bach, I haven't got all day. Better out than in, you know that's what this Weegie says.'

Inhaling quickly, she dived in. 'I was wondering about Robbie and his finances. Presumably he had a claim for personal injuries against the other driver after the car crash, same as his dad...'

A pause. 'Yes, he will have done.' Gavin's tone changed. Cautious? Certainly more serious. 'The name of the solicitors who acted will be in Jed's file. And you're asking, because?'

'Look, I might be completely off-kilter here, Gav, but it strikes me that Robbie has no money. He wears tatty clothes; he sleeps in your flat; he had a temporary career as a thief. He was eleven when his mother died. Surely his damages would've been a tidy sum at eighteen? Not only for his own injuries, but those relating to his mum's death. There would have been a claim for the loss of a parent's love and affection, for his financial dependency, his parent's services and the like. He's twenty-one now, so...'

Another pause, longer this time. 'What are you saying, Natalie?'

'I'm not saying anything, I'm just speculating...' She took another breath. 'Robbie was a minor when the accident happened, so presumably Jed sued on his behalf; he'd have been Robbie's litigation friend, wouldn't he? I know a minor's damages go into the Court Funds Office these days, but what about back then? Would it have gone to the parent with the usual undertakings to pass it on to the child at eighteen?' Wishing she'd kept quiet, she cleared her throat. 'Think of Jed's anger the other day, his fury. Maybe it was more than just the suggestion of restorative justice, maybe–'

'What restorative justice?'

Oh God. She shuffled her feet. This conversation was going from bad to worse; she'd forgotten Gavin didn't know about it. 'Robbie is considering going down that path. He learned about it in college and it appeals to him. He wants to meet and possibly reconcile with... the driver. That's what Jed was angry about, understandably so, but I'm wondering if it's more than that...'

Nat picked at her salad before throwing down her fork. The cherry tomato didn't want to be caught and she wasn't hungry anyway. She'd handled the conversation with Gavin badly. He'd said he had to go and abruptly finished the call. Bloody hell. Truth was she needed to see him in person, be brave and just say it all: that she suspected Jed hadn't accounted to Robbie for the damages he would've been entitled to at eighteen; that Robbie wanted to meet and possibly forgive his mother's killer at his own instigation; that Robbie's situation, his thoughts and opinions had no bearing on whatever Gavin decided for himself.

In the past she had blamed Jack for building Chinese walls, but she was constructing them herself in a way, creating invisible barriers to protect her friends and even her mum, but doing more harm than good; she'd become the 'C' in every flaming triangle. She needed to back off, step away and look after herself, just like Jack had said.

She dabbed her eyes. She knew he was right; he generally was. But suppose this conception had been her only chance? What then? In the past, Gavin had joked about her 'motherhood hormones' crying out. If that was the reason for her need to get 'fixing' and involved in people's lives, where would she be if she didn't fall pregnant again?

Reprimanding herself for more self-indulgence, she sighed. A baby had never happened for Catherine. Oh God; the poor, poor woman. She had suffered five miscarriages; five times of hope and anxiety, then the anguish, the devastation and the cruel, cruel loss. Nat's once was a drop in the ocean in comparison.

She picked up her phone and gazed at the screen. Could she really talk to Catherine as Jack had suggested? How nice it would be to say: 'I'm so, so sorry for misjudging you; I'm sorry for calling you Cool Catherine, for assuming you had no feelings when you must have been dying inside. It hurts, it really hurts. I can't image how you coped, how you put on a mask and lifted your chin high to the world. I'd like to say sorry; I'd love to talk. Can we?'

But she didn't; she might have had Polish parents, but she was buttoned-up British inside. Instead she sent a text. *I'm sorry for not getting back about Sunday. So glad to hear you're having such fun with your gorgeous grandson. Hope to catch-up for a large G&T soon!*

Still in her hand, her mobile beeped. For an instant she panicked, just knowing it was her. Oh God. Suppose Catherine mentioned Nat's loss? Could she speak without crying? Should she let on that she knew about her friend's own devastation? It was just too embarrassing. But after a moment, she twigged the caller was unknown. Bloody hell; she'd become completely irrational; the world didn't revolve around her and babies.

Remembering her desperate need for a call from Jose, she faintly smiled. That was a million years ago; another world, another person. Yet her heartbeat increased nonetheless.

'Hello?'

'Good afternoon. Am I speaking to Natalie Bach?'

A smooth, pleasant voice she couldn't place. 'Yes you are.'

'My name is Mr Hirsch.'

That sounded familiar. Someone had mentioned it recently. Work? Her mum? No, she couldn't quite grasp it.

The old professionalism kicked in. 'How can I help you, Mr Hirsch?'

'I'm hoping I can help you. Jack Goldman asked me to have a chat. I believe you're only down the road and I have a cancellation tomorrow if you'd like to pop down–'

Oh my God. The obstetrician Jack and Catherine had consulted. What the hell had Jack done? Embarrassing and wholly inappropriate didn't cover it; it was bloody insensitive and breaching a confidence. A step too far, even for Jack. She gritted her teeth. 'That's very kind of you, Mr Hirsch, but I'm fine.'

'And I'm sure you are, but I'd be happy to see you nonetheless.' He paused. 'I know this is a rather... unusual... way of going about a referral, but if you know Jack as well as I do, you'll be familiar with his reluctance to take no for an answer.'

29

FRESH AIR

Nat glanced at the crack through the curtains. Still inky black outside, it was too early to get up. Fuming wasn't a good recipe for sleep. Neither was tossing and turning and shouting out loud. 'Bloody Jack. How dare he? The final bloody straw.'

And she meant it. Why she'd gone back to Goldman Law after returning from Mallorca, she had no idea. Okay, she'd been away for five years and was out of touch with all things legal, but the law hadn't changed that much, and anyway there were catch-up courses available in Manchester. On the internet too. And why the rotten, flaming law anyway? She had tried her best with vulnerable clients in years gone by, but it wasn't exactly a caring profession, was it? She'd volunteered at a soup kitchen and helped disabled kids ride donkeys at weekends, but that was just scratching the surface of charity. To make her feel marginally less grubby about acting for the likes of Danielle and Frank Foster, probably.

But this *was* the final straw. Finito. No more Jack and Goldman Law. She'd offer her services full time to Gavin, and if she wasn't needed, she'd look for a job elsewhere, try something new. A teaching assistant or something part-time, because that would fit in with life as a mum. If she ever became one. Oh God.

She fidgeted again. 'Bloody Jack Goldman!'

'Has something happened, Nat?' Wes had asked when they chatted after dinner.

'What, something other than a bloody miscarriage?' she'd wanted to retort. But his eyes were shiny, his expression concerned.

She'd stared for a moment. Should she tell him what Jack had done, how he'd taken 'interference' to a whole new bloody level? But she'd kept schtum. Look how Wes had tried to take her to A&E on Sunday. She could see him saying, 'Jack means well, and if it helps for next time, why not?'

Well, neither he nor Jack would be body searched for 'tissue', or opening their legs to be prodded and poked, or whatever else the 'chat' with Mr Hirsch might entail. She wasn't born yesterday: simple conversation didn't need an appointment with an obstetrician-cum-gynaecologist at his clinic. A cervical smear was bad enough. And yes, if men had to have the embarrassing and uncomfortable procedure, they'd come up with something considerably less humiliating, wouldn't they? But they didn't.

'I'm worried I've offended Gavin,' she'd replied instead.

'How's that?'

'Long story,' she'd said, crinkling her nose.

He'd kissed it. 'Good job I have plenty of time...'

So she'd told him about her conversation with Gavin about the shooter and Heather's desire for reconciliation and forgiveness. Robbie's brave decision too. 'I don't think his is from a religious viewpoint, though,' she'd said. 'I think it's more about healing, moving on.' She'd sniffed back the emotion. 'He's had ten long years without a mum. Can you imagine that? We're both so lucky to have ours.'

Wes had gazed, a shadow passing through his dark eyes. Andrea of course; the mother of his sons. Her request to meet him wasn't something he'd decided on yet.

Anna's voice jolted Nat awake. 'Morning, Skarbie.' Then the drapes were opened, revealing a day as grey as Nat felt.

Her mum's pretty face hovered, looking doubtful. 'I didn't know whether to wake you, but it's late. I didn't want to leave without saying goodbye.'

Nat hitched herself up. 'It took ages to get to sleep, then I woke up at dawn and couldn't get back off...' She glanced at the clock. Heck, it was eleven! 'But I guess I must have done.'

She tried to shake away the grogginess. That's right; Anna and Borys were on a jaunt again today. A supermarket and its café; such was their new love! 'Sorry, you get going; I'll be up in a bit. Where did you say this new Morrisons was?'

Her mum didn't answer. Instead she stroked the hair from Nat's forehead. 'You're fretting about something.' She smiled wistfully. 'And it clearly isn't Wesley. It's so lovely having his company again.' She glanced down at her hands and took a breath.

Nat cringed; oh God, her mum knew. She wasn't ready for this conversation right now. 'The Morrisons in Hyde, did you say?' she asked. 'With your Prince Charming, of course.'

'Is that what's troubling you, love? I'm not replacing your dad, I never could. But...'

It took a moment to adjust. 'What? No, of course not.' Nat laughed. 'What are you like, Mum? Borys is great.' A bit of an old spiv with a waster son, perhaps, but considerably more affectionate and cheerful than her father. And he made Anna happy. 'Off you go and have fun.'

Anna's expression cleared before another small frown. 'But what about you? You've been cooped up in the house since Sunday. Promise me you'll get out?' She blushed. 'The same four walls can get you down. I know it's easy to hide when you're feeling a bit under the weather but...'

'Okay, will do.' Nat smirked. 'But suppose I need to fill the washing machine or feed the cats?'

Ignoring the teasing, Anna stood. 'Then it can wait. Your well-being comes first. I know it sounds old-fashioned, but some fresh air will do you good.'

The 'fresh air' turned out to be a veritable gale. Though Abney Hall Park was less than a kilometre outside the village, Nat wished she had driven. Tired both physically and mentally, she tromped home in the steady drizzle.

She put her key in the latch. Who'd have thought a simple trip out would make her so extraordinarily weary. High emotion, she supposed, and all those embarrassing tears.

Yanking down what was left of her umbrella, she pushed the door. 'Hello!' she called, shaking off her damp coat and boots.

Glad of the warmth, she padded to the kitchen. She expected to see her mum and Borys sitting companionably around the table, drinking tea as usual, but Anna was alone, her face pale and tense.

'You're late, love. I was starting to worry.'

'I went for a walk to...' Nat glanced around, expecting to see carrier bags. 'Have you put everything away, Mum? I would've helped.'

'We didn't go. We've been at the hospital.'

Feeling fragile, Nat stared. Could she handle more trauma right now? 'Oh no, not Borys. What on earth happened?'

Anna shook her head. 'Not Borys, but Michal, his son. It happened last night. Michal had no identification, so no one got in touch. When I arrived to collect Borys this morning, the call came through, so we went straight away.'

No identification? Oh God. Despite her sheer exhaustion Nat prepared herself for the worst. 'What happened, Mum?'

'Michal got beaten up. Badly beaten up on his own doorstep.' Anna's shock was plain to see. 'He was unconscious all night, but he finally woke up this morning, thank the Lord...'

Nat let out her breath. Thank God, not dead. But the prickling sensation was there.

Her mum was patting her cheekbone. 'He looks terrible, Natalie. Black and blue. He has facial fractures, they said. They're keeping him in overnight again. Why would anyone do that?' She sighed deeply. 'It's just dreadful, truly dreadful. I'm going upstairs to lie down.'

Her heart thrashing, Nat sat. God she hoped she was wrong, but she was certain she wasn't. Bloody hell, bloody hell! DFL Debt Advisers were meant to come out of the woodwork by sending a reminder letter to Michal, not send in a heavy right away. Yet she should have known, shouldn't she? If she was right and the Levenshulme Mafia were behind the loan management company, she had put poor Michal's life in danger. She knew too well how ruthless they were. Their 'debt enforcer' had repeatedly threatened, then assaulted, a heavily pregnant woman; it was blindingly obvious they'd have no qualms about a middle-aged man who'd suddenly stopped paying them.

Her mobile rang in tandem with the doorbell. She glanced at the screen. Oh God; Gavin. He'd be furious, of course. Where on earth should she begin to explain and apologise?

She answered him first. 'Gavin. One moment.' Then she stepped to the door to let Wes in, briefly holding his hand before facing the inevitable. Taking a shuddery breath, she went back to the phone. 'Gavin? I'm back.'

From his heavy sigh, she knew he was angry, even before he spoke. 'What did you think you were doing, Natalie?' he asked in a clipped voice. 'Putting Robbie in that position? The police have been here, grilling him with questions for fifty minutes. It's the last thing he needs. He's shaken and tearful, the stutter is back...'

Catching Wes's frown, she sat next to him on the sofa, trying not to cry as she continued to listen.

'...it took me half an hour to get the truth out because he didn't want to be disloyal or let you down. A man, no not a man, a *client* has been badly assaulted. The police seem to think it's linked to the advice a newly qualified paralegal gave him. Not just advice but a directive, one which was proffered under your watch, Natalie.' He huffed again. 'Robbie is barely an adult. I'm at a loss to understand why you would put him in that position and not do it yourself.'

She felt the weight of Wes's arms around her waist, pulling her close. The tenderness defeated her, the tears tumbled out. 'I know you're angry, Gavin, and quite rightly so. I'm so, so sorry. I deeply apologise – to you, to Michal and Robbie. There was a good reason, a good legal reason, I promise. It's complicated, but I can explain and I will, but not right at this moment,' she managed between sobs. 'I'll phone you tomorrow, but I need to talk to Wes and take things easy just now.'

A very long pause, then the tone of Gavin's voice changed. 'Is it a get-out-of-jail card from the doc?' he asked.

'Something like that.'

'Are you saying what I think you're saying?'

She smiled and wiped her face. 'I couldn't possibly comment.'

Finishing the call, she turned to Wes's puzzled frown. Her

emotions were still slithering all over. Elation, hope, anxiety, fear. She tried to blow them out. 'So... Jack arranged...' she began. She started again, the words tumbling out. 'Jack visited me on Monday and guessed about the pregnancy. Well, it seems he already knew from my pasty face when I last saw him. Anyhow, the next thing I knew was a call from Mr Hirsch. I definitely was not going to go, but Anna wanted me to get some fresh air. The grounds at Abney Hall were the obvious place for a walk, and just opposite, well it just so happens that his rooms are there. It seemed... I don't know, it felt like serendipity, so I went.'

Wes spread his hands. 'I have no idea what–'

'He's an obstetrician, Mr Hirsch that is, and some days he works from the Alexandra. Today included. He'd pencilled me in for an appointment at four. He called it a "chat", and in fairness we did, but after that he carried out an "MOT". I'm not entirely sure I like being compared to a car, but that's what he called it.' Wes's handsome face was a picture. She couldn't help but tease him. 'You know, oil change, spark plugs, brake check–'

'Nat–'

'And I passed, Wes!'

'So you're still–'

'Yes. He referred me to a colleague for an ultrasound scan.' Oh God, bloody tears again. 'And there it was on the screen. Our baby, a perfect baby with a heartbeat.'

30

COINCIDENTAL

It was a mistake to tell Anna about the pregnancy, of course. The doc had told Nat to take it easy for a few more days, not be banished to her bedroom and force-fed cabbage soup for the rest of eternity.

Nat had liked Mr Hirsch's pleasant and honest manner. 'I can't wave a magic wand, Natalie, but statistically you have a good chance of keeping this baby after twelve weeks and you're very nearly there.'

He'd explained there were a number of possible reasons why she had bled, including a blood clot or miscarrying a twin. Then again it could have been nothing at all; the body was a strange thing; some women spotted throughout their pregnancies, others had full blown menstruation. The best thing Nat could do was to take a couple more days of rest, then go on as usual, but to be sensible: no additional stress, extreme sports or alcohol.

She had wanted to enquire about the risks of having sex. Not immediately, but soon. Wes was now reading Anna's Sunday newspaper next to her on the bed. It turned out that her exile wasn't all bad; the father of her child was allowed upstairs for visits. Nothing had been said, but she instinctively knew an overnight stay wouldn't be approved of. Of course it was her house and she could do as she liked at forty, but she wanted to be considerate to her mum, and besides the silent fumbling was fun.

'Hey,' she said, flicking the tabloid. 'You're here to entertain me and tell me how much you love me.'

He laughed. 'Leave me alone, woman, I'm engrossed. I wouldn't be seen dead reading this rag in public. My eyes are literally boggling at the crap written. Listen to this headline...'

'Mr Hirsch says...' Nat started, drawling her words.

He threw down the newspaper. 'Oh yeah? What does Mr Hirsch say?'

'Apart from the need for constant adoration–'

'That's a given.'

'That tender breasts are a positive sign of pregnancy.'

He rubbed his hands and pulled a mock serious face. 'And you'd like me to check?'

The moment was interrupted by a call from Anna downstairs. 'Lunch is on the table.'

'My mother is psychic; she can read my flipping mind. Did I tell you that?'

Wes laughed. 'Just a few times. Look on the bright side. You've made progress with nurse Bach; lunch is downstairs today.'

Wes had left by the time Gavin arrived. It was only nine days since Nat had last seen him, but he appeared different again; he seemed to have filled out a touch and the beginning of a gingery moustache had made a comeback. The initial 'lip warmer' and his reconciliation with Heather had coincided last year. Was it a sign that relations between them had improved again? Nat didn't like to ask; the question seemed too intrusive, and anyway she and Gav needed to clear the air about Michal and Robbie.

He greeted Anna with an OAP bear hug. 'I don't think we've ever officially met, but I feel as though I know you,' he said. 'From my reliable seven-year-old source, I was anticipating someone who looked more like Natalie's sister than her mum and she's right.' He rubbed his chin. 'And if I'm lucky, I might be offered something that tastes like a doughnut?'

Nat rolled her eyes, but Anna disappeared, returning with a huge beam and a Tupperware box. '*Pączki*,' she said, handing it over. 'Made this morning for Ruthie, but do help yourself. How is she?'

'Bossing the staff around in the rehabilitation unit. Showing everyone her scar. Collecting football cards for Cameron. I've no idea how she's amassed so many.' He stroked his burgeoning fluff. 'Insisting on this wee fella.'

'I hadn't got you down as a major fawner,' Nat said dryly when her mum left them to their drinks. She sat opposite him at the kitchen table. 'Sisters indeed! And how did you know to ask about the *pączki*?'

Gavin tapped his nose. 'I'm not just a pretty face. You should know that by now.'

Nat took a breath. 'I'm over twelve weeks now, you can shout at me.'

'When have I ever shouted?' he asked, sitting back and folding his arms.

'You don't. Or you do, but you do it quietly. Anyway, it's no more than I deserve. Poor Michal. I feel terrible; I should have known what would happen; my God, being beaten up on your own doorstep.'

Gavin lifted his eyebrows. 'Every cloud – he'll have a nice claim to the Criminal Injuries Compensation Authority. A victim of a violent crime – he'll be entitled to compo for his physical injuries and loss of earnings. He could get a fair sum.'

Ignoring his comment, Nat continued doggedly. 'I also should have thought his case through without involving Robbie. I should've asked you, but you were...'

He put his large hands on the table. 'I know. Tell me now.'

Oh God. She'd been worrying all morning how to explain the complicated Goldman saga. Gavin didn't know about the illicit deal struck between Jack and the Levenshulme Mafia, so she had to tread carefully. 'Well... In a nutshell: Goldman Law client confidentiality, Chinese walls and Jack Goldman's personal affairs.' She looked at Gavin meaningfully. 'The Julian Goldman attempted murder case and more specifically Coma Man.'

She was referring to Gavin's own case. It was he who'd dubbed the debt collector-cum-enforcer 'Coma Man'.

'I'm not saying it was Coma Man himself,' Nat continued. 'If he ever came out of his coma. But–'

'The same lender?'

'Precisely. In Julian's case the loan company was DFL Financial Services; Michal's was DFL Debt Advisers. DFL both times. Pretty coincidental, eh?'

His expression thoughtful, Gavin tapped a finger on the table. Nat gazed as he narrowed his eyes. How much could he remember? For him the Julian Goldman case was one of many, but for her it was more than just memorable.

'The thing is, I can't tell you the whole story, Gav. I know it's a big ask, but you have to take it on trust that the D, the F and the L are very bad people and deserve to be brought down. But for a whole host of reasons, it can't be me who does it.'

He folded his arms again. 'So what was your plan?'

'God, I don't know. Find out exactly who and where they are for starters?'

Aware her cheeks were as red and hot as a pepper, she dropped her head. Her and Robbie's plan to flush the villains out had gone horribly wrong. But at least Michal was back home, enjoying a constant supply of casseroles and home-baked delicacies from the silver surfers. He'd become quite famous in his community and had even made the national press.

She rubbed the table. 'Maybe do more digging, get more information. Trading name, company name, registered office, directors.' She met Gavin's steady gaze. 'These villains are ripping people off, Gav, and they're clever with it. My bet is that they do some of the debt management legitimately, but carefully target their victims. People like Michal who bury their heads in the sand, who don't open demand letters when they fall on the mat, or worse, those people who can't read or who don't understand figures or interest rates. Don't tell me Michal is the only one who has fallen for it. There's probably a class action out there just waiting to be found.'

Gavin's ears had visibly pricked. His pencil had appeared. He pointed it. 'Class action, eh, Bach? You know how to get my attention.' He mulled for a moment. 'If it's a company, chances are it'll go into voluntary liquidation. There won't be any money.'

'Oh, if I'm right about who's behind this scam, they'll wriggle out of it, I'm sure.' Trying to shake off the image of Danielle Foster's sweet and innocent façade, Nat breathed deeply. She was supposed to avoid excessive stress; she had to stop.

As though reading her mind, Gavin stood. 'I'll have a think.' He nodded to her stomach. 'Congratulations, by the way. What are your plans work wise?'

She'd thought about this over the last few days. On the one hand she was tearing her hair out with boredom here – she'd bugged most people in her contacts for a chinwag already, and there were only so many rounds of *Words With Friends* one could play – but on the other, Jed's aggression still brought on a breathless feeling of vulnerability; suppose he'd had a knife? A new little life was growing inside her; she wasn't afraid just for herself any more. 'A bit of freelance, maybe? Working from home. Charging rate negotiable?'

Gavin smiled, but his eyes didn't match. 'Have I paid you yet?'

Sure he was also thinking about the Jed incident, Nat shook her head. It felt like a subject best avoided, but he cleared his throat. 'I think you might be right about Robbie's damages. I checked the file; Jed was his litigation friend and the trustee of the money. I should've thought of it before–'

'It's hardly your fault, Gav. You weren't acting for either of them.'

'True, but I took Robbie on. *In loco parentis* in a way. It's something I should have twigged before now and it's difficult...'

'I know. Sorry.' It was a tricky situation. Jed was Gavin's client; Gavin clearly felt sorry for the man; he'd looked out for him for years. And if Gavin confronted him, there was the potential of a seriously violent episode. She tried for humour. 'No wonder you don't pay me, I only make things worse.' She reached for his arm. 'Look, I may well be wrong; the damages could be stashed safely in a trust account earning interest. Maybe Jed thought Robbie wasn't ready for the responsibility of it yet. A quiet word that Robbie is old enough now might be all it takes.'

'I'll think about that too.' Gavin snorted through his nose. 'You're nothing but bloody trouble, Bach. Anyone tell you that?'

Nat followed him to the door. 'Unfortunately, yes.' She squeezed him tightly. 'I'm so glad to hear about Ruthie's progress. We've been chatting on the iPad and I can't wait to visit. And next week I hope to take the boys to the park, and then a cheeseburger as usual.'

He opened the door and turned, his expression clearly torn. 'The restorative conferencing, forgiveness, reconciliation...'

'What's right for Robbie isn't necessarily right for you, Gav. It may not work; it might be a disaster. No one can tell you how you should feel.'

He sighed and smiled thinly. 'I know, but why do I spend so much time thinking about it?' Stepping out, he lifted his hand. 'Take care of that bump, Bach. Freelance sounds perfect. Pay packet is on its way.'

31

PRIORITIES

Nat sipped her forest fruit smoothie. It was nice – and had all those vitamins she was now alert to – but when would her love of Yorkshire Tea return? She had never thought of it having a smell before now, but of course it did, Earl Grey more so.

She sniffed the coffee-infused air and swallowed. Perhaps adopting the Roasted Coffee Lounge as her new 'office' wasn't such a good idea. She'd had a call yesterday, out of the blue, from an unknown number. Yup, another heart flutter. But on this occasion it had been welcome, an excuse to have a break from Dorothea, Casaubon and Will Ladislaw (if her bedroom banishment wasn't the opportunity to finally read *Middlemarch*, when was?) and the caller was someone she had warmed to.

'Hi Natalie. It's Cassandra. Peter Woodcock's daughter? I'm in the area tomorrow. Would it be okay to pop in and have a quick chat? You're in Heald Green aren't you?'

'Sure...' The conversation had been tricky; Nat still didn't feel comfortable about returning to SS's offices, but she could hardly invite a stranger, albeit a likeable one, to her home. So she'd suggested meeting at the café before going on to her ante natal appointment.

After the two weeks of house arrest, the plan had been to walk from Cheadle to Gatley so Nat could take in her dose of fresh air and rub shoulders with the human race. Unfortunately it had turned into a battle with both the elements and the traffic on Kingsway. Each time she had thought it safe to cross the quadruple parkway, it wasn't. Still she'd set off with plenty of time, so she'd arrived before her date, spread herself out on the leather sofa, opened her laptop and taken advantage of the free wifi.

After spurning social media during the missing Mallorca years, she'd been making up for lost time since, and today was no exception. She posted pics of anything that moved (two pugs looking forlorn through the café windows) and anything that didn't (her Eccles cake and the quirky books surrounding her) on Instagram; she scrolled through Twitter, making arch or controversial comments, before deleting them; then she had a spurt of silly WhatsApp exchanges with Fran and Bo about a 'lost gin weekend' they'd had years ago.

Finally bored with liking Facebook pet and baby photos, she snapped the lid closed and stroked her small mound. Would that be her one day? Putting up snaps of her foetus from pea to prawn to... well, probably pork pie? God, she prayed so. Fran and Bo were her closest girlfriends, but she hadn't told even them her news yet. The hope and worry of today's appointment with Mr Hirsch made her breathless, but the tender boobs, the perfumed taste of tea and acrid smell of coffee made her hopeful that little he or she was holding on.

She looked at her watch. There was another ten minutes before Cassandra was due. It was a bit odd, really, her randomly calling Nat like that. What exactly did she want to talk about? Concerning her dad, was all she'd said. The usual speculation prodded, so Nat picked up her phone and scrolled through the news to stave off her mild anxiety.

'Cinema reinstates showing of gang film after brawl'; 'Man admits to stabbing two commuters'; 'EuroMillions winner convicted of child porn offences'; 'Met Police superintendent sentenced over indecent video.' Bloody hell; all a bit close to the bone, or what? It brought back thoughts of Issa, so she reverted to her laptop and spent a few moments searching for local newspapers in the Merseyside area, eventually finding reports by Kenneth Chen in the *Southport Reporter* archives.

She read for a while. There was no doubt Chen liked to make a headline splash; a number of cowboy builders, a 'double cheat' local councillor who had fiddled with both his expenses and his neighbour's wife, a 'butcher' dentist who had faked his qualifications. If they were true, they were good exposés. The need to make his name in a tough journalistic world was understandable, but not, surely, without checking his facts?

Sitting back, she gazed at a small photograph of the man. He had a striking face. What was really going on? Was he taking JP's version of events on trust like the police had with the fantasist 'Nick'? She thrummed her belly with gentle fingers. Maybe that was the way forward, a frank discussion between Issa and Chen, keeping JP out of the loop. It seemed that Chen was a massive influence on him; if Issa could put him straight about the addresses and dates, then maybe he could convince JP he was wrong. After all, the journalist wouldn't want to get in trouble with his editor – or the law – for libel. It was certainly a plan, but Nat shelved it for now; she was seeing Issa the week after next; it was best broached in person.

Plucking her vibrating mobile from her 'desk', she peered at the name. Oh God, it was Max. The thought of his police interview had bobbed in and out of her mind since his angry phone call. Would she forever associate heavy bleeding with it? Wes certainly did, the boyfriend Wes, at least. How was he handling it at work? Max was his assistant after all, so they had to communicate day in and day out. Wes had faithfully promised not to say anything, but could he hide the tension which always showed in his jaw? She doubted it.

She stared a beat longer. Should she answer it or not? Wes was adamant she wasn't to get involved any further, that the stress wasn't good for her. But to be fair, Max didn't know she was pregnant; he wasn't going to disappear and she was supposed to be his friend.

'Max, hi. How's it going?' she asked, automatically holding her breath.

'Okay, considering.' He paused. 'Look, I'm sorry about the other week. My parents were giving me a hard time; I was really stressed.'

'It's fine, I understood.' She cleared her throat. 'You didn't call me about the police interview, though.'

'It hasn't happened. I hope it won't, but if it does, you'll support me, won't you?'

She released the trapped air. 'Of course; I still feel really bad about it. It must've been a nightmare. How come they dropped it? What happened?'

'Dad's solicitor wrote a letter to her about malicious complaints, pointing out he had a duty to report a breach of ethics to the General Medical Council. I know it sounds harsh, but making completely false accusations does put her fitness to practise as a doctor into question. I couldn't believe it, Nat. Saying I hit her–'

Nat shifted in her seat; she'd joked to Wes about mad women in attics, but this was like Andrea all over again. It was too easy to make allegations; they were so difficult to refute. 'God, that's what she said?'

'Yes. Can you imagine how upset my mum was, thinking I go around slapping women? It's a joke that the police took it seriously. Dad's solicitor got some police officer he knows to look at the file or whatever they have. When she made the complaint, they asked for corroborative evidence and because she had zilch, she made up some bullshit about it happening weeks ago.'

'What about the...' Nat lowered her voice. 'The ammo?'

'The letter dealt with that too. It mentioned theft, copyright, the Criminal Justice and Courts Act. Belt and braces stuff. He's confident everything's contained, so you should see yours truly's name on the Goldman Law notepaper in a few weeks.'

The pleasure and relief in his voice was patent. Nat was pleased for him; she didn't care about partnership or fighting for the conference room any more. A tiny ultrasound beat had put that into perspective.

Max was still speaking. 'So, a drink or ten to celebrate, now I'm as free as a bird. How about Saturday? Same time, same place?'

She looked to the opening door. 'Yeah, sounds great. I'll call you.' She ended the call and stood. Appearing windswept and weary, Cassandra Woodcock was flopping down on the opposite sofa.

'Hi, how are you?' Nat asked. 'Can I get you a drink? Something to eat? I can recommend the Eccles cakes.' She laughed. 'Nah, you come from Worsley; you were probably weaned on them.'

The quip clearly didn't land. 'No, it's fine, thanks,' she replied distractedly. 'I'm on my way somewhere, so I can't be long.'

The young woman put her hands on her face and almost imperceptibly shook her head. 'Sorry, it's been a rubbish week. So, the reason I wanted a private word.' She leaned forward. 'About Dad. I think you'll have already gathered he's a very well-respected magistrate as well as a doctor, but he's due to retire next year to spend some hard-earned relaxation time with my mum. His medical career has been his life, his voluntary work the icing on the cake. His reputation means everything. If there was any suggestion of impropriety or negligence, it would kill him. Literally.'

Thinking of Harrow, Nat inwardly sighed. Another parallel; it seemed that life was full of them. 'I can't pretend to know all the ins and out, Cassandra; I was only assisting Gavin Savage while he was away, but I'm not aware of any suggestion–'

'There have been calls, Natalie, from lawyers, maybe from your office. Asking about Melanie's pain management plan, her prescriptions, her medical records, how often Dad visited her. He's trying not to show it, but he's worried. I know there are protocols for this kind of thing and it's asking a lot of you, but you seemed such a lovely person, I felt I could ask.' She took a deep breath. 'Off the record, is there something we should know or be concerned about?'

Oh God, Chinese walls, would they ever go away? But this time Nat was out of the loop, so she truly knew zilch. 'I honestly don't know anything. I'm sort of on sick leave, so I haven't been in the office. But I imagine it's simple fact finding and nothing more sinister.'

Cassandra tilted her head and finally gave a small smile. 'I'm guessing "sort of" sick leave is a euphemism for something else? Something much nicer than illness?'

Nat chuckled. She didn't mind looking dreadful, so long as her baby was thriving. 'Do I look that bad?'

'Not at all; I just have pregnancydar. Congratulations. How far along are you?'

'Thirteen or fourteen weeks.' Nat tapped the wooden table. 'I hope.'

Cassandra rose and brushed invisible crumbs from her coat. 'If you do hear anything and you felt you could tell me...' She pulled a business card from her purse and jotted a number on the back. 'We would both be very grateful. It was so tough for all of us to witness Melanie's decline, unable to do anything but watch. My father did nothing wrong or unprofessional. You've met him, so I'm sure you know that, but to be forewarned… Bye, Natalie. And the best of luck.' She briefly gripped Nat's hand before turning away.

Nat slipped the business card in her pocket. Her mind buzzing, she gazed absently through the window. What would she do if she found anything out? Another flaming moral maze. But her thoughts were interrupted by the sight of an attractive man striding to the door. Almost brushing shoulders with Cassandra, he stopped, then turned his head to have a second look.

The handsome man was her boyfriend. He leaned over to give her a peck. 'Was that your two o'clock appointment?' he asked, grinning.

'Stop taking the piss,' Nat replied, feeling a niggle of pique, despite his soft kiss.

'She seemed familiar. Do I know her from somewhere?' he asked.

'I certainly hope not. I don't want you mixing with attractive young blondes when I look

so–'

'Beautifully pregnant.'

She took his proffered hand and stood. 'You know you're not allowed to say the P word. We don't know for sure.'

'Yes, we do.' He glanced at his watch. 'And in fifteen minutes I will be proved right. I can't wait to tell Mum, then shout it from the treetops.'

A horrible thought suddenly hit her. 'What about Andrea?'

He shrugged. 'What about her?'

She touched her stomach. 'This.'

'If she finds out, fine, but I'm not telling her. I have no plans to see her now, or ever if I can help it.'

Her heart thrashing, Nat followed Wes to the car. 'Really? What about her threats?'

He climbed in and looked at her steadily. 'What will be, will be. Priorities have changed. I won't let her into our life. Does that sound okay to you?'

Avoiding the traffic, he drove the back way through Cheadle Village. They didn't speak until he turned off the engine in the leafy hospital car park. He dipped his head. 'Nat, is that fine with you?'

It was more than fine, but there were so many ifs and buts, she didn't know where to start. Still, only one thing seemed to really count. 'Does Andrea know about your decision not to see her?'

Wes's face clouded. 'Oh, yes, she knows.'

32

CIVIC DUTY

Nat woke up bright and early and scooped up her list of things to do. She hadn't slept that well, but it was fine. Her insomnia had been born of excitement, and she had filled in the wakeful interludes by scribbling memos on the pad by her bed. A call to Mr Savage was at the top.

She had intended to call Gavin yesterday, but buoyed by the results of the scan, she and Wes had travelled straight to Congleton to break the glad tidings to Kath and Joe. Although she'd already met them both, it was on their turf this time. Ridiculously nervous, she'd sat on the edge of her chair like a character from her current tome. Hesitant, mannered and polite, she'd nibbled cake and sipped lemonade, saying enough pleases and thank yous to satisfy Mrs Cadwallader. But she needn't have worried; as soon as Wes cleared his throat and announced: 'Natalie and I are going to be parents in the autumn,' Kath stood with arms raised and jigged on the spot.

'I knew it! I knew it,' she laughed, gathering both Nat and Wes, and continuing a three-way prance.

'I think she's pleased,' Joe said wryly, lifting his head from the newspaper, but smiling nonetheless. 'Congratulations, son.'

Then, with a glint in his eye. 'Congratulations, Natalie, though I'm not sure I recognise you fully dressed.'

The men had strayed into chatter about football – a new City signing and the ref's disgraceful penalty decision on Saturday – so Kath had rolled her eyes and pulled Nat into the chilly conservatory, put on a fan heater and sat her down.

'So, tell me everything. How far on are you?' she'd asked.

'Fourteen weeks,' Nat had replied, pleased to say it out loud. 'We had a scan earlier.'

There had been another peal of delight. 'Please tell me you have a photograph.'

'I have,' Nat had replied, digging in her handbag, but not wanting to hand it over just yet.

Kath had seemed to understand. Peering at it without touching, she'd sighed. 'Perfect, just perfect. So tell me exactly what you could see on the screen...'

Nat hadn't known if she'd been referring to a willy – or not – but it was nevertheless fabulous to describe what she'd seen on the ultrasound scan to someone who was thrilled to know.

She now peeped at the snap. Her eyes had been so glued to that beating heart, then counting the arms, legs and toes, that she hadn't thought about the baby's sex. She didn't want to know anyway; the fear of tempting fate was still creeping in. But all was good yesterday; she could breathe a tad more easily now.

'Second trimester,' she said to herself. How the heck did that happen? And more to the point, it meant she only had one more trimester to get used to the idea of an actual child, not one borrowed from Gavin or cooed over via an iPad screen. Bloody hell!

Infused with surprising energy, Nat finally settled down at the table. No more procrastination. Last night's master plans needed to be put into practice. First up, SS.

'Savage Solicitors. Chantelle Rochelle speaking.'

Rochelle? A rhyming surname? Really? Why didn't she know that? Reminding herself not to be surprised by anything SS related, she stifled the chuckle.

'It's Nat. Guess what?'

'Harry Styles is coming in to the office to get his will sorted. He'll immediately spot me and beg me to be on the cover of his new album. His gran lives near mine. Did you know that?'

'No I didn't. Try again?' Then, thinking Gavin might not be impressed by the two of them holding up calls with a guessing game for half an hour, 'It's fine; I'll tell you.' She took a big breath. 'I'm pregnant! I am going to have a baby in September.'

'Really? Wow.' Then after a beat. 'Are you sure? You're quite old to be having–'

'Excuse me! Forty is nothing these days.'

'You're *forty*? God, my mum's only–'

What the flip? People were supposed to be pleased, not put her in the same bracket as some old granny who'd gone to Italy for fertility treatment. 'Well anyway, can you put Gavin on, please?'

'Ah I get it,' Chantelle continued. 'You're accidentally up the duff with that dishy guy with the mad bitch wife?'

A bit close to the bone. 'Well yes, maybe, but... Just put me through to Gavin, please.'

He came on the line a little too quickly. 'Natalie. What can I do you for?' He couldn't hide the smile from his voice.

'You've been feeding Chantelle the lines, you bloody sod.'

'This wee laddie? As if.'

'I'll get my revenge,' she said when his chuckling had died down. 'I'm only phoning to offer my freelance services.'

'You mean you're bored already?'

'Pretty much. Tell me what's happening in the real world. Brian Selby, for starters. Doctor Woodcock's daughter came to see me yesterday. Have you been speaking to her father and asking for documents? She's worried he's going to be blamed for something.'

The line went quiet, then Gavin cleared his throat. 'Remember we act for Brian Selby, Natalie,' he said, the humour all gone. 'We do whatever helps him. If that includes slinging mud at the medic who prescribed the drugs, then so be it.'

The jolt of reprimand hit her as usual, but she knew he was right. The duty to do one's utmost in the best interests of the client was obligatory. Over the years she'd done it many times with gritted teeth. Yet she felt sorry for the Worsley GP. Perhaps she was getting soft. Hormones, probably, currently the answer to everything.

'I realise that, but you're not "slinging mud", are you, Gav? He seems a good guy.'

'As it happens, no. But there's no property in a witness, Nat. Anyone can approach him for information or a statement, including Khan and your mate Jack.' He paused. 'It might be our expert toxicologist, actually. Did you know he got bail?'

It took her a moment to shift focus. 'Who? Brian?'

'Yup, and Shirley. Both back home for now.'

That brought a smile. She pictured young Lucy's look of despair when her parents' 'absence' was mentioned. 'I'm pleased, at least that's something. Are they still both saying they did it?'

'Each of them say they held a pillow to Melanie's face. Who knows how that will pan out ultimately?'

'What do you mean?'

'For want of a better expression, the jury is still out. Brian and Shirley have yet to plea in the Crown Court; we need to get proper disclosure, look at all the police evidence, particularly toxicology. There's potential for murder, attempted murder or assisted suicide. That's just for starters.'

Nat laughed. 'You love your job, don't you, Savage?'

'Pretty much,' he replied.

She ended the call, flicked on the kettle and went in search of her mum. Following the sound of humming, she stopped at the lounge door and watched Anna polish the woodwork with a yellow duster. Every few moments she stopped to practise her steps. A waltz? Foxtrot? It was so nice to see her happy; thank God for Borys.

The thought of Michal Gorski popped up. She snorted to herself. What was she like? Mentioning him to Gavin had definitely been on the agenda. Bo and Fran had often complained about 'mumsnesia', but Nat was clearly starting her foggy headedness early. Thank goodness Anna's invisible dance partner had reminded her.

Retreating to the kitchen, she called Gavin back.

'Thought I'd got rid of you,' he said.

'About Michal...' she began.

Why she'd temporarily forgotten, she didn't know. He was regularly the subject of Anna and Borys's discussions over *szarlotka*, Lover Boy's favourite apple cake:

'Who would do such a dreadful thing?'

'The money men, Anna.'

'But why? He was working all hours to pay them, wasn't he? Who are these wicked people?'

Nat tried not to earwig; the stress wasn't good. On the one hand her feelings of culpability made her sweat buckets; on the other, it made her determined to stop the bloody thugs.

'What about him?' Gavin asked.

She took a breath. 'Yes, Michal. You were going to have a think about the debt management villains...'

'Ah, that.'

'And? What did you decide?'

'Let's just say Robbie has done a session of what Robbie does best.'

'As in?'

'His creative use of the laptop.'

'What? You mean hacking?' She had forgotten about this alleged skill. In truth she'd always supposed Gavin was winding her up about it; she still wasn't sure. 'Gavin! Just tell me.'

'Robbie found a trail which ended with a name.'

'Really?' She could feel her heart thumping. 'And it belongs to...?'

'One very respectable Mr Lewis Foster. He's a financial adviser who has some swish offices in Wilmslow, apparently.'

'Really?'

The word emerged far too high and Gavin chuckled. 'Did no one ever tell you acting wasn't your strong point, Nat?'

People had. 'So what now?' she asked.

'I've already done my civic duty. Reported everything I know to the police. Cheshire police's economic fraud unit, to be precise. Next up will be a nod to the Insolvency Service.'

The pounding in her chest cranked up another notch. 'And this has nothing to do with me or Goldman Law?'

'Absolutely nothing,' he replied firmly. 'In fact it might well generate some good publicity for the whistle-blower. He's tall and handsome with a terrific moustache. Tell you what, he'll look braw on the front page of *The Times*.'

With a grin, Nat remembered the magician's outfit. 'Wearing a cape and top hat with a little white rabbit, maybe?' She laughed. 'Hey, I could earn some dosh by exposing the "secret sorcerer life" of the Heald Green Solicitor.'

'Fame at last, don't knock it.'

'I thought your PC Plod case was going to make you famous.'

'Hmm... Not the type of fame I was hoping for. Nor him, I expect.'

Nat sat up, intrigued. 'What does that mean?'

'Well...' The chime of his desk phone interrupted his reply. 'Got things to do, Bach. Ask your buddy, Jack.'

33

ATTIC

Feeling a little on guard, Nat inhaled the delicious buffet aromas and listened to the hum of conversation around her.

She caught Wes's eye and smiled. He had asked for complete honesty and going forward that was fine. Backwards would not be helpful given his struggle to keep angst or annoyance from his face. Today of all days, she was particularly glad of her circumspection. It wasn't as though she had anything to hide personally, but the Goldman clan were another thing, and the whole dynasty was here at Catherine's Sunday brunch.

Nat's immediate instinct had been to say no to the invitation, or at least to dig deep for an excuse. There had been a smattering of pleasure when the text arrived asking her and Wes as a couple, but it had been rapidly replaced by alarm.

Wes had been more sanguine. 'Look, the whole thing is horribly incestuous, but they are our partners and friends, part of our lives.' He'd given her a peck. 'Unless you have plans to do a runner for five years again.'

'Not funny.'

Of course he was thinking about him and Catherine, her and Catherine, her and Jack, the strange foursome who'd been intertwined one way or another for fifteen years. Wes had no idea about the bigger picture, the Julian, Aisha and Levenshulme Mafia affair in particular. Still, everyone around the long bench had abided by the rules of civility so far: they'd sipped their Buck's Fizz, nibbled on smoked salmon blinis, and passed round the Goldman baby and pleasantries.

She looked around her balmy surroundings. In contrast to the ultra-modern cooking area, this room was more traditional with wooden beams, panelled walls, an open fire and the huge oak table. It looked like a genuine antique and probably was. Were the cool, high-gloss kitchen units and white sofas Catherine's choice, and this homely dining suite Jack's? Who knew? Nat's old 'nous' seemed to be faulty these days. She glanced at Max and relaxed a jot more; if anything went awry, the tribe could always turn on the new boy, who was flirting outrageously with Jack's usually sullen daughter, Verity.

Aisha was sitting on the opposite side. Without her pregnancy bump, she looked tiny. Nat had tried to squeeze in next to her, hoping that baby talk would break the ice after their less-than-friendly meetings last year, but Catherine had intervened. 'You're at the other end next to Jack, Nat. He's been missing you. Prepare yourself for a grilling.'

Her stomach rumbling, Nat turned to him now. 'So, what's going on with PC Plod and the taser case?' she asked, helping herself to several triangles of buttered brown bread.

'Ask your pal, Gavin.'

'He says to ask you.'

He lowered his voice. 'Seems your Mr Savage isn't happy with the racism angle.'

'What racism angle?'

Jack removed his glasses. 'Young black lad minding his own business gets tasered. I'd say it speaks for itself.' He polished his lenses before replacing them. 'We can't have our upstanding police force behaving that way.'

Nat narrowed her eyes. Of course he had a point, one she'd tried to explore herself, but Dwayne hadn't raised it, so it wasn't appropriate to pursue. And besides, Jack had never been that type of lawyer; he'd always done his bloody brilliant best for a client financially, absolutely, but never for a cause.

'What are you up to?' she asked.

He shrugged and spread his hands. 'Just doing your job, Miss Bach.'

Another platter was passed her way. Almost slavering, she stared at the selection of homemade pâtés, king prawns and quails' eggs. Typical; they were all on the bloody banned list. It was always the same; when deprived of something, one missed it so much more. She handed it to Jack.

'Eat double for me, will you.' She shoved in another triangle of Hovis and chewed. 'So, what about DeMille and his seamstresses? Did you check all the documents proving their entitlement to work here?'

'DeMille?' He paused. 'Ah, Cecil B. Very good. Of course.' He poured himself more wine. 'I don't suppose you're drinking alcohol either. Doing it by the book?'

She stared at his face. It was definitely shifty. 'Did *you* do it by the book, Jack? Those checks? If he's employing illegal workers, he'll get a shedload of bad publicity and a huge fine. which he'll pass on to Goldman Law for their failure to–'

'That won't happen, Natalie. Eddie, or DeMille, as you like to call him, is a good man. He's offering generous wages to those women, money they need for their families, a salary they wouldn't get otherwise. That isn't his only business...'

Nat sat back, astonished. Was he saying what she thought he was? That Eddie was employing illegal workers in several of his businesses, and that Jack was 'overlooking' it? She opened her mouth to speak, but he lifted his hand. 'You and I have something in common, Natalie. We're both children of immigrants.' He lifted his glass and stared with those incongruous blue eyes. 'We've been lucky, very lucky. Always remember that.'

He was absolutely right, but the surprise left her winded. She took a breath to say something, but he'd already changed the subject, nodding to the other end of the table. 'Verity seems charmed with young Max. I could do with getting her off my payroll. What do you think? Good husband material?'

She peered again at Max, but her gaze slipped to Wes, sitting next to him. Despite the facial hair, his tight jaw revealed his struggle with the boyfriend/partner divide. She smiled inwardly at the BF word. And he'd been right; she loved his beard now, couldn't imagine him without it.

'Max? Yeah, I think so,' she replied, bringing herself back to Jack. Sure, that phone call had shocked her, but Max had been stressed, it was clearly out of character. 'Nice-looking, private school, wealthy background. Partner-to-be. The sort you'd want your daughter to marry, I imagine.'

'And what about you when you have your daughter?' he asked. 'Is that what you'd want? Marrying her off to a rich kid, or have her standing on her own two feet, helping people, having convictions and making a stand?' He smiled. 'Even if it is in her own peculiar way?'

Feeling that poignant ache when Jack said something complimentary, Nat shook her head and snorted. 'What makes you think it's a girl?'

'Intuition,' he replied, adjusting his glasses. 'Talking of rich kids, Lewis Foster had a visit from the police this week.'

'Really?' Nat replied, staring steadily at her plate. 'What for?'

'Danielle was vague when she called. A misunderstanding with one of his businesses, apparently. A rogue employee not doing the paperwork properly, by the sound of it. Of course she's distancing herself from it, just in case. Much as she loves her son, business is business. She runs a clean ship, as you know. It wouldn't do to get "tarred", as she put it.'

Nat swallowed. It was disappointing, but expected. She hadn't for a moment thought Danielle Foster would allow herself to be associated by any impropriety, let alone be caught. She was a very clever woman; she'd never be found out. Nat didn't like her one jot, but had to admire her sheer determination and resilience.

A change of subject was in order. 'Anna sends her love,' she said to Jack. 'Did I tell you about her friend Borys?'

Trying to anticipate sharp bends and stray sheep, Nat negotiated the dark country roads with great care. Spring was supposed to be around the corner in March, but the trees were still starkly naked, the evenings winter black.

They were almost back at the cottage, at least she hoped so. She looked across to Wes, slumped in his seat. 'How was your end of the table?' she asked.

He opened an eye. 'Verity drinks at the same rate as her mother. She topped me up every time she helped herself to another glass of the Chablis. Think it made her feel better. It was hard to keep up.'

'Sweet of you to try,' Nat replied with a snort. 'I suppose you're planning to take advantage of this free taxi service for the next five months or so?'

He clenched his fist in a victory sign. 'I knew there was something I liked about you.'

She peered through the windscreen. 'Is it this turn or the next one?'

'Next, thank God; I need water.'

'What's Verity like these days? Apart from being a lush. Jack was asking if Max was husband material.' She pulled the car up at the barrier. 'You're going to have to work on being civil to him, Wes. He'll be a Goldman Law partner in less than a month.'

Wes grinned. 'I am civil.'

'Friendly, then. You know, moving on a little further than just yes and no.' She squeezed his thigh. 'Max is okay, really. He just lost his rag that once and we're forgetting about it, aren't we?'

'For you, I'll do anything, my love.'

Nat nodded ahead. 'How about starting with the gate? It needs opening.'

After rounding up an escapee hen, Wes held out his hand to guide Nat down the path to the stable door. Once he'd overcome the key's refusal to slide into the lock, he pulled her into his arms.

'Gate done and dusted, chicken caught, door open and we're finally in! What next? Anything your heart desires. What does it desire? We have an empty house. Mr Hirsch says...'

She laughed. 'Maybe a sit down and that water first.' The obstetrician had indeed said that there was no reason to avoid intercourse, but Wes was swaying; she doubted he'd get up the stairs let alone anything else.

He collapsed onto the sofa, hitching to one side to make room for her. He slung an arm over her shoulders. 'It was good today, wasn't it? Was I right to just... tear off the embarrassment plaster?'

'Yes, Wes, you were right.'

He was; she'd been thinking the same as him. The brunch, which had somehow merged into supper, had been fun; Max and Verity seemed a perfect match; Jack and Catherine were solid, doting over their pudgy-faced grandson. Julian had been friendly and even Aisha had eventually given her half a smile.

Life in general was hunky-dory too. Andrea appeared to have taken Wes's firm 'no' to any contact on the chin. And anyway, who would she tell about Wes and Catherine's fling? Everyone knew she was crackers, Jack included.

'Say again?' Wes was putting a hand behind his ear. 'Say again? I'm not sure I heard you properly.'

She smiled. 'Wesley Hughes was right, just this once.'

When his breathing slowed, Nat lifted his arm to slip away, but he tightened it again. 'Not so easily,' he muttered. Then after a moment. 'Oh, yeah, I forgot to say. I placed your two o'clock appointment.'

Appointment where? At the clinic? Or...? It took a moment to twig. 'At the café last week? My date with Cassandra Woodcock?'

'Think he called her Caz. Girlfriend in the attic. Seemed nice to me, but like you said...'

As Wes drifted off, Nat stared at the fireplace as the information soaked in. Bloody hell, Cassandra Woodcock was Max's crazy 'ammo' woman. No, that couldn't be right. Cassandra had seemed so grounded and nice. And Max had said his girlfriend was a doctor.

She gently raised Wes's hand and padded to her coat. Reaching into the pocket, she pulled out the business card Cassandra had given her. She stared at the handwritten mobile number, then turned it over.

A name and a business address: Dr C J Woodcock and the surgery in Worsley.

Completely winded, Nat flopped into the armchair. Bloody hell, Natalie; this was really, really bad form. The very same 'error' had driven her bonkers over the years: people assuming the man was in charge. Time after time she'd met a new client or taken a witness statement or gone to a different court with a junior male colleague, and *he* would be addressed as the boss.

Yet she'd done it herself with Cassandra. When the surgery receptionist had said, 'Dr Woodcock is waiting for you', she'd assumed it was Dr Woodcock senior, a man, not an attractive and friendly young female.

But that wasn't what bothered her the most right now. It was Cassandra that day, in particular her face. Her teeth clenched, Nat pictured it. Dr Woodcock junior had a black eye and a cut lip. She didn't need to do the maths to know that 'Caz' was still Max's girlfriend then.

34

SHOUTING

The journey to Heald Green was only a short one, but Nat got stuck in the Kingsway traffic. Why she'd gone that route, she didn't know. Autopilot, she suspected, distracted by her musing about Cassandra or Caz. No wonder the poor woman had looked so world-weary at their brief meeting. But it wasn't just the humiliation Max and his father's solicitor must have put her through – all but threatening to report her to the General Medical Council for being a liar – it was the traumatic assault itself.

Thoughts of aggressors happened to be topical today. Nat was now at Savage Solicitors, and though her visit would be brief, the apprehension about Jed was looming large. That tingle of icy fear was still at her fingertips, and the hopelessness that had gone with it. Of course she didn't know if Cassandra's bruised face was the result of a blow, or whether it was Max who had administered it, but the sense of violation was there.

The office door was locked, but Chantelle buzzed her in and sashayed over with open arms. 'Let's see your bump, then?' she said.

Nat unbuttoned her jacket. She had been wearing her

uniform of jogging bottoms or leggings over the past couple of weeks, but seeing as it was an office day, she'd tried on a work skirt this morning. It hadn't fitted, so now she was wearing an elasticated monstrosity loaned by her mum.

Chantelle wrinkled her nose. 'That's it?' she said dismissively. 'Typical. Bet I'll be huge when it's my turn.'

Nat looked at her bump. It was neat, but definitely there. 'I'm only four months, Chantelle. I'm told it'll grow if I water it. Is Robbie in yet?'

'Yeah, but he keeps disappearing to the loo.' She raised her eyebrows. 'Nerves.'

Too much information. 'Okey-dokey. Is Gavin free?'

Chantelle lifted her shoulders and pulled the face which suggested she wasn't best pleased with her boss. Poor girl; he'd probably been winding her up again. He should really be careful; behind the painted face, this woman was smart, a bloody good secretary; he'd be disappointed to lose her.

'I'll just go in then, shall I?' Nat asked.

Another shrug, so she made her way to the boss's office, tapped on his door and entered.

His shirt sleeves rolled up, Gavin was on the phone, so she sat down quietly and looked around the shabby room. Taking in the familiar smell of – figs? – and Gavin's aftershave, she felt a little sad that an episode of her life had come and gone. It had been replaced by another amazing challenge, but she'd felt at home here. Although a few things had gone pear-shaped and the majority of Gavin's clients were indeed 'Neds', there had been a feeling of... What was it? Yes, love. Love, care and concern, a desire to help and support, which one didn't often find in a lawyer's office.

Coming back from her reflections, she focused on her friend. His face was a deep rusty colour, his chatter had become heated. She casually glanced at the folder on his desk, then sat up and paid attention. The Brian Selby file. The Scot was indeed 'rabid' today; he was giving the person on the other end of the telephone a rollicking. She listened to his side of the conversation.

'Tell me, what is the point of the "golden rule" of disclosure if you and the police don't abide by it?'

'I don't accept that. They knew damn well the report was detrimental to their case so they deliberately held it back.'

'No, my client did not admit murder. He admitted to holding a pillow over his daughter's face, that was all. If you're in any doubt, I suggest you do your homework and listen to your client's own taped interviews.'

'We both know a charge of wasting police time is the best you can do. Be my guest and try it. I'm sure the press will have a field day after what appears to be a wilful refusal to come clean in the spirit of equity and fair play...'

Ending the call, Gavin made notes for several minutes before speaking. He eventually lifted his head. 'That's shouting,' he said.

'And very impressive too.' The colour had ebbed from his face. 'What was that all about?' she asked.

Gavin sat back and swung his chair. 'We finally got the police's toxicology report this morning. They've been sitting on it. Strictly speaking they're entitled to until the case management conference, but that isn't the spirit of the law when someone's liberty is at stake.' He tapped his scrawl with his pencil. 'Their expert can't say for sure what caused Melanie's death, whether it was the morphine overdose or suffocation. My expert is on to it, but I'll bet my granny's false teeth that his "fence" position means Melanie was already dead from the morphine before Brian – or Shirley – did the belt and braces pillow part. My guy says it's looking good.' He finally grinned. 'You can't murder a dead person, can you, Nat? Then any charge of attempted murder or assisted suicide isn't going to look pretty.'

Thinking back to what both Larry and Joshim had said about causation, Nat nodded. Not *who* done it, but *what* done it, or as Larry had eloquently put it: 'Did those hands cause her death?'

'So, what happens now?' she asked.

'I don't know. Murder is definitely off the cards, but they may stick to their guns with attempted murder and let the jury decide. But is that in the public interest? No, and especially not if our expert comes firmly down on the side of the defence, which he will.'

'Good news, then?' she asked hesitantly; Gavin was tapping his fingers and frowning.

'I'm hoping so. Brian and Shirley both made voluntary false confessions. The police might try to save face by charging them with wasting police time or perverting the course of justice, but that's not a major problem considering the time they've already served on remand.' He picked up the expert's report and wafted it. 'My only niggle is the huge amount of morphine in Melanie's body. Good for Brian and Shirley that it was enough to end her life before they intervened, but–'

'Brian told me she'd been saving it. Going without pain relief to accumulate enough for that final day. Dreadful, isn't it? Suffering to end her suffering. We don't know we're born, do we?'

Gavin gazed for a few seconds without replying. 'Her routine dosage was pretty high, Nat. Going without it would have been far, far from easy... The local doctor, Woodcock. Close friend of the Selby's. What did you make of him?'

'Like I already said, I thought he was a good sort.' Nat stared back, feeling hot. 'Not just that. I believed him, Gavin. He's of the old-school Hippocratic Oath type; everything strictly by the book. I don't think for a moment he did anything he shouldn't have done. Please tell me you're not going to upset the apple cart?'

Gavin threw down his pencil and smiled. 'And ruin my chances of one of your mum's *szarlotka* pies? Nope. Case almost closed.' He shrugged. 'And as you say, Selby's evidence is that Melanie stockpiled the drug.' He stood and plucked his jacket from the back of his chair. 'I hear you and Robbie are going on a road trip. Got time for a pint first?'

Nat was still smiling when Robbie passed her a scrap of paper in the car.

'The postcode,' he said, his first words all day.

'Right, cheers.'

She absently programmed it in and followed the satnav's directions. God, she loved the Rabid Scot. The drink with him had been such a hoot. He was back to his old non-PC ways, teasing her about her growing 'sproglet', noticing a 'definite waddle' already, and hoping Wes fancied fat women.

Though Nat had visited Ruthie at the weekend and had bumped into Gavin then, he reiterated the amazing progress she'd made at the unit, clearly thrilled her return home was on the horizon. Nat wondered whether Heather was still sleeping in Ruthie's bedroom and what would happen when her daughter needed it, but she hadn't wanted to pry. He hadn't mentioned his ex, forgiveness and faith, so neither had she.

It had been interesting to get updates on the cases she'd handled. Larry's hope that George, the mother murderer, would get off lightly wasn't looking good. Even his own psychiatric expert had pronounced him of sound mind, and it turned out he was more of a weasel than he'd first appeared. Larry had hoped for a loss-of-control, spur-of-the-moment type of defence, but days before strangling his mum, George had researched the internet, a 'how to murder your mother and get away with it' type of search. Poor old Larry had taken it badly; he'd decided retirement was overdue.

'So he'll just be sticking to his Christmas job,' Gavin had said, straight-faced. 'Which means I'll still need a freelancer if you fancy?'

Nat came back to the busy traffic and Robbie by her side. He'd taken to scraping his fringe back in a quiff. It suited him. 'I think I might have some sweets in the glove compartment if you fancy?' she said, breaking the silence.

On the basis of sugar being the SS cure to every malady, she'd bought a selection from the newsagents, ranging from Starburst to Smarties for her young companion. She felt stupidly nervous about today's outing; God knows what was going on in his head. Or indeed, in his bowels.

Robbie rummaged, took a packet and said thanks, but returned to his gaze through the passenger window.

Nat reverted to her thoughts. What *did* she fancy workwise? She was in pregnancy limbo and stupefied with boredom, but who knew how she'd feel when the sproglet arrived? What she definitely wanted was a home for her and Wes. Their current options were limited, namely squeezing in with her mouse-like mum, or having more room with Saint Bernard Sidney. Neither proposition was good. As much as Wes liked Anna, he'd hardly want to live with her, especially if he was banished to the tiny box room which was shorter than him. The idea of living full time in the dream-home-cottage was appealing, but it belonged to Sidney. Though he spent periods of time away, his messiness and jabber were exhausting when he wasn't.

Ideally she and Wes wanted to buy, but the problem was ready cash. Hers was still tied up in a Mallorcan bar. Or perhaps spent, or lost, or scattered in the Mediterranean Sea – another unknown. As for Wes, his petition for divorce on the grounds of his wife's unreasonable behaviour had been served, followed by the application to sort out their finances. Andrea had gone worryingly quiet. Her silence was helpful for the former. Wes had instructed a court bailiff to serve the papers, so she couldn't say she hadn't received them. Doing nothing would allow the decree nisi to go through by default. But the finances, including the sale of the house in Cheadle Hulme, downsizing, or at least the release of some equity, needed the Cling-on's co-operation. Nat couldn't see that happening anytime soon.

She glanced again at Robbie. He'd moved on from Fruit Pastilles to chewing his nails. 'Are you okay? Want to talk?' she asked. Then after a minute, 'You know you can change your mind.'

He nodded, so she took that to be a yes. That he was okay. And why the hell not? She'd been amazed by his maturity. His certainty too. Going through the family liaison officer who had looked after him ten years ago, he'd instigated everything himself. The PC had contacted the driver to see if he still wanted to meet and when he'd said yes, he and Robbie had done the rest by email, deciding to meet informally rather than through official channels.

As instructed by the satnav, Nat took the slip road off the motorway at Stockport. 'Are you still okay about meeting on his turf, so to speak?' she asked. She didn't want to fuss, but couldn't help it.

'Yeah, I'm fine,' he replied with a hint of a smile. 'It's where he works; it's not his home. I could hardly do it at my dad's.' He looked at his hands. 'By the way, Chantelle told me what happened when he came to the office. Sorry.'

'It's not your fault,' she said. 'Not your dad's either; not really,' she added, surprising herself. But perhaps it wasn't

Jed's fault, at least not entirely. Since coming back from Mallorca she'd discovered the old proverb was true; everyone said it, but didn't believe it: there *were* two sides to every question.

The satnav spoke again. They had reached their destination, apparently. Nat peered through the windscreen. Oh right; a side street in Stockport between two towering red mills. She sat back. Well, this was a coincidence; she'd been here before. Still, there must be any number of businesses hidden behind the rows of identical windows. Surely?

A horrible sense of déjà vu spreading, she parked up and turned to Robbie, but he'd already climbed out. 'Do you want me to wait here or should I come with you?' she called.

Taking his nod for a 'yes' to the latter, she scrambled from her seat and followed him to the old gated lift shaft. Even before he pressed the button, she knew it would be for the sixth floor. Oh God, really?

The lift came to a clunking stop. 'What did you say the driver was called again?' she asked.

His muttered reply was drowned out by the hum of sewing machines. Not knowing what to say, Nat opened her mouth, but it was too late anyway. She would have recognised that soft owl gaze from a hundred yards, but Mr DeMille was only a few strides away.

'Hello, Robbie,' he said, holding out a trembling hand. 'And Natalie, hello.' He might have been surprised to see her, but his eyes were so magnified behind his thick lenses, it was difficult to judge. 'Thank you both for coming.' He glanced at her. 'Do you...? are you...?'

Nat finally found her voice. 'God, no, I'm just the...' She almost said 'driver', but caught herself just in time. 'I'm Robbie's friend.' She pointed to the staff room. 'Is it okay if I hang around in there while you...?'

He gave a small bow. 'Absolutely, please help yourself to a drink. It's Samira's birthday today, so we have cake.'

She watched the two men walk away. What the...? The sensitive and altruistic Mill Man was also the drunk-driver-killer. Bloody hell. He'd have been imprisoned for sure. Causing death by careless driving when under the influence was definitely a custodial offence. How long had he served?

Yes, she needed a drink; preferably something stronger than squash. She headed for the kitchen, but instead she turned back, walking towards the thrumming sound of the machines. Hiding at the corner of a long window, she watched the women at work beneath the bright strip lights. Some elderly, some young, some brassy-haired, some black. Dressed in dark colours, several ladies wore headscarves, other pink-skinned girls sported shorts and vest tops. But above the steady strum, she heard chatter and laughter.

'A good man,' Jack had said.

Thinking about Jack and his own altruistic tendencies, Nat smiled and shook her head. When she'd discussed her working future with Wes, she'd mentioned the car, saying she'd have to give it back if she left Goldman Law. Wes had put her straight with a wry smile. It had never been a 'company' car; Jack had personally bought it for her, but she wasn't to let on that she knew.

She sniffed back the emotion. Of course, one couldn't compare herself and these ladies, but in a way they were connected; they had been given a chance to work and earn a salary when they'd needed it.

Deciding not to wait up here after all, she texted Robbie: *Take as long as you need. I'm going to listen to the radio. I'll meet you at the car.*

After half an hour he returned. 'Ready to go?' she asked,

noticing the scar on his temple. Then after a mile. 'Was everything okay?'

'Yup,' he replied.

Not a lot to go on, but there was no sign of nail-biting, stuttering or tears. 'Where shall I drop you?' she eventually asked.

'Dad's,' he replied, staring ahead.

'Okey-dokey.' She swallowed. 'Just tell me where I'm going...'

He finally turned to Nat at the Kingsway traffic lights. 'Thank you. You're a really nice person.'

She felt herself flushing. 'I've been named many things, but I'm not sure anyone would recognise that description.' Then after a moment, rubbing her tummy. 'Don't think I won't call the debt in one day with free babysitting!'

'I didn't mean that.' He was still gazing with clear, sincere eyes. 'I meant looking out for me. At work and the driving lessons. With Dad too.'

He went back to the windscreen. 'The lights have changed.' Then after a beat, 'Thing is, I already knew about the money, my damages. You know, through college. But he's my dad, so...'

Nat nodded and drove on. Not exactly a 'fix', but good enough. This young man was brave and bright; he had a great future and he'd deal with it his own way. And it was his private business after all. She was happy with that.

35

FEELINGS

Her foot hard on the accelerator, Nat shot past the Issa and JP service station, so musings about Chen were inevitable. But today she was thinking of him for another reason. Although she was chuffed the police had asked Lewis Foster to attend the station for a formal interview, he was bound to be as slimy as his mother.

What had Jack said at the brunch? That's right: Lewis was blaming the offending paperwork on a 'rogue employee'.

Nat groaned. Yup, she could picture the scene clearly: wearing his expensive suit and equally as expensive smile, Lewis would hold up his hands in surrender. 'Of course I must take the ultimate responsibility, officer, but the manager of DFS Debt Advisers had the day-to-day dealings. If he made unintended mistakes with the documentation, or if he was doing something underhand, which I struggle to believe, it was absolutely without my knowledge...'

Her jaw clenched at the thought. A year or so back, Lewis had been charged for a sexual assault. A woman in a nightclub had had the audacity (in Danielle's view) but the balls (in Nat's) to make a formal complaint about him forcefully pawing her.

Frustratingly, he charmed, smarmed or possibly bribed his way out of it, but what particularly got Nat was his attitude of entitlement.

She blew out the outrage. Perhaps it wasn't so surprising; Lewis had been brought up to believe he could have anything and everything he wanted; why would a girl he fancied for a quick shag near the bins be any different? God, she wished she could stop his meteoric rise and his bloody invincibility, but even if a civil claim was made against him by Michal or others, she just knew he'd wriggle out of it by claiming he wasn't vicariously liable.

'My manager went beyond the scope of his employment duties, and terrible though I feel about it,' he'd say, with a suitably apologetic smile, 'I'm afraid I'm not liable for his actions. But of course you do have the option to sue him. Indeed I encourage you to do so in the interests of fairness...' Goodness knows who the poor fall guy would be.

She sighed. At least Gavin was onto it. Hopefully he'd kick up enough fuss to encourage the police and the Insolvency Service to dig deep, but if all else failed there was the likes of Chen out there, investigative reporters who might be interested in a tip-off. Even a TV journalist? Get the bit between someone's teeth and who knew? Not that she planned to say such a thing to Issa. Today's plan was for a light-hearted, (slightly) boozy lunch, albeit with one baby in utero, the other in a highchair.

'Time out from all the angst,' Issa had said on the telephone; they were to talk about anything but *that*.

Keeping an eye out for road signs, Nat negotiated the Wirral streets. She stroked her bump at the crossroads. It had grown since the start of the week, she was sure, and though the fluttering movements were more pronounced, she still said a silent thanks every time she felt one. She hadn't yet mentioned the pregnancy to Issa, so that would be a starter for ten. She smiled; she and Jose's sister would be baby buddies – who would have thought.

As the roads became wider, the route to Lower Heswell and the Harrow home slotted in like a bolt. The first time she'd visited, she'd been struck by the obvious affluence of the area. Hidden by laurel bushes and tall trees, the Victorian houses were set back in half acre plots, a very far cry from her small childhood home in Oldham.

Turning into the long, leafy road, she shifted in her seat. The last time she came here, she was all but a member of the Harrow family. Should she have travelled by train and met in town instead of offering to chauffeur so Issa could have a few drinks? She blew the apprehension away. It was fine; Issa's parents were still away on their cruise, and anyway she didn't have to step inside the house. She could text to say she was outside in the car.

Wondering which property it was, she drove slowly. Had she ever actually known the number? Or was it baby fug? She'd always looked out for the postbox in the wall next to the iron gates. Her tummy flipped. God, there it was, the scarlet red colour almost hidden by ivy.

She pulled up and turned off the engine. *I'm here!* she texted. *I'll wait in the car.*

Sure, it might appear odd hovering at a safe distance on the road instead of parking in the large driveway, but she could live with it.

For a time there was no reply, so Nat listened to the news headlines before checking her mobile wasn't on mute. After two or three minutes she sent the message again. After another three, she called Issa's number.

Voicemail.

Unsettled and hot, she climbed from the car and peered over the stone wall. Issa's Mini was parked to one side of the pebbly terrace and lights were shining through the bay window. Okay, what now? She tried Issa's phone again. No answer. Maybe she had popped out? She looked over her shoulder. Pop out where, exactly? There were no local shops. And why wasn't Issa answering her mobile? She turned back to the house. Perhaps she was busy with the baby; maybe she was listening for the crackle of tyres or a knock.

With a sigh, Nat locked her Merc and crunched across the drive to the pyracantha-strewn door. The dark wood was a surprise. In her mind she'd remembered it as red. But perhaps that was the postbox. Colour association or false memories, she supposed; the mind could play all sorts of tricks. Lifting the lion-faced knocker she tapped a couple of times, but when there was no answer, a chill of concern settled in. She rapped much harder, then searched for the shrouded doorbell and pressed it.

Again no reply. Strange and unsettling, for sure. Tapping her foot, she stared at her mobile, willing a message to appear. What did one do in these circumstances? Call the police or go home? As if; she wasn't about to do either. The Harrow house was huge; Issa might simply be without her phone in a top bedroom or in the garden. She hammered one last time, then turned to the side gate. It was taller than her, so that was no good. Could she possibly climb around it? Maybe go via next door?

A rattling sound interrupted her inspection of the bushes at the side. Then a hoarse voice, a croaky male voice, called out. 'Hello?'

Her heart thrashing, she retraced her steps to the door. Wearing shorts and a T-shirt, a bare-footed man was standing on the top step. He was still tall and blond, but a blown-up version of the one she remembered.

The word came out clotted. 'Jose.' Trying to hide her obvious shock, she looked down at her feet. She hadn't for a moment expected him to be here. But it wasn't just that; his bony cheeks had been replaced with jowls and his skin was almost yellow; if she'd seen him on the street, she'd have unknowingly walked past him.

He snorted. 'You never could hide your feelings,' he said, turning tail.

She followed him in, her mouth dry from the whammy. Trying not to compare him to the twenty-something skinny bloke in the Harrow family portrait adorning the wall, she took a deep breath. 'Sorry. I just didn't expect to see you here. Issa said you were thinking of coming back, but I didn't know–'

'You're here to see Issa, then?'

'Yes, that was the plan, but if I had...' she began.

She sighed. She was going to say that had she known, then of course she'd have visited him. But what was the point of false civility? Lies, basically. So instead she opted for the truth. 'I should've come to see you in the hospital, Jose. For a long time I didn't know what had happened, but still, when Hugo told me before Christmas... My intentions were good, but I didn't see them through. I'm sorry.'

He smiled thinly. 'It's fine; I wouldn't have welcomed you.' Then after a moment, 'Not just you. I was in a bad place. Hugo got it in the neck every time he visited.' He looked at his trembling hands. 'It didn't stop him persisting, though.'

Feeling a stab of guilt, Nat swallowed. She'd let Hugo down too. 'How is he?' She tried for a smile. 'Still leading the ladies around the dance floor?'

Raking his hair like he used to, Jose returned the smile and for an iota Nat glimpsed *her* Jose inside the fat suit. 'He was good when I left.' He lifted his eyebrows. 'A wife appeared–'

'You're joking. A *wife*?'

'Not only a wife, but a long-standing one. No idea where he'd hidden her all those years. They're buying back the bar when they've sorted the valuation and finances.' He briefly touched Nat's shoulder. 'I left it in his hands, but I guess a cheque will be coming your way fairly soon.'

'The dark horse,' she replied, shelving the thought of her investment and the horrible assumptions she'd made.

Jose appeared to drift, so Nat took a breath to ask after his sister, but he rubbed his face and the focus came back. 'Have you been here for long? The doorbell's bust and I was asleep. The drugs make me tired. So, you're here to see Issa? I didn't know you two were friends...' He seemed to notice Nat's bump for the first time. 'Oh, right. I didn't know,' he said, his face flushing. 'So, yeah, Issa. Where is she? The kitchen probably, it's...Well, of course you know. I'll come too.'

Still shaky from surprise and emotion, Nat listened to the echo of her own heels as she accompanied him along the panelled corridor to the back of the house. Surreal, so surreal to see this man who'd been integral to years of her life. When he'd blanked her after Mallorca, there'd been anger and frustration, but most of all deep, deep hurt; her mum was dangerously ill; he'd abandoned her when she'd most needed him. Then she'd learned about his own illness and the anger had turned to apprehension and guilt.

How did she feel now? Sorrow. Yes, she simply felt sad.

'Issa?' Jose called, pushing a door. 'Are you guys in here?'

Jose's voice interrupted Nat's thoughts. She'd almost forgotten the reason she was there – a 'light-hearted' girl's lunch. Sniffing the sentiment away, she straightened her shoulders, armed her face with a smile and followed him in.

It took a moment to register why the kitchen felt odd. It was the absence of warmth and noise, smell too. Her memory was of a room filled with sunshine, the aroma of cooking, the constant sound of the radio, and of course Harrow's huge presence.

Apparently oblivious to their entrance, Issa was engrossed in a chore at the central island, but she abruptly turned when Jose spoke, her arms stretched as though hiding something behind her.

'Nat's here,' he said again. 'You ignored the front door. She was waiting.'

Her face almost white, Issa stared at them blankly.

Nat rushed to fill the silence. 'It's fine; I was early.' She gestured to Jose. 'And we've had a chance to catch-up so–'

But Jose was stepping towards his sister. 'What are you doing?'

Turning back to the granite, Issa hurriedly piled papers and packets with shaky hands, then clumsily pushed them into a shoebox.

Much like her brother, she raked fingers through her hair and didn't quite meet Nat's gaze.

'So sorry, Nat. Did you call?' She glanced around. 'My phone must still be... Sorry; I was absorbed, I didn't realise the time.' She tried for a smile. 'Harrow's seventieth is coming up. I was sorting stuff for a book of memories. You know what it's like once you start a job like that.' She scooped up the box and held it under her arm. 'Were you waiting long? The doorbell is broken and you can't hear a sound back here. I should have said.' Then blushing, 'Carlos usually alerts me. My own little chime. His nursery is in the front bedroom; he's asleep, or at least I hope...'

'What stuff?' Jose asked.

'Nothing useful.' She peered at her watch. 'Look at the time. Nat and I had better–'

'What stuff, Issa?' Jose said again.

'Some of Dad's old things: school reports, certificates. Nothing I can–'

'Let me see.'

Her face tight and pale, she clutched her treasure to her chest. 'It's just boring stuff, Jose. Nothing I could glue in a scrapbook. I'm going to put it back in mum's wardrobe.' She turned towards Nat, her chestnut eyes pleading. 'Besides, we need to go, don't we? Nat's on a tight timescale...'

Nat dumbly nodded, but Jose had already snatched the shoebox and upturned it on the table. Breathing heavily, he rifled through greeting cards, slim report books, folded parchments and photographs, scattering them with trembling hands until something caught his eye. He finally selected two items, stared for several moments, then thrust them at Nat, snapped around and violently vomited on the floor.

Nat didn't breathe. What the hell had just happened? Almost in slow motion, she turned from Jose's bent, retching figure to what she held in her hands. Photographs. Coloured images with white edging. She stared. The first was of Jose, aged seven or eight, solemnly standing next to a piano in school uniform. The second was an identical pose and expression. But this one wasn't of a lanky young Harrow. The hollow eyes belonged to a face she'd seen recently. This boy was smaller and clearly oriental. There was absolutely no doubt. This photo was of Kenneth Chen.

36

BLESSINGS

The sun-dappled flower beds were showing life: pearly crocus buds and green daffodil tips, sprouting like her stomach. Nat hadn't sat on the small bench under the kitchen window since mowing the lawn before Christmas. It had been a strange request from Anna, but she'd wanted everything to be perfect for the arrival of Philip, his two kids and pregnant wife. Though Nat wouldn't have admitted it to another living soul, she had cried as she stared at her handiwork. Tears as green as the grass. Her sister-in-law, lovely as she was, had two perfect children and another on the way; Nat had nothing: no boyfriend, no prospect of ever becoming a mum. It had felt so unfair. The sheer envy had turned to petulant anger, so she'd picked up a terracotta pot and hurled it on the patio. It hadn't broken, but the dry earth had risen on the wind, much like her dad's ashes.

She now put a hand to the base of her bump. Savouring the flutter, she silently expressed gratitude to someone for her blessings. Who was she thanking? She wasn't sure – her mum's God, she supposed. After years of being agnostic, it suddenly seemed important to believe in something, not for herself, but for her unborn baby.

Because sometimes life was dark, very dark.

A week had passed but thoughts of Jose and Issa had been a constant cycle in her mind. She told herself she didn't know for sure what those solemn, hollow-eyed poses meant, but deep, horrible dread told her otherwise. Rooted to the spot in the Harrow kitchen, she had watched the siblings. Like a silent movie, the scene and the characters had fallen mute. Surrounded by the reeking vomit, Jose had dropped to his knees. Issa had gone to him, but instead of comforting him as Nat had expected, she'd assailed him with her hands, slapping him repeatedly around his head and his shoulders. Sound had broken through then, not just Issa's animalistic howl, but another, more distant noise. A baby's keen. Stupid though it was, Nat had thought it was hers until reason kicked in. Little Carlos, of course. So she'd found herself sprinting down the hallway, following the shrill cry up the stairs, finally finding him sitting up in his cot, his features red and angry, a strange replica of his mother's downstairs.

She'd scooped him up, trying to give him some assurance that everything was fine, even though it was far, far from that. Then she'd taken in the fruity odour. A poo, yes a poo. He'd needed changing, so with fumbling fingers she'd tried to work it all out. Why hadn't she handled a bloody nappy before? Idiotic in the context of what was going on downstairs, she'd had to breathe deeply, force herself to keep calm. Baby mat on the floor, wipes and fresh clothes. Then little Carlos himself, lifting his legs in one hand to clean him with the other. How did the nappy work? And barrier cream, should she use it? His little bum looked pink and sore, but it seemed wrong to apply it. This wasn't her baby's bottom.

Oh God, oh God, what had those photographs meant?

She had changed him eventually, his soiled vest too, but still Carlos cried. Hunger; that must be it. So she'd crept down to the kitchen, overwhelmed by the responsibility of holding a flailing baby and fearful of what she'd find there. The rank-smelling room was empty, so she'd slipped the wailing child in a bouncy chair and flung open the fridge then the cupboards, frantically searching for milk.

The memory of Issa's words had hit her at that point: the poor woman's breast milk had dried up because of stress. How on earth would she cope now? But Nat had to cast it aside. This baby, this little man and his hunger was all what mattered right then. Formula milk, she knew that much, but not how to make it from scratch. She'd stared at the tin but the instructions had blurred. Her heart was charging, loud in her ears. She was pregnant and didn't know how to change a baby's fucking nappy, let alone how to feed one. But she got there in the end, finding a sterilised bottle and a latex teat from a steamer, adding powder and lukewarm water from the kettle, hoping for the best.

Not knowing what else to do, she'd stayed in the kitchen with Carlos on her knee. Her pulse finally slowing, she'd chatted to him, enjoying the feel of his damp fingers as he explored her face. But then she'd smelled something else above the puke stench. Burning? Yes, definitely burning, so she'd shadowed the whiff to the lounge and looked in.

Their hands entwined, the siblings had been sitting on the old Chesterfield settee. They hadn't turned from the snapping fire in the grate, or acknowledged Nat's presence. Issa had eventually reached out for her son, but neither of them spoke or focused on Nat, so she'd left, knowing she was no longer needed.

Bringing herself back to the hesitant spring sunshine, Nat stood. She waited until a woozy spell passed, then looked at her watch. Since breaking the news of her pregnancy, Wes's mum had taken to phoning her regularly for a chat and she'd suggested a ladies' lunch out in Cheadle or Didsbury. She hadn't met Anna and thought it would be nice to come in by train and share a bottle or two of fizz to celebrate 'happy times'. Her mum had been thrilled with the idea, but she'd insisted on making the lunch herself rather than dining out, hence Nat's escape to the garden.

It was still only eleven thirty; she wasn't due to collect Kath from the station until twenty past twelve. How to fill the next hour? She'd offered to help her mum several times, but Anna had politely declined. Nat smiled wryly. They both knew, for cordial relations, it was better for her to butt out. Which was absolutely fine; she wasn't doing *any* butting in any more. Not in kitchens, offices, pubs, courts or cafés. The human race was safe!

Nat had already planned on buying flowers, a huge bunch each for Anna and Kath which she'd present with a flourish at the end of the meal as a small thank you for their support and love. Not everyone had mums like that; look at Andrea. And what about Jose's mother? Was Chen's allegation, albeit made through JP's lips, really true? Had she known for all those years and turned a blind eye?

Nat shook the repellent thought away. Right, the bouquets; she'd collect them now and hide them in the boot of her car. Opening the back door, she stepped into the sweet-scented kitchen and spoke to her mum's profile.

'I'm just popping to the village before collecting Kath. Is there anything you need?'

Nat gazed at the cluttered worktops. Clearly not. Glossy pies and pastries, two different green salads, and bright buffalo tomatoes covered in mozzarella and basil leaves. Not to mention whatever was inside the tureens. A feast fit for the five thousand already. She hoped Kath would be very, very hungry.

Her mum briefly turned from her task with an icing bag. 'No thanks, love. Don't be late for Kath.'

'Don't worry, I won't. See you in a bit.'

Nat pulled the door closed and gave a little shiver. Funny, that; it was colder at the front than at the back of the house. As she climbed in the Merc, her phone rang. Expecting it to be Anna with a request for a vital ingredient after all, she scooped it from her pocket. Oh God, an unknown number; save for the call from Mr Hirsch, they had never been good. She took a quick breath. 'Natalie Bach speaking.'

'Hi. It's Cassandra. Cassandra Woodcock? I'm sorry to bother you at such short notice, but I'm in the area and I wondered if we could meet briefly?'

The anxiety upped several notches. It had to be about Max. The idea that he'd assaulted Cassandra was something she had shelved. She felt bad about it, but what could she do? Warn Jack and Verity? Tell Wes not to take him on as a Goldman Law partner because he was a violent brute and a liar when this was only speculation?

She glanced at the dashboard. Time was ticking. She'd suggest another day. But Cassandra had filled the silence. 'To be honest I'm already in the café where we met last time. Could you spare ten minutes?'

Inwardly groaning, Nat agreed, ended the conversation, then called Kath. 'I've had an SOS out of the blue from a friend. She needs a few minutes of my time. I shouldn't be late, but I wanted to warn–'

'Don't rush for me,' Kath boomed. As usual Nat had to hold the phone away from her ear. 'A friend in need, as they say. Tell you what, I'll just stay on the train and get off at Didsbury, then I can nip into Goldman's to see my youngest. It'll be a laugh to see the surprise on his face.'

'Great. I'll collect you from Wes's office as soon as I'm finished.'

Nat tapped her fingers on the steering wheel. Should she

alert her mum to a possible lunch delay? Nope, it would only add to her flapping. She smiled. It was nice agitation though; as Anna had put it at six thirty when she'd opened Nat's curtains, 'It's not every day you get to meet the other grandma for the first time. A happy day, Skarbie, one to remember.'

Humming with Friday chatter, the Roasted Coffee Lounge was pretty full, most tables taken and none, at first glance, with a single guest. Nat's gaze slipped to the sofas. No Cassandra there either. She reached for her mobile. Had she taken too long or assumed the wrong café? But she heard her name called.

'Natalie. I'm over here.' Next to the loos at the back, Cassandra stood from her wall table. 'Thanks so much for coming.' She nodded to her companion sat opposite her. 'You remember Lucy?'

Automatically holding out her hand, Nat tried to hide her surprise. 'Yes, of course I do. Hi, Lucy. How are you?'

Stiffly accepting the handshake, Lucy Selby rose too. As though unsure how to reply, she opened her mouth, then closed it again. She seemed younger than ever, pink-cheeked, blue-eyed and very, very sad.

Alarm spreading, Nat sat. Oh God; had something happened to her parents?

Cassandra reached for the girl's hand, but looked at Nat, her expression severe. 'Lucy wants to speak to one of the solicitors. In fact both of them,' she said in a low voice. 'She has for a quite a while.' Her eyes flickered. 'I persuaded her not to, but she's got to the point where she–'

'Where I can't bear it any longer,' Lucy blurted. 'I can't, I just can't.' She thumped her forehead with a fist. 'I know Caz says it's for the best and I don't want to get anyone into more trouble but I–'

'It's fine, Lucy,' Cassandra interrupted. 'But we need to be...' She put a finger to her lips.

Nat stared at the two women, one tearful and exhausted, the other pale and tense. What the hell were they here for?

Cassandra continued to speak in hushed tones. 'So I suggested it would be best to talk to you first. Before Lucy goes to the lawyers.' She rubbed the table. 'Or to the police.'

Nat was glad of the strained silence as she tried to catch up. Lucy was staring, her desperate eyes huge with tears. There was something she knew; it was clearly bursting to come out.

Cassandra squeezed Lucy's fingers again. She peered at Nat steadily. 'Can we speak to you in confidence?'

Bloody hell; Nat knew what that meant: off the record, a secret, a potential Chinese wall. Nonetheless she found herself nodding. She leaned towards the torn, unhappy child. 'What do you need to say, Lucy?'

No answer for moments. Then her whole body seemed to deflate. 'It was me,' she replied, her voice a tiny whisper. 'I did it; I killed Mel.' She dropped her head, her shoulders shaking as she silently sobbed.

Nat passed her a wad of serviettes and waited for more.

Blowing her nose eventually, Lucy took a tremulous breath. 'Mel. Mel's body...' she began again quietly. She frowned, seeming to search for a word. 'It twitched. And I had faithfully promised her that if the morphine didn't work I'd...' She wept again. 'So when she moved, I put the pillow over her face for ages. I was scared to stop pressing. Then later Mum came into her bedroom by chance and she called Dad.'

Nat nodded, her own tears threatening. Of course; it was obvious in retrospect. Brian hadn't been covering for his wife; they'd both been protecting their only living child.

Lucy roughly wiped her cheeks. 'It was awful. Mum and Dad had no idea of Mel's plans. They were so horribly shocked and upset. Then they felt guilty, wanting to know why Mel hadn't confided in them.' She gazed at Nat. 'Mel knew they would've tried to talk her out of it. And she didn't want to put them through more... agonising, I suppose. They already blamed themselves for her condition.' She swallowed. 'Anyway, after a while Dad said that I wasn't to worry, that he'd take the blame. He said he was the man of the family, that Mel was now in a better place and that he'd be happy to take the punishment. Mum insisted that I should agree and so I did.' She thumped her forehead again. 'But then Mum said she'd done it and they both went to prison. It was awful, unbearable.' She glanced at Cassandra. 'I felt so guilty and wanted to confess to make it all right, but Caz said to do nothing, to wait and see what happened. She said Mum and Dad would be angry if I told the truth, that their attempts to protect me would be for nothing. She said they wanted to give me–'

'The life they couldn't give Mel,' Cassandra finished for her. She looked at her young friend intently. 'And that's still true, Lucy. Which is why you shouldn't–'

'But they're suddenly so old and frail, Caz. They walk around the house like ghosts. They've had a taste of being locked up and they're scared. I can see it in their eyes. I'm sorry, Caz, I won't say anything about you knowing, I promise, but I can't bear it any longer. Sometimes I can't breathe from the guilt. Not for Mel, but for them.'

'Natalie?' Cassandra was now looking at her. 'What's your advice?'

Nat blew out. God, 'advice' was a strong word. Wondering what mundane conversations the other diners were having, she glanced around the café. Her guidance, her counsel, her help? Well, it might all go pear-shaped, but what had Gavin said?

'Case almost closed.' He was hopeful the major charges against the Selby's would be dropped. Perhaps her duty as a person, never mind a solicitor, was to report a crime to the police, but from what the expert had said, Mel was already dead before the suffocation, so there was no 'crime'.

A customer was passing, so she waited until the toilet door clicked to, then turned to the young woman. She didn't want to get her hopes up, breach client confidentiality, or get Gavin into trouble, but she had to lend a hand somehow. Clearing her throat, she found her voice. 'I too think you should wait, Lucy.' She bit her lip. 'You need to understand that I'm speculating here, but there's a possibility Melanie was already dead before you did anything, which means–'

'But she... trembled. I saw it.'

Cassandra touched her arm. 'Even after a person is declared dead, movements and sounds can still occur, Lucy. Muscles relaxing, the release of gasses, that type of thing...' her voice trailed off.

'Which would mean you didn't "kill" Mel, Lucy.' Nat spread her hands. 'We know there was a huge amount of morphine in her body from the stockpiling. My guess is that was enough for the end and if the experts agree, the charges against your parents will be dropped, or at least the major ones.'

Cassandra nodded. 'See, Lucy? You just need to hold on. You did nothing wrong and everything will work out completely fine. Always remember it's what Mel wanted, what she planned. To end it all, to be in a better place. And she is now, as painlessly as was possible. She loved us all dearly; she didn't want to get any of us into trouble.' She peered at her face. 'Yes? Are we good now?'

Realising the time, Nat stood. 'I'm really sorry but I have a lunch date and I have to collect my boyfriend's mum.'

Lucy's eyes widened. 'Sure, of course.'

Nat cringed; the word 'boyfriend' still gave her a small frisson, but the teenager probably thought she was far too ancient to have one. Oh well, who cared. What had her mum said? Today was a happy day. She smiled at her. 'I wish you the best of luck and future happiness, Lucy. You and your parents deserve it.'

Accompanying Nat to the door, Cassandra stepped outside and lifted her arms for a hug. 'Thank you, Natalie, you're a good person,' she said, her face finally filling with healthy colour. She softly put a hand on Nat's bump. 'Good luck with the pregnancy. It's shaping up beautifully. A little lady is my guess.'

The breeze cooled Nat's cheeks. 'Thank you,' she replied, vaguely aware a customer was approaching, but stuck to the spot, lost in thought.

What did Lucy just say? That Brian and Shirley Selby hadn't known about Mel's suicide plans? Mel lived in their house. With her disability, how had she stockpiled and hidden the drug? And, not having her usual dosage of pain relief, how had she concealed her severe discomfort, if not agony, from her parents? Had anyone other than her little sister known? It was a massive onus to put on a teenager.

Finally registering she was blocking the doorway, she stood to one side to allow the glaring woman in, then turned back to Cassandra. '*She loved us all dearly,*' she'd just said. '*She didn't want to get any of us into trouble.*'

Us.

'Mel was your friend?' she asked her.

Cassandra looked at Nat steadily. 'My best friend since primary school. Thanks again.'

37

SINS

Still tremulous from a mix of slithering sensations, Nat parked behind Goldman Law's offices and sent her mum a text.

Really sorry but we're running late. Now in Didsbury and collecting Kath from the office.

Don't worry, Anna replied. *The* zrazy *took me longer than I thought. No need to rush.*

Nat stared at the screen. Flipping heck, Kath was truly the guest of honour; her mum's beef roulade was usually reserved for first-born Perfect Philip. She smiled; it must indeed be a happy day.

Though an emergency was unlikely, she climbed out of the car to check she wasn't blocking anyone in. Six months ago, she'd had a spat with Wes over this very issue. The memory of his handsome, moody face made her chuckle.

It felt strange to slip into the rear entrance of the corner building and take in the old aromas. She sniffed. Today it was oranges, coffee and the lavatories, a combination that would have made her nauseous last month, but was acceptable now. She trotted up the first flight of stairs, pausing to let the dizziness pass before taking the next. It wasn't until she was standing at the conference room door that she thought of Max. She'd forgotten he used it these days. How did she feel about seeing him? Her emotions were so confused after what had happened this morning, she no longer knew what was real or imaginary. Did Max assault Cassandra? Did he blithely lie about his innocence? And what about Cassandra? Was she really the clingy, possessive girlfriend he'd described? One who threatened to expose a sex tape? More to the point after today: '*My best friend since primary*.' Would a 'best friend' allow another to be in considerable pain while she saved up the lethal dose? Indeed, was the drug stockpiled? Or did Cassandra supply or even administer it to end Melanie Selby's life?

Some probable, all possible, but what did Nat know.

She shook her head. It was so difficult to judge what went on beneath people's faces, that facade which hid emotions, evasions, lies. And was there such a thing as 'the truth'? No; it was incredibly subjective and everyone had their own spin on it – one only needed to read through a controversial Twitter feed to see that. Then there was imagined truth. JP's story had clearly been very real in his mind, but she guessed it had been skilfully planted by Chen. Who knew why? Perhaps he couldn't face making the allegations himself; maybe he hoped to rattle Harrow's cage enough for a confession, or find other victims through his exposé. Or perhaps nothing had happened back then at all. Maybe Harrow was just a kindly piano tutor who'd taken a photograph. But what about Jose? Why was there an identical image of him? She didn't want to dwell on his reaction and why he had vomited.

Taking a deep breath, she opened the meeting room door. It was empty but a steaming coffee, thick-framed spectacles and an open folder were on the table, like the *Invisible Man*. Sitting in her old chair, she peered at the file, then turned a few pages, quickly scanning the latest.

Dwayne, the young lad who'd been tasered, was now pursuing a claim for a racially motivated attack, a hate crime, no less. She whistled softly as she read. Poor PC Plod. His career in the police force was ending with a loud and public bang. She glanced up to see Jack watching her silently from the door. His eyes were electric blue and, for the first time ever, she wondered if he really did need those trademark glasses.

'So, what did this poor copper do to get on your wrong side?' she asked lightly, suddenly remembering the time.

'I thought you'd have worked it out by now.'

She smiled. 'Ah, so there is a reason?'

'There's always a reason, Natalie.'

Going back to the paperwork, she flicked through the pages as the pieces of the puzzle snapped into place. 'The taser PC was based at Wilmslow,' she murmured. She looked at Jack. 'Julian's case. You asked me to find out the name of the arresting officer. I'm not sure if I ever found out–'

'PC Abbot.'

She returned to the file and searched for the newspaper article she'd printed off the internet, the one which reported the outcome of the PCC's investigation. She tapped it with a pencil, Savage-like. 'Ah. The taser PC and the guy who arrested Julian are one and the same.' She smiled thinly. 'The young officer who didn't want to let Julian's arrest go because of the name Goldman. The one who dug and dug until he found something.' She squeezed her mind back to a conversation with Jack last year. 'A long story about bad blood, you said. You never did get around to telling it to me.'

Jack sat down. 'The sins of the father. Not mine, but Abbot's father, Detective Inspector Abbot. I acted for a client who made allegations of corruption against him. I had no doubt they were true.' He slipped his glasses back on. 'Like all bad cops, he took early retirement and a full pension, and to add to his satisfaction, he made a malicious complaint to the Law Society about me. It was rejected eventually, but you know how long these things take. It was... upsetting, both professionally and personally, so I'm sure he dined out on the tale for years. But the son. Well, you know more than anyone he made my life hell last year. Not just mine, but Julian's, Aisha's, Catherine's. My family.' He smiled grimly. 'And I'm glad to do the same for him.'

Nat inwardly sighed. Did Jack ever play by the rules? Still, she didn't know if he was putting ideas into Dwayne's head or words into his mouth. The young man might well have a genuine claim over and above the one for his injuries; if that was the case, it should indeed be pursued with fervour. If not; well, there wasn't a lot she could do about it now.

'I'd better go. I have two mothers coming for lunch,' she said with raised eyebrows. 'Who would have thought.' She pecked Jack on his cheek. 'See you soon and...' she cast a last glance at her filing cabinet. Should she ask him to tread carefully with her other cases? Nope; there was absolutely no point, '... be good.'

'I hope Anna's doing the catering,' she heard as the door clicked behind her.

Picturing her mum's kitchen delicacies, she glanced at Catherine's office. Should she pop in and say hi? On her and Wes's arrival at the brunch, Catherine had been sweet and charming, but had barely spoken to Nat after that. Had she given her and her bump a wide berth? Nat wasn't sure; she wanted to be friendly, she wanted to say sorry about her dreadful losses at some point, but would that be appropriate right now? Unsure, she shuffled her feet. To knock or not? A blast of conversation decided it for her. Catherine was either with a client or on the phone. Phew; a one-to-one could be shelved for now.

Bracing herself for another challenge, Nat tip tapped down the stairs to the first floor. Sharon was bound to have a thousand questions. She felt stupidly nervous; she hadn't rubbed shoulders with her, Emilia or the bench boys for over three months. The weeks had flown. The last time she'd stood anxiously at this entrance, she'd just learned that Ruthie had been shot. But her little friend had healed, thank God; she was now back home, eager to return to school after the Easter break.

Taking a breath, Nat swiped herself in, but she needn't have worried: the open-plan area was almost empty. She smiled wryly. How out of touch was she? It wasn't only a Friday lunchtime, it was end of the month payday, everyone on a high for the weekend, shopping or in the pub, enjoying their wages.

Christine was holding the fort on reception, so Nat spent a few moments catching up with her news. Her son's wife was expecting a baby; it turned out she would become a grandma the same month as Nat's debut. Flipping heck, they were around the same age. 'Who should be feeling ancient here?' Nat asked. 'You or me?'

'Probably old Granny here,' Christine replied. 'But I'll get all the nice bits, then hand him or her back. It sounds a good trade to me.'

Nat made for Wes's office. What, exactly, were the non-nice bits of parenthood? Her thoughts on the matter hadn't got any further than the birth. She peeped around Sharon's pod. Empty. Smiling at the thought of how disappointed her old secretary would be to miss out on the visit, she knocked at Wes's door and opened it. But she stopped in her tracks. Their faces both stony, Kath and Wes were sitting either side of his desk.

'What's up?' she asked, stepping forward to see what they were looking at. A mobile? What on earth...?

Wes turned and silently passed it to her.

She looked at the screen. Oh God, a text, a text from Andrea. Like an unexpected slap, the name winded her even before she read the message.

I meant what I said, Wesley. If you're not here by two o'clock, you will be sorry, very sorry.

Nat's heart thrashed. 'What does she mean?' She read it again, then looked up at Wes. 'She's spoken to you too?'

'Twelve minutes ago,' Kath replied with tight lips. She nodded at Wes. 'He stood firm, he told her he wasn't going.'

'Going where?'

'To the house.'

Wes's jaw, his expression, his whole stance was rigid. 'I wouldn't have answered but she'd changed her number or called from somewhere else.'

'Then nothing happened until this text a couple of minutes ago,' Kath added, taking the phone. Her features heavy with anger, she peered intently at Nat. 'He should ignore it, Natalie. She's a manipulative bitch who's playing him again.' She turned back to Wes. 'No more of her games, son. Don't let her, I beg you. Look what happened last time.'

Seeming to shake himself, he stood to give Nat his seat, then he stared through the window. 'Exactly,' he said, rubbing his face. 'Look what *did* happen the last time. If I hadn't turned up, she could've died. She might do something stupid again.'

Mother and son looked at Nat, the C in yet another triangle. But she felt breathless, her pulse racing. She couldn't think, let alone decide. Trying to clamber through the sludge in her mind, she spoke eventually. 'Two o'clock. What time is it now?'

'Nearly half past,' Wes replied, pacing the room.

Kath gripped his arm. 'You have to stand firm, boy. You have Natalie and a new baby on the way. Andrea is the past; they are your future.'

His expression torn, Wes stared and nodded.

His mum caught him again. 'I know you're thinking of the boys, but Matty and Dylan are adults now, Wesley. Before long they'll be living their own lives, which is how it should be. You have to live yours too. Give in this time, and she's won forever. She'll know she has the power to do it again and again.' Her mouth was set as she glared. 'Listen to your mother. You know I'm right, son.'

Desperation in his eyes, he looked at Nat. 'If she did something stupid, was harmed or injured, I'd never forgive myself.' He paused. 'Neither would my sons.'

Breathing through the nausea, Nat attempted to focus on what was happening here. Andrea; Andrea. Was this a hoax or would she really do something extreme? Like Kath, her instinct was to ignore it and call her bluff. But this was a woman who'd had the gall, the guts or the madness to throw herself down the stairs.

'What about calling the police?' she asked. 'Would they go if we said it was an emergency? A potential self-harming situation? They could check all was fine, intervene, call an ambulance if they had to.'

No one replied for a beat. Then the silence was broken by a screech and the blare of a car horn outside.

Kath abruptly scraped back her chair. She nodded as though making a decision. 'No. I'll go,' she said firmly. 'The police wouldn't get there in time, and besides that woman has wasted enough of their resources. There are people with real problems out there.' She dipped down to Nat. 'You're so pale. Are you all right, love?' Then to Wes, her tone angry. 'Get your priorities right, son. Natalie doesn't look well; she's having your child. This evil has to stop, right now.' She held out her hand. 'Keys, Wesley. Don't nag me about insurance.' Frowning deeply, she glowered at him. 'It's an emergency, remember?'

Scooping up her huge handbag she bustled from the room. Nat's eyes caught the two bottle bags she'd left on the floor, but the walls were closing in. She heard Wes's worried voice, 'Nat? Natalie?' Then everything went black.

~

A lovely smell. Lily of the valley or jasmine, Nat thought. Then she tuned into a voice. Catherine's. What was she doing here?

'How long has she been out for? I think it would be sensible to call an ambulance,' she was saying.

It took moments to focus on Wes's crumpled face and more to realise they were talking about her. What the...? Swallowing, she tried to shake the haziness away. She was still sitting in Wes's chair; he was crouched at the front, Catherine standing beside him.

She'd fainted. Yes, that was it. She'd passed out for a moment.

'No. Don't call an ambulance, please. I'm fine,' she said, remembering what had happened. The text from Andrea, strangely out of the blue after weeks of silence. The woman's implied threat to harm herself. Then the sudden rush of her own anxiety and fear.

Taking the proffered glass of water, Nat tried to sip. Her hand was shaking. Not just her hand, her whole body was trembling. From the panic, that was all; she was fine, wasn't she? No, something was wrong, something was definitely wrong. Her inner thighs felt sticky, her knickers were damp. She caught Catherine's eye.

'An ambulance is too embarrassing, but I think I should–'

Catherine nodded, understanding. 'Drive her to the Alexandra, Wesley. I'll call Mr Hirsch or a colleague and say you're on your way.'

Wes stood, his expression lost. 'Okay.' Then after a moment, 'Mum has taken my car.'

Catherine squeezed Nat's hand and smiled. 'Even better, I'll drive us.' She glanced at Wes. 'You can sit with Nat in the back.

I'll bring it round. See you at the door in two minutes,' she said, leaving the room.

Nat raised her eyes to Wes. The grief was there; already there in her chest. She was losing the baby, wasn't she. On this 'happy day'.

His eyes shiny, he held out his hands. 'Can you stand? Shall I help you up or...?'

'No, it's fine. I can walk.'

Yes, the sensation of leaking was palpable as she stood. She glanced at Wes's worried face. She wanted to howl at the injustice, but she had to stay strong, walk through the inquisitive eyes of the office with her head held high and pretend her world wasn't imploding.

Catherine was waiting in her SUV at the front. 'Hirsch is at his rooms in Bramhall today,' she commented once they were in. 'We'll be there before you know it.' An unimpressed driver leaned on his horn, but she smoothly slipped the car between the heavy lunchtime traffic.

Taking in the distinct smell of dogs, Nat rested against Wes's shoulder, closed her eyes and tried to float back into the faint's emptiness. The hopelessness was easier that way. She couldn't focus on Jose and Issa, the Selby's and Lucy right now, but she hung on to the certainty that their pain was infinitely worse than hers. Thrumming almost silently, the car softly swayed along its journey, then abruptly stopped. Surprised they had reached Bramhall already, Nat lifted her head.

'Are we...' she began, but Catherine was turning from the driver's seat and looking at Wes with a questioning expression.

'Should we stop, Wesley?' she asked.

Nat looked through the window. Their lights flashing, police vans and other marked vehicles were parked along the opposite pavement. And if she wasn't mistaken, there was the sound of a distant siren. A crime needing backup?

Leaning forward, she glanced at the street both ways. There were no cars nor an injured pedestrian, so it wasn't a road traffic accident. She followed Wes's gaze. Uniformed people were milling at the front of a regency style house and passers-by had stopped to watch. Mesmerised, she stared too. The front door was opening. A woman in a green shirt appeared and lifted her arm to wave in... an ambulance.

Bloody hell; an ambulance. Someone was hurt. And it was parking next to... a black Mercedes.

Catherine's words to Wes finally landed. Her sweat turning to ice, Nat snapped around to his face. She had never been to his Cheadle Hulme home, but even before she took in his strained expression, she knew this was it.

Catherine spoke again. 'Wesley? Should we–'

He cleared his throat. 'It's fine, Catherine. Drive on.'

As the car sped away, Nat turned to the rear window. Andrea. Oh God. What had she done? And why now after weeks of silence?

Looking down at her stomach, realisation finally hit. She knew exactly why Andrea had taken action today of all days. Like Cassandra had done this morning, she touched her belly with a soft hand. It felt too, too much like a spell, a malevolent curse. Not by the young doctor but the customer who'd glared at her in the café doorway. Nat had been distracted by her conversation with Cassandra, but even from her peripheral vision she should have recognised her. Blonde-haired and blue-eyed. And staring with undisguised fury at her bump.

38

HONEST

The cottage kitchen was warm, the sense of love and friendship even warmer.

'So basically, you pissed your pants.'

Ignoring Gavin's comment, Nat turned to Heather. 'Not wishing to upset the apple cart and all that, but why on earth do you put up with him?'

Heather laughed. 'Good question.' She put a finger on her chin. 'Let me think very hard–'

'So many qualities, she's spoiled for choice.' Gavin grinned. 'Good looks, height, talent, huge–'

'Ego,' Nat finished for him. 'It was fluid, actually. Turns out it can happen in pregnancy and it even has a name.'

With only a hint of a smile, Mr Hirsch had told her what the technical term was. She tried to recall. Flipping heck, baby brain or what? It rhymed with something equally unappetising. Oh that was it. 'Got it. Leukorrhea.'

'Oh, that's all right then.' Gavin swigged back his pint. 'It was *fluid*. That sounds so much better.' He reached over and squeezed his ex's hand. 'Next time I have ten of these, it's fluid, my love, most definitely not piss.'

Inhaling the delicious food aromas, Nat shook her head and smiled. Only Gavin Savage could tease her about a pregnancy scare and get away with it. The fluid had actually been vaginal discharge, ugly words she was definitely not going to use in front of him, but even if it had been hot love juice from Hawaii, she didn't care. It wasn't blood; it had not been a miscarriage.

She pointed at Gavin's beer glass. 'Only ten? You're slacking, Gav. Did you know that it wasn't until 1982 that women were entitled to buy drinks in English pubs without fear of being refused service?'

He turned to Heather. 'See how easily she did that? Changing the subject?'

Nat laughed. 'And God knows how the likes of you and Wes would have coped if women hadn't been given the right to enter the legal profession in 1919.'

Gavin squinted. 'The Sex Disqualification (Removal) Act, I believe. The year after you birds had been politically enfranchised by the Right to Vote.' He clinked Nat's tumbler. 'So how's the rampant feminist coping without the daily double gin?'

She threw a prawn cracker and rubbed her bump. Feminism and gin seemed a long time ago. The birth was inching closer, but she swung from complaining that the pregnancy was taking forever, to a panicky need to slow it down.

Strange though it was, her struggle with baby Carlos was more often in her thoughts than his mum and uncle's blank faces as they'd stared at the flames. Perhaps her instinct was blocking the traumatic trip out. A bloody good thing too; she didn't want to dwell on how potentially wrong she'd been about Harrow, or what those photographs had actually meant. The 'blocking' had been helped by Issa and Jose themselves, as they hadn't been in touch. She'd sent messages to Issa from time to time saying, 'Hope everything's okay' or 'Please feel free to get in touch if you want to', but she suspected she was now C in that particular triangle, the person who knew a terrible secret neither A nor B wanted to admit, even to themselves.

Holding a large wok, Wes turned from the hot plate. 'I hope you're all hungry.'

He dished out the sizzling steak into Nat and Heather's bowls, then spooned a tiny amount in Gavin's. 'If it's overcooked, it isn't my fault.' He gestured to the Aga. 'When Nat and I buy our place, we're not having one of these bastards.'

'Here we go again, blaming piss on fluids, chewy food on the hob.' Gavin deftly scooped up his beef and noodles with his chopsticks, chewed and swallowed, then pushed his dish towards Wes. 'Yup. Bloody delicious. You may spoon in the rest.'

Both women stared. 'Food critic at Chester,' Wes explained. 'If it didn't pass the Savage test, it wasn't worth eating.'

Gavin cupped his mouth theatrically. 'Don't tell Wes, but my standards were very low.'

Wes lifted an eyebrow. 'Did Gav never tell you about his little column in the local rag, Heather?'

'Not so little, thank you.' He snorted. 'How else was a poor laddie from Glasgow going to eat?'

Nat laughed and shook her head. Free food for writing reviews? Only Savage could have been so ingenious. And have the balls to ask. He shovelled in another mouthful. 'Aye, the cooking skills were a surprise to us all. We had no idea that Hughsie had even more talent than his left foot.' He turned to Heather. 'Course I don't need to tell Nat, she was drooling at him from the sidelines, but Wes was almost as good as me at law college...'

Listening to Gavin's prattle about his and Wes's sporting prowess, Nat glanced at Heather. She must have heard the same stories many times; Nat had to remind herself that she wasn't his new woman, but his old one, his ex. Nat was the new girl in the foursome who were chatting, laughing and eating dinner on a balmy May evening. The fourth used to be Andrea, the Cling-on who'd clung on, as only she could.

She glanced at Wes's grin. Did he mull about his ex-wife as much as she did? She supposed it would fade with time, but for a period she had almost believed the woman was capable of casting spells, maledictions and curses. Perhaps she still did in a way; Andrea's ghost was definitely loitering and creating chilly shadows. Still, there was humour, even if it was bleak. Gavin wasn't holding back on the quips, nor was Kath. Wes's mum had earned her entitlement to joke; she'd been the one who'd found Andrea swinging from the bannister with a cord around her neck; she'd been the one who'd struggled to hold her up whilst calling the emergency services.

'Try dialling 999 with your chin,' she'd said to Nat when they'd finally rearranged their ladies lunch. 'It's not easy, I'll tell you that for nothing.'

Yes, the Cling-on had clung on in the ambulance, but she'd died later in the hospital. Kath had travelled with her and stayed for some time.

'Just to make sure she'd really gone,' she'd said when Anna left the kitchen. 'Oh, I know one shouldn't speak ill of the dead, but I have to be honest with someone, Natalie. I can't say it to Wes and Joe doesn't listen. That woman was evil; I'm glad she's finally departed for good. There. Now top up my glass before your mum comes back in.'

The aroma of sweet pastry brought Nat back to the present. She reminded Wes about the apple pie in the Aga, then leaned towards Heather. 'How's Ruthie? Is she happy to be back at school?'

'She's great. They suggested leaving it until the new academic year, but she was itching to go back, so…' She glanced at Gavin. 'She's like her dad; basking in the attention.' Turning the stem of her glass, she paused for a beat. 'It's almost as though the shooting never happened.'

Her face stilled and Nat wondered about the 'almost'. And the 'shooting', as she called it, no euphemism there. Could she and Gavin ever reconcile their faith and forgiveness issues? It had been inappropriate to ask, but Chantelle had mentioned that Gavin was back in the flat above the office. When Wes invited his old pal for dinner, he'd joked, 'Nat says she doesn't like triangles, so bring someone with you, preferably female and not over seventy.'

'Bach has been telling tales about my silver surfer harem, has she? To be honest, I'm spoiled for choice,' Gavin had apparently replied, but he'd turned up with Heather, who was as pretty, pleasant and smiley as she'd always been. She and Gavin seemed affectionate, too. But who knew what was going on behind the scenes?

Telepathic, Nat was not, that was for sure.

Gavin and Heather had arrived with a stunning bouquet of thick-stemmed chubby roses. Nat nodded to them now. 'By the way, thanks for the flowers as well as the booze and chocolates,' she said. 'They're beautiful, but I feel a bit of a cheat seeing as I do nothing but sit around like a fat cat, purr occasionally and eat whatever Wes puts in front of me.'

Heather put her hand to her mouth. 'Oh, sorry, it wasn't me. Gavin–'

'Nah, can't be.' Wes topped up Heather's wine. 'Not the tight Scottish–'

'Delivered to the office yesterday for Miss Bach.' Gavin looked over his shoulder. 'There's a card somewhere.'

Nat felt her cheeks colour. It had to be Brian Selby. The police had dropped the charges of attempted murder against both him and Shirley, and a CPS solicitor had told Gavin, off the record, that he'd advised any further charges were not in the public interest. All eyes were on her, so she stepped to the bunch, plucked out the small envelope and slipped out the greeting.

'Share it with the class,' Gavin said.

She rolled her eyes. 'Thank you for everything, Natalie. More than just a "lucky lady"...' she read out loud.

Gavin stroked his moustache. 'And?'

Nat glared. The cheeky sod had obviously read it. She started again. 'More than just a lucky lady. Thank you especially for being a friend to Lucy.'

Gavin swigged his beer. 'A friend to Brian's daughter, eh? What has Miss Bach been up to this time, I wonder?'

She lifted her eyebrows and looked at him pointedly. 'Your magic repertoire hasn't expanded to mind-reading yet, Gav? I hoped you would grace us with the whole get-up tonight. What do they call it in the Magic Circle? A suit? One's finery? Uniform?'

Wes grinned and joined in the banter. 'Come on, Gav, spill the beans. Are we talking Harry Houdini or Paul Daniels?' He eyed him for a moment. 'God yes. My mum's old favourite–'

'*Old* favourite?' Gavin folded his arms.

'Yes,' Wes continued. 'I'm not sure he ever had such a fine tache, but the similarity is astonishing. Does this outfit include a red fez and–'

Laughing, Heather interrupted. 'And an expression, "just like that"?'

'Tommy Cooper?' Gavin shrugged. 'I can bide with that. He was tall, clever and he had some cracking jokes.' He chuckled. 'Here's a good one: "Somebody complimented me on my driving today. They left a little note on the windscreen, it said "Parking Fine".'

Nat smiled and squeezed Wes's hand beneath the table. There had been so much else going on at the time, she had initially forgotten to tell Wes about Lucy's confession, but in the spirit of honesty about things she knew for sure, she'd told him eventually.

What a Friday that had been. Lucy, Cassandra and Andrea, topped off by the miscarriage scare. Knowing something dreadful had happened at the house, Nat had tried to persuade Wes to call his mum, but he was resolute that she and their baby was his priority right then. After waiting for some time, Mr Hirsch had reassured them about the 'fluid'. He'd taken a blood sample but was positive the dizziness was simply fluctuations in blood pressure and a need for more iron.

Listening to the regular beeps from Wes's phone, Nat had felt such a time-wasting fool. But he'd finally opened the messages from Kath: she was at the hospital with Andrea, but she'd been too late to save her. Andrea was dead.

He had nodded and shown Nat the texts. Save for asking the taxi driver to drop him in Cheadle Hulme en route to hers, he hadn't said another word. Wishing she could help, she'd waited in the cab, watching him gaze at the handsome house before heading to the open front door.

He'd had to do the rest alone – the hospital, the identification, his sons – she'd known that.

She glanced at him now. He still did; they barely touched on the subject. But that was fine; he would share when he was ready. And anyway, this was one topic Nat did not want to poke and prod.

Only the dead woman knew exactly what had happened in that house. But Nat had her own theory. Two o'clock, Andrea had said. Kath had complied, gliding onto the large driveway in Wes's Mercedes in good time. But suppose Andrea had waited and watched from her front bedroom window? From there she wouldn't have seen the identity of the driver. She would have assumed it was Wes, due in the house any second. A man whose girlfriend was pregnant. A husband she was about to lose forever unless she took drastic action to keep him in her power. It was risky, of course. But no more perilous than throwing herself down the stairs. Besides, it was fine; Wes was there, just a moment away.

Did Andrea check herself in the mirror to ensure her hair was styled perfectly, her make-up just so? Did she softly step down the stairs, climb onto a stool and slip the silky knot around her neck, her timing exemplary as she kicked it away? Only it wasn't her husband nobly charging in to save her. It was his mum who'd said 'the evil had to stop'.

Nat shook her head. She wasn't telepathic; she didn't want to be. Nor did she want Kath to be completely 'honest', but she couldn't help wondering how long she had waited in the Mercedes before letting herself into the house.

What had Kath said at the café? '*I could kill her for what she's done to his family; I would if it didn't make things worse.*'

Yes, that mother love Larry had described: '*unconditional... that inbred willingness to go to the ends of the earth...*'

Wes's voice brought her back from her thoughts. 'Are you with us, Nat?'

Gavin laughed. 'Talk about dreamy, Wes. Your woman's gone soft. That sproglet is going to be the most spoilt little kid there ever was.' He lifted his glass. 'And quite rightly so. Here's to mother love.'

Nat blinked, lifted her glass of juice and smiled. 'Mother love,' she said. 'Yes, I'll drink to that.'

The End

ACKNOWLEDGMENTS

Thank you to all the lovely people who have helped me and Natalie Bach along the way, including:

- My fellow writers at the South Manchester Writers' Workshop, especially beta readers Peter Barnes, Liz Kolbeck, John Keane and Bev Butcher.
- The Bloodhound team, particularly Loulou, Tara, Heather, Betsy and Fred.
- So many fabulous blogger stars, but especially Steph Lawrence, Grace Smith and John Cowton.
- My brilliant agent Kate Johnson.
- Last but not least, my wonderful family and my author buddies Carolyn, Sam and Libby. Thank you for the support and laughter!

Printed in Great Britain
by Amazon